STICKING
POINTS

THE DREAMSEEKER FICTION SERIES

On an occasional and highly selective basis, books in the DreamSeeker Fiction Series, intended to make available fine fiction by writers whose works at least implicitly arise from or engage Anabaptist-related contexts, themes, or interests, are published by Cascadia Publishing House under the DreamSeeker Books imprint. Cascadia oversees content of these novels or story collections in collaboration with DreamSeeker Fiction Series Editor Jeff Gundy as well as in consultation with its Editorial Council.

1. Sticking Points
   By Shirley Kurtz, 2011

STICKING POINTS

A NOVEL

SHIRLEY KURTZ

DreamSeeker Fiction Series, Volume 1

DreamSeeker Books
TELFORD, PENNSYLVANIA

an imprint of
Cascadia Publishing House

Cascadia Publishing House orders, information, reprint permissions:
contact@CascadiaPublishingHouse.com
1-215-723-9125
126 Klingerman Road, Telford PA 18969
www.CascadiaPublishingHouse.com

Some Bible quotations are paraphrases from *The King James Version*; direct quotes from KJV
appear pp. 36, 68, 91, 95, 119, 121, 142, 191, 203, 216, 222, 246, 254. Quotes pp. 101,
118, 183 are from the *Good News Bible*. Old Testament copyright © American Bible Society
1976; New Testament copyright © American Bible Society 1966, 1971, 1976. Quotes pp.
174, 255, 260-261 are from the Holy Bible, *New International Version*®.
Copyright © 1973, 1978, 1984 International Bible Society. All rights reserved
throughout the world. Used by permission of International Bible Society.

An article by the author on Christmas form letters, "Friendship Can Survive 'Ugly'; But Will
It Survive Mass Marketing?" appeared in the December 15, 1992, issue of *Gospel Herald*. An
article by the author about her mother, Gladys Baer, "Isn't a Pulpit Just a Place to Spread
One's Papers?" appeared in the October 8, 1996, issue of *Gospel Herald*.

The author is indebted to Jennifer Murch (and her book club), Kathy Stoltzfus, Shirley
Coberly, Ervin and Joan Huston, the Ice Mountain writers, Connie Sutton, Ted Grimsrud,
Jeff Gundy, and Michael A. King. Credit goes to Zachary Kurtz who gave scholarly assistance
and to Christopher Clymer Kurtz for his photography.

Library of Congress Cataloguing-in-Publication Data
Kurtz, Shirley.
Sticking points / Shirley Kurtz.
    p. cm. -- (Dreamseeker fiction series ; v. 1)
ISBN-13: 978-1-931038-81-2 (6 x 9 trade pbk. : alk. paper)
ISBN-10: 1-931038-81-3 (6 x 9 trade pbk. : alk. paper)
I. Title.
PS3561.U74S75 2011
813'.54--dc22

                    2010054006

17 16 15 14 13 12 11   10 9 8 7 6 5 4 3 2 1

To Paulson, my love

STICKING POINTS

1

Not every blunder spells ruin—take last evening. After supper, spotting the foil-covered bowl in the refrigerator, behind the water glass holding some keeling-over parsley that would've stayed fresher in the garden, Anna realized she'd served her chicken-corn-and-noodle soup without the chicken. This had passed her right by, the whole time she was yammering at Wade and their son Todd and sipping up the spoonfuls of hot broth with little specks of floating fat and noodles swimming and chopped-fine onion and celery (the celery leaves, too, for their vitamin E).

"What in the world?" she wailed, bent in front of the refrigerator, letting all the cold air escape past her consternated face. Last Christmas's photo of everybody at Margie's, held fast to the freezer compartment door with a red plastic Coca-Cola magnet, fluttered knowingly, as did Todd's tenth grade final-nine-weeks' report card from back in June (two A-pluses), the grocery list (*RAISINS* scrawled by Wade in big letters, like he perceived himself on the verge of starvation), and the ancient valentine from all three of her children with its raggedy lace border she has to keep gluing back on.

Wade in the study let out a hoot, and Todd consoled, "Hey, it's not the worst thing ever." But how could've she forgotten good roaster chicken she'd pulled so painstakingly off the bones? The long pin bones on chicken drumsticks can choke dogs, she's heard, so why not people, too? Always, as the last bits of meat fall away, she examines for the shardlike projections. The tippy ends can't be snapped off, either, and she's careful about those knuckle-like cartilage things, either end of the leg bone. "All the work it took, getting that nice big bowlful!" she bemoaned, the fridge breeze fanning her cheeks gripped with chagrin.

But the next minute she dissolved in loud, giddy guffaws. "You're right," she told Todd. She stepped back and the door sucked itself shut. "It was just a dumb little mistake. If only my goofs were all this immaterial!" She was referring to last year's debacle—the article she'd written, one which brought on a true-blue life crisis.

At least, that's all past and done. She dug out of that hole, thank the Lord. Believe! she told herself. Just believe! Don't be a doubting Thomas! It took a number of over-and-over sessions like that, lots of raking herself over the coals, but eventually her faith took proper hold and she was able to start another article for *Gospel Truth* magazine in the spring, something to make up for the one the editor had returned, "A Two-faced God?!" It had been about Abraham and Isaac in the Old Testament. Now she set to work at her little round table near the kitchen stove, its checkered cloth dragging around her feet, and concentrating to beat the band, she soon had crumpled-up balls of paper snowed across the floor. Already she was bogging down, but at least it wasn't her doubts roiling her this time.

She sat there trying and trying to unjumble a sentence, crossing out and erasing, flicking away the rubbery shreds from her pencil, hooking and unhooking her feet on the chair rung, when suddenly behind her, *whoosh.* What in the world? Oh, the oven gas. Oh, the bread! How long had she left the oven to its preheating? The loaves still on the counter rising had puffed so high, now they would end up with dents in the top crust or even big sink-hole places.

She made sure to start the timer to ticking, after sliding the pans belatedly into the oven.

A more serious thing happened a week or so later, though. She was slaving in the study over the new article to hopefully send to Mr. Epp, the editor, keying a page of rough draft into the computer, and she had to pull herself away to put some water on to boil for another batch of bread. She returned to the desk, and sitting there staring at the lines on the screen, she got too caught up. The computer is old but its low-grade hum shouldn't have prevented her from hearing the water's hisses and pops! The boiled-dry pot, when she came to her senses and flew to the kitchen, was coated on its outer surface, on the copper bottom section, with a film of ash.

After scouring off the crud (underneath, the copper had turned a brilliant bluish orange) and putting more water in to mix with the oats and cracked wheat for the bread, Anna flipped the burner back on and stepped over to the door where she keeps her black Goodwill bag hanging on the knob. Somebody's souvenir from a Hadassah convention in Jerusalem ten years ago, the bag bears the words "Compliments of Bank Hapoalim" stamped on in gold. Who knows how something like this ever ended up at the Goodwill in Conoy of all places, along with people's old paperbacks, melty Tupperware, unraveling afghans and lumpen pillows, and dyed satin party shoes?

Anna was meaning to retrieve the hanky in her black bag, one of Wade's, along with the rolled-up old *Newsweek* she had yet to get around to chucking because of the interesting "My Turn" by some woman whose cat running around her bed in circles alerted her to a burglar or maybe a rapist on the prowl. Anna wanted to reread the piece. Partly she just liked how it was written—the woman thought initially that the scratching at her door, the man trying to pick the lock, was just another neighborhood cat, a stray. The fluid, conversational tone of the writing, Anna hoped, might afford her a needed shot in the arm.

That minute, though, something made her wheel around. Why, she'd turned on the wrong burner! The back one was flaming, underneath the glass pie plate she'd set on the burner grate instead of returned to the cupboard the night before when unloading the dish drainer. The lily petals of lit gas were pirouetting wickedly. Couldn't there have been an explosion, glass jaggers flying? Goodness. After the pie plate cooled she found the warning on its bottom, specifying in timid lettering, *For oven or microwave only, no stovetop or broiler, Corning NY.* So stupid of her!

Another day, wracking her brain over her article for Epp, hung up on a sticky point, she couldn't even match wits with a pesky fly. She was toying with her sentence at the table, trying to think herself through the jungle of phrases and order them into a lucid sequence, and the fly was buzzing above her on the hanging lamp that's painted to look like an upside-down tulip, and when she whacked irritably at the hard blue-and-gold plastic, sending the lamp swinging and its shadow undulating across the cloth's checks? Lucky fly, it simply hip-hopped onto her anemic potted spider plant to manicure its hooves and muster up new steam, and then it got back to its buzzing campaign—whereas she just stayed stuck.

She moved to the study where she depends on the trouble lamp clamped to the bookshelf over the desk, but despite the steady yellow downpour of light and the computer's industrious hum she could only fidget or drub her fingernail on one of the arrow keys, not hard enough to start the lines on the monitor to dancing. She needed a different but still incisive word, purely clarifying, and her orange hardcover thesaurus, its pages working loose from the rubbed-raw spine and the burlap peeking out, seemed of no help. Despite all the synonyms for "painful," only the word itself, *painful*, fit exactly. Say "painful," "painful," "painful" the whole way through? How dumb would *that* sound? She wished she were smarter. If she weren't such a goon, she never would've gotten herself so snookered over the Abraham-and-Isaac deal. Of course God could've done that! God could've asked Abraham to sacrifice his son Isaac. If God gave up Jesus to the cross!

"It all comes down to the matter of surrender," she said to Wade. "To the matter of believing—and trusting. That much is crystal clear to me now. In heeding, Abraham just acted upon a simple, trusting faith." She decided to title the article "Abraham's Take on Things, and God's."

Over the next month she plugged away at it, plugged away, plugged away. By the end of April, she felt she had her all-important pointers in place. "Pretty much so, anyhow," she told Wade. "I've had to take it peepee step by peepee step—but what's new?" Todd looked up from his bowl of mooshy ice cream when he heard that and studied her quizzically. "I'm just about there, just about!" she assured Wade. A few minor technicalities needed reconciling, yet. She didn't want any empty claptrap.

So close, so close! But there she remained, at an impasse. No amount of butting her head against the wall helped. She ended up squirreling the pages away.

Over the summer, whenever her unfinished business nagged at her, she shook it off. But yesterday she got to flagellating herself. Am I a quitter or what? she wondered. No. I don't *think* so. Bound and determined, she tramped into the study. File folder in hand, she studied the first paragraphs. She jumped to the section about how Abraham went jelly kneed and mentally railed before he let go and let God. Railed, she thought, yes. That part seemed fair enough. Then, no, she wasn't sure.

"Nobody knows about the old man's objections," Wade commented, on the phone. He was calling from school, between classes, to ask if he'd left his grade book in the study. Yes, ha! "People can only know how *they*'d feel. You can only know how *you*'d be destroyed. The torture *you*'d go through. You'd have to beat the sense out of yourself. Out of every last line of reasoning."

But in the evening, after she made her neglected chicken into salad and finished the dishes, when she sidled into the study and tried to bring up the topic again, he didn't want to get into it. "You'd do best to stick with your personal thoughts, Anna," he muttered, circling another wrong answer on a student's test. "Only, given your usual contortions, that would take a book."

"A book," she echoed. Such a thought sprouting caused a sudden cramp in the back of her skull. "A book," she repeated. "But how could I ever—" She hovered beside him, chewing dolorously on the inside of her cheek. The hurt in her head was turning to despair and filtering down through her shoulders.

After a few minutes she said slowly, "Sure, okay. I'll explain how I got so creeped and reduced in the first place, and then how—"

Five more minutes went by. She added, "I suppose I could use my Elijah on Mount Carmel story for starters. I mean, it sort of fits, doesn't it? Elijah's unswerving trust in the Lord, like Abraham's?" She took another nip on her cheek. "Isn't that funny. I've always *always* wanted to stay fast and firm as Elijah. It just goes to show. The road to hell is paved with good intentions."

Wade still wasn't paying her much regard. Silently she slipped upstairs for her mildewed cardboard boot box she's carried with her from one place to the next over the years, tied shut with an orange yo-yo string, containing her childhood stories she wrote at age fourteen and three of her diaries. Here at the Conoy Route 3 house she's kept it in the attic space above the bedrooms, tucked into the suffocating layer of shredded-paper insulation Wade got Conoy Home Improvement to blow in with hoses after he and Anna bought the place. They'd left her home area, made the big leap. She had the box in Daddy's old file cabinet at the time of the move, but the drawer's open-and-shuts were further eroding the cardboard, and as she watched the Home Improvement guys dumping bag after bag of cellulose into the hopper of their huge, clangorous blower, it occurred to her that now the attic would be an excellent hideaway, properly stuffy and choky.

Only a small hole in the ceiling of the hall, which nobody who's a tub could possibly wedge through, allows access, so last night she moved the wicker stool out from the bathroom and positioned it directly beneath, by the window overlooking the garden. She stretched her size 10 frame to reach, pushed up on the board that covers the hole, batted around in the insulation puffs, pulled down the box, fumbled with the yo-yo string, and hauled forth "The Mount Carmel Bonfire."

Especially in the light of day now, the pages are quite the mess. Anybody else privy would find them miserable to decipher. The old-typewriter botchiness doesn't exactly make for a literary treat, nor the spasmodic hit-or-miss effect and the run-amok xxx's. After all, she was a shrimpy teenager, writing. But now that she's spent some time putting the story on the computer, with her punctuation and spelling cleaned up, it seems readable enough.

The Mount Carmel Bonfire

Mama asked, "You just using a cake pan?" Thirteen-year-old Annie said, "It'll work fine and dandy, yep." Mama was letting her be in charge of Sunday night children's meeting for once and she'd got herself a novel idea. Mama had tried out a recipe for flaming peaches out of Verna Pyles's cookbook, see, it said empty a jar of peach halves in a dish and in each peach hollow put a sugar cube that's been dipped in some almond extract and then light the sugar cubes with a match, and when Mama'd sat the peaches down on the table, Herbie and Wesley went bug eyed and it was good Margie'd got baptized and didn't have her braids hanging down anymore to get their tail ends caught afire. So Annie's plan was to make a sample altar like Elijah's up on Mount Carmel. Out of brown sugar. Use those sugar cubes, she'd thought first but Mama said no, too expensive, she just mostly had them on hand for people to dunk in their Sanka coffee.

Sunday night Annie toted her Bible and grocery bag up front like Mama always did and soon as she put the cake pan on the song leader stand all the children on the front bench quit their squirming. "The prophet Elijah back in the Old Testament was disgusted I guess," she said solemnly. She daren't look back at Margie who might get her to start tee heeing and lose her self control. "Everybody else was turning away from God and worshiping Baal instead, some silly idol. So Elijah said let's fix sacrifices and see who's more mighty and trustworthy, let's see if God or Baal can send fire down.

"So Baal's prophets built a stone pile and laid out their bull sacrifice and started their praying, louder and then louder. They danced around and even cut themselves with knives, needing Baal to grant some attention. Elijah said, he's maybe sleeping. Maybe off on a trip.

"After a long spell of that, he said it's my turn now. He went over and started repairing the broken down altar of the Lord that was there, nobody'd used it in a long while." While she was saying this she upset in the cake pan her measuring cup of brown sugar, it stood up by itself firm and uncaving.

Next thing she got out was a plastic cow to lay on, it was from Wesley's Noah's ark set he never played with anymore. That Wesley! "Huh-uh," he'd shouted, seeing her take it out of the toy box, and she argued back, "Don't be so selfish. Somebody big as you, seven years old, possessive about an old cow? For shame." She informed her young lookers-on, "Elijah arranged his firewood on the altar and then some cut up pieces of bull meat. We'll just pretend about the wood. And the bull part. And Wesley didn't want me to chop up his thing."

Someone partaways back on the ladies' side tittered but were the children ever ogling. Not hardly budging on the bench.

Mama'd said no using up her almond extract but rubbing alcohol would work as good. So a jar with alcohol in and the cap off the Jergen's lotion for dipping it out were the next to last things Annie got out of her bag. "So children, what Elijah did next must of made folks think he was off in the head. He sent helpers down to the creek for water to besotten the wood and stones and all. Four barrels, he instructed, and four more and four more. How many in all? Eleven did you say, Billy? No-o-o."

She unscrewed the jar lid and counted while she doused the altar, "One, two, three, four." The little streams of alcohol carved out paths going down the brown sugar. "Five, six, seven, eight, nine, ten." She made sure the cow got good and wet. "Eleven, twelve."

She said, "No peeking now, you children. I mean it." They pasted their eyes shut and she dived in the bag one last time.

It was tricky trying to get things going with the match and at the same time read Elijah's whole prayer out of the Bible. "Lord God of Abraham, Isaac, and Israel, let it be known this day that thou art the God in Israel, and that I am thy good servant and I have done all these things at thy word. Hear me, O Lord O Lord hear me, that this people may know that thou art the Lord God and" but she didn't make it to the end quite. Somebody was oohing out loud, probly that cheater Billy Grogan, and big flames were shooting out of the pan, she had to step back away.

Then brown syrup was blurping up, it was like candy syrup bubbles, and she couldn't much pay heed to people's gasps, shaky as her insides felt. But the alcohol was bound to get lapped up soon so she stuffed away her jar and stuff. "You can go back to your parents now," she said. "Don't you children ever forget about Elijah, his courage and faith. When the people saw what happened, that fire flashing down out of heaven like it says and eating up the bull and wood and stones, they fell down flat and hollered, The Lord he is the God! The Lord he is the great God! Go on now, go back to your parents. Billy, you too."

Still she stayed up front herself till her bonfire was pretty died down, just a weakly blue flame that sallied along the edge of the pan. The cow was laying sideways in the gunkish candy goo, all blacked up but not consummated.

After church was over and the last stragglers were gone Mama helped her push the song leader stand back to its regular place and she tried to pick up the pan, but for a little it stayed stuck. It left a ripply black patch in the shellac. In her startlement Mama almost couldn't speak. "You should of used a hot pad underneath," she said, "you should of thought." "But didn't it get across the point?" said Annie. So she was okay once she got past her fright, because that good old Elijah and his doings, she'd got that across anyhow.

Anna guesses she sounds like some kind of a pyromaniac—her kitchen-stove mishaps, and now this! But when has she ever meant to flirt with catastrophe?

One good thing, though: Wesley never even missed that cow of his. She pitched it, afterwards.

Car-a-mel, she muses to herself, quietly chipping the word into parts. *Mount Caramel*—that would've made a better title, ha. She picks off the desk a page of the original version of her story and peers at her childish goof-ups. For example, one single wrong letter in "altar," every time she typed the word, wholly (not holy) altered the definition. The way language can be twisted and tampered with—it's just too crazy. Just as bad is the way every little sticking point throws her for a loop. She got too foiled, trying to expound about Abraham. But if she can chronicle her own struggle to accept the deep truths and stay humble and yielding, this might encourage other people who are tempted with faithlessness, who long to be as staunch as Elijah and Abraham. It's harebrained, though, to be setting her sights on a book. Really harebrained.

2

A week later, looking over her first chapter, Anna frowns.

She ponders that grocery list specifying raisins. Still on the fridge, it also includes "torlet paper" written jokingly in her hand, and "glaham clackers," and "Colby chizz" (not Velveeta—she never buys Velveeta anymore). Her maiming of the language can be deliberate, sure. She's dallied already with the idea of requesting bo-log-na (with a hard *g*) at the grocery store. Saying it out loud. "Bo-log-na, please, a half pound." She'd like to do it just for the look on the deli clerk's face.

But in the most trivial of situations, the inherent fraughtness overtakes. She can get frustrated just labeling cookie dough for the freezer. "Chocolate chip dough," she'll print on a strip of masking tape, using black permanent marker. But that second *o* in "chocolate" might be dragging a tail like an *a*, choc*a*late. She'll scissor away the section of tape instead of rip it, so as not to leave a ragged edge, and try again: "chocolate chip." Then in parentheses she'll add, "I used cracked eggs, so please do not eat raw," because otherwise Todd, spooning out the dough for her onto trays some night at suppertime, might get it into his head to snitch the last glob in the container.

At least, the eggs come from Wade's layer hens, not the store. Their coop sits up in the field, a slipshod construction of scavenged windows and tin and old boards, and every evening he strolls up through the clover and wild mustard to pen the biddies in for the night, carrying an old dented coffee can full of scratch and coaxing, "Here chickchickchick." Eggs from hens like his that run all day outdoors—aren't confined in stifling commercial layer houses—don't pose as much of a threat of salmonella poisoning as the store-bought kind. Nonetheless, anytime an egg is cracked, or at least, cracked badly enough that it leaks, the person is running a risk. Anna now figures that the cardboard flats the Overholts used over and over, for the eggs they brought from their farmette to the mission where she grew up, must've been hotbeds of iniquity. The flaky, crystalline seepage stuck fast to the cardboard must've teemed with pathogens replicating at a fever pitch.

That masking-tape label of hers, Anna will need to wind it around the face of the carton. Her parenthetical sounding bells will have made it too long to fit on the lid. She's so cautious, so cautious.

AND YET, TONIGHT in the car with Todd after his youth meeting at First Evangelical Brethren in Conoy, Anna nearly imperils their lives.

She shopped for groceries at Pantry Pride during the youth group's volleyball game in the church parking lot, played with a net stretched between two poles set in cement-filled tires, and then she drove back to the church with the plastic and brown paper bags whispering in the back seat, and she took advantage of the wait time to do some catch-up reading. Still somewhat of a greenhorn at driving, Todd is at the wheel now, and paused at the last of the stoplights in Conoy (the town boasts three), he hits the turn signal, intending to take a right to cross the town's aging concrete bridge spanning the Catawally and head the six miles home. Perhaps steam is rising beneath the bridge to mingle with the dusky September air, and perhaps in the water, turbid and lashed with bark from the paper mill upriver at Bricksburg, the disaffected crappies are vying for territory, but the rolled-up car windows are putting at a remove such signs of the night underworld. Anna is only fiddling with the straps of her black Goodwill bag, but as the light changes to green, she suddenly realizes she didn't get bagels. Impulsively she reaches across her son and pushes down on the turn lever, activating the left blinker instead.

"Hey!" yells Todd, momentarily losing his grip on the steering wheel.

She claps her hand over her mouth. "Sorry! That could've scared you into pressing on the gas and shooting us out into traffic. What ails me? Can you run us back to the store for a minute? I forgot to check out the bakery markdowns."

But the bagels are still humped in their trays in the display case, not packaged into bags on the counter, six for $1.59. "They're not on special yet?" she questions the bakery woman, careful about not sounding pushy.

The woman looks up from polishing the stainless steel ovens. Her apron is grungy with Crisco and spattered icing, and the strings above her bulgy hips are coming untied. "I've been so darn busy, hon. Just pick out all you want and I'll put the half-price stickers on."

Anna loads up on the garlic-speckled kind, onion, blueberry, raisin (with swirls of cinnamon), sesame and poppy seed, even two banana-nut ones that might be gross. At home she rearranges the bagels more compactly in their bags, pats at the empty spaces to drive out the air, and fastens the twisties back on. On account of the thinness of the plastic, she slides each bagful into one of the sturdier, opaque plastic bags that held the groceries, with QUALITY! SELECTION! SAVINGS EVERY DAY! printed on the side, and she closes up the outer bags with more twisties. But now anybody retrieving this food from the freezer won't know which bagels they're getting, raisin-cinnamon or blueberry or what!

So she plucks her masking tape and black marker pen from the drawer near the telephone. "Sesame and poppy seed." No, sesame and p-*o*-p-p-y seed. "Garlic." No, g-*a*-r-l-i-c. Almost too tired to see straight, she persists with her tedious lettering. Upstairs Todd is banging on the bathroom door, impatient with his dad, wanting a turn in the shower. The only child still at home, Todd likes to think the bathroom is his own personal domain. She hears the sudden shudder of the pipes, Wade shutting off the water. He'll take his good old time drying off, she knows. He has the habit of slapping his wrung-out washrag all over his body to sop up the wet and then scraping the towel over himself so hard the hairs become statically charged.

Fuzzy-headed with exhaustion, the labels completed, she presses them across the plastic, rubbing with her thumbnail, apprehensive that they might pop off in the freezer, their sticky sides dried out. But she gives up on *that* thought.

Of course, things are worse when she's fatigued. Telling herself firmly that she's not going to obsess, not going to, not going to, doesn't make a dent, because already the neurons are spinning out of control. But maybe it's all for a purpose. Maybe this embarrassing affliction keeps the dangerous side of her in check—the pride. A certain pleasure can creep in, when she's been grinding away on a paragraph and suddenly a big word she's eked out stands in front of her, uncharacteristically bold and vigorous and bright. Using big words, is she being too nervy? Even braggartly? She must *must* stay faithful in her spirit, stay constant and humble.

3

Here at home the breeze ordinarily blows fresh and pure. A person doesn't get Conoy's smells: the fast-food restaurants' fat; the sickish-sweet breath that forcibly exhales from people's clothes driers and out the wall vents; those solvent fumes coming from the dry cleaner's on Pearson Street; the stink of the newspaper company's unscrubbed ink barrels that line the alley a block and a half over; the petroleum-y reek from the grease-monkey garages and self-service gas stations; the belches of smoke from the over-loaded logging trucks as they crawl through the short stretch of town, fol-lowing Route 46 west toward Bricksburg and the paper mill. No, here the rural air, chlorophyll filtered and spacious, rarely ruffles the senses.

It blows mostly silently, too, at this distance. The spread-out valley's calm and the piney green woods' wordlessness complete the painterly pic-ture. But Anna's not always down-on-her-knees grateful for the quiet. Sure, it gives her a chance to hear herself think, if she needs this. But the hush, no external stimuli competing, also makes it easy for her to spin off on one of her dotty mental rampages. Or the opposite thing happens sometimes— the quietness presses and presses in, and the weighty encumbrance muffles any ideas or gumption. This morning it's been like that, and even after a couple cups of coffee she's still languishing, second-guessing herself. To just be writing about some doubts, one insignificant little person's trip-up over something right there in the Bible, so plain and clear? The question has been hanging in the paralyzing silence. Who'll even care?

The big-shot conference people wanted a speech from her, though, didn't they? It went over all right, didn't it?

At last, she ups herself from her chair to go for her copy.

The Sprunger guy contacting her came as a shocker, she remembers. Chasing in from the wash line, through the mudroom, to get the phone, she hit her crazy bone on the boot rack and nearly flopped onto the floor. Probably a telemarketer, she thought in the kitchen as she seized the receiver, her dander mounting. "Hello?"

It was nobody she knew, all right. "Excuse me?" she asked, still out of breath. "Sprunger? Melvin Sprunger, did you say?"

"You're no doubt aware, Mrs. Schlonneger, that the annual meeting of our regional Evangelical Brethren conference is slated for July 9 through 11. The conference center at Rawlings Lake is only several hours south of you, if I'm reading my map right—am I correct in this? Our executive planning committee would like to know if you'd be willing to speak.

"The decision to invite your participation was unanimous," he added, and Anna let out a small squeak.

"We'd like to hear something about your experiences, writing for publication," he said. In a spurt of panic she straightened her spine and sucked in her belly flatter, as if the phone had eyes instead of punch buttons and might feed her dumb-housewife flip-flops-and-blue-jeans image back through the circuits. The effort made her light headed and dizzy. "More specifically, we're interested in hearing why you write for *Gospel Truth* and what role your Christian belief plays."

Swimming in confusion, she grabbed fifth-grader Todd's jelly marked arithmetic paper lying on the counter by the fridge, to scribble on. "You'll need to keep it brief," Mr. Sprunger was saying. "Five minutes, ten at the most."

"Five to ten minutes, fine," she repeated. Her juggling act now, note-taking *and* striving for the appropriate telephone manner, demanded every ounce of concentration. As he spoke, she furiously scrawled. The wet, brown circle on Todd's paper from the coffee drip on the counter gradually widened in diameter.

"For each of the three days of the conference," Sprunger explained, "we're planning a short feature like this to precede the keynote address, on the theme of how the person's faith intersects with their work. Personal anecdotes are always of special interest to our conference attenders, and they'll enjoy hearing from professionals in the church who've—"

"Oh," she gasped, "I'm no professional." What in the world? Didn't he realize? "I just send stuff to the editor, willy nilly."

"That's all right, Mrs. Schlonneger." His voice had turned bassy deep and smooth. She noticed office noises now, too, faint clicking sounds, and the *glub-glub* of a water cooler. "We like your articles," he said. "We like your down-to-earth perspective."

We? The committee, or who?

She waited till everybody was home from school, around the supper table, to spring the news.

"Yeah?" said Wade, putting down his fork and breaking into a wide grin. "That's wonderful, Anna."

"Tell how you antagonize, Mom," Jonathan suggested. Antagonize! He knew the proper word. "Tell how you throw down the scratch-paper balls."

"Tell about the weasel getting my chicken," offered Todd who'd missed out on the salient details.

"No, no, no," said Anna. "It has to be *spiritual.* Not any old thing just to be entertaining."

After spending weeks producing a draft, she practiced on the children. She sat them down on her new flowered sofa in the living room and handed out pencils and sheets of paper laid on top of encyclopedias so they could record their criticisms. At that moment, for all practical purposes the sofa represented a judge's bench—she wasn't wasting her attention on the handsomely curved, tufted back, sink-down cushions, and old-fashioned bearpaw feet, or thinking about her sister Margie's assessment. Anna'd had her qualms, choosing something that posh, brand new from the store. But Margie had approved. She'd stood there in the living room rubbing her pudgy forearms and mutely admiring, and then she'd announced, "It's like in the Rembrandt paintings, isn't it? Like what the naked ladies recline on."

Now, though, no Margie, just the children lined up in a row, Anna nervously instructed, "Say whatever you think. Be as hard on me as you want."

"From my point of view," Todd wrote across the top of his paper in his labored cursive, but that was all the farther he got. Jonathan put down, "Say era the right way. It's not air-uh. And don't huff and puff when you're reading. You should take some long walks to build up your lungs." Mary Beth, in gym shorts, taking up more than her share of sofa space, one shiny, shaved leg draped across Todd's lap, kept tucking her long blond hair behind her ears or coiling the ends around a finger while observing Anna shrewdly. "Aren't you trying too hard to sound intelligent?" she wrote.

"Can't you use regular words? I think you mispronounced era. Also, memorize some parts so you can look up more often. Don't read it word for word."

On the drive to Rawlings Lake with Wade, Anna tried to relax her jaws—she'd heard clenched teeth could bring on a headache. Sometimes she hummed little snatches of made-up songs. Her black bag she'd found that very week at the Goodwill sat hunched on the floor behind her seat, and every so often she twisted around to feel in it for her papers, as if they could somehow escape. Or she flipped down the visor mirror and patted at her growing-out bangs. She was sorry about the oppressive early evening sultriness, the heat sticking in the air. She'd blow-dried her choppy front strands to a decent sleekness, but she knew that the minute she stepped out of the car, they were going to kink up and frizz unmercifully.

Given her butterflies, she was able to take only a few bites out of Wade's ham-and-salami sub from the Stop-n-Go in Preston. "Too much mayonnaise," she grimaced, the lettuce shreds clinging greasily to the corners of her mouth and daring to drop on her skirt, which would've left regrettable smears. Then the lunchmeaty aftertaste bothered her. She wanted to brush her teeth, but when they neared the junction at Route 156 and Wade slowed to turn in at the only gas station, a hicksville kind of place where she'd probably have to request the restroom key, she said, "Never mind, I'll take a few swipes with the toothbrush dry." She let out a moan. "Why does it have to be so humid?"

At Rawlings Lake, Wade eased the car past the conference delegates streaming up the main drive or cutting across the lawn, coming from the dining hall, cabins, lodge, and solar guesthouse. He nosed into the one empty parking spot by the meeting pavilion, where Melvin Sprunger was motioning, stumbling over himself and just about knocking down the *Reserved* sign. Reserved for them? Right away, Melvin led them to their seats.

"We're too crammed," she whispered to Wade, because somebody had set up the folding chairs too close together and the knees of the man behind were practically knobbing her in the back. "Oh me," she whispered after a moment, "I should've read you this—read you my last little fix-ups. I should've taken a little more time."

As she sat there barely holding herself together, she recalled how Mama's throat went dry anytime she gave a talk at the mission. The words came out pasty and sticky, causing Mama to turn pink. I should've requested water, thought Anna. They could've allotted me a little plastic cupful. They could've hideawayed it behind the lectern.

Well, she would avoid swallowing.

With effort she joined in the hymn singing led by a corpulent woman. She half listened to the young married couple up next at the mike, zestily reciting verses out of Proverbs they'd committed to memory. Soon she would be lifting one foot after the other up the platform risers, please God, not crashing on the steps, and crossing to the lectern and situating her papers and—

Before she quite realized, she was hearing the echoes of her own voice. Her mouth was practically grazing the soft black microphone ball. Below her, yellow light was glinting off people's glasses, necktie clips, silvery hoop earrings, balding heads. The noses looked oleaginous in the heat. "Anybody who thinks the words come spilling out, that all I do is click more lead out of my mechanical pencil as the pages pile up in reams, is sorely deluded," she heard, the words bouncing back at her. "If you only knew the half.

"The risk of failure hangs over any writer's head, of course—when mailing a manuscript, they're expected to send extra stamps and a self-addressed envelope so their effort can be returned if it's too dumb, so this tends to put a pall on things. At least, it does for me. I always wonder, What if I can't say it right? Or can't say the right thing?

"Saying it right involves chiefly the mechanics—making sure of my grammar and punctuation and so on. Is there clarity? Consistency? A catchy beginning? Tidy ending? In the part in between, no deviating? And my worrywart habits compound the problems dreadfully.

"Then of course, saying the right thing is even more critical—being honest at every turn, and standing up for the truth and guarding it.

"I got into trouble one time over an article for *Gospel Truth* in which I went back to my childhood in Pottstown, 160 miles north of my present home, Conoy. During that simpler era in the church my parents, Ralph and Myrna Farber, served at the Evangelical Brethren mission there in Pottstown, and in my article I told about Mama dressing us modestly, and about Daddy's sermon he gave on women's buns and prayer caps, at the mission and elsewhere. He'd go down the verses in 1 Corinthians 11 and explain why women must submit and never take a scissors to their hair. Whipping two hankies out of his pants pocket, he'd illustrate the Bible verses' exact import.

"Relating this in detail in my article, I never outright suggested that Daddy had been mistaken in his interpretation of Scripture. I wasn't sorry the church wasn't taking the same stand anymore, but I wasn't making a big jab at it. Daddy's demonstration was just so interesting. Well, a couple of weeks after I sent off my article, here came a fat envelope, my own I'd addressed, oh dear!

"In with my article, the editor had enclosed this letter. 'Sorry, but I'm returning "Daddy's Hankies." You realize, I'm sure, that some among us still feel strongly about the prayer-cap teachings. Out of consideration for such persons, the subject cannot be treated lightly. Would you perhaps be interested in systematically researching the differing views on that Scripture passage and presenting them in a more objective article?'

"I'd long ago done the research. Well, a little research. The thing is, it would've been wrong of me to hurt people's feelings. I was really struck by the editor's concern about the constituency. I'd never really thought about the readership. I'd always just written about what I felt and believed! Now I had to come to terms with the fact that upset readers could cancel their subscriptions."

Anna longed, so, for her cup of water. The skin on the underside of her lips had gone parched and was making unpleasant suction-like noises against her teeth. But maybe this was audible only to her. A few times, laughter had erupted. On each occasion it had come at her like an explosion, the mouths in the faces distending crookedly and letting out cackles, catching her up short. She'd not meant to be humorous. At her mention of buns, a man in the front row had bent way over and slapped at his knees. His neck, where the hairs were clipped close, had looked the same purplish red as Mama's petunias in the mission flower bed back in Pottstown.

Anna pressed on, though. "I put that letter and my article away. I guessed I didn't have any business trying to tackle that kind of theological subject. I would just stick to the common everyday things. But didn't I go and get myself into a pickle again, some years later, when I decided to write something about TV.

"Travailing over this article, I went to great lengths to explain why I thought television to be society's worst cure, and why my husband and I felt it necessary to spare our children from a couch-potato fate. I said that Mary Beth, as a baby, ate our *Newsweeks* instead of slobbering before a TV. Jonathan, when he came along, liked to empty the bottom kitchen drawer of every last plastic container and then clop around the kitchen with his feet stuck into two yogurt cartons. Todd, in his turn, banged randomly on the piano or climbed up on the washing machine. From such pranks, our children went on to build roads and bridges and parking garages out of the blocks their daddy sawed from 2x4s, and they finger-painted and colored and pasted, and they tore around outdoors.

"We preferred anything, almost *any*thing, to them sitting in front of a TV, I said. Their early years, permitting them to habitually watch would've harmed—tainted—their developing little bodies, not to mention their souls. It's not like we never took them to see movies, but a TV in the house would've inured them to banality and worldliness. What beat all was the fact that even though all three were in school now and hearing constantly about this or that show, they weren't coming home and begging us to stop being such old fogies.

"And you know what? The editor returned the article. He said I was being too judgmental. That hurt."

The audience had turned still, no jollity. Anna licked her lips urgently. "I worked hard at making repairs, trying not to outright decry television's vacuousness and unhealthy influence. Because everybody has TV. You all have TV, right? So I'd been insensitive. I wondered if I'd been *so* much in the wrong by just being frank and earnest, but maybe that was sour grapes.

"I finally got the article to where the editor could accept it, but it didn't seem all that interesting anymore. It was more just an encouragement to people to spice up their family life with homey activities. You maybe don't even remember it. But really, Mr. Epp had to do the best thing in the interests of the church. My pride took a beating, that's all."

Anna noticed folks were relaxing again, whew. "In tenth grade at Pottstown's small township school I had an amazing English teacher, Miss Lois Fritz. Gifted in every way, dignified and eloquent, she put us to reading the best biographies. And, oh, the poetry she quoted! It gave me chills. I could see the billows frothing like yeast in Longfellow's 'Wreck of the Hesperus' and Bessie swinging from the clapper of the bell in 'Curfew Must Not Ring Tonight.' Miss Fritz explained that with the pen you could give vent to your heart's every shaded longing. You could lay bare both the tragic and lofty.

"She said you just had to allow the imagination free rein. You just had to surmount the constricting cords of exactitude. Well, I didn't know about *that* part. 'Exact means exact!' I said to Mama. But a yearning was growing in me, a tremendous urge to compose some stories about my own woes and tragicomic adventures. At last I decided, Well, just stories, that can't be *wrong. Clear wrong* can't matter. If I call the girl Annie, that'll make the wrongness clear. If I spin a little more, even that won't matter.

"I was already taking typing, so I got Daddy to let me carry his clunker Remington over to the Bible school room on the mission's second floor, and fancying myself the poor starving artist up in her garret, I hacked out my tales. I perceived them as riddled through with significance. Maybe I wasn't dredging up the perfect particulars, but neither was I lying. The project took me months. The night finally came when I gathered up all my pages to take them to Miss Fritz the next day at school, and then's when the sordid reality hit home. What a state of arrears—all my typing botches—there were so many! I stood there, shattered by self-doubt. Miss Fritz would just think, You dummy.

"So she never knew.

"She got married after school left out, too. She didn't come back to teach in the fall.

"Me, I buried my dreams. Writerly wise, I mean. And for a very long time, I stayed good and squelched. But after Daddy's wrenching death to cancer, I sat down one day and wrote a brief essay about the regrets he'd expressed not long before he took his last breaths. My husband said, 'Why, Anna, this would be good enough for *Gospel Truth.*' And that's really how I got started. I'm just so glad for the editor's supportiveness. He's been long-suffering and patient. He's allowed me to bumble along, bumble along. Everybody has their cross to bear, so maybe my cross is my proneness to pick everything apart and worry and mess up. Anyhow, it's what I live with. A much worse thing would be if I faltered in my beliefs, went out on a limb. But I'm committed to the truth. I'm committed to persisting for the right—to trying. 'I'm *trying,*' I often tell my husband, and he says, '*Very* trying.' But living the Christian life, isn't that just how it is?"

A peculiar snort came from the second row, from her startled husband, there at the end. There followed lots of rustles and clearing throats, and as she scraped up her papers, somebody started clapping. The noise rose and swelled and rolled across the pavilion. It astonished her and flooded her to the gills with self-consciousness.

"Refreshing, very refreshing!" barked Philip Delp, the man with the petunia-hued neck, as he pumped Anna's hand and Wade's after the meeting. This was the district's new moderator-elect, mind you. He'd taken the platform after Anna and delivered the lengthy keynote speech. People were just milling around now, not necessarily seeking her out, so him bumping into her and Wade was more circumstantial than anything. "You have to realize how that prayer-cap talk comes across to anybody who's younger," Delp chortled. "When you said 'buns,' there for a second I took it as 'bums.' Ha ha!"

"Well, I didn't intend—" Anna trailed off. She swayed closer to her husband, taking strength from the brush of his sleeve against her clammy, bare arm. "Daddy had a lot on him at the mission," she said. "We had that little green rulebook, you know, and the bishop who came to Pottstown to instruct the converts read down through all the doctrines and ordinances. So Daddy upheld the teachings. If Josie Clark and Verna Pyles would've balked about the prayer cap, the bishop would've put off baptizing."

Philip Delp's eyes were darting. He was pivoting his head like a turkey, considering the crowd, the most feasible route through. She added, "The important thing, really, was Mama and Daddy's burden for the unsaved. Both my parents had a real heart for the lost." But Delp ducked to slap someone on the shoulder, another fellow loomed up in his place, and a woman trying to squeeze her way through inadvertently clonked Anna's elbow and sent her scrambling for her speech papers she'd not pushed down deep enough into her bag. Anna had to pick them off the pavilion floor, the one page slightly trampled. All these years later it still bears a faint, rubbery shoe mark.

IN THE AFTERNOON, wheeled backwards in the swivel desk chair to return the papers to the file cabinet, Anna takes pains to not coax the drawer the furthest possible extent open. It's too tippy a piece of furniture—once, with three-year-old Jonathan at her side, she caused the whole thing to topple frontwards and upchuck a portion of the contents. The sharp corner of the drawer nearly chopped off Jonathan's toes. "I thought I warned you!" exclaimed Mama, when she found out. "That upper drawer is a dilly!" But Anna couldn't remember Mama offering any such caution the day Wade and she had driven off with it sticking out of the trunk. Already the battered metal had grown little trails of rust from the disuse.

Just as old, probably, is her easy chair flanking the file cabinet, from Davy Jenkins's Saturday-night auction house behind Pantry Pride. A decidedly un-naked-lady style, it's upholstered in gray velour except for the carved wooden arms, and the nap is seriously defaced, especially on the lumpy, bowled seat. She bought the chair only a few weeks after the Rawlings Lake conference. "It'll be for when my fame spreads," she joked to Wade, snickering through her nose, as she cast about in her black bag to find out how high she could bid. "It'll be for the *Newsweek* and *Time* interviewers lining up." She cocked her hand over her mouth and shook with glee over her own silliness. The mere memory now, the mirth of it, comes pushing up from her lungs in dangerous bubbles.

Huh, flattery sure gets you nowhere, she tells herself. And, oh my, she just must get to her canning.

That's the job she's at when Todd comes in from school, when he enters the kitchen and shoves his backpack across the dining table. The tomatoes she's dropped into the kettle of boiling water on the stove have started to crack—left in till the skins tear in this way, they're easier to peel. Next she'll chop the tomatoes into sections and pack her jars and add salt, and then they'll go into the canner. Waving away the steam, she greets her son jauntily. "So how was your day?"

"Got a barrel of trigonometry homework again."

"Oh dear. Well, it won't hurt you."

"Yeah, you wanna do it?"

She clucks in sympathy as she chases a plump specimen with her slotted spoon, lifts it through the haze, and deposits it in the dishpan of saggy, already blanched tomatoes. She retrieves a second one, equally large and smoldering hotly. Scooping up a third from the water, she comments, "Just be thankful for your mathematical genes, because you didn't get them from me."

"Or I did, Mom, and that's why you don't have any left."

Spoon midair, she retorts, "You're the works!" The tomato is wavering and she mustn't let it go rolling on the floor, squirting juice and seeds. And the rosy, rent skin of the one still not fished out is curling hard along the fissure. Better hurry, she thinks, dumping the irresolute biggie and diving once more. "Anyhow, I don't even pretend to know better. I never was a whiz at those equations and what-all. I never had a head for computing. Never understood $E=mc^2$ and other such hooey."

"Mom, that's Einstein. That's physics."

"Oh, right. Oops."

These are Big Boys, a bright red variety. She never wants Wade to grow those dusty pink hybrids some people prefer. Pink tomatoes are sweeter, lower in acid, but for common ordinary home canning, for water-bath processing, foods must be high acid. If a food is low in acidity, botulin can develop in the sealed-tight jars; in the anaerobic conditions, the *C. botulinum* spores that are omnipresent in nature and for the most part harmless can go on a breeding rampage. Anna has read somewhere that several tablespoons of the toxin, straight, could kill the entire population in the Western hemisphere. Only high-temperature pressure canning assuredly destroys all viability, so since she doesn't own a pressure canner she freezes the low-acid vegetables like corn, peas, green beans.

Of course, fruits do fine with water-bath canning. And besides the true-red tomatoes, anything pickled does, too.

Near suppertime, as Todd over at the table absorbs himself in punching more and more numbers into his calculator, Anna notes the faint chirpings of towhees or grackles in the sugar maple—their happy-go-lucky take on such a golden September afternoon. Theirs is the only outside sound she can pick up. In the stillness of the kitchen, the warm tomato aroma is suddenly too much. Knifing apart a deflated, blanched fellow and letting the chunks slide between her fingers and plop into the jar, she straightens her shoulders tiredly and decides the second basketful still sitting out in the mudroom will have to wait. Tomorrow's another day. Tomorrow she'll make those tomatoes into juice. Maybe she'll can the hot peppers, too—maybe she'll try out her new recipe.

4

Perched quietly while Erma Lee Showalter reads the opening Scripture, Psalm 23, before dismissing everybody for Sunday school, Anna notes the sickly tint of Erma Lee's soft bread-dough cheeks. But she can't be any more flattered, herself, by the squeaks of green light the pocked church windows allow in. She feels a touch of sympathy for Wade beside her. He's always complaining about not being able to see out—what's nature for, in its myriad beholden glories? For a change, here's something that bothers him more than her; clear windows in the sanctuary would be fine, certainly, but she wouldn't take advantage by monitoring the geese flights and insect life. On special occasions when the candles behind the pulpit are lit, flickering atop their wrought-iron legs and reflecting in the angular mosaic panes of the front window that's fittingly designed in the shape of the cross, opaque green like the side windows, it takes her back to her and Wade's wedding. Only at Jackson Road that evening, in the church Mama still attends, the multicolors of the cross's fractured glass gave off a more poignant aura—the darting shadows of turquoise, amber, chartreuse, and pink.

Oh, and the day of the wedding, to add to the colorfulness, Wade's mom placed upon the organ lid a kidney-shaped basket with a high loopy handle, holding full-blooming stalks of blue and purple gladioli she'd brought the whole way from Hawk Knob where she and Dad Schlonneger

3 4   S H I R L E Y   K U R T Z

and a bunch of the clan still live, two counties over from here. Watching as
Mrs. Schlonneger conferred with Sam Bollinger, Jackson Road's pastor at
the time, over the positioning of the basket, Anna worried about what Mrs.
Shlonneger might be making of Sam's one notable idiosyncrasy. He had this
unnerving way of lapping his tongue around his gums—was it a chronic
case of gingivitis, or what?

Overall the church here at Conoy is less of a showcase, Anna guesses.
Plain pews, while at Jackson Road the pews, blond to match the piano, are
lined with velvety maroon cushions. For the benefit of any passing traffic,
the Conoy church has a narrow slatted-wood tower sticking up a few feet
above the roof, whereas at Jackson Road a steeple overlaid with hammered
copper juts into the sky, tarnished to a salt-wave green.

Hm, salt wave, thinks Anna. Well, that's apt. Except ocean water isn't
like a river's. After she started college, after Mama and Daddy moved the
family away from Pottstown to Jackson, three years later the town took a
pounding from the worst hurricane in fifty years. The Jackson newspapers
told how the vicious brown, boiling flux from the normally sluggish
Elkhorn River, which had risen fourteen feet above flood stage, surged
down Frederick Street and pummeled house foundations, splintered front
doors, and slapped at the wainscotings and parlor wallpapers, and left in its
wake mud-coated floors warped beyond repair and rotted legs on all the
downstairs furniture. Much of the south side of the town had to be razed,
including the mission building, and in time the Evangelical Brethren district office commissioned the construction of a chapel up on the hill and a
parsonage alongside, sturdy yellow brick.

A week before their wedding Anna induced Wade to drive her over. She
wanted him to get an inkling, at least, of her old life. By now a number of
the buildings had been leveled in the damaged section of town—a yellow-
blinkered road-construction barrier still prevented access. The scene almost
made *her* feel expunged. "This doesn't tell a whole lot," Wade remarked,
leaning back against the hood of his Mustang. He'd parked the car snubbed
up against the trestle's crossbar with CAUTION painted in glaring letters.

"You're right about that," she said ruefully. "It's like my past is in wrack
and ruin."

But of course no flood has demolished the basic, staying truths. The
church still upholds the big important things. The peace teachings—nobody's let those fall by the wayside. At Jackson Road, Conoy, or any other
congregation in the Evangelical Brethren denomination, no silky, ripply
Stars and Stripes hangs on a pole up front, smack alongside the Christian

flag like in other churches, as if the national one should be accorded the same cross-your-heart-and-hope-to-die loyalty. Pacifist Christians, all the ones Anna is acquainted with, see no use in those bumper-sticker slogans about God and country, and no place, *no place,* for the glorification of war. So the memorial signboards are missing in the church lobbies, too, with their bronze slide-in name tags honoring soldiers who died a bloody death on some battlefield, ridding the world of Nazis or Communism.

Thou shalt not kill, period. That's the thing! Is it any wonder she nearly lost her way last year, all in a stew over the way God put Abraham through the mill?

But—now wait—no no no no no no—that's too much like excusing herself. Goodness.

Down in the Sunday school classroom, next, in the basement, Anna settles in contentedly as Susan Nussbaum, her study guide on the table along with the two Bible dictionaries she always brings, begins the lesson on the prophet Jeremiah's captivity in an empty cistern. Jeremiah's forecasts about the horrible fate soon to befall anybody who doesn't surrender to the Babylonians have made him appear traitorous and gotten him where he's at, sunk down into the mire. "Picture it as a brackish, deep sludge, if you can," suggests Susan, her face chipper and animated. She's so good at laying out the background like this, making a story come alive. "And what's more, they were starving him!"

Suddenly she spots Nelson Rhodes's copy of the latest *Faith Confession* lying atop his zipper Bible. Every five years or so, the Evangelical Brethren publication board puts out a new batch of these booklets, basically spelling out in snazzier print the long-held doctrines: the Trinity, original sin, the divine plan of salvation, heaven and hell, and so forth. This time though, the church's peace position is promulgated in a lengthier, annotated essay. "Do you mind?" she asks Nelson, stepping over to where he's sitting at the table. She scoops up the glossy softcover pamphlet and waves it like it's her filled dustrag she's shaking out the window.

"Pardon me for straying a minute, but has anybody else here noticed the same thing I've noticed? Have you read, in the ordinances section, the statement on footwashing? No? Well, they've toned it down. They make it sound like a useful exercise but not an outright command from the Lord— which I find perturbing, to say the least. Is the Bible no longer our authority?"

She grabs hers, open at Jeremiah, and scribbers her thumbnail down the length of ribbon, tacking it deeper into the pages' dip so she can take off on a search. "Don't we believe that everything here is faithful to history and inspired? And didn't the Lord stipulate that we're to wash feet?" She flips the pages in chunks, on ahead to the Gospels, to Luke, John, John 8, John 13, skims down a column, and begins reading in her precise, nonmushy voice Anna always envies. "'If I, then, your Lord and Master, have washed your feet, ye also ought to wash one another's feet,' quote, unquote." Susan looks up, looks around. She's blinking rapidly, a habit of hers Anna finds endearing, though not Wade. He says it reminds him of a hummingbird. But he does get on well with Susan—sometimes he helps her out by filling in as teacher. "Tell me please," she demands, "what excuse could there be for disregarding this command from Christ?"

"Oh," Anna butts in, "I don't think footwashing will ever go. The concept—it's a key concept. We need that reminder to be practicing a life of servanthood. Sure, some of the ways we do things have changed—"

No girdles, for example. Communion nights back at Pottstown, after Bishop Strite returned the uneaten bread to the front table, and the two tin goblets of leftover grape juice, the men's and women's, and after he gave Daddy and Herman Overholt their signal to carry in the footwashing tubs, the church members duly followed the example of the Lord when he put aside his garments: the men over on their side removed their shoes and socks, and the women filed chastely out to the anteroom to take off their nylons. Or, most of the women—just not the bishop's wife and the deacon's. Right there at their seats, Ruby Strite and Mildred Overholt felt through their skirts to pop their garters, and then, *shlish,* down slid their nylons.

"Like, who wears a girdle anymore?" says Anna. "And we don't necessarily do the skin thing, either."

Justine across the table gives one of her squawks and Anna hastily puts in, "You know what I mean. Where I grew up, anyway, the ladies always shed their stockings. Mrs. Strite and Mrs. Overholt did it right out in the open, in plain view. Margie and I, we'd roll our eyes. Too public! But the point is, you got everybody in their raw skin."

Into her head jumps a memory of the time she got stuck footwashing with Josie Clark. Josie smelled oily and sour, like she'd been frying onions, and when she realized her hem was dipping in the water she snatched up her skirt and Anna caught a close-up flash of dimpled fat-lady thigh, whoa. "The old way was just more homely, I guess," says Anna. "We'd gird up like the Lord in special towels with ducking tape sewed on so they could be tied around the waist, and we'd unceremoniously get on with our slosh-sloshing, rub-rubbing, pat-patting, and after our God-bless-yous and holy kisses, we'd hightail back to the anteroom. Mrs. Overholt and Mrs. Strite, though? They'd just shamble back to their seats and repair themselves, as if—"

Wait a minute. Can that be? Them coaxing up their nylons and revealing their spongy, white, upper-leg flesh, while floundering for their girdle elastics and grappling with the clamps and garter buttons? She witnessed *that*? Huh. It sounds too implausible. But she can't remember ever seeing Ruby and Mildred out in the anteroom afterwards amid the companionly, shushed hustle and bustle of women putting themselves to rights. "Um, just a minute, I'm not sure about that part," says Anna, rushing her words together. "I maybe got that part wrong."

Susan, restored to her usual vivaciousness, quips merrily, "Thank the Lord for *some* changes!"

"Like you said, Anna, the meaning's the thing," offers Peg Heatwole. "I've not forgotten that really good article you wrote about your mother— what you said about her servant attitude. So interesting, I thought. Servanthood should be our constant goal."

"Well—" Anna manages, caught off guard by the flattery, and fortunately, Justine takes over. "Oh, nuts," she says with a huff, "the details don't matter. What matters is that we're still footwashing."

"Pantyhose washing, you mean," Anna amends, but she fails to get another squawk out of Justine.

Upstairs after Sunday school, after Scott Forry's sermon and the partaking of the communion emblems in the warmer light, for the sun is taking a higher path and creating a green glow, the footwashing proceedings begin. Like her friends, Anna only kicks off her shoes—strappy, dressy heels. She doesn't inchingly shuck her control-panel pantytop, ply the clingy nylon folds downward, and molt free of the last stretchy sections of footing. Past her move the first several women, flat-footed and comfortable but still confined, and generously she ignores the synthetic *shhh-shhh* sound of somebody's porky thighs rubbing.

Waiting in the line of women, Anna picks off a curly sprig of stray hair on the back of Peg Heatwole's blouse, beckoning like a beetle's antenna in the air-conditioning updraft. "Thanks," whispers Peg, turning and smiling. Peg is extremely pretty, with perky boobs, the kind Anna would choose if this were possible—if a person could pluck from a display hook in Wal-Mart, back in the lingerie department, her exact preference among the numerous sets of knockers in their little snap-shut plastic bags.

As she watches Susan knelt at a tub, paired with Donna Rhodes, Anna is wistful. Susan's appearance is so spiffy and perfect. Her bathroom ritual way early this morning, she must've pumiced her soles and smoothed on lotion and tweezered the wrap off a brand-new packet of hose, maybe the L'eggs brand, Silken Mist, causing a flyaway piece of the plastic to whirligig unseen into the commode—if Jack Nussbaum is like Wade, he never puts down the lid. Switching her thoughts to Donna's suit, Anna wonders about the fabric. Shantung, maybe? It's beautifully nubbed. Donna is a sweet one, too, just more reserved. Or not reserved exactly, maybe restrained. Her kindness always shines through.

"You sit first," Anna whispers to Peg. Planted at the tub, Peg extends one foot over it, not down in. Anna's dolings of water trickle over Peg's stocking and separate like mercury escaping a broken thermometer—the water splits into wee, uncertain globules. The wet can't penetrate except where a tiny run has started, where Peg's toenail gloss is glinting through the shredding nylon. Mostly the water dritzes back into the tub. But carefully, with a great deal of tenderness, Anna pats with the towel. Then she turns her attention to Peg's other lissome, clad foot.

Her turn, Anna plunks her feet deep down in, flat against the tub's cool zinc. As the water paddles at her ankles, she centers her mind on the just-completed communion service—on the flesh-and-blood reminders of the Lord's suffering, and the pastor's murmurs as the church members filed past, *This is my body broken for you, take and eat; this is my shed blood, take and drink.* Jesus bleeding and dying—oh, dear God. That Jesus gave his life for her—it always puts her to shame.

Yes, she thinks affectionately, Mama provided a precious example. Mama running the bathtub for drunk Mrs. McCulley so she could soak her whole soused body, now *that* was footwashing—the archetypal lowly, servantly, high deed. A fresh appreciation for the church people here, too, for their unbudging stand on the Word of God, washes over Anna, a from-the-bottom-of-her-heart thankfulness. That's another crucial thing to include. Without these spiritual pillars to model after, how much lower might've she sunk during her season of unrest and desolation? Were it not for their influence, how could she ever be embarked, now, on a book?

5

Again this morning the bucolic backwoods balm has settled down onerously around Anna's head and clobbered her to mush. She despises this inertia—the way she always goes to pot, just slumps in her seat and grows more and more numb, unable to haul herself out. Her brain circuitry is stuck on "uneaten," this one single word in her Chapter 4 printout. "Uneaten," Bishop Strite returning the "uneaten" communion bread to the front table, makes it sound like everybody refused their portion, like they proceeded right on past him as he pinched off pieces and shushed in a low tone the timeworn words, *The bread which we break, is it not the communion of the body of Christ? The bread which we break, is it not the communion of the body of Christ?* Not like they held out their obsequious, grateful palms and received. But what word can she possibly substitute? She's been nubbing her pencil eraser circlewise against the paper and poofing at the shredded black tails, and fruitlessly pondering.

Even one of those battery-driven cattle prods would do. Almost any interruption would be a mercy—anything to propel her. Say, the shrills of the phone in the kitchen; or the stove timer's ding (but there's nothing in the oven), or else the smoke alarm's screams (if a pie were bubbling over); or the mail carrier's Jeep out front, spitting gravel. Something to get her blood running, that's the crux. Even if she just needed to go to the bathroom—the clip upstairs could act as a trigger. That headlong action after the lengthy period of immobility, with her mind going duller and duller and clotting hopelessly, could fire up the neurons, enough to alleviate her fixating, and in the bathroom the words could commence to bumping around behind her skull and rearranging themselves.

Hm, "unused" bread, she's thinking, no no no, when the quiet churning of the washer out in the mudroom abruptly breaks off and the first spin cycle erupts. Todd's jeans in the depths begin racketing around and around, *wop, wop, wop, wop, wop,* and she lifts her eyes. So that's a start. Minutes later, after the rinse cycle's turn and the second spin, hearing the washer quit with a huff and a thump, *hff-ump,* she upheaves herself from the desk chair. Outside at the backyard lines she plops her wash basket and clothespins bucket in the grass, and just that act, the stooping motion and the sudden downswing of her head, causes somewhat of a rush—she senses her brain prickling. As the blood cells get to galloping, she thinks, Maybe "remaining"? The "remaining" bread, could she say?

"Psst," she hisses at the cat, scramming him, because he was about to climb in with the clothespins. Pleased with her new pellet of thought, she raises the first pieces of laundry to the crisping sun. Okay then, "remaining," she concurs with herself silently.

Unlike the cat, Wade's loose hen is naturally keeping her distance, scrabbling underneath the raspy, dead dill umbrellas in the garden and clucking over each newfound seed, pinchbug, earwig, and gourmet larva, but the dog, Popper, prefers company, and as Anna goes on routing and shaking the clothes and advancing down the line, she allows him to remain underfoot, lounging in the sloppy wet grass, muzzle planted on his paddy forepaws and his rolled-up eyes on the alert. Or maybe "half-loaf of bread"? proposes Anna to herself, her headcloggedness thoroughly ameliorated. Would "half-loaf" convey even better? Or how about "the leftovers"? Except, no, that might evoke a few little snitches, not the sizeable hunk Brother Strite covered over with Mama's fringed linen cloth. That part of the loaf, the amount that didn't get plucked off in small turkey-stuffing morsels and dispensed, reverted right back to regular bread. Mama made toast the next morning.

Back in the house again, Anna wheels herself up close to the desk, eager to scratch out "uneaten"—but now the term seems perfectly fine. There's nothing wrong with it. All that time she wasted, fixedly boring her eyes! In embarrassment she gives the page a good shake.

She reads through the rest of the scene in Sunday school, finding little to pick at. It's interesting enough, probably. But should've she included the Sunday school lesson's outcome? The end of the cistern story, where rescuers come with a rope and old rags? They throw the rags down to Jeremiah, yelling that he must wad them under his armpits, because he's horribly emaciated, and forthwith they haul him up. Soon thereafter, King Zedekiah, who ordered the rescue operation, meets with him. "I need your advice," the king says, "and you mustn't hide the truth from me." Jeremiah replies, "But if I tell the truth you'll kill me. You won't listen anyway." "No, no," the king protests. He gives his promise not to betray Jeremiah. So, as before, the prophet urges that the Jews must surrender to the Babylonians.

"And did the king heed?" asked Susan, Sunday in class. She gave a tug on the ribbon in her Bible, and the big round fake ruby brooch pinned on her front wobbled slightly, sharing in her indignation. "Did he? Just give a guess, if you've not read the passage. Brenda? Did Zedekiah take Jeremiah's words to heart?"

Brenda Arnold, not the best person to pick on, thrust out her cheeks in speculation. "No?" she ventured.

"Actually, that's correct—he didn't. And look at the destruction that befell! You'd think folks would learn."

Oh, right—Susan's pin. Yes, here's another change among the Evangelical Brethren—the wearing of jewelry. A number of verses in the Bible warn loudly against adorning yourself, so the bishops in the past handed down stringent rules. But aren't the Bible's injunctions really against pride? Against exalting yourself more highly than others, or showing off? Lord knows, the most plain-dressing, drabbest of souls can still be a preener. An ugly wrinkled-up prunish person can still be harboring destructive, self-glorifying attitudes, as can a dumb-dumb self-fancied writer. So that's the point—the pride.

Certainly, though, people's concerns about slippage in the church are understandable. There always exists the possibility of backsliddenness. Susan *should* feel a little jumpy about the new wording about footwashing in the *Faith Confession* booklet, about the church relaxing its position, because if *that* practice isn't quote, unquote, scriptural anymore, what might go flying out the window next? What really big, mainstay belief?

Except, just because a person is convinced something is scriptural, does that make him or her a special possessor of the truth? Not necessarily. The person might be misguided. Simply because the church leaders in former times were dogmatic about the prayer cap, did that make it an instrument of salvation? A woman's black gauze bun-warmer thingy encasing the back of her head, held fast with straight pins and bagging at the bottom from the load—did it put her right with the Lord? Or could a bed sheet instead, like in another of Anna's childhood stories she wrote, assure that the Lord would hear and save?

ANNA HAS DECIDED the readers won't understand beans about the sheet unless she digs out "Fist Lady." Her printout of Chapter 4 laid aside, upstairs she again retrieves the wicker stool from the bathroom, and she balances herself on the seat to sort through her decrepit old boot box. After she's back on solid footing, a stir of breeze from the hall window helpfully whisks the crumblies off the top page, the powdery bits of cardboard.

What she said in her speech at Rawlings Lake about Miss Fritz was no exaggeration—about her teacher's eloquence and dignity of bearing. It's no wonder Anna's pluck failed her. She'd collected her stories into a pile, with her cover page titled "Oh, the Trials and Tribulations of a Girl Growing Up," and she was all set to hole punch everything and string in the shiny, stiff scrap of stationery ribbon Mama had given her, when, without warning, a horrible misgiving drenched her and jellied the very bones of her soul. Miss Fritz might laugh. Musical little titters might come floating up out of her pearly, thin throat. Deflated of purpose, Anna crept to the cellar, to the under-the-stairs shelves where Mama kept old boxes, and she found one the right size for secreting her trove. Wesley's orange string lay behind the box, wedged in the crack between the shelf and the stone foundation wall, still in the same tight, scrimping ball she'd wound it into after his yo-yo accident.

Her "Fist Lady" pages, when the breeze completes its dusting, appear all the more pitiful. The lines are totally hatcheted up with mistakes. The soupy typing, too, would rouse the pity of any readers, if they could see. The *b*'s are soot-bellied, and the bottom lobe of every *g* is all-the-way blacked in.

The Fist Lady

Eleven years old Annie on the bench saw how Daddy's cuffs,
how he was holding up his Bible to read, stuck out like his suit was
shrunk, but not bad shrunk. He was saying his syllables separate
and clear, he had this part memorized. "Every man pray-ing or
proph-e-sy-ing with his head covered up dis-hon-our-eth his head.
But every woman that pray-eth or proph-e-si-eth with her head un-
cov-ered dis-hon-our-eth her head, for that is even all one as if she
were shav-en."

Daddy said, "And look at the next verse too. Look how it says, For if the woman be not cov-ered up, let her be shorn." That word "if" he said slow, and "also" he said slow too.

He laid down his Bible and fished in his pants pocket for his two dress hankies Mama'd bleached good and ironed. Onehanded he shook the first one open. "Follow close here, people." Floaty floaty down it came over his other hand made in a fist. He draped the corners, explaining, "Here we have the woman's hair." Next he shook out the second hanky and arrayed it over top. "And here we have the woman's covering, her cap." It was almost like the fist lady was breathing out little puffs, the way the hankies were quailing.

He checked in his Bible to read again. "For if the woman be not all cov-ered up," he said like before, and pulled off the top hanky, "let her also be shorn," and then he pulled away the other one. This made his fist as bald as Mrs. Overholt's chicken eggs. Probly up close his little black knuckle hairs were flicketing, appreciating the fresh air. "But if it be a shame for the woman to be shorn or shav-en," he said, because now he was finishing up the verses and returning the hair hanky over his fist, "let her be cov-ered," and down flappered the cap hanky and settled on the hair one.

He said, "How can it be any plainer? Why's this ignored in other churches? We're taught in 1 Timothy women should learn in silence with all subjection, so where's any call for putting women in the pulpit and subjecting the men, either? How much longer will we remain the faithful remnant?"

Well, that night in bed Annie heard Mama still in her church shoes come tapping tapping down the hall and then the footsteps stopped. "Annie?" On account of how her head was wrapped up in the sheet the sounds came through muffly. "Annie?" She said in her mind, In Jesus' name, amen, and flung off the sheet.

She dandied the edge nice and smooth over the spread's little chenille bumps, Mama not saying a peepsqueak at first, only watching. "What were you doing?" said Mama. "Just finishing up my praying," said Annie.

Mama had Herbie's ripped trousers she'd got off the dirty wash pile and Wesley's scuffy high tops with the laces half fallen out, and she turned on the dresser lamp and ploppered down. Annie felt along the sheet fold in case the little air rushes had tousled it and for a while Mama just stayed sitting, doing the lace on a high top and doing the other one and swing-a-swinging her foot and jiggering the bed. "It's easier praying in bed," confessed Annie. "Guess I'm just lazy." She'd tried keeping her prayer cap on but it got too mashed.

"Nobody cares if you're in bed," said Mama. "Just talk to the Lord."

"You know how we're supposed to pray without ceasing," Annie remindered Mama. "Except Preacher Yoder said seizing."

"Seizing?"

"In Bible Conference. That's how he said that verse, 'Pray without seizing.'"

"Oh," said Mama.

"It means be ever ready, right? Does it matter if I substitute with the covers?"

Mama said, "Annie, just pray anyhow you want. The prayer cap is for a public sign. It's our witness out in public, showing we're trying to be pure and in submission." Mama's foot speeded up. "What counts the most is the heart. God sees in our hearts. God hears our very thoughts rising up to him as prayers."

"But Mama, if God's looking and seeing."

"No, now you're carrying things to extremes again." But wasn't Mama herself careful? If Annie had to go the bathroom after Mama and Daddy came up to bed, if she looked in going past and they were down on bended knee praying, here's the sight she'd see. Mama's bathrobe slopped across the chair and her scuffs underneath and her hairpins laying this way and that on the dresser, an untidy sight, and Mama's hair pouring down her back like honey, but still she had her cap stuck on top. Crooked and not straight pinned but still on. Was she out in public? No! So how could Mama preach? What she said didn't help Annie none. The only help would be to be a boy. A boy, ha ha.

Obviously, by "So how could Mama preach?" she only meant "expound." Privately expound. Not preacher preach, gracious.

By the hall window, musing, she picks at a page corner. Shucks, ingrained as the thinking was back then about women's underling role, it's understandable if some in the older generation are still having trouble making the switch. If they had that belief pounded into them, why shouldn't they resist the notion that submission is the man's job as much as the woman's? The two holdouts at church are Erma Lee Showalter and her sis-

ter, sweet old Birdie King—being of the mind that women should keep to
their place, they still wear the cap.

Well, there's Peg, too. She and Jay have a farm east of town, the only
full-fledged dairy operation in the area anymore; day in and day out she has
to help milk and it's no prim, prissy life, and yet, Sundays when she gets to
church she pins a cute little scrap of black lace over her corkscrew curls still
damp from her trying to shampoo out the barn smell. She's Evangelical
Brethren now, but she had a very different past, growing up in a Catholic
home—so mightn't the lace doily be more a holdover from the Catholic tra-
dition?

Peg is plenty feisty, though. Not only does she routinely roll out of bed
at the crack of dawn, on Sundays she also takes extra pains with the family's
breakfast, their custom of Sunday donuts. She deep-fries the donuts in vegetable oil in her roaster pan and serves them up hot. They're really just those
pop-out biscuits that come in cardboard tubes—she cuts out the biscuits'
middles, drops both the holes and the rings into the boiling oil, and after
they puff up and turn brown, she rolls them in a sugar-cinnamon mixture.
To this day Anna can recall Jonathan, when he was just a little squirt, coming home and blabbing about those donuts. Dudley'd had him over for a
campout behind the sofa. "We had cocoa, too," Jonathan reported, swag-
gering with importance. "And as many marshmallows as we wanted. Dudley's mommy put the cocoa scum in the cat dish."

Peg's ability to take herself with a grain of salt is what Anna most envies—her calm, no-nonsense, matter-of-fact practicality. And for all her
conscientiousness about her doily, she's not the cowed, groveling type of
person. Anna can't imagine the little-girl Peggy clogging herself up in the
bedclothes while doing her rosary beads or worrying if she mispronounced.
That night Mama on her way downstairs stopped in her tracks by the doorway to peer in at the lumped covers, Anna was mentally chanting her cus-
tomary wrap-up "I'm sorry" line: "And forgive me for all my sins, dear God,
please dear God, please, in Jesus' name, amen." At any moment Jesus might
return, the sky shooting quicksilver lightning jags from east to west, and if
she didn't frame the words right? Though Mama, Daddy, Margie, and the
boys all whooshed up to meet the Lord, mightn't she be left behind to blaze
forever 'n' ever in hell?

Anna gives a huff, sighs. Story pages in hand, hitting on the window
screen to shoo the ladybugs migrating across, she thinks, Unfortunately
some of us are born extra sensitive. Poor Mama hardly knew what to do
with her shrinking, difficult-natured daughter. Maybe the problems even

stumped the Lord. Doesn't the Lord shudder, watching his children learn of his ways, overseeing as they bungle along, bungle along, deciding what to hold fast to and what to release? That's always the trick, isn't it? Knowing what meaning to assign? Besides, of course, obeying then with the same alacrity and trustfulness as Abraham's when he forayed up Mount Moriah and laid down his boy?

Some behavioral differences between people are innate, Anna feels sure. Wade's mom, for instance. "Yeah, she calls it her bee bonnet," Anna can remember Wade telling her, soon after they started dating, when she asked if Mrs. Schlonneger still wore the prayer cap.

"Honest?" asked Anna, her mouth dropping open. She pulled it back shut and tamped down the giggle welling up. "But doesn't 'bee in your bonnet' mean hot and bothered? Does she act all snooty and bugged about it?"

"Nope, she just pancakes it on and says, 'There, now quiet down yourall's buzzing.' She's quite the card."

"My mama, never," said Anna. "And when you've been taught the prayer cap is called for in God's Word, ditching it isn't the easiest thing." She still couldn't believe it, somebody like him in her European History class. An out-of-state junior-year transfer from some backwoods place, Hawk Mountain, who was a dyed-in-the-wool Evangelical Brethren, plus tall and virile and rippling with smarts—and attentive to dumb little her?

"It's peripheral, Anna." Wade clamped his arm around her and pulled her over onto the hump between the Mustang's bucket seats. "Look, I'll take you down to visit. You'll like my family, I promise."

Mrs. Schlonneger attended the wedding prim and pinned. She gave herself several more years before giving up the cap. She did it rather blithely, though, Anna bets. She's never actually questioned Wade's mom, but at what point did Mrs. Schlonneger know without a shadow of doubt that she wouldn't be condemned for it? How much do happy-go-lucky people like her dither over what beliefs to let go, let fly?

"Fist Lady," anyhow, isn't about to go a-sailing, forgotten on the wind. The window screen isn't slid up on its tracks. Anna only raises it if she's cleaning up here in the hall, needing to shake out her mop laden with the floorboards' lint and dust bunnies. So there's no chance a surprise gust will whip the pages from her grasp and send them scuttling across the roof of the mudroom and lofting out over the yard and garden, casting bird shadows on the grass, the burgeoning heads of late-crop broccoli, the still-dutiful tomatoes, and the spotty collection of hot peppers—those she didn't pick to can the other day, not reddened yet or a deep-enough yellow.

As the filmy voile curtain lifts and sags, lifts and sags, lifts and sags, under the sway of the gentle but willful breeze, she notes a few unchastened ladybugs, ones who spattered onto the sill at her mean knocks but then rightened their tiny bodies. They're advancing across the screen's hopscotch holes again, the very audacity. An especially adventurous critter hesitates mid-trip, levers out its ticky wings, flies into Anna's hair, and rambles toward her scalp.

6

The tall oak hutch in the kitchen, the upper doors fronted with glass and exhibiting her summer canning, came years ago from a farm sale down the road from the Schlonneger home place at Hawk Knob. Only fifty dollars. It was lathered all over with hideous black shellac. Wade about worked the skin off his bones, refinishing. In the thick of canning season, Anna can't squeeze everything in—the overflow goes to the cellar and gradually makes the trip back upstairs. But she's strict about not using everything up from one summer to the next, hiding the accumulating empty jars in the rear and maintaining the bounteous front-row display of yellows, reds, greens, and purples glimmering shoulder to shoulder.

"You don't think it's deceitful of me?" she asks Wade sometimes. "No, Anna," comes the weary reply. But what about overweening and vain? Her peaches, cherries, tomatoes, soft-fleshed apricots, prickly pickle slices, Concord grapes made into pie filling (the grape skins pinched off and set aside, the slithery eyeballs boiled to a pulp and sieved to eliminate the seeds, and then the skins put back in with the pulp), tender whole beets in a spicy vinegar brine, sweet sugared applesauce—isn't this all too grand and glorious?

Yet, couldn't anybody else achieve the same thing? If they'd run around all summer as she does, like a chicken with its head chopped off? That's what she asks herself this evening while emptying the dish drainer. She returns a washed applesauce jar to the hutch, pushing it to the back where it will stand upside down but hopeful, and she turns her eye to the lineup of tomatoes and tomato juice and slides a finger along the side of one quart, bumping over the ridged lettering, B-a-l-l with a fancy huge *B*. Furthermore, to take the tomatoes as an example, how would it be frugal of her or responsible, healthwise, to settle for store-boughts instead, those dismal things that had to sit out their lives in vast pesticided fields only to get harvested indiscriminately, in one fell swoop, by gas-hog mechanical pickers and trucked to the cannery by the tonload, mashing hopelessly and offering up their dubious nutrients to the baking-hot highway air?

Not that she's such a sucker for the hard work. Just one more day on tomatoes, whew.

Back at the sink, reaching for the plates in the drainer, she catches a glimpse of Wade through the window—he's striding across the back yard toward the garage carrying the holey-lidded jar he uses to spread his Reet pesticide, a pyrethrins compound. Though it's organic, the dust takes a few days to break down to a harmless state. "Hey!" she yells. "Hey—Wade!" She drops her dish towel, races for the mudroom, and flings open the door to scan the garden.

Thanks to him the two rows of tomato plants, seriously bedraggled by this late in the season, are now as powdery and ashen as the ruins of Pompeii. "Wade!" she screams. "I was going to do one more batch of juice tomorrow! I wasn't going to let that job drag into next week! I wanted it over and done with! You! Now look what you've done! Now I'll have to wait till Monday for it to be safe!"

Backtracking, he rounds the corner of the house waving his jar at her. "It's okay. It's not Reet. It's just some lime. Dad said that's what he's doing for the deer this year. The county agent over there told him deer won't even snuff at the stuff. I thought I'd give it a try."

He walks over to the edge of the strawberry patch and gestures. "The deer are really moving in. Look, droppings. You *want* the tomatoes, don't you? Did you want to give up on them before frost?"

"Oh. All right, then. Just lime, you say."

"I'll pick you all the tomatoes you need. Don't be so all-fired accusing."

Mollified, she steps back to shut the door. Instead, she suddenly yanks it wide again and sputters, "But—but lime? Won't that change their pH? Reduce the acidity?"

"Nah, Anna. Just wash it off."

Finishing her kitchen chores, she's only halfway shamefaced about getting so upset. But later, regret niggles. Looking at the spiritual side of things, if she had a full, full measure of faith in God's protection would she be such a worrier? If she'd always just trust the Lord? Wade has never offered that suggestion, no. But doesn't she understand all too well what happens when a person doesn't lean completely on the Lord? After her backsliding feat of last year, shouldn't she know to be more on her guard?

NEXT AFTERNOON, hearing the screech of the school bus brakes, she pauses from pushing the boiled, soupy slop around and around in the strainer to catch her breath. She's ragged from all the exercise. She hunkers down to work again and only nods a hi when Todd comes into the house.

He swipes a sample of the thick pulp smushing through the strainer holes. "Yeech, Mom," he teases, "are you sure that stuff's all washed off?"

"I did my best. It certainly wasn't nice. Practically every other tomato was all gunked up." Starting in on the juice, easing the basket onto its side on the drainboard to roll the tomatoes into the sink, she was struck by a fear that the lime could've permeated the skins. Beset with the heebie-jeebies, she rubbed the tomatoes individually under the water, kneading hard, and she rinsed them, and then rinsed them again. But what difference would her efforts make if the skins allowed passage? Then she noticed, when she was cutting up the tomatoes, that every time she held her knife under the spigot after coring out a bad section, water droplets splashed into the kettle, diluting the tomato content and maybe diminishing the acidity level more. That Wade! How could he be so convinced of the safety? She wanted to smack him!

"I'm *not* sure," she tells Todd. He gives her a hooded look and she adds, "It's okay, though. I called Marlene Wagler at the newspaper office because I thought I remembered something in her column about tomatoes, about what to do if you're less than 100 percent positive they're not an acid-reduced variety. Marlene was very nice about it—she said to just add a tablespoon of lemon juice to each quart. She said it wouldn't affect the taste. Let me tell you, that was such a relief!" Taking another break from her frenetic stirring, she straightens and touches a hand to her aching back.

Todd examines the lifesaving jug of ReaLemon prominently guarding the jars that are still standing empty. He picks up a filled quart of warm juice and practically sticks his nose inside to sniff. "Don't do that!" she glares. "Nose hairs, yet. That's all I need!"

ONLY AFTER SUPPER, after the juice is canned, does she get around to swiping her floor sponge at the sticky tracks she's made. But she's buoyed by the popping sounds of the lids as they seal. In a day or two she'll place the jars alongside their fellows on the shelves that hold the rest of Wade's Big Boy beauties, altered but still laden with sun-and-rain vitamins: the chunkies crowding their jar space, dotted with swimmy yellow seeds, the blushing picture of health, so unlike Pantry Pride's sadly bloated, tinned variety floating in a wan sea; and the juice not at all akin to the suspiciously smooth, dense substance Pantry Pride sells under multifarious labels and obscured behind metal, but consisting instead of a lusty, substantive pith and a thin lymph, the two salubriously suspended, gorgeous through the glass.

From the porch door, now, she takes in the action in the driveway: a spread-eagled Todd partway underneath the car, assisted by the ash pan Wade uses for draining the oil, and Wade coaching. "Your wrench, okay— go counterclockwise. You got it? Then you'll have to take out the filter—"

Wade disappears into the garage and emerges with another junk rag. "You'll see it's mounted on a threaded post, so don't just hit at it. Get a grip on it and turn hard." He notices Anna. "Hang on," he says to Todd, "I'll be right back. Get that filter off, next."

In the kitchen, Wade lowers his tone. "I wanted to tell you. When I—" With the rag he makes an attempt to remove a splodge of grease on his wrist. He's wearing the oddest expression.

"Such a strange deal," he says. "I don't know what to make of it."

"Deal?"

"It's nothing. I sure hope it's nothing."

"Hon?"

"At RG's. When I stopped in town for gas, after school."

"Yes? So?"

"The pump didn't print out my receipt, so I had to go inside, past a white Corolla parked by the entrance, the same model as Beckers'. Their Corolla, I realized. So when I came out I thought I'd knock on Frank's window, he and Justine were just sitting there talking, and then I saw it wasn't Justine, it was Brenda."

"Brenda? Brenda Arnold?"

"He had his hand on her leg."

"What do you mean?"

"It was—bizarre."

"Like—like—? Well. I guess a person can be in another person's car. I guess they don't have to not touch."

"You'd want me doing that?"

"No, but—oh, Wade. Look, neither Frank nor Brenda would—"

"I didn't stop and get their attention. I don't think either one of them saw me."

"Well, it wasn't anything. I guess you didn't say anything to Jerry." Jerry Funkhouser, she means—the physics teacher at the high school who carpools with Wade.

"Of course not. Why would've I done that?"

Not Frank, thinks Anna. Not Brenda. That's ridiculous.

She tips her head low, at the very edge of the kitchen counter, quite close to her jars exuding such a savory, mellifluous goodness, to assure herself of the tiny concave dots in the centers of the lids that indicate they've sealed. Here's another advantage with homemade, uh-huh—the lids will just pry off neatly, come time to put the food to use. No hairbreadth metal shavings slipping down into her juice, from a jaggy can-openered can top.

7

Broo-oo-ooch, thinks Anna, a page from Chapter 5 on the table in front of her, her countenance pickling. Broo-oo-ooch, she repeats, mentally sounding it like br*ew*ch, with the double *o*'s drawn out, rhymed with pooch. She takes another dramatic, prolonged sip from her first cup of coffee for the morning. Watch her overdo it again today. Lately she's been acting like a lush, almost. Why can't the caffeine help her over the humps, dissuade her from going back and back and rethinking her words over and over?

"Huh-uh, huh-uh," she used to fuss at her sister, "like this, br*ew-ew*ch." Dolly, their friend Wanda's aunt, had herself an entire collection of such pins, some as weighty as that red ruby stunner Susan owns. Dolly needed something to help clinch the gap in her blouse that was always about to bust its buttons. Her plumpers swelled above voluptuously, her quivery, ripe Bartlett pears.

"Uh-uh, it's br*oa*ch," Margie would remonstrate. "Wanda said so. You're just a big silly."

Todd interrupts her thoughts, brushing past her to get at the breakfast cereal in the cupboard. "What're you screwing up like that for?"

"What? Oh. I was just thinking. About Susan, I guess. Um, Aunt Dolly, really."

"Who's that?"

"Back in Pottstown—Wanda Nickel's aunt who lived above the grocery store. Did she ever slap on the makeup. On her cheeks, big clowny patches. And she wore this Luscious Cherry lipstick, drawn in the shape of a kissy heart, and so much eye shadow it looked like she'd bumped into the bedpost. Then her high heels yet, patent leather. She had to hang onto the handrail, tripping down her apartment steps. She greased those shoes with Vaseline, according to Wanda. But I bet Wanda made that up—it sounds too wacky. Every little puff of sidewalk dust would've clung."

And the shoes kicked off, lying indolently on their sides on Aunt Dolly's flowered carpet in her parlor? Wouldn't they have left inauspicious spots of slug slime?

Her fruits jostling in her blouse, though—that's what took the cake.

Somebody buxom like Brenda Arnold, thinks Anna, sitting back— why, a person like that must get awfully tired of the winking and jokes. She'd hate that, herself. She'd have to wonder if the shifty-eyed garage man or overly voluble Wal-Mart manager was actually working on her problem or just sizing up her jugs. Brenda doesn't need people's false hunches on top of everything else, no. But why would she get into a car with somebody else's husband? With Frank Becker?

Well, Wade just wasn't seeing straight. "I never would've expected it from Frank," he said, mentioning his sighting again, later on last night. "And out in public, right there at RG's. Him on the make like that, it's a wonder the windows weren't steamed."

"Fondling her?" Anna asked. "Hon, no. I believe you're completely off base. Completely."

She leans in and takes one last pepper-upper swallow of coffee, ah. Todd has pulled a dining chair over to the little round table and seated himself near her, and he's anointing his outrageous portion of Cheerios, one paw cupped overtop to contain the mountain and thwart any runaways as the milk level rises in the bowl. "Sometimes I think you eat more than Jonathan and Mary Beth put together," she scolds.

"Yeah, yeah."

"Actually, why don't you just pour the milk into the box? And eat all sixty-five servings that way? The BHT stuff in the wax paper, yum." She motions at the picture of the suggested serving on the box front. "Peg says they use white glue in their photo shoots. The cereal can't sog down in.

Elmer's glue, yet, in with your Cheerios, you wouldn't have to worry about any escapees, for sure. Some of that nice Elmer's silage, yum."

"Not silage," he snorts. "Mucilage, you mean."

"Oh. Okay." Abandoning her work and rising from the table, in a burst of fondness she thumps his ruffed-grouse head not enough recovered from his buzz cut, prickled all over with a stubby one-quarter-inch growth.

He's emptied the orange-juice carafe, too. As she holds a can of frozen concentrate under the spigot to start it thawing, from behind her, above the rush of the water, comes the sound of her son attacking his meal, avidly clacking his molars. How can he abide the jaw noise? The reverberations inside his own head? She turns in time to catch him also helping himself to her papers.

"No no no," she pleads, dropping the can. "Don't, okay? Don't. Let them be, please. Here, give them to me." Wetly she rescues her property and tucks it under the spider plant pot. "Hey, are you watching the clock?"

"Duh, Mom. Shouldn't I be allowed to read something?"

"Well, sure. Once I've made enough progress. I'm just so nervous. You know, clueless me. My dim wits." Busily she clears her throat. "I wonder how Mama will react. If this book ever sees the light of day, I mean—won't it bring back all the grief of losing Daddy, make her feel old and bereft? But she'll appreciate the parts about Pottstown. I *think*. I *hope*."

Minutes later, still at the sink, hearing the tinks and clangs of Todd scraping the bottom of the barrel, she surfaces from another spell of reverie. "Mama lived so sacrificially back at the mission. You know? Such a stick-to-it attitude, too. The example she set played a big part in keeping me from going completely off the deep end last year—I'm convinced. Living there in Pottstown she could've confined herself to the detergent-ad housewife routine, but no. Doing the Lord's work, helping unfortunate souls, she persevered. She—she'd—"

Anna gasps, smites her forehead. "Gracious me, why don't I just put in my *Gospel Truth* article? That one I wrote about her? No need to be standing here yackety-yacking like this!" And into the study she hastens for her author's copy of the magazine in the file cabinet from eight years ago.

The slam of the kitchen door reaches her from far away, and the complaints of the school bus rolling to a stop to load her boy.

My Mama, Myrna

Sunday nights at the mission, Mama sorted into piles all our soiled, vile clothes, and she devoted Mondays to their redemption. I think she derived a

happy satisfaction: the duds cramped through the wringer, bled of their sins.
And she spent umpteen hours cleaning. She knocked a bottle brush around the
radiator coils, brought down the spider webs with her mop, dusted the balky
venetian blinds, polished the windows—and having vanquished the swill and
corruption, she pronounced herself pleased. Oh mercy, thinks Anna with a
frown, dropping into the gray velour chair and glancing at the window, its
panes clouded by insect scuzz.

Mama didn't bemoan the repetitive nature of housework, nor was she
paranoid about the seamier aspects. No, winsomely she applied herself. A gentle
piety underpinned; her devotion drove her on. She scrubbed the floors with her
skirt pleats puddled chastely around her. Anna pauses again, bites her lip.
Does Mama come off, here, like somebody with a scrubwoman fixation—
does she sound psychologically unbalanced?

After Clyde Bailey's visits, she faithfully assailed the skid marks in the hall
from his army-issue clodhoppers. Clyde's one foot dragged—the shoe made little
squealy peeps and laid down rubber. So here, too, ridding the linoleum of the
ugly streaks, she was trouncing evil's inroads. But I don't mean to be disparag-
ing of Clyde. He was seriously handicapped—blind, deaf, and missing part of
one arm (he wore the sleeve doubled up over his stump)—and he didn't realize
about his tracks. "How're ya, Ralph," he'd ask Daddy, the query dragging out
instead of turning up at the question mark. "Are ya doing good, Ralph. How's
Myra. Is my Myra doing good." Daddy would catch hold of the cruddy hand
feeling in the air for an answer and wave it to signify yes. That made Clyde
happy; it made his eyeballs roll around every which way in his milky sockets
like spilled marbles.

Maybe at the veterans' home in Waterbury they served the same old soup
every day, because Clyde always seemed famished. "Isn't it a pity," Mama would
say. If I wrinkled up my nose at the supper table, she'd chide, "Remember, insti-
tutions like at Waterbury, there's only certain nights for baths." After the meal
he'd pat along the oilcloth until he got to me, then he'd lean in close and confide
something. Phew, his breath. He'd say, "I brung your favorite licorish again,"
and dig in his pants for two pieces and juggle them in his paw to tease me. "Go
on, Anna," Mama would gently prod, so I had to accept. "Now tell him thank
you," she'd say, but I couldn't. My sister who possessed more derring-do would
come over and take hold of his hand and fingerprint T-H-A-N-K Y-O-U, un-
concerned about any trespassing cooties.

"Doesn't the steel plate give him a headache when he's outside in the cold
winter?" I asked Daddy. The army had patched Clyde up, after the war, by fit-
ting a plate into his skull. "Headache?" said Daddy. "That's a good question."

He looked over at Mama. "Myrna, what do you think?"

"I wouldn't know any more than you," she answered. "He's no doubt suffered. And he's deeply in need of the saving grace of our Lord Jesus."

Another visitor recipient of Mama's ministrations was Mrs. McCulley. When the doorbell rang, Daddy was upstairs studying. Mama hurried out to the vestibule. "Why, yes, certainly," I heard her say. She came back to the living room. "Up to bed, children. Anna, you settle the boys, but first tell Daddy to come right away." But she couldn't wait. She called up the stairs herself, "Ralph, Ralph!"

As I scurried everybody past, I caught a putrid whiff of upchuck.

When I sneaked back down, Daddy was holding the woman by the elbow to prevent her from pitching over. She had on twisted pink stockings with holes, and bedroom slippers that had lost the pompoms, and her hair looked like Mama's worn-down pot scrubber, all scraggly and matted. "Steady now," Daddy was saying. "There, there." But she just went on jabbering.

"She's gonna stink up the whole living room," I whispered to Mama. "Is she drunk?"

"Shh."

"Why's she—?"

"Shh, shh. Daddy wants to pray with her."

From my bed a while later, I heard Mama scrounging around in the bathroom. Soon she came tiptoeing down the hall and whispered in to me, "I'm having Mrs. McCulley take a bath before she goes."

"In our bathtub?" I sat up fast. "Mama!" But the woman was already starting up the steps with Daddy, and I had to duck to stay unnoticed.

She scuffled past. Mama steered her back the hall and into the bathroom. The splashing and sloshing started up. Mama's sousing her even worse, I told myself. Then it grew quiet, so maybe she thought she was on the beach, under her umbrella. But finally I heard the gurgle of the pipes, and before long, here came Mrs. McCulley on her own two legs. Slowly she traveled down the stairs and then the vestibule door banged shut.

I found Mama over in the bathroom pouring some of her Egbert's Cleaner into a pail. "Shouldn't you be asleep?" she asked. She wiped down the commode, then she kersplashed the Egbert's Cleaner full strength around the ring in the bathtub and scoured every inch of surface. "You never know," she said. "The diseases people carry."

"Venal disease?" I hissed.

"Venereal? Maybe. It's so very, very sad. The sins catch up. But we can't just remove ourselves. Our calling is to love and serve the down and out no matter what."

Mrs. McCulley never returned. But you see, Mama's actions spoke. She loved the Lord and energetically served. In children's meeting, too, she pressed God's truth indelibly upon our hearts. She always had a grocery bag containing some little object to hold the attention of even the youngest and help illustrate the Bible story or the anecdote from more recent history about somebody Christian who'd stayed true to the Lord. I loved the one about the conscientious objector during World War I. They sent him to army camp anyway, despite his peace beliefs. When ordered to don the uniform he balked, so the officers dressed him like a little baby, buttoning the jacket crooked and letting the pants hang open. And out on the drill field, when the sergeant blew his whistle—and here Mama produced a toy whistle and pretended to give a little toot—the boy just stood there. "Push him! Kick him!" the sergeant ordered, so the other recruits on behind bumped into the boy and pulled on his arms and stomped on his toes.

She made it all so vivid without ever once raising her voice. Me, though? Many years later, relating that same story to our Bible school assembly here at Conoy, at the indicated moment I took from my handbag a real referee's whistle and shrilled on it, much to the astonishment of the Becker children, the Hurst girls, Marvin and Dudley Heatwole, and the rest. Why my flamboyance, I'm not sure.

Clear in Mama's mind was her lot in life, her place in the work of the mission. She grew flustered if she had to do a Sunday night topic, because compared to children's meeting, "topic" held a risky connotation. She wrote out her speech word for word, and then up front at the song leader stand, not the pulpit, she read her lines. This way she wasn't outright "speaking," lording over the men. The preaching was for Daddy to do, or any itinerant who came through.

One traveling minister, Stanley Yoder, owner of a deep Southern drawl, would wave his arms and whoop and rock on the balls of his soles, and his messages enthralled us. If he'd twisted a verse wrongly, would've Mama contested, do you suppose? Planted her hands on her round little hips and demurred? No, that was about as liable to occur as her mutinously whacking the porcelain belly of the wringer washer some blue-drear Monday, scuttling the machine on its rollers down the hall, tipping it over in the vestibule, and gooshing the gray bilge down the front steps and sidewalk and street gutter, the sodden mass of clothes floating, glug glug.

But I ask you now, wasn't she a preacher, herself? Is the preacher's job supposed to mean something special and lordly? A pulpit versus a stand—what's the difference, if we take submitting literally? Why should sermonizing be seen as some particularly high and mighty task? If we believe in humbleness of heart and servantly deeds such as washing one another's feet, how is it right to ever set up categories? Isn't lordliness itself sinful?

After we left Pottstown, Mama took a job at the Saturday farmer's market in Jackson, clerking at Lily Zimmerly's stand. I was tackling my first college courses, not paying too close attention to her stories from work. But one day she accidentally stepped into a bucket of Lily's pickled red beets and eggs and came home early, her foot squishy and the juice streaked up as far as her dress hem and slip. "So humiliating," I groaned.

"Oh," she replied, "Lily and I, we laughed so hard. Look at this shoe! It's probably ruined for good!"

"Mama," I asked, "don't you ever mind just waiting on people, slicing their half pounds of baloney and cheese and dishing up their little cartons of pineapple fluff?"

"What's got into you, Anna?" she cried. "It's a good *pineapple fluff!"*

A few weeks before my wedding I got into a minor argument with Wade, which Mama overheard but maybe not Daddy. I don't know why Wade and I were even looking in the Sears catalog. Our income would scarcely cover the rent, let alone buy a brand-new Kenmore appliance. But there we were, contending over which would be preferable: the regular kind of refrigerator with the freezer section above, or the big fancy side-by-sides. He was so taken with those side-by-sides. He was being thickheaded.

Mama stayed out of it. But later she said to me, "If there's something to decide and you can't agree, just let him make the decision. Even if you think it's a bad choice, it won't be the end of the world. He'll learn from his mistakes."

"Mama," I ventured, "are you so sure women must always defer?" By then the belief about male leadership sounded a little cooked. People were rebelling.

"I am," she declared. "The man is supposed to be the one wearing the pants."

"Wade and I—um, he says we're not having that kind of marriage," I said slowly. "Submit to God—isn't that what the Bible's really saying? Just submit to God?"

Her understanding has broadened, I'm glad to say. When we go back to Jackson, she gives us the sleeper sofa down in the basement room that used to be Daddy's study, and in the very early hours, I waken to the creaking of the floorboards overhead. When I climb the steps to start some coffee, she's already buttoned into her dress and sitting in the pink recliner with her Bible, having her prayer time. Her wispy locks are captured in a knot, like an iced honeybun—but no cap. So what does that tell you? But the diehard doctrines are a different story—her convictions about the authority of God's Word and the atoning death of Jesus haven't changed. Thank goodness for that. Believe me, she's still preaching her same old sermon, extemporaneously. It's not the formal speechifying kind, but so what? A bulwark pulpit or not, take your pick. The words scrupulously drafted or breathed straight from your soul, you choose. Isn't a pulpit just a piece of furniture to lean on? Isn't the way you live your life your sermon?

Anna relaxes her hold, flops the magazine into her lap, frowns again.

Peg's reaction, well. Peg did enjoy the article when it came out in *Gospel Truth.* Sunday morning before class, in the ladies' room, she gushed, "That was super! Not because you mentioned us, though that did kind of give me a shiver, seeing my boys' names staring up from the page. No, I just think your mom is one great lady. To be honest, you're a corker, yourself. You, your mom—the both of you."

"Oh, don't say that," Anna protested, squirming. Her rib cage was knocking and bloating up in unfounded self-importance. "I can't ever get my facts straight, even. Mama called me about the beets. It was just beets, she said. Miniature ones the size of those runty green apples. No eggs were in the bucket. One more goof of mine! So now what do I do? At least it wasn't intentional." Anna rolled her eyes sorrily. "What if my tattletaling puts a hitch in Lily's sales? She still owns that stand. Any Evangelical Brethren customers, now they're wondering about her sanitation policies and maybe sniffing for a bunion flavor."

Peg laughed, and Anna grabbed at her friend's shoulder. "Mama *is* something else, though—I agree. She still thinks pants are obscene on women. If I'm down on all fours washing the floor she'll say, 'Where's your dignity? Your sense of modesty?' I guess she's right, in a way. It's not exactly the picture of propriety—my butt flared up high like a cow's in heat, alerting the horny bull."

When Mama telephoned, Anna asked, "Why did I think eggs? Was I subconsciously embellishing?"

"I don't reckon so. But if we would've refrigerated them together for too long, the beets would've taken on an egg taste."

"Oh-h-h. Yes." She nodded at the receiver, still in a ruffle. "Otherwise do you like the story?"

"Oh—I—well, you calling all that attention to me. Daddy and I just wanted to obediently serve in the Lord's vineyard." Mama's disembodied long-distance voice turned hesitant, almost plaintive. "I got confused a couple places, so maybe other folks won't understand, either."

"Maybe not. I was just throwing out some ideas to chew on, you know. We really should keep asking how's a pulpit important. A person shouldn't be holding sway, thinking they're the pope." Anna took a moment to ponder. "I guess *my* sermons are just these articles. Hm. Isn't that strange. How's come it's only now occurred to me? Isn't that the oddest thing?"

She jumps slightly, remembering, and the magazine slides onto the study carpet. Goodness. The irony. It would be a mistake to keep up this fussing about her spiritual frailties, and mental. She shouldn't go on castigating herself for her inferiority if what she's trying to do here isn't any more important than anything else in the world. If she'd start posing like she herself were the pope and infallible, well *then*. But she's already confessed her fraughtness and abject failures, so *that* can't happen. Huh-uh, huh-uh.

8

It's Worldwide Bible Sunday and Conoy's avuncular, good-natured pastor, Scott Forry, has themed his sermon accordingly. The congregation's smothered, humid puffs of restlessness and hunger stirring the green air, he slides his gaze fondly across the sanctuary—over his wife, Lorna, and their three kiddies, the Hursts, the Nussbaums with their twins, Frank and Justine Becker, Birdie King, Heatwoles, Brenda Arnold and her son Larry, and the other folks clustered. "So there you have it, friends—my eight reasons why a person should have devotions daily, not allowing anything else to pre-empt." *Elts* is how he says it, "anything elts," his voice thick, grainy, burdened with Adam's apple. Anna always wonders what makes people do that, pronounce it as "elts." Beaming a hearty smile of encouragement and passing his large, kindly hand over the pulpit in a wide sweep, he adds, "In conclusion, I offer you a chance to make a fresh start. I invite anybody who can pledge to read the Scriptures faithfully, on a daily basis, to do so now. Will you rise to your feet, please?"

Promise? Every every every single day? Never skip? Never ever forget? But how can she not oblige, stationed in her family's usual spot, the third row from the front? As Todd and Wade rise and the sounds from behind reach her ears—the agony of the benches suffering hairline fractures from everybody ungluing themselves—she pulls herself to her feet. Stuffing her bulletin into her black bag, she braces herself against Wade.

At lunch, she's quieter than usual. But over her piece of pie, a frugal slice, not hulking like Todd's and Wade's and spilling itself out and dangerous, she rouses to remark, "That was a good idea of Scott's. Him challenging us like that to a higher level of commitment."

"I suppose a person could feel manipulated," says Wade.

"But if it works!" she exclaims. "Look at me! I needed spurring! I've been too lax about devotions."

She dabs her napkin at the crumbs on her lip. "I liked Justine's story, too." Once a month there's a little something special for the children immediately before the sermon, up beside the pulpit. "Justine's good with youngsters. She's so expressive."

But she's nobody you'd ever want to go up to and say, Um, your husband—does he make it a habit to sit in cars with other women? Anna wishes she could've stayed oblivious to all this hokum. Why did Wade have to plant distrustful thoughts in her mind?

Doggedly Todd forks up his last glob of thickened peaches and tender crust, then he shoves back his chair and goes for the candy tin on the counter. She stocked it yesterday with that same black licorice Clyde Bailey kept stashed in his pants, the squat, chunky kind resembling cut-up tractor tires. Pantry Pride carries it in their serve-yourself candy bin, and to her it smacks of dirty pockets, but all three of her progeny love it. Just to torture her, now, Todd crams a huge handful into his mouth like it's his chaw and leans back to chomp on it and let the spittoony slime wander down his chin.

"Ugh!" she squeals. "Smelly!"

In response to his guffaws she jumps up and runs to the sink, grabs the dishcloth, and slaps at him. "You! That is so sick!" She flails the dishcloth a couple more times, laughing, but she feels too giddy. Her laughter is too high pitched and forced.

"Aren't you getting a little bent out of shape again, Anna?" asks Wade.

She slumps weakly against the counter. "Oh dear. Am I? What's wrong with me?"

"Nothing's wrong with you. Nothing's wrong with anybody. You're tired, I think." He's piling together a few messed plates and the water glasses. "Take a vacation, why don't you? I'll do the dishes."

"Really?" she squeaks.

She stands by as Todd joins in clearing the table, but when he props her "Say nothing and look like a fool" mug on top of the askew forks, knives, and spoons, she sucks in her cheeks in trepidation. "Careful!" she scolds, because it's wobbling. "If you break that—"

Wade affectionately pats her on the rear. "Go, Anna. Go."

"It's my favorite! He can't just sling it around!"

"Anna. I said go. Why don't you take a nap?"

But a few minutes later, instead she's lifting the hall-ceiling board to take down the boot box with its peeling label, "Tingley Rubbers." The size can't be distinguished, but Daddy had quite small feet, maybe size 8 or 9. Readying to pay his afternoon preacher calls, if the rainwater from a thunderstorm still ran in Pottstown's streets, turning potholes into tar ponds and swamping the sewer grates with cigarette butts, he'd eee-eeek the Tingleys—sober black, thickly treaded—over his shoes. Where the sidewalks consisted of lumpy, upheaved bricks, the puddles lingered, with floating, dead leaves, and the concrete pavement out front at the mission slickly gleamed. Or maybe "slickly glistened," thinks Anna, recalling.

This time it's not a story she's after. She wants one of the childhood diaries. Of all those she once possessed, remaining are only the tiny, red leatherette volume Mama presented to her the Christmas she was seven, hung with jingly keys and a lock that broke right away, and the blue leatherette one from when she was nine, and the green notebook decked with gilt curlicues on the front, which she wrote in by spurts the year she got baptized and joined church. As for what happened to the rest, she has no clue. The three make for pitifully meager leavings—they're more famine than feast. But shouldn't there be something here to help juggle her memory? Er, jog. Juggle, duh! Didn't Clyde Bailey first show up on the mission doorstep about the time she turned nine?

Intent, she shuffles the blue diary's pages. June. July. August. Hm, here's mention of him, anyway. *Not myra!!* the entry begins. Anna slides down onto the floor of the hall, close to the window, and the dishwashing racket downstairs in the kitchen fades to nonsensical clacks in her brain as she mulls over the memories her diary elicits, and as she fills in the details that pertain.

In light of the fact that Clyde didn't have Mama's name right, were Mama and Daddy being truthful with him? This question plagued her. "Is my Myra doing good," Clyde would bawl, his chancy legs waving out the taxi door and finally stabilizing on the curb, and wasn't Daddy fibbing, pumping Clyde's hand piston fashion in answer, Yes yes? Wasn't Mama being devious, plunking down her iron or her scrub brush and hurrying to Clyde's side when he stirred in his seat and summoned for Myra? Or when he quizzed, "What's that I smell cooking, Myra," or "Myra, are they calling for rain anytime soon," how could Mama just compliantly extend her reply?

Mama might be fixing scalloped turnips with little bits of carrot and celery added, or chicken and biscuits, and too busy for a word-for-word explanation, she'd rightfully abbreviate, *T-U-R-N-I-P* pat *C-A-S-S-E-R-O-L-E*, or *C-H-I-C-K-E-N*. Or she'd glance out at the slain grass in the yard, brown and crackly as twigs, and accommodatingly bat Clyde's hand to and fro, No no, no rain in sight. But she wasn't Myra!

That August day, Clyde spent a long while rocking in the rickety chair Mama had pushed into the corner for him, out of reach of Wesley's cradle. He talked to himself sometimes, his sandpaper chin buried in his chest. Once he mumbled, "Myra, you're tops," and gave a lovesick sigh. He started several mostly one-sided conversations. It wasn't till after supper, when he was snoozing into his buttoned-crooked shirt, that Anna at last confronted Mama who was busy cleaning up. "Isn't it lying if you're pretending you're somebody else?" she burst out. "Making like you're Myra?"

Mama's elbow stopped its jerking. Her dishrag lay marooned in Clyde's slops of hamburger gravy on the kitchen-table oilcloth. "Somebody else? I—I—" she faltered. "Well, honestly."

She recovered enough to drip more dishpan suds on the mess. "I did tell Clyde. I told him 'M-Y-R-N-A' when we met. Daddy and I were going room to room at the veterans' home, passing out tracts, and we ran into him in the corridor poking around with his cane. 'Wag his hand back and forth for no, and up and down for yes,' the orderly told us. 'Put everything you write in capitals and signal between each word with a pat.' But Clyde didn't catch my *N*. He just said, 'Myra and Ralph, why, them's right dandy names. Pottstown Mission, haw. Never heard tell of an old folks' place by that name. I'll get me drove over one day to say howdy-do to the help.'

"Of course, now he knows we're a church. But I've never thought to rectify about me." Mama pushed up her soaked sleeve and got back to her scrub-a-dubbing. Her round-and-round swipes made the claw feet of the table chatter in their castor cups, but the oilcloth rose into its usual humps, making it appear as if moles were tunneling underneath. "So 'Myra' is how he knows me. If I up and told him 'Myrna' now, wouldn't that be a humiliation?"

"But Mama. Still."

That night, taking pains, mashing her pencil stub across the page, she wrote, *Not myra!! Thats not her but mama never Lets on!! is this rite? clide makes freindly with mama, he says myra this and Myra that, and she just goes yes yes or no no, all nice and polite as pie.* There, she'd gotten it down.

She put her diary back in its safekeeping place, turned out the light, and curled up, eyes squeezed shut and long braids splayed awkwardly on the pillow. But she wasn't sleepy enough. She flopped onto her tummy. On the blackboard behind her lids she traced the circuitousness of her logic. If— But if—

Oh. Huh! She scrambled up on her knees and felt around the headboard again, beneath the torn flap of wallpaper. That very moment, Mama rounded the landing. "Wait, Mama! Wait! C-l-i-d-e, is that how you spell it?"

Stopped short, Mama peered into the dark. In the glare from the hall, Wesley lay squelched against the diaper on her shoulder, making little snort-snoots in his sleep, his mouth pudged like a fish's. "Shh. You'll wake Margie. Why aren't you settled yet?"

"Soon, Mama." She turned the lamp on, found her pencil. "I promise, Mama." So she had to hurry the rest. In these tacked-on sentences here, her lettering shows up choppier, more spastic: *Oopsie. he's clyde. I thought Clide or else Clied. Like lied with the c up in front. and I gess if he thinks mama is myra its true in his mind. Yay.*

Dimly Anna notes the clanging of kettles, and Wade's heavy-handed banging on the salad bowl, and pieces of silverware boinking into the dish drainer. She wrinkles up, unsatisfied. Interesting maybe, but this isn't the big nugget she was needing, something to put to rest the qualms she's had since Thursday after resurrecting that article about Mama. What Anna needs is something to assure her about Clyde's eternal soul. Did Clyde—? Did he ever—? Now why in the world can't she recall?

9

She's sticking to it. This will be her third day in a row, dipping into Daddy's Bible. His, not hers, because mightn't this help to keep up her steam? For too many years she's kept it shelved like a museum piece. She's finding that the cracked black leather and the shlishy feel of the pages brings him back physically, almost. It's reassuring, but sad, too.

He gave up pastoring with the move away from Pottstown but kept on with his commentaries and concordances, preaching the occasional sermon, up until the cancer diagnosis. It came as a terrible shock—in two months he was dead. Not until three years later did Mama feel up to the task of disposing of his papers. The Saturday Anna and Wade went over to help, when Wade was carrying out the file cabinet to take it across town to their apartment, leaving in its ghost space only the corroded dents in the study carpet, she asked Mama, "Do I *deserve* it? That's what I really wonder." So maybe it was greedy of her to request Daddy's King James, too. Up on the stepladder, sweeping everything off the top bookshelf for Mama to pack into cartons, she fairly pounced upon it. "Oh Mama, can I have it?" she begged. "My my my—look at this. All his notations."

Daddy's script marking up the margins struck her as uncharacteristic, too jabby and exacting. Here and there he'd underscored a verse for emphasis, or a worthy detail. In the first two chapters of Amos, she saw he'd slashed the transgressor tribes with green ink, and in Joel, in chapter 2, she discovered "cankerworm" blotched with the same green, and "caterpillar," and "palmerworm, my great army."

"He wore it clear to a frazzle, didn't he?" murmured Mama. Studying Daddy's signature trawling jerkily across the flyleaf, Anna could feel her throat clogging up. Mama had pushed back the olefin drapes, and the dead leaves tamped outside in the window well were *tick-tick*ing against the screen, rebelling at the bustle coming through after the long time of neglect. From up in the living room came Mary Beth's stuffy-nosed naptime wheezing.

Mama said no more, just reached for the next armload, and Anna swallowed her sob and continued on with her job. But she brought the Bible along home with her, chocked in with Mary Beth's dry pairs of training panties in the diaper bag.

Shouldn't just the associations, the lingering bittersweet impressions, be a big boost? Won't this instill some gumption? Alone in the house, hunkered all to herself on the sofa, the 8:00 a.m. sun creeping across her neck, Anna caresses the tattered cover of the Bible and nods. She's deep-down glad now for Scott's nudge on Sunday. Wade isn't being appropriate, that's all. When she asked last night, "Are you keeping to that promise you made?" he only *umph*ed testily in the dark, mooched more of the quilt for himself, and turned his back. Was she bugging him for no good reason? No! He could've acted appreciative. Not like he wanted her to just see to her own beeswax.

She thumbs a few chapters, scrabbling at the Bible's frail, slippery leaves. She realizes it's not very systematic of her to be reading any old page she lands on, but commencing at Genesis 1:1 and almost right away tangling up in the begats would be too daunting. Besides, what's so terrible about allowing for an element of suspense? Um, let's see, something here in Luke, maybe. Here's Jesus' prayer service up on the mountain, with just Peter and James and John along, until— Okay, yes, this will do fine.

Wha-a-at? she questions, partway through the transfiguration story, where Jesus suddenly turns spookily radiant. How did "glistening" end up mangled like that? *And as he prayed, the fashion of his countenance was altered, and his raiment was white and glistering.* "Glistering," is that a full-fledged word?

It must be.

In the study she pulls down the dictionary. Huh, "glister." Glitter, it means. How about that! Well, she should've known. Hm, couldn't she maybe put it to use in that part in her manuscript about Daddy going visiting in his rubbers? *Readying to pay his preacher calls after a big rain, he'd eee-eeek on his Tingleys because the concrete pavement out front glistered slickly.* "Glistered" rather tidily conveys the idea, doesn't it?

She scoots back to the living room. When she's done reading, she'll bring up her computer file. And for an even bigger improvement could she say "tractor-tire-tread rubbers" instead of just plain "Tingleys"? *Readying to pay his preacher calls after a big rain, he'd eee-eek on his tractor-tire-tread black-licorice rubbers because the concrete pavement out front still slickly glistered.* Put it like that, maybe?

NO. NOT SO GOOD, after all. "Glistered" is too archaic, or something.

And that whole rant of adjectives in front of her nose, on the computer screen, just looks pandering and silly.

Grumpily she leans back and allows her eyes to wander to the window and beyond, past the going-naked limbs of the quince bush, past the meaningless tree-branch-blurred span of atmosphere, far over to the field where one of Wade's hens appears to be bent on a crazy-course pursuit of, what, a flying fluff of milkweed? Anna can't quite make out. She takes a swipe at the window to see better, but this doesn't do much for the flyspecks and ladybug-poop trails. Yu-uck.

Maybe she ought to clean the worst downstairs windows—just the inside panes.

That little bit of extra strain might bump her spirits up a notch, too.

A worn-out washcloth, a bucketful of plain water, and several pages from an old *Conoy Gazette,* and she's equipped. Mama taught her this window-washing trick—there's something about the newsprint ink. First, however, Anna studies Marlene Wagler's face accompanying her once-a-week "Soup's On" column, and Marlene's recipe for Hearty Herb Loaves, a German bread fortified with bulgur and rye. Hm, interesting. You're supposed to sprinkle on the loaf tops some parsley, snipped chives, caraway seeds, and one level tablespoon of chopped, dried dill stems. *Table*spoon, though—can that be correct? With the *Gazette,* a person never quite knows. Routinely, even glaring typos get by. Once the "Soup's On" readers were instructed to put five—five!—teaspoons of salt in the buttermilk-pancakes batter, which would've been enough to float the flour the recipe said to add next. "But I guess anybody that fell for it couldn't even swallow their first mouthful," Anna still remembers telling Wade. "I don't guess they ended up in the hospital dehydrated and on life support."

Just because a thing is printed—published—doesn't make it true. She should know!

She slaps water over the bug gunk on the bottom pane of the study window, the part that shows below the bamboo roll-up blind, and then bunches her newspaper drying rag into a loose ball and mops up, turning a corner of the paper back on itself when it rubs thin, and another corner, and another (like she used to do when wiping her children's runny noses on toilet paper—"Blow! Harder!"—and catching up the clogged sections). There, that's much better. Next she moves to the front window in the living room. She pushes aside the ficus plant and the battered steamer trunk, takes a few drippy clouts at the window dirt, rubs for a bit, and sops up the streaks of water. She drops her spent chunk of newspaper, the columnist's countenance crumply and miffed at the disgrace, and with a couple of grunts and a heave-ho or two she shoves the furniture back into place. If she keeps this up, she'll soon be as charged as Mama. Mama even sang along sometimes, cleaning at the mission. She'd go around warbling like a little wren, *Christ our redeem-er died on the cross,* her face a glowing pink, the tune bubbly and joyous.

When I-I-I see the blood, when I-I-I see the blood, when I-I-I see the blood, I will pass, I will pass over you, Mama sang, disinfecting the stinky vomit spots on the couch after Mrs. McCulley's visit. On the one cushion, Mama's round-and-round-the-mulberry-bush swabbing left a permanent, beaten-down donut of discoloration. "Vee—veer—that disease, doesn't the person go insane?" she wanted to ask Mama, watching anxiously. Mama was using her trusty Egbert's Cleaner, but its smell, too, was an assault to the senses.

Phew, a product with that strong of a germicidal reek wouldn't even be marketable anymore, Anna bets. It wouldn't stand up to the competition— the present-day cleaners available, with their relatively benign odors, such as Mr. Clean, The Works, Softscrub. Why, even Lestoil is a rose in comparison. *Less toil,* ha. She knows better now, but back when she was pregnant with Jonathan could've she been any worse of a twit?

They were still occupying the Jackson apartment and she was trying to spiff things up for Christmas despite her morning sickness. Ordinary dish detergent wouldn't budge the grease marks around the kitchen cupboard knobs, though. So one day at the IGA she searched up and down the cleaning-supplies aisle for something industrial strength.

The Lestoil, when she spied it, won out. "That'll be great," she decided. Oh. Oops. She'd read the label wrong. Less *toil,* it meant, not less *oil.* But she examined at length the list of ingredients. "I still think it'll work," she informed Mary Beth, as if her two-year-old riding along in the cart gave a fig. "It better would."

Back in the apartment, her belly pressed against the kitchen counter, she ran her soaked dishrag around the first knob. Any improvement? The strong petroleum vapors were rushing up her nose, stinging her eyes. Uncertainly she took a few more swishes, trying not to breathe, in case the fumes could somehow harm the baby. But couldn't not breathing be dangerous, too—couldn't it reduce the baby's oxygen? Another swipe, phooh! She had to blink back the tears. Her lungs about to rupture, she raced to the bedroom and gobbled up some nonnoxious air.

Like a dodo, she returned to her chore then—she put herself through the same paces. And she did it again. And again. And again. Each time, she dammed up her breath, flailed desperately at a cupboard, and galloped out of the room. She did this over and over, even though, in the kitchen, overexerting, she always ended up gasping involuntarily and taking in more fumes.

For the duration of her pregnancy, this was the part that most tormented her—the way she'd persisted. After that first whiff she could've stopped! She could've left the cupboards as they were! Now her baby, exposed at such an early stage, would be born deformed, with an extra esophagus maybe, or prehistoric-type flippers for arms. Wade couldn't convince her of the harmlessness. For months she quietly harbored the dismal knowledge—the wrenching, sad reality. She had to carry on, bear the dread, up until the July afternoon when Jonathan slipped from her, coated with cottage cheese and robustly squalling.

Wade tried to blame the hysteria on her ramped-up hormonal state. But can a person be reduced to just a bundle of chemicals and nerve endings? If such is the case, then can't *any* sorry behavior be chalked up to the person's physiology, as if it's simply their unlucky fate? What about their spiritual responsibility?

The other window in the living room, looking out to the garden's brittle cornstalks, frost-blackened lifeless tomato plants, and dried-up melon vines, must be the grungiest in the house. Anna splashes water on it and works at the scat and the proboscis slime. Unfortunately, once the pane is slippery clean, that won't dissuade more flies from trekking across, equipped as their feet are with clingy pads, pulvilli. She notices the Monarch butterflies fluttering up from the wrecked popcorn patch, resplendent in their orange-and-black-dusted jackets. Their broccoli-worm cousins will soon belly into the soil and spin chrysalises to winter over, but like Wade said yesterday, the Monarchs' heyday is almost past. He'd just gotten home from his day of teaching, dropped off by Jerry Funkhouser, and he beckoned her out to a swarm of them hanging off the hickory stump on the other side of the driveway. "They won't be here long," he said, "so drink in the sight while you can."

"Yes," she said, "it's all so momentary, isn't it? The vainglory? Any vain thing—it's always so short-lived."

Using a fresh piece of *Gazette*, a full page of ads, she wipes away the window's water drops. She weasels a fingerpoint's worth, *RICKY'S AUTO SER-VICE, LUBE, OIL, AND FILTER, ONLY $29.95* into a corner of pane scoured of its bug leavings, whereupon a torpid late-October ray of sun suddenly ignites the glass. The gleam, too, is ephemeral, but it's a fine-enough result, a passable glister, jing-bang enough to suit her.

10

A twig off the sugar maple out front, on its dark-of-night descent to the earth, scritch-scratches the house clapboards as she cozies up to Wade and struggles to shut off the words cropping up, one of her sentences full of drivel. She's got to calm herself down, a challenge diametrically opposed to the one she faces mornings when she's needing a pep talk. She's learned from years of experience the necessity of putting on the screws. Look out, otherwise, because the mental tinkering will lead to new phrasings scrolling past her mind's eye, one idea giving way to the next, her dither increasing, her nerves racheting into higher and higher gear, till she's much too tight-wound to sleep. She *must* get herself reined in.

The mishmash she's made of things is bothering her, too. She should make a note to herself about that. She shouldn't let the perception float away, *poof*. The *Newsweek* probably has a stapled-in subscription card, or the library book under the bed might hold her loans slip. For something to scribble on, either will do. But the pencil is on the night table by Wade's side of the bed. Oh, and so is the *Newsweek*.

Wade has already drifted off, his breath escaping in teakettle whistles, but she thumps him on the bicep. The tooting from his nose quiets. She senses him tensing, doggy-paddling to the surface. "Can you do a note for me?" she pleads in a whisper. "Pretty please? I just need a little reminder to myself. Do you mind very much?"

His arm lifts a notch, falls. "Anna, no."

She clubs him again. "Wade?"

He feels around for the lamp and she has to clench her lids against the sudden send-up of yellow glare. "The *Newsweek*," she murmurs, keeping her voice small and abject. "Use the *Newsweek*. Just put, 'In the next chapter admit that the plot is confused and I might be even more addled than I thought.'"

She waits while the pencil scrapes along. The bed heaves, and with another click of the lamp switch, blackness once more muffles the room. The covers jerk in Wade's direction, but right away he turns, slamming his body into the mattress, to cram his arm around her.

Anna wriggles slightly, so that her nose is almost butting his, and confides, "I don't know what I'd ever do without you. It's almost like you're my salvation. Not in the spiritual sense, I don't mean *that*."

He smooches the cold cave of her shoulder hungrily, pulls her hard against him, grovels his jaw along her cheek. "Another thing I don't get," she says. "I mean, about Frank and Brenda. Why would she find him appealing?"

"To each his own."

"Exactly."

Anna slants her eyes, in the dark. "I can't even imagine it—being with somebody else. You and I split up."

"Nope."

Nonetheless a picture rises in her mind, Wade in shirtsleeves and his loose-fitting, light blue pair of jeans she especially loves, striding down a sidewalk in town toward her, but on the opposite side of the street. A stranger, almost—remote, yet familiar. His once-reassuring figure, still brawny and rugged, but lost to her. "If any one person stands for manly goodness and strength, it's you," she says. "None of that lily liveredness."

She sucks at her teeth. "Plus, promises are promises. I don't know what's wrong with some people."

"Sure you do. Life's not all cake. Hopes and expectations get dashed."

"Like for Brenda, I guess. She has it hard—I do realize. Somebody ornery as Bill. You think *he's* out running around?"

"Let's not make it your problem, Anna. Not right now."

"Don't you want to get to the bottom of this?"

"I've thought of saying something to Frank, sure. The time never seems right." Wade's chin digs at her shoulder bone. He seems to be thinking, weighing his options. She stills her rustles, waits for more. But he shifts sideways and the pressure of his hold eases off.

Then he's going under, tootling again. She can never understand it— the speed with which her husband, *pfft*, on a dime, is able to fall asleep. The callous, less-developed nervous system of the male which she's read about in the marriage books—it's utterly, entirely true.

IN THE SUNNY reality of midmorning, her dictation up the side of the cartoons-and-quotes page of the *Newsweek*, now that she's remembered and run upstairs to recover it, is surprisingly legible. But what did Wade do with the pencil? Oh, there it is, partway under the dresser, coated with slut's wool. His flails in the inky pre-dawn when the alarm started up its beeping must've sent the thing rolling.

She takes herself back downstairs and plops into the swivel chair to stare dumbly again at her verbiage on the computer screen. Get your wits collected, lady, she scolds to herself. The industrial-weight coiled iron spring beneath the seat of the chair, which allows the back to slant, groans as she lists steeply for a moment and studies a crack in the plaster near the ceiling. She paws idly at the mouse. Meanderingly she fools with its noose of wire.

She turns a few degrees, just enough to make the spring protest, and plucks at a seam in her jeans. She draws her chin into a pickly, sour knot. She shakes her lamebrain head. Does *any*thing here make sense? Is it just one huge useless hodgepodge? Still, mustn't she drag all the issues out into the open so the readers can get the big picture? But once she's gotten all her wrong and right angles construed, then what? She's started jotting down each new chapter's bugaboo details on looseleaf notebook paper—she plans to Scotch-tape the pages together, accordion style, and then she'll be able to stretch them out into a long, jouncy timeline to review—but the points and particulars still want to swim together in her head. Aren't things far too higgledy-piggledy?

She hasn't resolved the Clyde question, even. Did Clyde—did he—?

The chair gives her up with a reluctant croak, and in the kitchen she lifts the phone receiver from the wall to dial.

"Mama? I'm having the hardest time remembering something. If you think back to Pottstown, can you say whether—"

"What? Anna? Is that you? Speak up, I can hardly hear."

"Okay, Mama. Is this better?" She envisions Mama's gnomish figure backlit by the dining room window, with the streaming-in sun electrifying the wispy white frazzles of hair not caught up in her sweet-roll bun. "Mama,

I've been wondering about Clyde Bailey, about whether—"

"Anna, what?" It sounds like Mama is transferring the receiver to her other hand, as if she mistakenly got her good ear switched with the bad one. Or maybe the funny noise means she's endeavoring to adjust her dress where it's frumped around the waist from her sitting too long with her crocheting.

"Clyde, Mama. I'm just asking did Clyde ever get saved? Did you or Daddy—?" But the receiver's sound has gone flat. Mama isn't there anymore. She's not breathing into the holes, straining to make out Anna's babble. How did I do that? wonders Anna. How did I disconnect us?

In her impatience, when she hits the hang-up trigger she bumps her elbow on the coffeepot basket, almost knocking it off its hinges and relieving it of its ground-bean mud. She punches the numbers again, 1-727-118-4417. But she gets a busy signal.

She dials again. Again. Again. Always, the same rude, grating blats. But she didn't hear the phone go crashing. What if Mama is on the floor, in massive coronary failure, fibrillating and weakening and turning cyanotic, her moans washing helplessly up the four walls?

What do I do *now?* wonders Anna.

Maybe call Snyders, the folks who recently moved next door? Rosalie and—Ramer, is it? Raymond?

But the operator can't produce a number, a Jackson listing for a Raymond Snyder *or* a Ramer Snyder.

Not for Raymond or Ramer Sn*i*der, either.

"Then how about Ray?" urges Anna. "Or Randall? Russell? Roger? Is there a Roger? Say that again, please? 727-118-5899?"

She gets a recording on Roger Snyder's answering machine. "Please *yap yap* leave a message *yap yap*. Me and Greta aren't here, but Spot says hi *yap yap yap.*"

Anna thinks of her siblings. Obviously, Margie in Finn City can do no more to resuscitate Mama than can Herbie seventy miles north in the town of Bucks, or Wesley in Vancouver. Nonetheless Anna dials 1-277-823-7144 for the bank where Margie works, and 319, Margie's extension. The synthesizer hold music fritters precious seconds. At last comes her cheery greeting, and then, "Anna, what's wrong?"

"Mama won't pick up her phone. I *know* she's there. She spoke to me— she was fine. I can't get her back on the line."

"Ask those new neighbors to run over. They're so friendly and nice. They won't mind a bit."

"But there's no Raymond S-n-i-der *or* S-n-y-der!" Anna is nearly shouting. "S*i*der? Oh. Oh my! Dumb me!"

But Siders' phone is busy, the same as Mama's. *Blat, blat, blat.*

The church pastor, thinks Anna suddenly. Bud Derstine—or Millie, the secretary—one of them will be in the church office, surely, and Jackson Road isn't all that far from Mama's house. This time Anna reaches a more efficient operator. Fingers twitching, she dials the provided number.

"Millie? It's me, Anna Schlonneger. No, I'm not around, I'm at home. Mama isn't responding. I mean, she *was,* we were talking, but then, zip, nothing. Do you suppose somebody could drive over and check on her? See what's going on? She's there, I promise. I know she's there!"

It's another knuckle-biting half hour, though, before Anna gets Mama off the dining room floor and the color restored to her cuticles. At the first ring, she snatches up the phone. "Millie?"

"I'm back!"

"Is she all right?"

"Her service is out, that's all. Most likely a backhoe hit a cable over on Niland Avenue where they're putting in a new Sheetz."

"Oh. Well then!"

"She was a mite befuddled about not having a dial tone. It had you worried there, I know. She's such a dearie, isn't she?" Millie's voice still has its musical lilt, and her permanently spread, chapped-cheeks smile is carrying warmly over the line—her imperturbable, consistently kind nature. She must be sixty-five by now. Bud inherited her from the former pastor, Sam Bollinger; she more or less came with the ministerial contract. Anna thinks of Millie's hairdo, the way it travels in a sculpted, corn-silk-smooth path down to the scruff of her neck and then springs out astonishingly in a fat, turned-under knockwurst. How she achieves this is something of a mystery. Does she put in pin curls every night? Nestle them along her hairline—a single tier of tight, slicked snails, *x*-ed with the bobby pins she once needed to keep the frizzies around her bun tidy?

"I'm always amazed at her vigor," Millie is saying. "You don't often see that much bounce in somebody her age."

"I know. She's pretty remarkable."

"And you, Anna? Are you still writing articles? I haven't come upon any lately in *Gospel Truth,* and I'm not one to miss out. Anytime I spy a piece from our Anna Farber, that's the first thing I read, even before the letters and obituaries. I always know it will be something provoking. Provoking in a good way, something spiritually challenging. Your courage and conviction, that really blesses me."

"No, I—" A fizzy feeling of discombobulation is taking over. There's an itch starting in her throat. "The truth is, I don't—"

"I've said it to Myrna and I'll say it to you: the two of you have inspired in me a deeper loyalty to the Lord."

"Oh, Millie, you don't know how much that means. I—I'm not sure I can live up to that."

MAMA IS PROBABLY still stranded. Those repair crews can be the biggest slowpokes. Anna maneuvers the phone's long, kicky cord past the coffeemaker to jab at the numbers, imagining the overquota of foremen in hardhats moseying around, kicking shiftlessly at the sheared wires, tending to their chaws. But lo and behold, *br-r-r-ing*. And Mama's stout, "Hello?"

"There you are! You gave me quite the scare, Mama. I thought you had a heart attack."

"Millie came by. Isn't she the most considerate friend? You got yourself in a lather all for nothing, Anna."

"I know, I'm sorry."

"I couldn't catch what you were saying. Something about Clyde."

"Clyde Bailey, yes. Do you know, Mama, if he ever got saved? Did anybody ever lead him to the Lord?"

"Oh my, 'deedy, I've asked that, too. Daddy tried and tried to help him understand his need for Jesus. Clyde said he was born and raised a Baptist and wasn't that good enough? He called himself a Christian. The army chaplain always preached on John 3:16, or so Clyde said." Mama stops to evaluate. "I guess it's something a person has to hand over to the Lord. We have to rest in the Lord's mercy and grace."

"So that's all the farther things went," says Anna.

"Do you remember what Herman Overholt said?"

"About Clyde?"

"He said somebody should've right-out asked Clyde, 'Did you kill? Bomb people?'"

Anna recalls Herman's words now, yes. The phone line goes silent again, holding out the questions at length, brutal and blunt and unanswered. Wanly she rubs along the nib of her chin.

11

In the fallow quiet of Friday afternoon, hunched over the desk where she's getting riffs of air from the window she cracked a few inches, Anna winces over this or that line of twaddle in her manuscript, shuffles the papers, gulps coffee, heaves her sighs. Why does she do this, keep shying away and shying away from simply laying out her article the editor didn't want and letting it speak for itself?

She slacks off on her browbeating for a moment to tippy-tap her pinky nail against the adage that scrolls around the midsection of her special mug. It's another of her spoils from the Goodwill, although in this case Jonathan gets the credit. She badgered him back in August into accompanying her, hoping he could help hunt for several pairs of jeans for him to take along back to school, and maybe one of those goosey lamps. But he was just standing uselessly in the aisle—this nerdy, handsome hunk, humoring her mother-hen thriftiness. "Hey, there you go," he said, pointing past her shoulder. "Get yourself that cup."

She turned to look at the shelf of dishwares and slowly took in the mug's caption: *Say nothing and look like a fool, open your mouth and remove all doubt.* Stepping back, stumbling over her sandal, she squealed, "You meany!"

"Oh, come on. It's a joke. You're my best and smartest mom. How do you think I got this smart?"

"That was from your dad, not me. Oh well, it's true—the saying fits. It fits perfectly. It's a wonder the editor didn't just put *that* in his rejection letter. Sending his polite, supportive condolences, how could that undo my dingbat actions? 'Lady, let's not spill our guts all over the grass, okay? Let's hang on to a shred of dignity, okay? And ask the Lord to open our spiritual eyes.' He should've been more upfront with me."

All her namby-pambying and beating around the bush, forestalling the inevitable—what's the use? She's just got to blunderbuss through. She'll unearth the article tomorrow. She's hearing the familiar chugs of the school bus conquering the curves on Coldbrook Road, bearing down on the house. All at once the phone jangles, too, joining in.

It's Jay Heatwole on the other end, with a favor to request.

"Fever?" she asks, after a minute. "High, you mean? Didn't Peg get a flu shot?"

"She's hot all right. A while ago, she was going on about the walls tilting and the floor being too far down from the sofa. And she's been throwing up. I hope it's not asking too much—you and Wade supervising the campout on such late notice."

"Oh no, that's fine. It wouldn't be right to cancel and ruin everything for the youth group. We should help out. You guys do tons with the youth—you're so dedicated and involved. Is Peg, um, anything like dire?"

"Naw," chuckles Jay. "You know her. She's tough enough."

While he clues Anna in on the evening plans, she jogs the cord around the fridge to the kitchen door to watch Todd disembarking from the bus. She's warm, herself, but it's just her coffee hot flash. Ick, the last bit in her mug seems too dreggy. I-i-i-ick, it tastes like dead bugs. Maybe right before she dove out of her chair, some squashed remains on the bottom of the window sash came unstuck and rode over on a fluff of breeze and fell in. She nods, and nods again. She smiles a hi to Todd coming in. "Okay then," she tells Jay. "You just leave things to us. Just take good care of your honey, how about?"

"I get the car tonight, right?" inquires Todd, as soon as she hangs up.

"Do you care too much if Wade and I come along?"

"Huh?" Her son is heading for the stairs.

"Because Peg is sick."

"Oh."

"I dread the thought—no sleep." But if she would've turned Jay down, that wouldn't have been very Christian.

When Todd, in short order, comes back down with his paraphernalia and drops it by the kitchen door, she eyes it with alarm. He's sloppily choked his pillow and his packs of jelly beans into the folds of the rolled-up sleeping bag. "No way," she announces. "Your stuff will fall right out."

With an exaggerated air of resignation he unrolls the sleeping bag full-length on the kitchen floor and unzips it to fit the pillow inside. But she frowns at the elastic bands looping beyond the bottom end of the bag, like a trapper's snares. "Somebody will trip," she scolds, wagging a finger. "Larry Arnold's got shoebox feet. He'll be up to something in the middle of the night and catch his foot and plunge headlong—he'll get a concussion."

"Aw, Ma."

"Promise you'll push the bands underneath, out of the way. Except— no. They could still weasel out. How about we cut them off?"

"Ma-a-a."

What's with this "ma" bit? she wonders. Is this some new craze? Is she Todd's old lady, now? Stepping over the mess on the floor to help him reorganize, she thinks suddenly about Marvin—Heatwoles' Marvin. Tonight she'll have to keep an eye on him, too. He might be coming down with the same flu. The whole youth group might catch it.

HEATWOLES' BARN sits sprawled on a gentle slope, sided with peeling boards, a quaint red by day but blurred and gray now against the night sky. The cavernous upper level houses the farm tractors and wagons, and at the far end, bales of hay that are stacked to where the roof begins its musty, steep ascent. The lower level holds the stanchions for the Holstein dairy herd. Earlier when Anna poked her head over the edge of the hay hole, after her eyes adjusted to the gloom she was able to discern the cows' mottled, sprawled forms, with the hindquarters tuckered sideways and the udders blobbed on the concrete like dumped Jell-O desserts.

She doesn't mind so much the rustles and pokes of the hay with every shift of her body, but at this late hour the teenagers' tongues are still flying. Also the cows' lowing is filtering up, signaling their unease and fitfulness. The intrusion probably has them lactating depressed curds instead of sweet unchurned gallons, 5% milkfat minimum. The unsettledness is reciprocal, but to be fair, shouldn't any vexations be the perpetrators' cross to bear, not the lesser beasts'?

As for the other lamentable deprivation, Anna is keeping handy, between her and Wade, the only reliable flashlight anyone's brought, Marvin's. "This thing stays with me," she informed Crystal Becker next to her and the rest of the girls down their half of the row, when they were spreading out their sleeping bags, getting themselves bedded. "Guys, do you hear? It's available only if there's an emergency. And I don't want anybody crawling over me. If you've got to go, wake me." The way the restless, lumpy cocoons are lined up now, parallel, at least she won't have to obsess in the middle of the night about anyone getting garroted in their sleep by another person's bag bands.

Rooching nearer to Wade, creating for herself a bit of distance from her neighbor's vigorous potato-chip chomping, Anna says softly, "Didn't I see you speaking with Frank? When he dropped Crystal off?"

"Frank?"

"Yes. What were you talking about?"

"Don't remember. Oh, I guess he asked about the pick-up time tomorrow."

"I don't want him even getting near me."

"Frank Becker's not going to bother you. I daresay he knows his bounds."

"That's sure not a foregone conclusion. How can you think that?" But an explosion at close range, the startling pop of Crystal's emptied potato-chip bag, forces Anna to tuck her head into her sleeping bag, turtle fashion.

She notices a dullness in her one ear, like it has suddenly plugged up with wax. "Wade." She pushes her face back out. He ought to make Crystal apologize. "Wade, do something." But no, he's grabbing for the flashlight, training it in the boys' direction. "Hey!" he yells. "Nuh-uh! Nuh-uh-uh!"

On all fours, Larry is almost to the haymow ladder with his Mountain Dew empty. He throws up his arms snarkily like somebody under arrest, blinking in the glare of the paddy wagon's headlights. He was intending to lob it down the hay hole and scare the cattle? "Why's he always the bully?" she mutters under her breath. "Well, I guess I know. Anybody with a dad like his."

"We don't trash people's property," Wade calls. "We don't trash anywhere, period. What's more important, we don't behave maliciously toward animals."

"It's just a bottle," grouches Larry, crawling back to where he belongs. "They're just moron cows."

"Sure, they're morons. They'll *eat* plastic."

"Won't neither."

"Not the number 2 recyclables," says Wade. "But the steers my dad used to raise ingested the plastic bags that blew into our pasture from people littering."

"*In*gested?" asks Anna. "You mean *di*gested?"

"No, the plastic passed through and wound up in the manure. All chewed up, in scraps."

"You went out and picked through the cow pies?" asks Larry.

"Cow piles," says Crystal. She's pedaling her feet, trying to work her potato-chip crumbs down to the bottom of her sleeping bag. "Not pies."

"Oops," says Anna, "I forgot. Pies—that reminded me. Everybody, Jay wants you to be thinking up fund-raiser ideas for the youth-group officers to consider at the next planning meeting. Wouldn't whoopie pies really bring in the money? If you want my opinion, I say do a big bake sale. You could freeze the whoopie pies and then go around selling them in the school cafeteria. You wouldn't even have to take orders."

"I vote for cow-manure pies," says Larry.

"Oh, come on. You all, listen. I seriously want to encourage these efforts. It's awesome seeing you supporting a missionary program, putting your energies into this. Look, bringing other people to Christ—there's nothing more important. When I was your age I *lived* at a mission."

"What, Anna?" Nicole Nussbaum down the row raises up on one elbow. "Like, for the homeless?"

"No. Well, we *were* situated on the poor side of town. We held regular services and Sunday school, Bible school, street meetings—that kind of thing."

"Meetings out on the street? You dragged the chairs outside?"

"Not like that."

"Tell about it, Ma." Fooling around with his dispirited penlight, Todd wavers its leaky yellow beam across to her.

"Street miming, then?" asks Kimmy Rhodes. "Did you have mimes and clowns and all that?"

"No no no. The mission owned this transportable amplification system and my father would load it in the car, with the loudspeakers tied on the roof, and go the few blocks down to the empty lot by Simpson's Grocery and set up there, just put the mike a ways back in the grass and thistles. It was just us and Overholts and Werts, mostly. We'd do our songs—it might be all the grownups, like in a sextet, or just my sister and me—and then one of the men would do a sermon. Oh my, Coca-Cola bottle caps in the grass, I remember, and old carnival tickets, and popsicle papers coated all over with ants trying to eat the sugar off. And you could see the long long cord from the microphone stand, writhing through the debris. Snaking back to the car, like somebody had let it out of the zoo."

"Ha ha, I get it," says Nicole. "A rattlesnake, ugh."

"No, black snake." Anna is irritated, suddenly, by Todd's horseplay. The penlight's furred trajectory is zooming in arcs between the nest overhead built by swallows, where the joist is plastered with mud and droppings, and the papery remnant of a hornet's nest further over that's held on with chew-up and spittle. Is he even listening? He knows only the barest details, himself. "Todd, please. Will you stop that?"

"Duh, Ma."

"Please don't aim at me, either."

"All *right*."

"Now what was I saying? Oh, yes—the thing is, outdoors like that we could reach a wider audience. Mrs. Conklin—she lived above the laundromat on the opposite side of Grackle Street, and she was too obese to leave her house very often—could just arrange herself at a window, with her snacks around her to munch on, and take in the proceedings. Though, I guess she could've even heard from the closet."

"The closet?" questions Nicole.

"I suppose so, sure. 'GOOD EVENING ONE AND ALL,' my father would boom out, and right off, the regulars would start collecting, and any kids who'd been straggling past on the sidewalk, and whoever else. Oh, 'Whosoever Will,' that was one of our songs." Out of the blue, Anna takes off on the number. "'Who-so-ev-er hear-eth, shout, shout the sound.' And 'Jesus Saves' was another. 'We have heard a joy-ful sound, Je-sus saves, Je-sus saves—'" But the notes are too gargled and she can't carry on with her operatic performance. It feels like there's a buildup of glottis cartilage in her throat, or like she's too sunk into her pillow.

"It was pretty neat," she adds. "Except, one time Mrs. Conklin—"

"Oooh, Anna," Natasha Nussbaum whines dramatically, "ants, you said, but I bet yellow jackets, too. And rats." Her eyes materialize in the dark, beyond Crystal. "Oooh, rats would be the worst. There's some up here, I betcha." She's pulling her sweatshirt hood up and tying it around her face like a laundry bag. "That big huge kind with fangs, like in the pied piper poem. I know for a fact there's some that'll chew off your hair."

Waylaid, Anna is about to say there's no need to worry, that farmers starve their barn cats on purpose, when she remembers the cocoa scum Jonathan talked about. Heatwoles' cats, who knows? Mightn't Peg still be feeding them her leftovers? She wonders if Peg is improving any. Peg almost never gets sick. She says people who milk cows can't afford that luxury.

WHEN THE BLADDER urge nudges Anna back to wakefulness, armed with Marvin's light she pitches her way across the hay to the ladder and clambers down, lets herself out the massive, cranky barn doors pulleyed with concrete blocks for counterweights, and follows the tractor ruts down and around to the milkroom entrance at the barn's south end. Inside, she guides the beam past the stainless-steel bulk tank's polished belly, its paddles a-hum, and past the ponderous poker face of the walk-in refrigerator where Heatwoles' few private customers—Forrys, Rhodeses, Anna's family, and several others at church—can expect to find their weekly order waiting in half-gallon jars, raw and thick at the top with cream. In the small unheated toilet, she makes certain sure none of Natasha's scurrilous vermin are lurking.

Lowered onto the weather-bubbled seat, her skin crawly from the cold, she meditates upon the mystery of Mrs. Conklin's mashed sandwich that time at street meeting. As the first hymn of the service, one she and Margie knew by heart, bounced off every nearby facade, *BRIGHT-LY BEAMS OUR FA-THER'S MER-CY FROM HIS LIGHT-HOUSE EV-ER-MORE, BUT TO US HE GIVES THE KEEP-ING OF THE LIGHTS A-LONG THE SHORE*, high above the sidewalk a hammy arm walloped at the tattered lace curtain and more of the woman moved into view. Soon she was involved with her white-bread sandwich—taking little pinchy bites, drawing out the process, chewandswallow, chewandswallow, chewandswallow, and parsimoniously licking the mayonnaise smears off her fingers. A second sandwich waited on the sill.

But after the song, just as Mr. Wert stepped to the microphone and started in on his crackly prayer, *OUR KIND HEAVENLY FATHER, whomp,* down slammed the window. "Don't," Anna whispered when Margie nudged at her and pointed. "Don't call attention." But the impact had, indeed, flattened the extra sandwich to a pancake. A robber bumblebee was beginning to circle with interest the teeniest bump of bread sticking out.

"Somebody like Mrs. Conklin wouldn't accidentally on purpose waste her baloney and pickles," she contended, later. "The window catch must've just, bam, broke."

"Nope-er," Margie argued, "that fat old hippopotamus was stoppering up her ears."

"Lookie here, that's not polite! Saying hippopotamus!" Still, Anna feared she had no business scowling so self-righteously. *Let the low-er lights be burn-ing, send a gleam a-cross the way,* the chorus of the song was supposed to go, *some poor faint-ing struggling sea-man you may res-cue, you may save,* but her head had played a dumb trick. One of the diagrams in the book under Mama and Daddy's mattress showed the semen paddling around in the sperm—wriggly, swarming black tadpoles, vying in their milky pond, trying their hardest—and unexpectedly that very picture had popped up. Each time through the chorus she'd had to stand there beside her sister and flub along helplessly, *SOME POOR FAINT-ING STRUG-GLING SE-MEN, YOU MAY RES-CUE, YOU MAY SAVE.* "Some" wasn't even right. Only one little peeper out of the pack maybemaybemaybe might hit on the egg. The rest were plain doomed, she knew. No res-cue for them.

Of course, thinks Anna, pumping herself a stringy orange drool of antibacterial hand soap from the jug on the toilet washbowl, that "sperm" word is misleading. It ought to be "spermy"—singular, to distinguish—and "spermies" in the plural. Look how a single switched word or twisted concept can throw a person off!

She makes it back to the barn's nebulous upper story and her sleeping bag. There, lost in the black-as-plums obscurity, only vaguely intuiting the drifting motes of hay mold and the roof's slant toward the creepy netherworld eaves, she's bothered by a curious buzzing behind her eyes. Has she already caught Peg's flu? Crystal has migrated too close—every time she tosses, her ponytail marbles grind—and she's letting out jerky, startled breaths, as if a venomous electrical cord in her dream is flicking its tongue at her or shivering its rattles.

Plagued by the swirly mental sensations, Anna scrounges for a comfier position atop her bed ticking. Maybe she's just too cranked up—and if such is the case, how will she ever manage to get back to sleep? Tangledly she turns onto her other side to reach for her husband, for the soft jut of his jaw line, his solidity, and just this simple act of reorienting, this small defying of their unwonted situational rift, eases her anxiety a bit. Nothing is ever *exactly right* right, she tells herself. The obfuscations and boggler wordings in her manuscript at home start crowding into her hayfevered mind, but then they clot up even more and run together, and before too long a yawn collects in her chest and escapes, ho-hum.

12

Oh, something else, yet. She wasn't planning to go into this—tell about the hot peppers—the quirk with the recipe, and hiding them. But after last night's run-in with Wade, she's too scattered and uneasy to get down to the real business.

Back in September, daily he was taking one of his burny little crunchers from the garden in his lunch—he'd slice it up at the lab sink in his classroom for his cheese sandwich. Did he ignore the Reet (gone defunct, supposedly)? Not bother to wash the peppers under the plastic hose thingy hooked to the giraffe-necked lab faucet? And did he just use a dissecting knife, one that had seen the preserved, rubbery maw of a frog? He autoclaves his equipment, sure, but who else would even commandeer such a tool? Well, that's beside the point. Or no, maybe it isn't. At any rate, one day Joey Snipe, who'd been sent to Wade's room for a noontime detention because of unfinished homework, came sidling over to where the teacher stood carving his pepper into long, skinny pieces. "Hey, my grandma cans them things."

"Yeah?" said Wade. "They're good canned?"

Joey laid the recipe on Wade's desk the next day, a greasy card with spidery handwriting: *Boil ½ c. reglar oil, 1 cut up Garlic clove (1 good size corn, not the whole knocker), 1 C. pickling vinegar (cider kind), ½ C. Water, ½ C. reglar Domino's white sugar, 1 scanty teaspoon Salt. And pour over the peppers in the jars and boil them 10 minutes ample.* Did Joey hope this would get him extra-credit points? Maybe so. He's the kind of kid, Wade says, who can't seem to make normal sense of a situation. For example, Wade's number-one rule in the classroom is: no *I don't know*s. "What's the name of the multiplication cycle whereby viral DNA attaches to the host-cell DNA and becomes dormant?" he'll ask the twelfth graders, interrupting his lecture, the overhead projector notes cast whitely on the screen behind him. "Annette Knotts?" He's singling out Annette even though she hasn't raised her hand. Actually, nobody's put up their hand. Chad Pritts could probably reply right off the bat, "Lysogeny," but Chad is in the principal's office explaining a forged excuse note or changing out of the wifebeater shirt or handing over his pack of cigarettes.

"Nuh-uh," Wade will caution if Annette shakes her head. "Not *I don't know.* What *do* you know, Annette? C'mon, c'mon. *I know that* what?"

"Uh, I know—I know—I knowthatvirusesareobligatoryintracellularparasites." Good girl. She'll get this much of the concept, anyhow. And Rosie Deavers, if Wade calls on her next, will respond with, "I know—I knowthatvirusesconsistofaproteincapsidwitheitherDNAorRNAinsidebutneverboth." She'll manage to come up with something. But Joey Snipe, if Wade were to pick on him? Joey would be so far afield he wouldn't even realize it. "I know more'n is good for me, hardy har. That's what my pap says. Them DNAs, ain't they what're in that there picture in the book? Ain't they them damn things what're strunged up in chains and Ferris wheels?"

For Joey, the only Christian answer would be *Idunnonothing.*

Wade kept after Anna to try the recipe. She knew the vinegar would make the peppers high in acid, so between her tomato-juice sessions she fit the job in. But lifting the hissing pints out of the canner, the reds, oranges, and yellows drifting together artistically, she wondered if it was okay for the oil to be separating from the brine and rising to the top. The pepper tips weren't fully submerged in the vinegary part anymore. They were thrusting up through the shallow brim of oil. "Might there be a chance of the *C. botulinum* spores taking off on a spree?" she asked, when her husband came home. "If the vinegar isn't permeating through and through?"

"Don't the grandma's jars do the same thing?" he replied. "Have any Snipes succumbed?"

"Wade, you're nasty. What's the use in asking *that?* Even if nothing's ever happened, what's the guarantee? Mercy! If that toxin stuff ever developed, there wouldn't be anybody left to tell the story—it's just about the deadliest substance there is. You know that! *You're* the expert." And the next morning, once Todd was on the bus, instead of putting the jars in the hutch or taking them to the cellar she scrunched herself into a fetal position and scooted them way, way back where—

Well, someplace secret.

Fortunately Wade still had a lot of peppers hanging on out in the garden, an abundant supply. Then in October, the night the radio predicted the first hard frost, he picked a pile, along with the mottling tomatoes and a few last-ditch psoriasis-y squashes, and dumped his stash in the refrigerator, and he drew on those for a while. Noting the dwindling numbers though, last week, she had to squirm.

Maybe, last night, he wanted to *commit* her.

She'd already showered, but he hadn't even gotten around yet to packing his lunch. He was just puttering around, the way he likes to do, relaxing and jamming along with his oldies station. Music like this isn't what she grew up with at the mission, that's for sure, but for him and his family it's always been part of the air they've breathed.

"Those Schlonnegers, they're a different stripe, I guess," she informed Mama after Wade first took her to Hawk Knob, letting out a pinched, squeaky giggle and rolling her eyes. "They're quite the jolly pack. More live and let live." In Wade's Mustang, dark evenings, the low, smoky tunes from the car radio curled around the black-vinyl padded interior, or some wild beat thumped away, and she'd fold contentedly up against him in the green glow from the dash lights, dazed and quiet.

Even all these years later, with his kitchen-radio music, when he turns up the volume and the hard-driving rhythms pour through the house—or songs more twangy and haunting—she mostly just tucks into her neck and goes along, tame and subdued herself but glad he's so swashbuckling and playful. He has this way of growling out the lower-register notes, his voice rough and gravelly, with lots of esophageal air mixed in, and for the high parts converting to a tragic wail. So at first, last night, it was business as usual—he was yowling along with "I'm a Believer," *dum dum dum dum dum, dump-de-dump-dump-dump, dum dum dum dum dum dum, dump-dump-dump,* slightly off pitch—and his laughable antics made her want to tell him she thought she might get somewhere this week, might finally get past the pity-partying and procrastinating, but then he soared into an ear-splitting *dum dum dum, ooooooooo,* and too unsure of herself, she turned from the kitchen and shuffled upstairs.

She tapped on the bathroom door. "Are you naked? Can I brush my teeth?" Granted entrance, she squeezed around Todd cutting his toenails into the wicker wastebasket and peered at her blowzy image in the cabinet mirror—the sloppy heave of her bathrobe collar, her flattened mop of hair. Anyhow, I'm still kicking, she thought.

"I don't know what possessed that Brenda Arnold, telling Peg in Sunday school this morning she looked like death warmed over," said Anna. "Though, it wasn't all that far from the truth. Peg should've stayed home. I would've." She levied herself a smidge of toothpaste and recapped the tube. "Two days of fever, I would've been whipped."

Todd arranged his other foot over the lip of the basket and bent again to his snipping. "That's not the nicest habit," she grumped around her toothbrush swishes. "The shreds fall right out on the floor. Every time I clean in here I find the yucky leavings. Couldn't you do that somewhere else?"

"Is it a big deal?"

"Not really. Well, yes it is. Sort of." A foamy bubble was forming at the corner of her mouth. "Thome conthiderath—" She hastened her swishing, spat, and rinsed. "Some consideration would be nice, that's all."

"Consideration?"

"Yes. A little kindness goes a long way." She gave a shrug in his direction. Above his shorts elastic his backbone stood up in an obdurate ridge. "Although I guess I could just line the bottom of the basket. I could put down a paper towel or something for a liner."

He unclogged the clippers with a huff and reached around her to grab for his washcloth. "You done in here?"

"I'm going, I'm going."

In the hall, concerned that maybe nobody had fed Popper and the cat, Anna leaned over the banister to call down to Wade. He was into another oldie now, drowning out Percy Sledge, *doo doo doo-oo doo doo dooo-doo, doo-doo-doo-doo-doo-doo-doo-doo-oo-oo-oo*, and collecting his lunch fixings, and she heard the crisper drawer of the fridge bang open and abruptly shut. Uh-oh, she thought, no more raw peppers? Wade's soulful yipping and whining broke off. Was he looking in the hutch? Uh-oh. Next thing, she heard him go charging down to the cellar, and what sounded like the potato crate dragging, like he'd accidentally hooked it with his foot in the underworld shadows and was trawling it along behind him on his way over to the canning shelves. "An-na!"

She tore downstairs in time to meet his glowering face at the top of the cellar steps. "Wade, look. Please. *I know* the pepper jars aren't down there." At least she obeyed the classroom rule. Fluttering, wishing he wouldn't automatically turn belligerent, she pleaded, "You're not allowed to open any yet, okay? I'm still so uneasy. Okay? Can you try to understand? Don't do this to me. Just don't. I'm going to call around and try to find somebody who has the information. Somebody who knows what to do when the brine is separated like that."

"This is ridiculous, Anna. There's *no* problem. You're being 100 percent irrational."

"Wade," she implored, "ple-e-ease. Wait. Wait till I can get some assurance. Have a little patience, okay? What about pickles instead?" She clutched her robe more tightly around her and stepped over to the hutch. "Here," she said, pushing a quart on him, seven-day sweets. "Take these. Take the whole jarful. Keep them in your prep room fridge. They'll be ever so nice and handy that way." The radio was still playing, but "When a Man Loves a Woman," the singer's ardent, sweet-sad crooning, had given way to "Hound Dog."

Now, Monday, Anna bets he's only put the jar up front on his school desk, and he's promising handouts. That's the kind of thing he'd do. He's known for throwing his swirly, cellophane-wrapped pinwheel peppermints at students who get their answers out before the count of ten, so who knows what he might try with the pickles since they're not exactly the zippy hot stingers he was after? But how can she be expected to blindly trust his judgment? Trusting in God is one thing. *Trust in the Lord with all thine heart; and lean not unto thine own understanding,* she read in Daddy's Bible this morning, and *What time I am afraid, I will trust in thee.* A person mustn't let their faith crumple. In her period of dark spiritual wandering last year, what more desperate need had she than to trust, to abandonedly lean on the everlasting arms and not stop to question every little glitch? But the trouble was spiritual related—it concerned spiritual beliefs. In these more quotidian, everyday foul-ups that seize her with apprehension, mustn't she muster her frail powers of reasoning? In these small, fraught, domestic situations? If the husband is just the mate, not some fervent lord-it-over pulpit thumper?

"I know," she told Wade last night, "*I know* I ought to be taking a little token something to Mrs. Snipe in return. It can't be in appreciation, exactly. Well, I'm appreciative of her friendly gesture, I guess. What am I supposed to say when I see her? 'How's come none of you-uns has gave up the ghost?'"

So this is something else hanging over Anna's head, however dopey and inconsequential.

13

Well, all right. Now everybody will blanche, maybe honk behind their hands, but here's what she wrote. It only further confirms the tragedy of having boob brains.

A Two-faced God?!

I'm telling you, a person can get into hot water without ever planning to. And I don't mean corn-boiling water, either.

Our church has a practice every August spending a day together at Jay and Peg Heatwole's farm, preparing slushy two-gallon freezer bags of sweet corn grown by the Heatwoles, which we then donate to a rescue mission in Bricksburg. It's a really neat, fun operation and a great service opportunity. This last corn day, a blistering hot one, Jay had us huskers and silkers stationed under the gnarly old maple next to the milkroom driveway, and while the youth group kids picked and delivered the corn (and, between wagon loads, hogged drinks at the barn hydrant, slopping themselves hilariously, and sprinted around stocking our crates), we tried to keep abreast. Other adults were stoking the fire beneath the huge iron pot, or transferring the cooked ears to the cool-down tubs fed with garden hoses, or slicing off the corn in toothy strips over at the cutting table, a boards-and-sawhorses affair.

Susan, Brenda, and I, our lawn chairs pushed together so we could share the same crate, got to talking about Brenda's husband Bill who's openly skeptical about our Evangelical Brethren peace beliefs. He'd started bugging their son Larry about him joining the army. What if he were to sway Larry? Induce him to make such a grave choice? Brenda said Bill was even getting on her case for making Larry attend our church.

"He keeps saying that letting me switch my membership was a big mistake," she confided, as Larry dashed past us with somebody's piled-high dishpan of cleaned corn, his Popeye muscles bulging under his T-shirt. "Why he has to hound and hound, I don't know. I tell him, 'Bill, you ought to visit. Nobody'll bite. Why can't you be the weeniest bit open minded?'"

"I still think he'll come around," I said, attempting to be optimistic. "We'll win him over, yet."

"He just barks back at me, 'What's to be open minded about? Defending our country is our Christian duty. They're all draft dodgers.' I say, 'Bill, if you're such a good Christian how come you're attending at First Mattress now?' We were such regular attenders at Victory in Jesus Baptist when Larry was little. We went every Sunday."

She released a big sigh, then picked some silks off her corn and knifed out a bad part. "He's forever bringing up the Old Testament. 'Talk about fighting,' he says. 'God ordered the Israelites into battle. God told Joshua to go ye up and possess the land. God said to utterly destroy the heathen.'"

"Oh, I know," I nodded. "It does get gory." My mind went to the five Amorite warlords who get hauled out from the cave at Makkedah by Joshua's officers to be savagely executed. Joshua orders the officers to stand on the necks of the men, and then he slaughters all five himself and hangs the bodies on trees.

Susan said to Brenda, "But you've explained, haven't you?" About the Old Testament and New Testament dispensations, Susan meant. She teaches our class at Conoy except for the rare times Wade, my husband, substitutes, and she's well versed in the Scriptures. "Why can't Bill grasp the important difference, understand how Christ's teachings supercede the Old Testament codes?"

"Well, I can see why people who've not grown up hearing that emphasized would be confused," I offered.

I snuck a glance over to where Wade and Frank and Nelson sat. The corn husks were flying off, and the wormy sections of cob. "I mean, just that episode where David mows down the two hundred Philistines? You know? It's horrible."

Brenda gave me a quizzical look. "Remember?" I said. "About David killing them for their foreskins? Oh, come on, you know. David asks to marry

Michal, Saul's daughter, and Saul establishes as the dowry price one hundred foreskins off the Philistines because he doesn't want his upstart rival coming back alive. And David bags two hundred, instead. The thing is, that's when Saul realized the Lord was with David, not him. In effect, God lent David a hand at—you know—at lancing the—"

"But that's the Old Testament way," said Susan as she chucked her ear of corn into the crate, rescuing me from my blathering idiocy. I leaned back, glad somebody still had their wits. "Yes," I agreed, "thank goodness. Still, it's horrifying. Without the Sermon on the Mount, without Jesus' teachings, we'd still be advocating an eye for an eye, a tooth for a tooth. Well, without Jesus' death, too. God's incredible mercy and love in sending him to die on the cross."

This part always twists up my insides. The crucifixion, I mean—the shed blood of Christ in exchange for our salvation, in fulfillment of the sacrifice laws God handed down along with the Ten Commandments. Unlike when Abraham set out to offer up his cherished Isaac on Mount Moriah, there was no panicky last-minute rescue. I was sitting there thinking about this, and about Abraham, all the while struggling to work a blackish blob of smut off my corn. I felt a little nervous tic starting in my eye. Or more like, insistent jabs. I turned to my two friends. "Thou shalt not kill," I said, quoting it in a deliberate way but not vengefully, not really. "Wasn't that a little two-faced of God? Giving that commandment even though he'd told Abraham to slay Isaac?"

I didn't realize how loud I'd gotten. My question had carried across the worn-down patch of ground and lumpy tree roots and attracted the men's attention. I looked over to see Frank aiming at me with his corncob. "Hey, God could say whatever," he objected. "God providing Abraham the ram instead, that's the whole point."

"But just saying it?" I returned. "Just, God saying to offer up Isaac? If God later on was going to specify in the plainest of terms, 'Thou shalt not kill'?" Suddenly it didn't make one little figment of sense. "I—I can't believe it," I sputtered. "It—it just sticks in my craw."

"Aw, child sacrifice was common back then," Wade pitched in. "So naturally the idea hit Abraham, too. He thought he was hearing from God." Wade is always trying to get my goat, always throwing out some alternative half-skewed theory, so I knew not to give him the time of day, but Nelson's forehead was pleating into a mass of deep creases, like now he had two heretics to deal with. "Please, stop the smart-alecky games," I said to Wade. "I'm seriously asking."

"Yeah, ha," said Brenda, "that's bosh for sure, Wade." She smiled, patted my arm. "Girl, you're a real bird. The stuff you come up with!"

Susan seemed scarcely ruffled. "Nobody ever said it's easy, believing. 'Now faith is the substance of things hoped for, the evidence of things not seen,'" she recited quietly, ever the one to have the needed passage on the tip of her tongue. "That's the wonderful part. If everything depended upon our sure knowledge, what place would God's grace hold? The salvation that comes by faith?"

"Right," said Nelson, "that's it in a nutshell. God was only testing Abraham."

"You're all such stalwarts," I said weakly. "You're the people I can put stock in." And I meant it. I count it such a blessing to have friends like these. But I still feel like I'm floundering. That day at Heatwoles we were just being ourselves, not formal like at church. Susan had corn yuck under her nails, and Brenda's shirt was sullied with corn squirts, and below my shorts cuffs the entire exposed surface of my thighs bore the same grimy byproducts (except for where my legs squished down through the lawn chair webbing like pale marshmallows). I guess in such a setting I felt freer, so I ended up, without warning, blurting out every random, flukey thought. But I was being honest, right? Aren't we supposed to be honest? And transparent? Especially with our church family?

Wade is always advising, "Be more generous, have a more generous attitude. There's always another side to things. You're no know-it-all." And I say, "You're telling me? I know that much!" But was I being a dweeb, questioning if God maybe acted in a fickle way with Abraham? If God might be somebody a person can't fully count on? That still puts me in a froth. Doesn't anyone besides me quail, knowing they could spend an eternity ruing their mistakenly placed trust?

The day the editor's reply showed up in the mailbox, Anna remembers, she noted instantly the weed thinness of her self-addressed envelope. No manuscript padding it. She stepped the whole way off the road, closer to the neighbor's steer fence, and ripped it open. The very first sentence, her chest clutched up. "Dear Anna, I'm sorry to say that I cannot give this article space in *Gospel Truth*. It's not that others haven't wrestled over God's call upon Abraham, but usually the tenor of your work is more contained and reasoned. Besides the fact that the central topic here is broached only superficially, your approach is too melodramatic, almost maudlin. But please don't let this dissuade you from submitting more articles. I'll be looking forward to receiving them. Sincerely yours, Harold Epp."

Maudlin. She steadied herself. *Melodramatic.*

The barbed-wire fence mournfully screaked in the wind as she slowly folded the paper back into thirds.

Why in the world didn't he send back the manuscript? she wondered, crossing the road, trudging up the drive to the house. He'd sent back her prayer-cap article. And her too-preachy one about TV.

Of course, she now grasps all too keenly Epp's concern about the superficiality. She needed to seriously delve into those faith questions. But only with a humble heart! Like she bumbled and bumbled around trying to say in her subsequent attempt at an article (after she got herself patched back up and her spirituality restored), measly human beings cannot begin to comprehend each and every devising of an omniscient God. It's human nature for a person to want things to tidily line up and make normal everyday philosophical sense. But if the person's reasoning is self-seeking in any way, then they deserve getting their goose cooked!

Anna gnaws on her knuckles, soberly reflects. Writing about her little tantrum on corn day, airing her dirty laundry like that, was she on some kind of egotistical, self-important quest to make *Gospel Truth* her bully pulpit? Oh, mercy. She almost wonders if she's ever had solely pure motives. What about that brown-sugar altar of hers, up front at the mission—her rendition of that other sacrifice story? How could've she tried so hard to sound interesting, doing her dippy children's meeting, that she just about melted Mama's cake pan and burned down the song leader stand?

Rising off her duff, she clumsily knocks her hip against the middle drawer of the desk, oof, ouch ouch. She takes a lo-o-ong stretch. In the kitchen she pulls the Maxwell can from the refrigerator and rattles through the silverware in the drainer for a tablespoon. From the sink window, Wade's apple and peach trees in the open reach of field beyond the backyard appear quietly stoic, lifting their stripped arms heavenward. Up the steep, densely wooded back hill, autumn's deciduous riot of color has gone, leaving only lackadaisical daubs of green from the cedars and pines, and the squirrels are berating the birds and chipmunks and chasing helter-skelter, doing what they must to survive the coming months. Despite the perfect clear-blue November sky, an inner harbinger is driving them to hurry for their bitter winter acorns. Or else it's just their gumptiousness. Either way, they'll get the job done—she should take a lesson.

The boys' old decayed fort in the wild-cherry tree, now visible through the clumps of skeletal timber, puts her in mind of a memory, now. How old was Todd? Four? Hearing a frightful caterwauling coming from the boys' building site, she went puffing up the path to find Todd scrunched into one of Wade's chicken-feed buckets, and Jonathan on the half-built platform,

preparing to pulley him up. Jonathan had been using the bucket to haul up
his boards, and the piece of rope he'd tied to the handle was severely frayed.

"I don't wanna go for a ride," Todd was blubbering, "I don't wanna."

"Boys!" she shouted. "Jonathan!"

"He climbed in himself," Jonathan told her. "I didn't make him get in."

"I changed my mind!" wailed Todd.

She put them both on a time-out. She sat Todd on a stump and
Jonathan on one of the slats he'd nailed onto the tree trunk for a ladder, and
she made them warm their behinds for a good ten minutes. "Think!" she
ordered. "The next time, think!"

Which seems, at the moment, the most pertinent of all possible
morsels of advice. Impatient to get back to the computer, she adds a heap-
ing spoonful of coffee to the damp grounds in the filter, pours a mug of
water in, flicks the switch to "on." The perky pings of the liquid hitting in
the pot, and the smell, ah-h. She chafes her arms vigorously and sucks in
some air between her teeth, a tad shocked about the headway she's made.
Though, her whole long sorry coming to account is still waiting in the
wings.

14

Why in the world? she remembers repeating to herself, back in the house. He'd not even returned it. Of course, she still had her own paper copy, and the file on the computer. Spreading wide the lone page from the editor, she stared once more at the words. She took from the file cabinet her folder labeled *Two-faced? to Gospel Truth September 18* and labored slowly down the paragraphs, white faced and unmoving, her insides in a miserable knot.

Several times that afternoon she ran toward the phone but stopped mid-flight. She waited to call Wade till 2:30, his last-hour planning period. He'd maybe be busily setting up a lab experiment for the next day—peeling away the rubbery agar in his petri plates and wiping the old dates off the lids, bottle-brushing the test tubes, concocting a fresh batch of nutrient agar—but she'd held off long enough. "Mr. Schlonneger, please?"

He finally picked up the phone in his classroom. "Did Epp junk it, or what?" she cried. "Was that very nice?"

"Your article?"

"What else? I feel awful!"

"I guess so. Did he offer anything constructive?"

Wade couldn't linger for her response, though—he had to go. She hung up, thought a minute. She hurried to the desk for paper and a pencil. *Dear*

Harold, I put what, four? stamps in with my article,"A Two-faced God?!" But you didn't include it with your letter. So I don't know if you trashed it—made paper jets or something—or only mislaid it (but I have my strong suspicions as to which). Listen you, doesn't everybody have emotions? I'd say if they never feel anything deeply, then secretly they're robots. I dumped out my soul, I asked some heretic-type questions I guess, and you went, Oh ha, a hysterical woman. Well, you'd better examine your sexist prejudices. And your own spiritual weaknesses. You higher-ups in the church prefer to hide behind your three-piece suits and act staid and perfect and composed, but it's high time that stops. I was only laying myself bare, and look what I got for it. Is it possible the church is a place of t-r-u-t-h but not h-o-n-e-s-t-y?? The second question mark, she punched down on the dot so hard her pencil lead broke off and went skittering. She put her head down on her arms and allowed her spine to cave in between her shoulder blades.

Dimly she served supper. When Todd volunteered to wash the dishes, she waved him off. After her long, solitary session of clattering and banging, she wandered into the study. Wade twisted the desk chair a half turn and dangled in front of her the scribbled-up paper he'd happened upon. "You didn't mince words, anyway."

"Oh," she gasped, reaching for it, "I wasn't going to send it."

He drew back, leaving her clawing at the air. "I guess not. Anna, you're no heretic, rest assured. You can be blunt at times, that's all." He pillaged through the mess on the desk for her *Two-faced?* folder and slid her impetuous note inside. "Epp just didn't know what to do with something that personal and inflammatory."

"Inflammatory? No, he's decided I'm wacko. The jig is up. I've shown myself up as the poor pathetic sap I really am."

She sagged down onto the mangy velour chair awaiting the interviewers from *Newsweek* and *Time* and studied her shoes. "Mary Beth liked it. I read her my rough draft, it was still needing a lot of fix-ups, and she said something about it not being all lofty and teachy-preachy. Like she approved of that."

"Call her," said Wade.

"Load her down with my dumb woes? Huh-uh. I'll just e-mail sometime, let her know."

Wade strode to the phone in the kitchen to dial Mary Beth's apartment in Houston, twelve hundred miles away. After speaking with her briefly, he called, "C'mon, Anna. Get yourself out here."

Too aflutter to care she was leaning her shoulder into the children's valentine on the fridge, Anna cradled the phone tightly, hungry for any snippets of consolation. Against the usual background of sirens far below on the clogged streets, Mary Beth's voice, soft with sympathy, filtered up the line. "Oh, Mom. I'm so sorry. I *did* say it was good. I wasn't just fawning and flattering. No, no, there's no way he thinks you're a bimbo. He can't think that. Nobody can think that."

A new thought struck. "Oh-h-h," Anna groaned, "I know what happened. They sent it to somebody else. By accident. Epp's secretary was stuffing her envelopes—her renewal notices, or those capital-funds donor solicitations—and she got her piles mixed up, and now somebody has received along with their proper formal business letter my pathetic story all loaded down with angst." A-a-angst, she pronounced it. "What a pretty kettle of fish this is!"

"Mom, that copy doesn't especially matter."

"I know, I could've submitted by e-mail. But I didn't."

"You probably forgot the extra postage. You didn't send the stamps."

"Forgot? No."

"Maybe. It doesn't help a thing to automatically assume the worst. You have a terrible habit, you realize."

"The worst?" asked Anna. "So you're saying being a dunce isn't the most evil bane?" Her ear was starting to hurt, plastered under the receiver.

"Mom, please. Be reasonable. Stand back and think. You don't want to make a mountain out of a little molehill failure. Everybody gets a bunch of chances to goof up. You're not anywhere near your quota."

"What's that supposed to mean?"

"Relax, Mom. Maybe it was too good an article to print. I'm sure you can salvage some of it. Try developing better your idea about the importance of having good Christian friends to bounce off of. Try that. What was it you said about the church folks being so supportive? Stalwart, or something? Read me that part again, will you?"

"Oh—"

"Just that much, okay?"

Anna dropped the receiver onto the table, the cord's coils blipping against the corner of the refrigerator, to go for her manuscript. Back again, though, she hedged. "Look, why don't we forget this? Let's don't get all analytical. Let's skip it, how about? You really don't want to bother."

"Mom."

"Mary Beth—"

"*Mom.*"

"Why do you insist? What's the use?" Anna sighed. "Oh, well. All right. I was just trying to point out the church people's dedication. Susan and everybody's. "'*You're all such stalwarts,' I said weakly. 'You're the people I can put stock in.' And I meant it. I count it such a blessing to have friends like these. But I still feel like I'm floundering. That day at Heatwoles we were just being ourselves, not formal like at church. Susan had corn yuck under her nails, and Brenda's shirt was sullied with corn squirts, and below my shorts cuffs the entire exposed surface of my thighs bore the same grimy byproducts (except for where my legs squished down through the lawn chair webbing like pale marshmallows). I guess in such a setting I felt freer, so I ended up, without warning, blurting out every random, flukey—*"

"Mo-om, that is so hilarious. Marshmallows."

"Hilarious? My thighs? No. That's just the human condition. Any woman my age, I mean. Just you wait." Anna went silent. She scowled at the mouthpiece's toothpick holes. She let out some useless lung wind. "Oh, me. It's all making me bleary in the head. I guess I'm pretty pooped. Can I hang up now?"

"Let me talk to Dad again," said Mary Beth sternly. "He's probably the only one who'll be able to whack some sense into you."

Late that night Anna thought about that word she'd used on corn day, bloviating to Susan and Brenda: "lancing." She crept out of bed. It had been a coon's age since she'd actually read the story about David collecting the booty required to win his bride. She turned on the lamp by the sofa, but the living room was cold. The fire Wade had lit in the wood stove to take off the evening chill had frittered down to bitsy, unconcerned coals. Just worming her toes down between the sofa cushions wasn't enough. She found a flashlight in the mudroom and went back upstairs, and jockeying for some blanket for over her shoulders without denying her slumbering husband his half, she scoured for the verses in her Bible. *Before the day set for the wedding, David and his men went out and killed two hundred Philistines. He took their foreskins to the king and counted them all out to him, so that he might become his son-in-law.* Well, so it never said "lanced," or "slit off the corpses' genitals' tippy-tips of their hoods." But that was the upshot, not so? What had she misrepresented, writing about it? Nothing! As she lay cramped in an uncomfortable ball under the covers, a cross, put-out feeling washed over her frame and lodged deep in the pit of her stomach. Wade went on senselessly slurping up his sleep in ample, nonchalant doses.

FOR LONGER THAN she cares to admit, Anna has been lolling here in front of the computer. The tiny gridlocked letters are no longer twitching at every tap on the keyboard. Instead, the screen saver's pinpoint stars are methodically traversing their black-night sky—springing from nowhere, hurling whitely through space at an amazing clip, extinguishing. Good Christian friends, Mary Beth said. Yikes, thinks Anna, was something already afoot between Frank and Brenda back then on corn day? Yikes—was he sending Brenda corncob signals?

I count it such a blessing to have friends like these, she wrote, but she's never let on to any of them, Peg included, about the article and the abysmal nosedive she took afterwards. Turmoiled and shook up as she was, divulging seemed too big a hurdle. To just let it all splat? Spill herself all over everybody?

She's told both her older children what she's up to now—yes. Not even her family at home, though, has gotten more than peeks. She's shrunk from allowing anything more.

The other week, Mary Beth tried to wheedle her into sending a few chapters. "I'll keep everything confidential, I promise! I need the distraction!" But Anna said, "No no no, not yet." Just the suggestion made her squeamish. Should've she been more amenable? she wonders. But every new child they add to Mary Beth's caseload at Evangelical Brethren Family Services means she's saddled with that much more paperwork. Why should she have to rub her nose in Anna's, yet?

Last night Jonathan's dorm sounded like a madhouse. Guys were bellowing out in the hall, and she could hear raucous TV laughter. It's always like this when he telephones—she always feels like she's somebody's withered old auntie. "Are you going to show me some pages over Thanksgiving vacation, Mom?" he questioned, before his roommate, Crater, a third-year engineering major, too, interrupted with a series of catcalls.

"How can you stand that?" she asked. "Is he trying to flag down some girl halfway across campus? What's going on?"

"Crater's not so bad." Jonathan's voice faded, came back. "He slept through our biggest calculus test, so now he's setting three alarms every night—his watch and radio, besides his clock. He's got the clock masking-taped to his bunk, which is what caused the problem in the first place, but now if he knocks the snooze button inoperable again in his sleep, the others will kick in."

"Really?" She hesitated. "I don't know about this book. It's more of a crazy conglomeration than I expected, and there's so much yet to tell. I'm only now getting to all the flailing I had to go through after Epp turned down my article. My whole long slough of despond, when you children thought I was definitely off in the bean."

"No, Mom, I took you for depressed."

"Despondent, really."

"And the way I see it, people who never question their religion are just being ignorant."

"Well now, that's a little harsh."

"Examining your beliefs is strengthening, in the end. That's what *you* told *me*. Remember your worried-mother lecture before I left for my freshman year?"

"I said that? Huh."

Maybe she'll grant him a sneak preview.

It makes her cheeks flame, anytime she considers with her set-straight mind the annoyance—or disgust?—scorn?—her article must've provoked in Harold Epp. Judging by his photo on the editorial page of *Gospel Truth*, he must be taking vitamin B_{12} for some minor ailment, because his eyebrows are especially moppy, even for a man. Doesn't B_{12} enhance follicle vitality? Except, then wouldn't he be extra hairy everywhere else, too? Chest tufts aren't poking out of his shirt collar. She thinks his eyebrow bushes must've clumped up even worse as he scanned down her lines, but at the end, commiseration overtook and he was swept by a deep, abiding pity. He determined to handle her as mildly and delicately as possible. He had the article lying face down on his desk as he scratched out a response on his notepad, and, oh, who knows, maybe he had to leave his cubicle for a minute and some underling dashed in, hunting for regular office paper with one side still clean, good for drafting memos. Or something. Something like that happened. Whatever! It's not significant!

As the computer drones on and on, its face blacked out, just more pindot stars flinging past and winking out, winking out, she remains in her trance, whiling away at nothing, her mind grasping idly at straws.

15

Scoop the meat out of the halved baked potatoes and arrange the skins in a 10x13 pan. Mash the potatoes by hand. Stir in softened butter, salt, sour cream, and shredded cheese. Mound the mixture in the skins. Sprinkle with additional cheese, bacon bits, parsley, and paprika. Another part of her, the part not working down through the instructions for her dish for the Thanksgiving meal at Hawk Knob tomorrow, keeps straining for the sound of Dudley Heatwole's rattly Toyota pickup with Jonathan aboard—for the slowing-down hiss of the tires on wet, splashy Coldbrook Road and the spitting of driveway gravel.

"Jonathan is a good driver, I've always thought that," she remarks, "but you know Dudley."

"Aw, Ma," says Todd. "Dudley's no cowboy."

"Well, I'm glad the boys can trade rides. But he's a little too clownish and show-offy. There could be ice on Keezer's Ridge." The five-hour stretch on the map between here and the university in Brownsville on the western border of the state, the highway is mostly interstate, but up in the mountains any inclement weather can spontaneously turn extreme. "Remember that accident Mary Beth told us about? The three girls?" These classmates of Mary Beth's when she was at Brownsville, who were traveling home on a high, icy pass on I79, skidded onto the shoulder of the road and rolled their

VW bug. The first people on the scene had to bang on the upside-down vehicle and instruct the hysterical driver to roll down the window so she and
her friends could climb out. The rider in back, weighed down by the seat
that had come unmoored from the floor, was in a panic about her glasses
that had flown off, and she kept scrabbling around for them, refusing to
emerge.

"Nah, Anna," says Wade from the study, "it's too warm for ice. They're
getting rain all the way."

"Remember when Fred hydroplaned?" she asks. Margie and Fred's first
trip down here, they hit a patch of heavy rain on Route 81 and Fred suddenly couldn't steer. He took his hands off the wheel and allowed the car to
careen insanely between lanes until it went jolting and bumping down the
grassy slope of the median strip and came to a stop, with them deposited in
the opposite direction, shaking but unharmed, and the children still buck-
led in back. "Does Dudley know not to go over 50 miles per hour in such
conditions? Maybe they're having windshield-wiper trouble. Visibility
problems."

"Anna, there's no point in—"

"Oh, thank the Lord," she breathes, dropping the cheese grater, as the
coughs of a motor reach her. Twin streaks of light are striking the side windows of the kitchen and twinkling off the raindrops that the gusting wind
has splatted across the panes. "They're here, they're here!"

"I say this calls for popcorn," Wade announces, coming into the
kitchen and making tracks for the lower cupboard next to the refrigerator
where the popper is stored. She blanches. She dodges past him and clangs
around in the cupboard herself to produce the kettle.

"Here you go!" she chirps. And then her middle child is stamping his
feet on the rug at the door, rumpled and smelling of truck heater and wet
hat, but self-possessed as always. He's throwing his coat and cap on the floor
and grinning easily at her, and though he's in need of a shave and his head of
curls is a frisky mess, his eyes are their usual calm, limpid state, emanating a
quiet intelligence. Conscious of his brainy gaze, she comes to a decision.
When he troops upstairs with his first load of gear, she goes to the study for
her hacked-out chapters and schleppy, quivering, taped-together plot notes
and stuffs them behind Wade's teacher-edition textbooks lining the shelf
above the desk.

OH GOODY, your potato boats, Anna. I was hoping!" Mom Schlonegger
relieves her of her baking dish and places it on the mahogany buffet with

curvy polished legs, already groaning under the weight of its bounties. The standard enormous, clove-pocked ham. A roaster pan of Sharon's baked beans, and a kettle of the ever-popular green beans gussied up with French-fried onion rings and cream of mushroom soup. Nancy's Reuben chicken specialty—deboned breasts, sauerkraut, and Swiss cheese, doused with a bottle of thousand island dressing. Mom's fabulous cloverleaf rolls. A long pan of LeAnne's scalloped corn, and another holding baked zucchini. Aunt Arbutus's standby salad of lettuce and hard-boiled eggs and thinned-down mayonnaise, and the mandarin-orange fluff Arbutus always brings too, sprinkled through with baby marshmallows. Cranberry relish, store-made, contributed by Monica. Applesauce. Peanut butter cake, Hawaiian wedding cake, tunnel of fudge cake. Beverly's divinity candy. Anna always has to wear her baggiest sweater and slacks to these dinners.

Afterwards the women sit around the table like beached whales. Most of the menfolk, not the kind to linger, have followed Dad Schlonneger out to the barn, and the children, too, have scattered. Anna is still marveling over the zucchini casserole. She must've taken four helpings. "You made it from scratch?" she asks LeAnne.

"Sure, how else?" LeAnne flicks her used-up napkin at the cake crumbs caught in the ditches of her green silk pants where they cross below her middle. "I can the zucchini in the white sauce, see? So for the casserole all I had to do was grease the pan, empty in three pints, and layer on the cheese and crushed cornflakes. I rolling-pinned the cornflakes in a bread bag."

"You canned the zucchini?" She *canned* it? "In a pressure canner, you mean?" asks Anna hopefully.

LeAnne makes a face. "Oh my, no. Of course I heated the casserole in the oven till it was good and bubbly."

"But you're supposed to pressure can anything low acid!"

"It's the easiest thing," says LeAnne, waving her hand in the air. "It's perfectly safe."

"Oh ha," says Monica, "I don't know any scratch foods I'd call easy. How anybody still finds time to freeze and can is beyond me. Or time to cook, period. Am I the only one completely swamped? I come home from the office, I'm exhausted. Every day, it seems I fall more on behind. Really, it's getting to be too much." She clicks her tongue at nobody in particular. "And now, Christmas. Wal-Mart's had their stuff out for how long already? I believe I saw it cropping up even before Halloween. What's the point? How can anybody even *think* of Christmas this soon?"

"Well, I'll be starting on my cards first thing next week," Mom Schlonneger says.

"Cards!" exclaims Monica. "Who's got time?"

"I think they're important," says Mom stoutly. "Anna's been an influence on me." Anna whips her head around, puzzled. "Your article, hon, remember? How long ago *was* that? For Christmas that year I planned to take a load off my back and try one of those nice chatty form letters, not work myself up to a migraine writing a whole host of cards, and then didn't the *Gospel Truth* come with your piece in. I saved it, Anna. It got me back on track. If I'd done a letter I probably wouldn't have resisted the temptation to paint an over-rosy picture."

"Saved it?" says Anna. "You never said. Well, I'm sure honored."

"Yes. In with my Christmas card list." Mom is pulling open a drawer of the highboy that takes up a corner of the dining room, the same dark veneer as the buffet and table, and the same spindly legs. With the table stretched its entire length, she needs only to hike around in her seat to reach. "See here? What did I tell you? My, has it been that many years? You all remember this?"

Mom fingers along the first line of the article and beams. "Listen here. 'I love it in December when the cards start dribbling in.' Now see, Anna, even that. 'Dribbling,' that's so nice." She glances over at Anna and observes the hot flush creeping up her neck. "What's wrong? Hon? Are you being modest? Don't be modest. You mind me doing this?"

"No—well, I guess I do. Everybody's already read it. They shouldn't have to sit through it again. Something that old hat."

Mom's laugh rings out. "Well, if you say so. Here, anybody that wants their memory refreshed can take a look." She pats Anna benignly on the shoulder and plops the *Gospel Truth,* folded back on itself, by Anna's dirty dessert plate, smack on top of a cranberry spill on the tablecloth. So now the underside pages will be all smirched. The women's jabbering veers off on another path, more cackling and lively, and despite herself Anna permits her eyes to travel down the first paragraphs of "How About Not Tooting Our Horns?"

I love it in December when the cards start dribbling in. Homemade ones with stenciled scenes or childish crayon drawings or cute pasted art with half the glitter fallen off and stuck down in the corners of the envelope. The huge, gaudy kind with gold-foil-lined envelopes and foil seals. Some that surprise you out of your wits by starting up their tinkly "I'm Dreaming of a White Christmas." The glossy, bright-colored photo cards (the greeting is "Noel," or "Silent Night," or "Feliz Navidad," but it's the sender's family in the picture, not Mary and Joseph and the wrinkly baby in swaddling wraps). I take great pleasure in hearing from our relatives and friends and find reassurance in the fact that we've not been forgotten. Gradually my basket piles up fuller.

But sometimes I find, stuck in with the homey or silly or glitzy card, one of those form letters. I'm sorry, but this is distressing. To begin with, it wasn't written to Wade and me. Maybe it just says, "Dear friends," or the sender has filled the blank space behind the "Dear" with "Wade and Anna" or "Wade and Anna and family," with the aim of personalizing their message. No! They've written this to practically the whole world! I don't know how to respond. I can't write a letter in return. That wouldn't be a conversation. It would be like talking back to the radio announcer.

Somebody was too important and busy to sit down and write a personal note. Caught up in their hectic daily pace, they figured that by composing a generic epistle and printing out sixty copies they could kill sixty birds with one stone. Maybe they did hit sixty birds, but how did it bring any special happiness? And how will this frantic, rushed sender find enough spare sit-down moments to read the form letters that will surely come his way? What a waste! All these letters passing back and forth in the mail, words upon words upon words, clogging up people's lives even more!

But the worst thing is the puffed-up reporting. They're enjoying their new hot tub; the children never once fell off the honor roll; the parents climbed Pikes Peak to celebrate their anniversary; and during the family vacation in Mexico they took in this and that and this and that and this and that awesome historical sight. All very wonderful, but aren't they giving a one-sided picture? What about the inevitable normal miseries? Or am I deluded about what constitutes "normal"? Much of the time my family, anyway, leads a humdrum existence. We're not relentlessly successful. We catch colds. We argue. Wade can't motivate a certain few recalcitrant students. Our children wangle out of their chores. The corn gets eaten by raccoons. I flounder around wondering what I was put on earth for. The refrigerator we bought secondhand eight years ago stops keeping the contents cold and we learn that the Freon has all leaked out and we've been, what, getting gassed? The youngest still sucks his thumb.

You people shouldn't be tooting your horns, see. It doesn't seem Christian or honest. If you'd—

But Anna doesn't flip the page for the rest.

She toys with her dessert fork, its tines sticky with chocolate, as the conversation weaves and drifts around her. She has to wonder, Was "A Two-faced God?!" any more maudlin than this? Wasn't she shunning pretentiousness, like here? Showing up her unsavory side? Speaking candidly instead of dissembling and posing? She's bothered, suddenly, by an uncomfortable rubber-band tightness in the back of her skull, like the cells are too stretched and suspended. Of course, she tells herself, that topic was of such grave consequence. Maybe her attitude was dangerously shrill, and—

"Anna?" Portly Arbutus, curiosity spread across her face, is bending her way. "What new articles are you writing?"

"Oh, I—I—" The fudgy fork clatters from Anna's hand onto the plate. She darts a look around the room and is surprised to see Jonathan standing in the doorway, watching, one eyebrow perked. Thoroughly rattled, she dispels a rush of air. "I'm working on—on a—on something that's going to take me a while. I don't—I'm not—well, I—" Anna bangs back her chair. "Oh my, these dishes. Are we planning to sit here all afternoon?" In a sudden housewifey flurry of industriousness she stacks up some crusted dinnerware and silver, and with loaded arms she flees for the kitchen.

On the way home in the evening, Anna feels slightly sick on the stomach. What if it's not just the winding mountain roads? "Listen," says Wade, "I took some of that zucchini, too. You're okay. If something was wrong with it, we'd have keeled over by now."

"We could've *all* been poisoned. Even those who only tasted a tiny little bit on the end of their tongue!" She can imagine the headline. MASS DEATHS AFTER FAMILY POTLUCK, BOTULISM DETERMINED TO BE THE CAUSE. She barely stifles a belch. "We wouldn't have even *detected* anything off in the flavor. The poison isn't *detectable*. If a person were able to *tell* it was present, well sure! Who'd worry? There'd be something concrete to go on. Do you know how much I ate?"

"Nah, Anna."

"Zucchini, yuck," Todd mutters to Jonathan, in back.

16

She pat-pats at the brown grocery bags—straightens each at its creases, flattens it, and doubles it over, to add it to her store of reusables in the mudroom—while her eyes follow the drama framed by the sink window, up the hill, beyond the property line, where a vulture is circling the sky, maybe attracted by the remains of a distempered opossum, or a bobcat not yet turned stiff. What shall she do about her peppers? Please, what?

Her assertion last week about botulin toxin wasn't all the way true. It *can* be undetectable—it's *possibly* impossible to detect. On the other hand, there might be signs in the jar of food, such as the lid bulging, or a cloudiness in the liquid. Home from the Schlonneger get-together, lying awake way late, she had to admit to herself she'd exaggerated somewhat. Regardless, she most certainly didn't want Wade finding her peppers the next time he took a hankering for popcorn. But she didn't sneak down to the ghostly kitchen, illuminated at that hour only by the two dusty, furry-beamed electric candles tacked by their cords to the sills of the double window; she didn't hunker by the lower cupboard next to the fridge and reach past the pots and lids, mixing bowls, and the Whirley Pop kettle from Margie with its cogged stirrer that helpfully shuffles the exploding kernels; she didn't stretch back, back, back to the farthest end of the shelf to withdraw her suspect pints. She considered such a foray, yes. She wavered over the idea while the night wind swept the house and badgered the rain gutters. But she could just imagine herself knocking down the stack of kettles, causing a terrible clamor and bringing Wade and the boys on the run, only to find her inspecting for portents. Wade would snort, "So that's where!" and open a jar on the spot and down a slice just to prove the harmlessness. That would be his kind of stunt.

The rest of vacation, she mostly managed to keep her predicament at bay and function on a more complacent level. But Sunday afternoon her anxiety returned. She stared down the road after Jonathan and Dudley in the departing red pickup, watching them take the potholes, bounce up over the knoll, and disappear, and then stepped away from her post by the door to try to tease forth any ideas. Who would be authoritative enough to turn to for advice?

And Monday, yesterday, everybody back in school, as she bent her head over her scenes in her book that same question kept flaring up: who to ask?

But this morning when she was on the way into town for groceries, an inspiration hit. What about the farm bureau people? Well, not Darnel Gaines. Darnel has come out to advise Wade on his gardening dilemmas— the asparagus beetles, for instance, and an insidious mold on the grapes that made the new stems droop and fall off, and a mysterious blight that afflicted the cucumbers one summer—and he's always been folksy and friendly and concerned. But there's also a nutritionist in the office, a Carol Feaster who's occasionally pictured in the newspaper promoting such events as an aquaculture seminar for the 4-Hers, or the Knobley Valley Homemakers' ham breakfast—happenings of that nature. Of all people, wouldn't Carol be informed about the conditions necessary for *C. botulinum* to taint foodstuffs, and about safe canning procedures?

Anna hurried through her shopping and loaded her groceries into the car—cheese, Hellmann's mayonnaise (buy one, get one free), celery, tuna, moose tracks ice cream, three new untried flavors of Alberto VO5 shampoo besides her usual pick, Kiwi & Lime Squeeze, on special for 99¢, and so forth—and buzzed over to the farm bureau located three buildings down from the Davy Jenkins auction place. A few extra minutes' wait wouldn't defrost the ice cream down in the bag with the yogurt—not the brief snitch of time it would take her to stick her head in the office door and ask the one quick question. She maneuvered into the space closest to the building and was about to let herself out of the car. It would take her only a minute. "Um, ma'am," she would begin, "with canned peppers, if the oil—"

No.

This way, then: "Um, ma'am, I canned some hot peppers according to the exact precise specifications in the recipe, adding garlic, sugar, salt, and oil, plus the vinegar and water in a highly safe two-to-one ratio, but—"

No. Just the facts—the honest, unflourished details. Never mind Carol's bothered dum-de-dumming pencil. "Um, ma'am, would you have any idea what the chances of *Clostridium botulinum* growth might be if the oil separates from the other ingredients in a jar of canned peppers?" Never mind Carol's eyes raising, and down alongside the careful, scarlet-lined corner of her mouth, an impatient tic kicking in. "Actually, to tell the truth, I have a jar of pickled beets down in the cellar I'm not sure about, either. One slice is pressed up against the glass in such a way that it creates an air pocket, so maybe the pickling juice hasn't entirely penetrated, and if—" By now Carol would be gawking, and the door of the adjoining room would be inching farther open and the eavesdropping secretary would be leaning around to see.

Anna pointed the key back into the ignition, got the motor to quietly clearing its throat, and backed out of the parking space.

Turning in at home, she thought about upturning a jarful over the chicken fence. Hm. If the chickens didn't go into convulsions or respiratory failure and topple over dead, their scaly toothpick legs pointing toward the sky, okay. Except—no. Not okay. Couldn't their gizzards circumvent the danger? She came to a hard stop in front of the garage, rocking the car, the driveway stones clinking against the bumper, and nearly burst into tears.

Defeatedly she moved around the house putting away her purchases. The two jars of mayonnaise banged into the cupboard above the toaster. The can of black olives rolled onto a different shelf. The parsley flakes, vanilla, and olive oil noisily met their appointed spots. The bundle of toilet paper landed on the bottom staircase step in the living room to wait till she went upstairs later, and so did the shampoos with their contents listed in teeny tiny print. She thought for a second, then picked up the Pear Mango Passion and brought the label close to her nose. *Cocamidopropyl betaine*, phooh. *Sodium laureth sulfate. Ammonium xylenesulfonate.* She asked herself, Even when it comes to shampoo, how can a body rest assured? How is *any*thing positively, conclusively safe? Nobody's going to *eat* this—it's not supposed to be *edible*—but still, mightn't it pose hazards? Mightn't these horrid-sounding compounds be brain-cell soluble and carcinogenic?

She checked the other three bottles, the Sun-Kissed Raspberry, Free Me Freesia, and Kiwi & Lime Squeeze, and found the same ingredients listed, and the same big-deal claim: *This product not tested on animals.* She said to herself, See that? The manufacturer isn't taking risks either, isn't even experimenting on chickens equipped with gizzards!

Folding another Pantry Pride bag now, here by the sink, she can't squelch her despair. The vulture, sinister and dark against the morning sky, seems an omen. The all-surrounding natural world seems shot through with pessimism. Can equanimity even exist in God's creation? Up there on the hill, the fundamental starkness is taking hold. The leaves have dropped, the earth is going stone cold and corrupt. Even when summer held florid sway, every piece of petrified crinoid and every bitty fiddlehead fern fossil witnessed to the inevitability of the takeover, and every chestnut stump riddled with the ubiquitous fungal blight. With autumn's wane, the ugliness is on the march. The season of death is digging in, heartless. Soon the woods will be the very incarnation of ruin, of the physical world's dust-to-dust, muck-to-muck, rot-to-rot mortality—

Oh.

Why, goodness.

Just dig a hole. A regular old hole. Let the peppers be swallowed up by the forest floor. Let them join in the infestedness and decay and death, follow the way of all flesh. Why not? What could *that* hurt?

She'll confess to Wade tonight—no getting around that. But he'll survive. She'll stash these bags and put herself to a few hours of concentrated work on the book, chronologically mapping out the rest of it, sparing none of the low points of last winter's grim spiritual odyssey. And in the afternoon, when it's warmed up enough, she'll see to the jars.

SHE FEELS LIKE an overfed, waddly duck, crossing the back field, suited up in Wade's chunky brown coveralls. By the time she reaches the woods, she's huffing.

Climbing, planting one foot, then the other, she lets out little snorts through her nose. Her temples pound. The jars in the bag under her arm are tipping and knocking, and the shovel she's hugging in the crook of her other arm keeps trying to clonk her in the neck. Abraham's donkey, she thinks. His ass—*ah-ahss*—not pronounced like the swear word. Party to God's plan, it willingly clambered up Mount Moriah bearing the wood for the sacrifice. She could use such a beast of burden shinnying up the incline ahead of her now, clicking its hooves on the rocks, unfazed by the parceled danger bobbing along on its back.

Not so far from the wild-cherry tree and the boys' falling-down fort, she props her bag against the trunk of a tall pine mottled on its north side with gray lichens. With the shovel she scrapes around in the dead leaves where the tree's roots haven't spread, and she uncovers a patch of moss that might be keeping the soil more friable. She stomps on the shovel's heel, dislodges a load of the peaty, sheltered humus, and spills it close by. She evicts another ladleful. She shovels again and again, badgering up more and more dirt and letting the twigs and old needles and rotten acorns go skidding and tumbling. Whenever the shovel balks, she wrenches it backwards and takes another stab. Sometimes she must bat away her hair falling in her eyes or blink to clear her contact lenses of the spat-back flecks of soil. Scoopful by scoopful, the hole overtakes its bounds.

Crouching, breathing heavily, she pries the lids off her jars one by one and watches the contents slip free, *glub glub,* and scud recklessly into a bright pile. Each time, the brine swells and recedes, leaving behind the beached seeds and brackish, oily slices. Pint number five. Six. Seven. Eight. Nine. Ten. Wade is going to hate this. He's going to lecture her.

A twiggy rustle reaches her. A rodent? Or might that vulture still be in the vicinity, poaching on the property at closer range? Another rustle. Is it the donkey nuzzling around, searching for grass? Anna peers against the sunlight glinting off a clump of wild-raspberry canes a short distance away, denuded but still prickery. Her squint tightens. She flinches. For a fleeting second, her imagination catches on a ram tangled in the branches, twitching his hide, punting with his scary forelegs, shrilly bleating.

It happened in the nick of time, yes. Thank heaven. As Abraham stood with upraised knife, about to plunge it, God provided. God substituted the animal. The old man frenziedly picked loose the knots of the rope binding his boy, grabbed him off the firewood, clasped him to his breast, and crumpled into a blubbering heap on the ground. Struck again by the fright of it all, Anna passes a dirty palm across her forehead. She heaves, needing to supply her collapsed windbags, and sways precariously on her haunches. She rakes her hands up and down the rough coverall sleeves.

Stilling, she frowns. *Kill your son.* God said that. Kill. *Kill.*

Huh-uh, huh-uh.

Oh no, not again.

Mightily she tries to clamp down on herself and muster her forces.

PROBABLY, UP ON THE HILL, the furtive lesser species are drawing near, nosing at the grave mound tracked all around with her sneaker prints. Morosely she rinses the jars at the outside faucet behind the garage and lingers for the water to seep down through the gravel and vanish. In the garage she pitches the jars into the recyclables bin under Wade's workbench. She chucks the rubber-ringed lids, too—Wade has been finding rat turds out here lately, so conceivably the rats will snitch tastes of the rubber and die the chickens' forestalled deaths. Last thing, she smashes the grocery bag and takes it over to the burn barrel. She's just one big squashed bag herself, leaked of her steam. Of her shameful flatulence and puffery, if that's what made her think she had some kind of insider knowledge on what it takes to become a spiritual giant.

17

Blab blab blab blab blab. Blabber blabber. Blabberblabberblabberblabberblabber. That's about all the sense things make. Everything's muddied. On occasion she notices the same sensation as at Thanksgiving—back in the rearmost part of her cranium, a pull-ull-ulling, strai-ai-aining elastic-like forcedness. Then even the skin over the area goes all pinchy and stretched.

"I can't think right," she tells Wade today. "I was mixed up enough, already. In the writerly sense, I mean—my digressing—all my unimportant little offshoots, my frayed little threads and tie-ins."

"Yeah."

"How could God do that? Not exactly tempt Abraham, no, but—more like—well, how do I even word it?"

"Anna, I don't—"

"God doesn't change. Does, not, change."

"And?"

"Excuse me, but how am I supposed to believe that?"

"In that bit you showed me from your first chapter, didn't you say you'd be chronicling your straying and struggling? It doesn't sound to me like now is any time to stop."

"But—"

"But what?"

"Oh, I don't know. I just don't know. I was supposed to be all repaired, planted on higher ground, lending a helping hand to anybody bogged down by doubts or pride. Mostly, I was *fine,* mostly I was *okay*—and now this. Tripped up all over again!"

"Then just say so." Wade rubs his hand across his beard stubble and grunts.

"I *have* said so. Now what? Just more doodling down the bunny trails, doodling down the bunny trails?"

18

"So I checked in my topical index," Susan is burbling, "and under 'deceive' I found scads of references, only a few of which we'll have time this morning to explore. 'The Deceptions of This World'—what a timely lesson! If we want to single-mindedly serve the Lord we must be constantly discerning between good and evil." The high neck of her pink wool pullover sweater is plumped fluffily around her slender, striving throat cords and she's all blinky and pert and full of her usual sunshiny optimism. But Anna is having trouble with the fluorescent lighting. One of the bulbs hidden in the drop ceiling above the Sunday school table keeps flickering, flickering, flickering. It's a good thing nobody in class is epileptic, because doesn't the rhythmic flashing of light sometimes trigger seizures in people suffering from that disorder? She wishes Wade could just hop up on the table and disconnect the tube. But she can just see him accidentally bashing it in and flooding the room with the poisonous mercury vapor.

"Let's start with Ephesians 4:14," Susan suggests. "Nelson, can you read it for us please?"

"Verse 14, alrighty." Nelson thumps his Good News Bible around on the table, unzipping it. "'Then we shall no longer be children, carried by the waves and blown about by every shifting wind of the teaching of deceitful men, who lead others into error by the tricks they invent.'"

"Thanks." Susan pats along the blackboard trough for the chalk holder she always uses to avoid stubbing her nails. "I find the language a bit spicier in the King James, actually. There we're warned about the 'sleight of men' and 'cunning craftiness.'" She jots the terms on the board and turns. "Let's make this practical, now. What about in our modern day and age? In our society? What deceptions do we encounter in our daily lives? Anybody? Frank?"

"Well, right off the bat, I think of that billboard ad encouraging young people to enlist in the armed forces. 'Be all you can be.' As if there's something noble about flying bombers."

"That really gets me," Peg chips in. "It's just a dressed-up lie."

"People call this a Christian nation," says Jay. "Warmongering is more like it."

"Surely that can't be." Wade's humor, again. Tipped back in his chair, a behavior he forbids of his students, he's drumming on the metal seat. "Isn't 'In God We Trust' our ever-present motto?" He brings the chair down on all four legs with a whump. "Ha, we're sure not taking any chances on God *not* defending us, if our arsenal is any evidence, and our military budget. Our military spending exceeds that of the next forty-two highest-spending countries in the world, combined."

"Yes," says Susan, "'In God We Trust' is quite the euphemism." She twirls the tip of her chalk against her chin as she sorts through her mind for any additional astute spiritual applications. "And think about this. Think about money, period. Isn't wealth a deceiver—the idea that material things can bring security and happiness?"

Stepping back, she motions with the chalk holder in the direction of the bulletin board. "Justine, I like this. I meant to say so last Sunday." For December Justine has created a nifty display of Christmas presents, some with crinkle ribbon glued on, tied into bows. Anna has been noticing how the curly ribbon ends springing away from the wall wink every time the faulty fluorescent bulb emits another death flash. The largest package, luscious red foil, prettified with jingle bells and frillier ribbon, has its lid raised suggestively and a tag. THE GREATEST GIFT OF ALL! *For God so loved the world that he gave his only begotten son, John 3:16.* Susan mouths the lines in a pensive fashion, then nods in approval. "A good reminder. And it fits right in with our lesson, considering how the world has deceived itself by turning Christmas into a secular holiday. For so many, Christmas has been reduced to a riotous commercial event."

"You can say that again." Peg's doily decorating her squeaky-clean, scrambly hair bounces in accord. "Conoy's parade, for example. What's that all about? The high-school band, the floats, the candy for the children, fine, but the procession of cars with business signs? Every bank and store and civic organization advertising? It's too blatant."

"Shoot," says Frank, "the year we took the kids to the Reston parade, the VFW had a float—rickety old guys in uniform sitting on a wagon. Worse than that, the last vehicle, after the fire trucks and ambulances, was an army tank chewing up the asphalt. I dunno, they must've hauled it over from the National Guard armory outside of town. Two guys in combat fatigues were riding in the hatch, behind the machine guns, throwing down candy. I said to Justine, '*Christmas* parade?'"

Donna remarks mildly, "Well, even Santa Claus."

"The commercialism of gift-giving, you mean?" says Anna. "Or because Santa's a deception, just a big trick?"

"Trick?" says Justine. "So what! I love Santa Claus. We always played Santa. Till the kids got too old."

"You *did?*" Anna twists in her seat to face Justine and Frank. "You said he came down the chimney?"

"Gosh, it was only a game," Justine replies, tossing her head. She's gotten a spikier haircut and the color is redder, splashier, not her natural carrot shade, so maybe she's been experimenting with henna. "It made Christmas fun and magic. Magic isn't the same as deceit."

"What happened when they found out the truth?"

Justine screws up her freckled pug nose. "They were sad—for about ten minutes."

"They still trusted you?"

"It didn't scar them. It didn't make them psychologically impaired. And you know what else? The next year they still begged to do the cookies and milk. They didn't want to give up believing."

"That's often the case, isn't it?" says Susan. "Our children do trust us, for better or worse."

"Maybe I was too strict," says Anna uncertainly. "Back in Jackson I even avoided those bumptious Santas in the stores. I didn't want them giving my children candy canes and suckers on paper sticks that could skewer their tonsils. At the IGA I'd make a big detour, go down a different aisle."

"Sounds paranoid to me," says Justine.

"I guess so." Stung, Anna sends a silent appeal to Wade. He shrugs. She claps a hand to her mouth and exhales too loudly. "Oh, something weird did happen one time. Jonathan and Mary Beth were along one night when we were Christmas shopping for a wagon, and at Higsons' Hardware they had a Santa hut out front in their parking lot. I don't know, somehow my usual determination failed me. I said to Wade, 'Oh, what'll it hurt?' Not that he cared so much. I asked Mary Beth, 'You want to talk to Santa Claus?' Well, for a four-year-old she acted so skittish and shy. I had to charm her into doing it. She finally got up on his lap but she was still bashful. She looked all pop-eyed and stiff, not unhappy though, because her lips were stretched the whole way across, almost to her pigtails. As soon as we got out of there she screeched, 'Mommy, Mommy! He doesn't have scratchy claws!'"

"C-l-a-w-s?" says Brenda. "Ha ha. Who would've thought?"

"You never know, do you?" Susan puts in. "You can never tell what's in a child's mind."

"Well, I guess I got a little off the subject," says Anna. "Sorry."

"No, it was interesting," says Susan.

Reluctantly she deposits her chalk and returns to her lesson quarterly and notes. "Let's see, where were we? Oh, yes. Moving on now to 2 Timothy 3." Ruffling through her King James, she blows busily on her upper lip. "Let's look at verse 13. 'But evil men and seducers shall wax worse and worse, deceiving, and being deceived.' So the seductiveness of sin is one thing, and to make matters even more daunting, as we reach the end times we can only expect an upsurge in human depravity."

And on she goes in her bright, bubbly, stimulating voice. Bolstered by all the discussing, Anna remains heedful, sometimes narrowing her lids to shut out the unnerving jolts of light, until those two words that are up on the board, "sleight" and "cunning," knock around long enough in her noggin to hit home. Huh, what about God's crafty ploy with Abraham? God conning him into—? No—wait—never mind. That's no way to think. It sounds too nefarious. But even—just—God leading Abraham on? Stated like that, even? How was it justifiable? God toying with somebody, rigging their dark night of the soul?

JUST SHE AND WADE ARE GOING HOME after church, not Todd, and next to her husband at the coat rack, in the cold, nearly vacated top landing of the stairwell, she says, "Spaghetti. I'll quick heat up that spaghetti from yesterday. It'll have to do for lunch—I'm conked."

"Fine by me."

Hat arranged on his head, Wade edges away from her only to back ungallantly into Susan. "Excuse me, ma'am. Didn't mean to run you over."

"You two, hey." Susan glances around. Her demeanor has dampened. She pulls at Anna's sleeve and cajoles her and Wade into the murky corner where the metalwork and freed-up coat hangers meet the wall. "Will you please keep the Beckers and Brenda in your prayers? I can't say anymore than that—just that there's reason for concern. I'm confident we'll get things worked through. Some people just have so much to deal with."

"You mean—" Anna presses closer. "Good grief. Why's everybody always so upbeat in class? You don't get a clue about the troubles—nobody acts remiss. My goodness. There *is* something going on, isn't there? This—this is really major. Wade, listen."

Wade has started toward the main lobby but he reverses himself and seemingly inspects the top stair tread, its worn, black ridges. He turns back to their friend. "I'm not sure why you're calling this to our attention. Is somebody seeking our help? Anna's help and mine?"

"Oh! Well, it's not like that, exactly—I just want us to be there for each other. Going it alone can be unbearably difficult. Frank's evasive, he tried to stonewall when I repeated to him what Justine told me. Yet he keeps coming to church like nothing's ever happened, and Justine can't—"

"Frank and Justine want us in on this?" Wade fixes a look on Susan.

"Just pray, I said. Hold them up in your prayers."

"Well sure," Anna answers. "If there's anything more we can do personally, we're willing. I'm maybe not close enough to Brenda and Justine, either one of them. I don't figure they'll come to me on their own. But I'm available—I'm—"

"Let's go, Anna." Wade hauls her with him toward the church door.

Driving home, he's tight lipped at first. He tells her to can it when she tries to tell him Susan meant to be discreet. He says he was wrong to have fostered Anna's suspiciousness. And then he warms up and really gets going. When she finds a chance to get a word in edgewise and feebly offers the suggestion—in much the same vein as Susan's—that nobody should have to suffer through the throes of their spiritual unfaithfulness in secret, he gives a disgusted honk.

"It's juicy, yep," says Wade. "It's juicy talk. But now somebody's on the case, okay? We're keeping our distance. Don't you go and get yourself mixed up in it."

TODD STAYED AT CHURCH because the youth group is making hardtack candy this afternoon, for which they've been taking orders. As with their other fund-raisers, the proceeds will go to the missionary center in Tegucigalpa, Honduras, *Instituto Bíblico Evangélico del Bueno Samaritano.* After lunch, her hands still dishwater damp, Anna enters the living room smearing on lotion. Horsey, guzzly splutters are coming from Wade's mouth. He's taking up the entire sofa to nap. Gingerly, using her nongooey wrists, she grasps his feet and swings them off the cushion, and she sinks into the cleared space.

He shuts down, chewing on his saliva. "Yeah, okay." He rolls into a sitting position and oafishly yawns.

She massages her knuckles and slaps her palms together, working the lanolin into the pores. "I thought you said you have a backlog of reading."

"Yep."

The warmth from the wood stove is soaking into her bones. She takes a finish-off sniff at her hands, then watches the flames licking lazily around the single log, dancing halfhearted jigs, ragging sideways, lapping at a corner of stove glass speckled over with char. "I wonder how they're coming along at church. Remember Mary Beth's hardtack, all her varieties?"

"Yeah, now that you mention it."

"I can't believe I let her do that by herself. So young, only thirteen. What a mess." Mary Beth boiled each sugary batch in Anna's biggest heavy kettle, spread the syrup into a thin puddle on a cookie sheet to cool, and cut the brittle, glassy results into pieces with a scissors, shards flying everywhere. But she was a pleased little flibbertigibbet, handing around her bagfuls to all the relatives at Christmas. "Can you imagine what the church kitchen must look like by now? That stuff stuck to the soles of everybody's shoes? Poor Peg and Jay. Such good sports—all their supervisor responsibilities. We should've offered to help out."

Wade stretches. He makes a move to get up. Anna tugs at his elbow. "The youth group peddling candy, what about that? Isn't *that* commercializing Christmas, too? Well, it's for a cause."

"Sure."

"Did Justine have to snip at me like that in class? Was *she* raised on Santa Claus? No! Or anybody else Evangelical Brethren, back then? No!" Anna isn't saying times can't change, of course not, but people going along with the Santa hooey? "Mama and Daddy were right to forbid that sort of thing. More than ever, I'm glad about that. I *appreciate* them protecting us children from the worldly emphasis. It's not like we were pathetic hothouse plants, never exposed. Margie and I—we'd spy behind the living-room blinds."

"Spy?"

"When Santa came to town, to the firehouse to hand out presents. We'd watch."

She thinks about how the yellow light streamed from the tall, wire-reinforced windows of the firehouse those nights. It sat catty-cornered across the street from the mission. The wiggly line of children waiting, freezing their feet off, reached down the ramp and on around the side of the building as far back as the ladies' auxiliary entrance, until the door of the hook-and-ladder room rattled upwards and everybody pressed forward with a howl.

"She got a Tiny Tears doll, I bet," Margie speculated one year, when their friend Wanda reappeared on the street. "No," countered Anna, "a china doll, I say. Very beautiful, with a velvet dress and puff sleeves and a queen crown." Wanda was holding the package out in front of her like it needed guarding. "And you're not supposed to bet." Instead of arguing, Margie smashed her nose up against the pane and started blowing fog circles. Anna said, "Don't go and covet, now. Besides, you don't know what dandy little something you're getting. Mama's been acting all hushy." Mama always laid their presents on their plates Christmas morning.

But one Christmas the fire department's fliers on the telephone poles announced that Santa would pay house calls. The night the Pritchard Mattress and Furniture Company truck cruised through town, dumping out Santa at every stop, what could Mama and Daddy do? Act ungracious? Not answer the doorbell? There went Herbie, racing through the hall and squealing, and Wesley chasing after. Daddy didn't think to shut the vestibule door after he let Santa in, and while the Pritchard Mattress driver out front ground the gears impatiently, the visitor trooped with his sack from child to child in the drafty living room, tracking street-gutter snow and *arrgh*ing his sinuses and booming stuff and nonsense.

Collecting the box shreds after he was gone, Mama tried not to slip in the puddles of slush and crankcase oil. "Was that Clarence Nutter, I wonder? That voice—it had to be Clarence. Well, I'll say this much, he and Vivian are faithful about getting their boys to Sunday school."

"Yes, they are," agreed Daddy. He'd already dropped Herbie's dart gun into the waste can.

"Why'd he give me checkers?" Anna asked. "We already have checkers."

Wesley couldn't get his orange yo-yo to spin back up on its tether and nobody saw when he took off for the cellar stairs. He must've forgotten to loop the cord around his finger before he lobbed the toy over the handrail. Mama, hearing his screams, made a beeline, Anna on her heels. "Lookie,

Wesley, lookie," Anna said, gathering up the slivers of yo-yo wood scattered across the concrete, "you can still use the nice long string for pulling your tractor and baler." But he just kept on bawling. She wrapped it into a penurious, tight ball and placed it on the cellar shelf.

Anyhow, that string has come in handy, Anna reasons to herself, loafing on the sofa next to Wade.

When he finally unseats his butt, she murmurs, "Well, anything that detracts from the gospel should be a concern, *anything*. The worldly revelry that skips right over Jesus' poor, lowly birth is only one sin in the sea of transgressions. I just think Justine could've had more regard and respect in Sunday school for somebody else's spiritual cautions. It's so important, *so important,* to be sticking to the bedrock meanings. To the Bible's truth, period."

Abruptly she strikes the flat of her hand against her cheek. "But, oh dear, what am I saying? The person to worry about is me. I don't have all that much right to be critical." She fingers along her earlobe, musing. "Justine did do a good job on that bulletin board. She went all out. 'For God so loved the world,' that was altogether apt. Wasn't it, hon?" she calls after Wade. Already in the study, he's picking through his stack of *Science Newse*s. "It totally drove the point home," she calls. "The fact that God sent Jesus to bleed and die."

She tells herself, Of course, that was worse. Way worse. God *not* pulling off some tidy trick by providing a substitute sacrifice. God *not* switching course in a last-ditch burst of mercy. But God couldn't relent. It had to be that way.

She rubs hard across the back of her head, letting up only at that soreish spot, and utters a sigh.

After a spell of squirmy silence she's still stuck on those last thoughts, sitting by herself in her long slit corduroy Sunday skirt and matching cardigan, her control pantyhose riding up her crotch and causing further discomfiture but keeping her passably sucked in.

So far, the only applicable doodly things that have come up haven't helped one whit.

19

Anna's history with Randy Treadle, the pharmacist at Rite Aid, goes way back. Soon after the move to Conoy, in for medicine for Jonathan's bronchitis, she slid her eyes across the man's name tag on his coat and proffered timidly, "Sir, um, excuse me, we're new. This Bactrim? It's not penicillin related, is it?"

"No ma'am, it's a sulfa drug."

"Because as a nine-month-old, Jonathan broke out in a rash on his abdomen after he took amoxycillin for earache, and isn't amoxycillin in the penicillin family? Mightn't he might be allergic to penicillin, too?"

"Possibly, yes, Mrs. Schlonneger. You've notified your doctor here, haven't you?"

"Uh-huh. I listed amoxycillin on the questionnaire. I mean, even if that rash was years and years ago—"

"I understand." His uncurried, tawny headful of hair and the crook-shaped cleft in his chin made for a certain boyish appeal.

"What is it with allergies, anyway?" she asked. "They'll manifest in the most insidious ways—there's too much uncertainty. Shouldn't there be some way to detect that a child is allergic to bee stings beforehand? Before the anaphylactic reaction?"

"Indeed so. I would hope the research is being conducted."

"Peanuts, too. The packages carry warning labels now, but what good is a warning if you're clueless until the onset? I saw somewhere that in particular cases the allergic child can't even be in the same room with somebody else eating peanut M&Ms. My, that's pretty serious. The school cafeterias here have stopped serving peanut-butter-and-jelly sandwiches, I've heard. Well, I'm glad."

"Yes ma'am."

"At any rate, you're not in doubt about this Bactrim for Jonathan?"

"As with all medications, watch for any deleterious results. In the event, notify your doctor. If a reaction manifests, any number of drugs can be substituted."

It was with the utmost courtesy that he spoke. He didn't hurry her. He didn't brush her off.

Soon after, she trucked into the store again, this time with a prescription for Mary Beth's infected toenail. "I guess you can make out that handwriting. Cedlor? Oh, Ceclor! Let me see the dosage again, if you don't mind." The small bulge of skin between her eyebrows dimpled up as she scrutinized the paper. "Five hundred milligrams twice daily for nine days? Couldn't that much antibiotic make mush out of a ten-year-old's liver, Mr. Treadle?"

In his cordial way, he assured her of the unlikelihood. He didn't look at her like, Lady, you're sure not one to leave a stone unturned. She told Wade later, "For once, here's somebody who doesn't begrudge the customer their tedious little iffy concerns."

"Oh, sir, are the expiration dates on over-the-counter medicines meant to be strictly heeded?" she inquired another day, picking up a tube of Neosporin. Behind his little window for passing out the prescription bags with their printouts stapled on, their dire side-effects information about diarrhea, hives, hypertension, renal failure, thrombosis, even cardiac arrest, Mr. Treadle was studiously shuffling his pill bottles. "Aren't those dates more for the benefit of the stock clerks?"

"Products such as what you have there, Mrs. Shlonneger, aren't known to turn toxic with age. But they do lose their potency."

"Really? Well *then*." She double-checked the date on the Neosporin. She would go through the medicine cabinet when she got home. "That's true of Pepto-Bismol, too? And Tylenol?"

"Generally speaking, any medicine."

"Tylenol in whatever version, you're saying? Caplets? Capsules? Well, I guess so."

"Yes ma'am. And tablets."

"Maybe this is dumb of me but I try to stay away from the tablets."

"Ma'am?"

"To me they seem more obstructionist. Likelier to plug the person's epiglottis."

"I can't say I've seen any studies indicating such a risk."

"No, it's just one of my phobias. Oh, if you don't mind my asking, do you personally think taking Tylenol for fever is actually the best course? Isn't a fever advantageous sometimes? I don't mean one so high the patient goes into convulsions, goodness no. But isn't fever the body's way of combating infection?" She had to step aside, though, for another customer and didn't obtain Treadle's opinion.

Many times since, she's sought his advice about what-all different pharmaceuticals, but approaching the counter this morning, a package of Robitussin CF in hand for Todd's cold, she isn't laboring over the product's potential dangers. At the cash register she forks over the cough syrup and holds her question until Treadle has finished ringing her up. Hedging, she asks, "Are you especially familiar with vinegar, sir? Wine vinegar, I mean— I guess." The soldiers at the crucifixion put some on a sponge for Jesus. *Spunge,* it's spelled in Daddy's King James. S-p-u-n-g-e, yes. She stumbled upon this yesterday in the Matthew account. When she leafed to Mark, there it was again, the same spelling. The soldiers impaled the soaked sponge on a stick and held it up to Jesus. "Can you point to any known, verified medicinal uses?" she asks. "I've heard already of elderly people taking ordinary cider vinegar with honey for their chest congestion. What sort of healing propensities might be attributable? Could vinegar serve as a painkiller? It's high in acid, I know that much, so would the acidity itself help palliate? Or the fermentedness?"

"You've got me there, Mrs. Schlonneger. I haven't a clue."

"No? Oh."

She wants to ask, "Do you have any pills in stock for the spiritually dyspeptic? For a person's spiritual constipation?"

IN THE SOPORIFIC AFTERNOON QUIET, a flurry of crinkled wads on the kitchen floor, her elbows digging into the checkered tablecloth and her chin buried in her palms, she questions whether she's just as brain dead as the pointy-headed elf on top of the carton Wade dragged from the living-room closet last night. Its two jiggle eyeballs are ogling her blankly from the doorway. It spilled out when Wade was grappling with the box's weakened cardboard flaps and trying at the same time to back himself out without getting hung up on the ironing board or the bag of sewing scraps from Mama or the mare's nest of coats—hence its privileged lookout spot on the box.

Offhandedly she wonders which child the trinket actually belongs to. Didn't it come from Erma Lee Showalter? All three of the children had Erma Lee as a Sunday school teacher. Originally a note was attached to the yarn loop, "Squeeze my cheeks and I'll give you a kiss," and when you pushed in on the sides of the yarn-laced plastic netting face, the mouth popped open to reveal a Hershey Kiss, like an overblown silver filling. There was a bag of extra Kisses, too. Kisses, oh, thinks Anna. She should've picked some up at Rite Aid.

Wade said last night, "C'mon Anna, buck up. It's time you're getting into the Christmas spirit." After hauling out the box of ornaments he promised, "I'll come home early enough tomorrow to go up the hill before supper for the tree." He asked her, "Want a hemlock again? Same as last year?"

"I guess. Okay."

"Not a ten-footer?" he joked. He was referring to the lunker item he towed into the apartment their first year of marriage, so tall he had to saw the top off.

"Please, no."

For her, their first married Christmas, just having a tree was a step. They'd spent Thanksgiving at Hawk Knob, and traveling back to Jackson they'd passed a truckload of trussed just-cut evergreens. As Wade cut back into the driving lane, she gave a sprightly squeak and proposed, "Let's get us one, okay? Can we? Do you think?"

"Sounds good by me."

"Oh, but I don't know. It'll disappoint my parents."

"You've left home, Anna."

"I know. Still, we should be sensitive. Mama'd say whenever Margie bellyached about no tree, 'If it's supposed to remind folks that Jesus died on one, then why aren't they accepting him as Lord and Savior?' Of course, Mama was right."

She waited till an overtaking tour bus rolled past, spewing gray soot across their side of the highway. "But, same as Margie, I loved the magical-ness—the total star-struck effect. Aunt Dolly's up in her parlor had that fake snow squirted on. Loads and loads of tinsel and frosted-glass balls."

"Yeah."

"It's the kind of thing that's neither here nor there, really."

"Yeah."

"And it's not like Mama and Daddy haven't already had to adapt."

"I'll say."

She took a long, drawn-out, acquiescent breath and let escape a cheerful cluck. "Won't it be fun? I'm so excited."

Anna thinks of the miniature ceramic tree Mama has now, with colored bulbs bugging out from it, lit from inside. Herbie's wife, Rita, gave it to her. She puts it at her front window and keeps it plugged in all night. Bless that dear mama of mine, thinks Anna, stirring from her pose, whonking her arms down onto the table with surprising vigor. And it's sweet of Wade to be trying to get her sparked, it really is. Him setting them up for a cozy, fun evening—that's sweet. They'll have a fine time unpacking the homemade paper snowflakes, each year a little flimsier and more yellowed, and the starched-lace stars and spray-painted walnut halves; the gilded Japanese lantern from Wade's mom; the Baby Jesus manger Mary Beth made in second grade with shredded wheat for the hay; Jonathan's third-grade picture in a jar-lid frame, and the elephant Todd carved out of Ivory soap when he was eleven; the funny doodads contributed by the children's playmates. Anna's favorite addition last Christmas, a wee angel made from uncooked pasta, came from Megan Funkhouser, Jerry's wife: a piece of rigatoni for the choir robe, with two elbow macaronis around the middle for sleeves, painted with pearly white nail polish, and for the head, a popped kernel of popcorn with a gold-sequin halo. "You're so creative," she told Megan. "It's just precious." When she hung the angel next to the jiggly-eyed elf it looked almost bawdy—too cheap.

No, not Erma Lee. Anna remembers, now. Lorna. Lorna Forry is who bestowed the thing. Even by its lonesome, sending empty-headed leers from its roosting spot on the box in the doorway, the elf seems no less tacky. It's almost salacious. It half gives her the creeps. Lorna taught Jonathan's Sunday school class one year, that's right, uh-huh. That bag of Kisses for refills, Jonathan thought he'd hit the jackpot.

But why candy? thinks Anna abruptly. Why a dumb, cheeky toy?

Who's the bamboozled one, here? In a muddle, she chews on the barrel of her pencil and clinks it against her teeth. Who's the ignoramus?

Why a big spangly tree? Whatever for? What could be more vacuous and nonsensical—and more of a gibe? Confounded, she drops her pencil onto the table. They gave Jesus the vinegar for his thirstiness. On the cross he cried out, "I thirst." But that spongeful couldn't ease the torment. Because God had to extract a price, Jesus suffered and paid.

Maybe a sad, ragged tree is what's needed, thinks Anna. She lifts off her seat but smacks right back down again and tussles with the tablecloth to free her legs. Sad, now that would *mean* something. Scrawny and stunted—she can handle *that*.

She moves about collecting her paper rubble. Next she scuffs around in the mudroom and climbs again into Wade's coveralls. She'll bring in her own pick. One of those malnourished itty-bitty scrub cedars, with the sap bleeding at the cut. Minutes later, she's trundling up the hill, a chumpy, solitary figure, carrying an ax.

20

"You got it? Oh good." Mary Beth's voice circles up the phone cord, joshy and fun. "Open it up, Mom."

"Not wait? I thought we were to wait."

"Oh, pooh. Make Dad and the boys hold off on theirs, if you want."

"Well—okay—"

From the newsprint-wadded depths of the box, Anna draws one of the separately wrapped packages. *For Mom, FRAGILE.* The Christmas paper falls away to reveal a mug, floridly engraved. *If wisdom's ways you wisely seek, five things observe with care: of whom you speak, to whom you speak, and how, and when, and where.* "Mary Beth, it's beautiful. Oh, and what's this? Its own little lid? So nifty!"

"It's supposed to be the second piece in your 'great aspersions' collection. Something better than that 'Look like a fool' thing. Isn't this one cheerier? More inspiring? Hold on a minute, Mom."

A coworker must've stopped by Mary Beth's desk. While they confer, Anna traces her palm across the pebbly cobalt-blue glaze. Aspersions? Aphorisms, did Mary Beth mean?

"You still there, Mom? See, I found this really neat catalog—all mugs. So you can expect more."

"I guess, though," says Anna, "if somebody has to deliberate every time before they blab, they must be hiding something. Honesty *is* the best policy."

A hurt yip. Anna quickly adds, "No no, it's a be-yoo-ti-ful gift. I love the blue. I'm just saying a person should be straightforward and Christian in all their dealings. Not sly."

"Well, I'm going to find you other artsy ones, too, all right? Is the coffee okay?"

"Coffee?"

"Dig around a little more. It's in there somewhere."

"What? Oh." *Also for Mom,* the gift tag instructs. "Oh yum. Yum. Godiva, sumptuous."

"You're more fun pumped, you know. So go tank up."

"Shouldn't I wait to imbibe? Out of fairness?"

"It won't matter in the least, Mom."

"Well, we'll see."

"Are you done with your shopping? What're you giving Dad?"

"Oh, I'm in a bit of a fix. I thought another field guide, but how can I tell for sure which volumes he already has if he's always taking this one or that to school? Twenty-one titles are listed in the Peterson series but some are regional. He hardly needs a book on Mexican birds, or on the mammals of Britain and Europe. Do they have mammals different from ours, you think? Are there special stripings on the zebras, or what? I thought I heard him say he wished he had the one on animal tracks, but when I looked, there it was, up on the shelf."

"Can't you get Todd to snoop around in Dad's classroom?"

"Get Todd—? Oh. Silly me. Why didn't that even occur to me? Now it's too last-minute to order anything by mail." Anna presses her head into the shabby lace of the valentine on the fridge and lets out a sigh. "You're always so sensible. How'd I ever spawn anybody sensible—three rational-minded progenies, all totaled?" She sighs again, noisily. "I miss you. I hate this, you not coming home for Christmas."

"I know. Me too. It's even the wrong weather here. Another thunderstorm today."

"It's that warm?"

"But Trisha fixed up a tree for our section. It helps, even if it's fake."

"Fake!" cries Anna.

"Don't worry, there's a real one out in the lobby. Huge, huge. We're putting paper chains on, paper lanterns, things like that, crayoned by our kids and parents. They need some busywork during their supervised visits.

Poor Willard, though—the maintenance man. It fell over yesterday, so he's in a snit. We helped fix it back up, but the carpet is all gummed from the piney stuff that was in the water."

"It's sticky?" Hm, Egbert's would do the trick if it were still available—Mama's cleaner. Anna bets it could've removed the Vaseline in Aunt Dolly's rug. "Surely Willard has something that would work," she says. "Paint thinner, maybe? Tell him to try that. Except—wait—no, don't. It's flammable. Some client might walk in and light up their cigarette. Don't suggest paint thinner, hear? Or anything else flammable."

"Paint thinner, okay. I'll have Willard douse the spots."

"No! Oh you!" But Anna can't keep from laughing along.

"Mom, you're a scream."

"I guess. If you say so. Huh, you should see our pipsqueak tree here." Listing slightly, it's on top of the children's old toy chest at the far end of the kitchen. No baubles, not a one. No blinkies. Tied on are just some clumps of firethorn berries. She happened upon them on her scouting expedition.

"Pipsqueak? Is it nice?"

"Nice? We-ell." Meaningful, anyhow. Nice isn't the term, no. *Merry Christmas*—why is that everybody's big chirpy greeting?

Like her, Mary Beth seems in no hurry to get back to the deskwork. When she launches into a story about a pair of runaway foster siblings, Anna fits the receiver more amenably into her neck, flopping the jumbly cord out of the way of her Goodwill tins and baskets. The small brother and sister, Mary Beth says, pushed their shoes and teddy bears and pajamas in a play stroller all of twenty city blocks and then helped themselves to a hank of bananas at a 7-Eleven. As her daughter yammers on, Anna nods and um-hums. Every so often she lifts from the dish drainer a bowl or juice glass and finds it a home. Sometimes she pulls the cord full length, wiggling and sinuating behind her, to stand in the middle of the kitchen and watch at distant range the speeding celestial bodies in the study. Her accumulated prior chapters, mumly harbored behind the computer screen's relentless, starshot midnight sky, seem more nutty than wise. If wisdom is what she's been seeking to impart, she's unwisely blown it.

IN THE LATE AFTERNOON she alerts to Todd shucking his sneakers and coat and throwing his schoolbooks onto the dining table—and yelling in annoyance, "Ow! Hey, Ma-a-a-a."

She comes running to find him hopping around on one stockinged foot and clutching the other. "Oo-oo-oops," she brays. "Sorry about that. I wasn't intending to crucify anybody." She plucks from the floor the cluster of orangish-red berries beset with spiny thorns, fallen off her sad-sack excuse of a tree, and a peppery sting rips across the skin of her thumb. "Me, too! Ouch! Well, that's what I get." A bright blurb of red rises and she dabs at it with her tongue—at the hot, sour flavor. But another drop surfaces, and another.

"You need a tourniquet, Ma? You gushing?"

"Gooshing, huh-uh."

Goosh, she used to put it. She asked Mama, "Does the blood goosh?" Up in the bathroom, dripping into the washbowl and peeling the paper off a Band-Aid, Anna ponders that pad story she wrote so long ago. She mulls the angles, the applicability. Humph. The pent-up air releases in a rush from her nose.

Bandaged up, she carries the wicker stool into the hall. She brings down from the hidey-hole her string-tied collection, loosens the bind, knocks off the lid, and bungles around with her uninjured hand for the pages.

A Split Second Miss

"Where'd Wanda get lost?" whispered Annie, she was squashed in the pitch black with her younger sister Margie under Mama's hung up dresses and getting heat bumps. "Don't know but my buttocks hurt bad," Margie whispered back, because see, Mama always admonished her daughters aged nine and seven to use the right words, not butt or behind or rear end or other vulgar substitutes. Margie was squatted right on top Mama's everyday shoes but if she changed position Wanda who was it might catch the noise.

Wanda'd rung the doorbell during their company dessert and Mama'd said, "Pull up a chair." Mrs. Overholt'd just kept swallowing down the coconut cake, no friendliness, acting like she didn't prefer for Mama to charity feed somebody in shorts. Mama didn't like immodesty neither but she never said things like, "Tsk, tsk, just so it don't rub off." In a jiffy Wanda had her fork licked clear of every cake crumb and off the girls went to play hide and go seek. Wanda got to counting and Annie and Margie fled upstairs, but then where? "Twenty, ready or not, here I come," she said and quick they piled in the clothes closet.

Margie hit at Mama's smothery dresses and all at once toppled against the closet door and toppled out and splatted face down. The

dresses were swinging around Annie's head with their hangers clinking but she could see Margie roll over and repair her skirt, she didn't
let it stay hitched up. "Cover your knees, girls," Mama'd admonish
and anyhow who wanted to see scabby knees?

Mama's dresses slowed down down and sluffed against Daddy's
stiff strict suit and then lined up prim and according. Annie peered
around and saw Daddy's good hat on the shelf was too pitched and
might fall down beheaded any minute. And Mama's mashed everyday prayer cap was up there too, she wouldn't change out of her Sunday one till the company went. Margie was still flat on her back and
Annie got curious about why she was moving her lips. Oh, she was
trying to read Mama's stocking box where it said 5-0 d-e-n-i-e-r.

"What's that other box?" asked Margie. It was big, blue with big
white letters. "M-O-D something."

She got up and went for Daddy's desk chair and pushed it over to
the closet with the castors wobble-screeching, wobble-screeching.
"Shush," Annie said, "quit that noise, what's the matter with you?"
But Margie didn't care anymore, she got the chair up next to the
jambs and got up on the seat.

"M-O-D-E-S-S," she spelled. "So ha."

"What of it?" said Annie. "Anyhow so what?"

"Just some white somethings or others," said Margie, feeling
around in the box. She dragged one out, it was long and punchy with
ends that petered out, and turned it over and over, putting it up in
front of her face. "What's it ever for?" She climbed down off the
chair. "I'm gonna ask."

"Wait," said Annie, leaping up and reaching out far but just
catching the thin air, and in that same split second Margie escaped.
"Wait! No, wait!" Margie went out in the hall holding on the sanitary
pad and calling, "Mama, Mama!"

Annie could overhear Daddy and Deacon Overholt's serious discussing but nothing out of Mama and Mrs. Overholt apparently rest-
ing their tongues. That Margie, she skipped on down the steps ahead
of her and ran into the living room shouting, "Hey!" Herbie was
putt-putting his tractor and on the couch Mama was holding Wesley
in her lap. Margie shouted, "What's this, Mama?" and went over and
flappered the tail ends at Mama. Mama went beet red. She sat Wesley
down on the linoleum. He started up a loud wah-ing but Mama
didn't pay him any mind. Deacon Overholt got busy clearing his

throat or else choking and Mama rushed Margie right back out.

Upstairs Mama smushed the pad back where it belonged. "Oh oh," she murmured in a namby pamby state, "oh oh me," and collapsed down on the bed unheeding of her nice brown Sunday dress with eensy weensy brown geometry shapes. "It's a very private thing, Margie," she said, all hoarse, "it's for the blood."

"Blood?" said Margie, all innocent. Mama's shoulders were shaking and she had to stop and blow her nose like a boat horn. Probly Margie thought, What's so disastrous? But Annie knew. Kind of. "Now now, it's nothing so terrible," Mama'd said when Annie discovered one in the waste can not wrapped up right, she'd sat down and explained about girls' monthlies. "It's just messy, is all. But don't say anything to Margie, she's still too little. Don't you go telling her."

Annie should of grabbed fast. Sat on top of her till Mama came and then this unseemly scene wouldn't of happened. Maybe told her, except Mama'd said don't tell. "What you don't know won't hurt you," her teacher at school always said, Mrs. Klinestiver, the fourth-grade teacher, when somebody was too nosy, asked how old are you, other questions like that. Sometimes yes, but what you didn't know could put you in a serious pickle. Or put somebody else in the pickle. So how true was that saying? Not very.

Did the period blood just drizzle, or more like dump, goosh? Annie wondered, she would have to check with Mama. Not now, Wanda was coming, not around Wanda, but soon as she got a chance she would check. So she wouldn't not know and just get wrought up.

At the end, her page-turning stilled, Anna remains slouched near the hall window in the milky, waned afternoon light, the cold of the wall plaster grinding into her shoulder. She's decided this story will go in, too. Goosh—gush—either way, there's that bloodiness. At the soldier's stab, water and blood spilled from Jesus. The worldly Christmas-tree frivolities only vulgarize the sore truth of the cross.

The scratch on her thumb sets to throbbing and she's besieged with a new notion. Santa doesn't have c-l-a-w-s, but what about God? Is God the one with claws? In haste she stanches the prickly, rebellious thought, but not fast enough to retract it.

21

Crimping crusts, she's too hurried and harried to be making wholesale sense, yet her college boy backed up against the counter is good-naturedly nodding, devoting attention. "'Pies again?' I asked Margie when she called. I asked, 'What about apple, like last Christmas?' But no, she wanted grape crumb. 'No,' I said, 'the crumbs will muck up.' 'Muck up,' she said, 'what do you mean?' So I explained about those pies, they always go washraggy by the second day—I'd need to do the baking on Saturday. It would help, sure, if I could keep them sitting out. If they didn't have to suffocate in the car trunk all through church and the drive up. She said, 'Phooey, that won't matter. You're such a pick.' I said, 'Okay, all right, fine. If that's what you want.'"

Anna wheels the pie plate a quarter turn with the heels of her hands and resumes coaxing her pastry edge into a ruffle. "So does she think I'm proud about that? The pickiness? I'd like to know! Because I'm not. All the suffering in the world—wars and famines and mud slides—and I piddle around worrying my head over pie crumbs."

"Mud slides?" inquires Jonathan.

"When was that avalanche? Last year? That hurricane in Nicaragua, when mud sluiced down off a mountain and caused thousands of deaths? Well, you were at school. The Jaycees' campaign for donations was what opened my eyes to the *campesinos'* poverty. Anytime I'm reminded, like now, I feel so petty. It seems wrong to twitter over a paltry problem like sogginess."

"Good point, Mom."

"Combs. Toothpaste. Antifungal cream. They were requesting the merest, most basic necessities. Toothbrushes. Tylenol. Packed in a plastic five-gallon bucket or just bagged up. I thought I was doing something just buying laundry soap. That's what I *thought*. You know what Susan did? Not only did she load up on a bunch of each item, oh no! When she couldn't find any place that sold the buckets, she took it upon herself to drive around to all the new-construction sites to bum some empty spackle containers. Can you believe it? She collected ten I think, let them clunk around in her car, and scrubbed them out down in her rec-room bathroom. I guess pushed back that black-glass shower door with the gold bulrushes painted on and ran the tub full blast and scraped away. She bleached them, too. Bleached—when the least little splash would've ruined, absolutely ruined, the carpet! Did she let nitpickiness deter her? Nope, huh-uh."

Oops, when Anna dumps the first of the two quarts of canned grapes into the kettle, a juicy blip flies up and lands on the sleeve of Jonathan's polo shirt. "Look who's talking!" she scowls. "Look who's the slop!" She scoops up the dishcloth and rubs at the spot. "Oh dear. Well, grape stains aren't permanent. You children used to go around wearing mustaches from your jelly toast or your grape Kool-Aid."

"God's-blood Kool-Aid."

"God's—?" She rears back and frowns at Jonathan. "Oh. Oh, I get it." When he was a little tyke, it was his most asked-for story. *Mommy, Mommy, tell about the popsicle. The popsicle? Well, let's see, it was su-uch a hot day, hot enough for you and Mary Beth to be splashing in your pool, hot enough for one of the Kool-Aid popsicles I'd made—whee! goody! You can each have a halvesie, I said. But what did you do? You squatted down, your swim trunks were glued fast to your roly-poly bottom, and you laid your halvesie right on the burny hot sidewalk and said very solemnly, When it melts it'll be God's blood. You were so, so cute. You were remembering about communion at church, weren't you? Yes, you were.* "In case you don't know," she says to Jonathan, "that's not exactly the best joke anymore."

"But Mom, those buckets?" He's watching her measuring the cornstarch. "Shipping relief items in heavy-duty polyethylene that takes decades to decompose? Doing that would only compound Nicaragua's environmental problems."

"So Wade thought, too, until the person he reached at the Jaycees' national headquarters told him the refugee family would especially prize their bucket. Because of the lid, the lady said. No spills, hauling their cooking water from the river. See what I mean? The destitution?"

Her dry ingredients mixed in, she starts the pot of filling to cooking. At the first *phlup-phlups*, she test-drizzles a small amount. Mm, just about the exact right thickness, in her judgment. She boils the kettle half a minute longer, then tastes a dab off her spoon. Her teeth crunch on something hard. "Ugh, what was *that?*"

Spotting dark specks in the pot, she switches off the burner. She spoons up more sauce. Jonathan edges close. "They're pieces of stem," he says. "Some of the stems didn't get picked off."

"No, what I bit down on had a brittle texture, not woody. Like it was something foreign. I bet a chemical reaction occurred during the canning—poisonous, I bet. It could've been a crystalized microorganism."

"Poisonous, no." Jonathan swipes at the spoonful and examines his specimen. "If they're not stems, then they're pieces of grape peel," he decides, taking a lick. "No big deal."

"You don't know! Don't do that!" Before he can sample more, she hurls the spoon into the sink. Her veins are thrumming, suffusing her with dread and indecision. "We can't take something iffy like this." But, waste the grapes? Chuck the whole batch? The idea is too mortifying. Her mind in a roil, she drums on the stove. She toothpicks a dried fleck of something off the knob of the potholder drawer. She retrieves the purpled spoon, powders it with Ajax, and rinses it. She mushes an overlarge lump of brown sugar in the bowl of topping crumbs and holds her sticky hand under the faucet. "What do I do? What do I do?"

At least, Wade and Todd stacking firewood on the porch can't hear. "That's enough, Mom," says Jonathan. He relieves her of the dish towel, takes hold of her by the shoulders. "Out. Out." Steering her toward the living room he orders, "Tell me how to finish. How long in the oven?"

"No, no."

"Get done with your packing. Go do that."

"Maybe don't use all the crumbs," she whimpers. "Just sprinkle them around thinly." Obediently she starts up the steps. "Don't let the oven go higher than 425 degrees. And make sure the crust and crumbs completely brown, you hear? The pies must be on the bottom rack."

Then a few minutes later she barges from her bedroom into the hall and calls, "No, wait, Jonathan! When you think they're just a whisker away from done, let me come check. Okay? Okay?"

PARTWAY THROUGH the Sunday-morning Christmas service, a ripped-off piece of church bulletin gets passed down the laps—Todd's, Wade's—to Anna. The note from Jonathan reads, *Those God's-blood pies will be a hit, mark my word.* She sends him a look and quickly turns back to her hymnal and "Angels We Have Heard on High." Not until the close of the song does she venture another glance in his direction, whereupon he makes a self-congratulatory circle with his thumb and forefinger and discreetly pumps his chest.

That boy!

But at the din-filled family gathering at Margie's in the evening, Anna jumps at the chance to lose herself. After the whopping supper, when Jonathan is telling Mama about the panic attack, Anna laughs so hard the tears cascade from her screwed-shut eyes and cause her to run for Wade's handkerchief. "Another of my ignoramus capers," she bleats. "I don't know why I didn't have the heat turned lower under the kettle. At least there wasn't all that much black char to scrape off."

"I suppose not," says Mama. She's covering the two leftover slivers of pie with a paper napkin. "I didn't notice a hint of burn."

"I know, I know," agrees Anna, blotting her face. "Why didn't the taste carry? The crumbs did go mushy—you noticed *that,* I guess. But, oh well!"

Spatters of glee are coming from the archway where Rita is attempting to rearrange the cousins in yet another shutterbug pose, framed by the strung-up Christmas cards. "Put Mama in the picture," Anna urges. "Rita, stand Mama in the middle. You'll send reprints to Wesley's family and Mary Beth, won't you?"

"Yeah, make them sorry they missed out," booms Herbie, rubbing his big meatball of a belly. Anna punches him playfully. She pulls on his tie, holds it out like a jump rope to admire it. "I should've gotten Wade one like this," she says. "Why did I pick out something so staid for him?" From Rita, Herbie's tie is striped with different shimmering reds. It's almost phosphorescent.

When Rita puts down the camera, over the hullabaloo Mama asks about one of the Christmas cards. "Margie, who's this? Whose cutie-pie children?"

"Who's who, Mama?"

"Kyle, don't play that thing," Rita scolds. "Allow us some peace." But the ever-beloved music box on Margie's coffee table, plinking out the

"Twelve Days of Christmas" tune while the ceramic partridge on top re-volves, will have to wind itself down. "Kyle, shoo. See if Uncle Fred will run his train set for you."

"Oh, whose children?" says Margie. The photo card Mama is looking at, GLORY TO GOD IN THE HIGHEST, shows three chubby-cheeked imps in matching pajamas. "That's Gavin and Kent and Christine. The Brenne-man kids. Valerie and Jim Brenneman's kids." Turning, Margie yells, "Yoo-hoo, Herbie! Your pet verse, 'GlorytoGod'nthehighestandonearth-peace,' remember that? Back at Pottstown?"

"Sure, Herbie went for it because it was short and sweet," says Anna. "Hey, Wade, there's an idea—a memorization program like at the mission. We should suggest that at Conoy. Donna would be good at running it, or maybe even Erma Lee."

"Memorization program?" asks Rita.

"Anna, what?" says Wade, obliging her as she wiggles for room in his armchair.

"It was all Mrs. Overholt's doing," says Margie. "Credit where credit is due. She had these posters she'd hold up, one after another—the picture side showing, not the side with the verse unless it was a new one and no-body had it down pat—and somebody would stand up where they were and recite. And then somebody else and somebody else. Except we all knew not to take Herbie's verse and disappoint him. Everybody stayed put for that one. He'd jump right up and rattle it off like a world-champion memorizer. What were you, Herbie—four?"

"Sounds about right, yeah."

"And there was her artwork, too. I can't say Mrs. Overholt lacked all spontaneity and vision." Margie leans toward Rita. "Like, to illustrate the 'Put up again thy sword' verse she drew a flashy ornate-handled one. Gold foil for the blade. And for 'Thou shalt not kill,' her two tablets of stone had the commandments written on in gobbledygook hieroglyphics."

"'Put up again thy sword into his place, for all they that take the sword shall perish with the sword,'" Anna chants. "But it was more of a dagger, don't you think? Sword, dagger—I'm not quite clear on the differ-ence, myself. Mrs. Overholt coached, if the person forgot what came next. 'Shall per—per—per— That's right, that's right. Shall perish with the s—s—s'"

"Mama, how many can you still say?" asks Margie. "'Lay not up for yourselves treasures on earth,' remember that one? How about 'Bring ye all the tithes'? That big long stringer?"

Mama is pursing up in thought. Margie prompts, "'Bring ye all the tithes—'"

"Wait, ah, wait," says Mama, working the soft, seamy corners of her mouth. "'Bring ye all the tithes into the storehouse, that there—'"

"Go on. You know it."

"'Bring ye all the tithes into the storehouse, that there—'" Mama stops with a grunt. "'Bring ye all the tithes into the storehouse, that there'—that there—that there—'may be meat in mine house, and prove me now herewith, saith the Lord of hosts, if I will not open you the windows of heaven, and pour you out a blessing, that there shall not be room enough to receive it.'"

"You're a whiz, Mama!" shouts Margie above everybody's cheering.

"You know what, though?" says Anna, after things have quieted down. "The picture Mrs. Overholt made to go along with it? Just a collection plate with coins in, remember? I thought she should've drawn the meat. Plucked chickens with their feet still on, and ham hocks, and baloneys like in the meat case down at Simpson's, sewed up in stockings."

"Baloney?" says Herbie. "Doesn't that verse refer to the sacrifice meat?"

"For on the altar?" Anna's eyes widen. "Oh—why yes, I guess so."

Margie adds, "But that woman sure could be a sourpuss sometimes."

"Oh, now Margie," demurs Mama.

"She didn't like Wanda. She didn't extend Wanda any leeway. Wanda's bubble gum, Anna, remember? The used wads she'd glop on the underside of the pantry shelf?"

"Of course I do. Sometimes I got lucky and found myself a piece that still had a little flavor left. Honestly, somebody else's saliva. I don't understand what allowed me to chew on those old cuds."

"That's not my point. I'm talking about Mrs. Overholt—her behavior. The way she treated Wanda."

"Huh? Oh-h-h. That time she came to help with the catch-up housecleaning."

"You girls." Mama is becoming agitated. "I don't know what you're talking about."

"You were upstairs, Mama," says Margie. "You didn't get to see her just about drop her britches."

Mama gestures helplessly. "Margie, what?"

"She was in there in the pantry, banging away at what little dirt, I'm sure, and thinking she was being such an irreplaceable godsend. We heard her call, 'Girls, girls!' Here a gob had come off in her rag. Which in itself wouldn't have been so bad, just some gum, but your Egbert's Cleaner must've dissolved it. She came stalking out with the rag held out in front of her and the slime hanging off in long strings. 'Who, please, can I thank for this?' So I indicated Wanda and Mrs. Overholt snapped, 'Such a nasty, filthy habit! I should've known. I wonder whether Myrna realizes the influence.'"

"Dearie dearie me," Mama manages, sagging in surprise. "You never told."

"And how about that day you two were up to some big canning job, with Wanda there too, hanging around Mrs. Overholt's elbow?" says Margie. "You don't recall? When Wanda let slip the 'darn' word? Or 'dang,' was it? Oh lordy, did our sweet, sainted soul go off on a lecture. 'Now now, young lady! No slang!' She quoted that 'yea yea, nay nay' verse, and she—"

"Matthew 5:37, I imagine," says Mama, rallying. "'Let your communication be yea, yea, nay, nay, for whatsoever is more than these cometh of evil.'"

"But how was a little kid off the street supposed to know any better?"

"Don't you guess Mrs. Overholt just wanted to plant the seed?" says Mama.

"There was some other verse she spouted, too—something about the final judgment—and then she—"

"Peaches," interrupts Mama eagerly. "We were canning peaches. It's coming back to me now. The verse was Matthew 12:36. 'Every idle word that men shall speak, they shall give account thereof in the day of judgment.'"

"And then she shook out her apron," Margie's voice is going higher, almost cracking, "shook it out hard enough to make that big raisin mole on her neck wobble, and she said, 'Young lady, you'd best pay heed!'"

"I remember," says Anna, nodding vehemently. "Idol word, I thought that meant. I-d-o-l."

When the room explodes in mirth, she joins in. Rita is holding her sides. Herbie can't hold his—the flab is jouncing. Even Todd and Jonathan are plastered with broad grins. How long have they been listening? The hubbub swirling about her ears, Anna flops back weakly against Wade, and for a change she basks in the nonsense and in her insipidness and plain inane discombobulation.

MAYBE THIS CHAPTER is bloating up too much, but back home on one of those dank, hungover afternoons between the two tail-end-of-the-calendar holidays, when the boys are at the auto-parts store and only her husband is around, something else happens. Anna has usurped Wade's ugly, misshapen slippers, as big as boats on her, so to begin with, she could be mistaken for an extra-lucky Nicaraguan refugee, blessed with a donor's hand-me-downs in addition to the bucket of hygiene supplies, *gracias a Dios.* Years ago, she ordered the slippers for Father's Day from the L.L. Bean catalog. Size 12 should've been right, but Wade had to positively cram his feet in. His phalanges bones made ridiculous, individually pronounced bumps. "Let me re-order," she pleaded. "They'll ship another pair postage free. Please let me return these." "Nah," he said, "they'll stretch out." Which they certainly did.

No socks despite the frigid wind squealing around the north corner of the house, just Wade's slippers that extend from the backs of her feet, Anna flop-flops up the stairs to produce from the hall's overhead hole the Tingley Rubbers box and her blue diary she kept when she was nine. The peach canning would've been in August or September. She can still picture Mrs. Overholt in her flowered apron with armholes, her knife adamantly circling the peach halves and flicking off the skins, while Mama forked the peeled ones from the dishpan and packed the jars. "More, girls?" Mama asked cheerily. Their chins were dribbling. "Wanda, would you like another?" To which Wanda replied, "No'm, I'm darn full."

Owing to the steaming heat, Mrs. Overholt had rolled down her stockings, and all through that stern little sermon, Wanda kept her head ducked and studied the scraggly purplish webbing of veins on Mrs. Overholt's legs. Margie and Wanda bolted from the room when the woman stopped for air, her mole still quivering. She looked down her glasses at Anna. "You, too. Let that be a lesson. It behooves us to watch our tongues."

Don't I know full well, thinks Anna, paging through to August, finding the right day.

Contrasted with the entry about Clyde Bailey, her handwriting here appears more crabbed, ridden with endeavor. *Mama had pecks of peaches, Mrs. Oveholt came. Proply she was worryed About wasteing and whatnot and when Wanda said somthing dumb and wreckless Mrs Overholt chided. About slang, all that, but I dont know what idol Words.*

As she remembers it, for quite a while afterwards the mystery dogged her. Idols' names? People weren't to say the names out loud? Or was the verse warning about idol worshipers' hokey prayers, such as when the children of Israel hailed their gold calf by prostrating themselves with their noses buried in the dirt and mumbling, mumbling, mumbling their strange repetitions? "What would those idol words be?" she finally asked Mama. "'Hocus-pocus,' or what?"

Mama shook her head, perplexed.

"Idol words. You know, for praying to statues. In that verse—Mrs. Overholt's verse."

"What? No, no. Idle, i-d-l-e. But different from lazy. Extra words, ones that aren't useful." Mama smiled. "Oh, Anna, you and your mix-ups!"

Sure, and look at her now. Talk about mixups. This imbroglio of a book—no plot anymore, even. Dour at herself, battered with discouragement, Anna ponders the difficulty of it all. Everything is so complicated. It's too much. It's just too much.

She ascertains a strange numbness in her toes, maybe because she's standing so close to the window, with the fronts of Wade's slippers tipped up against a crack in the baseboard where a piffle of icy air is stealing in. She backs away, shakes off a slipper, and tentatively bats her toes against a floorboard. Glancing down, she observes they're a strange color, too. She doubles over to see at closer range. Wha-a-at?

She drops the other slipper and the diary and hobbles down the steps hollering, "Wade, Wade!"

One foot perched on a chair in the kitchen, she takes a few pokes. "My toes are like—dead. They're just stumps!" Even if she pinches the underpads, pinches them tight, no feeling registers. "Diabetes. It's diabetes. Oh no. Isn't poor circulation a sign? Don't the doctors sometimes end up amputating?"

"Nah, Anna."

"Look at the skin. Pure yellow. Like wax!"

"Anna, no. Sit down." Wade moves another chair next to her. He cups her feet snugly and begins kneading but she pulls away. "Call Randy Treadle," she cries, wrapping the baggy end of her sweater sleeve around one set of toes and pummeling at the others. "Ask him about the symptoms. I know what—it's that hardtack! I must've eaten a whole pound yesterday. See? What kind of youth-group project was that, anyway? Not just perverting the Christmas spirit to grub for money, but encouraging hypoglycemia. Or hyperglycemia. Whichever. Call Randy!"

"You're no diabetic, Anna," says Wade, going for their standby manual on the study shelf, *Family Health Care.* He leafs through the volume. "Diabetes, let's see, diabetes. All right, now. You listening? Here are some signs. Frequent urination. Excessive thirst. Excessive hunger. Unusual weight loss. Fatigue. Blurred vision. Nothing about yellow toes."

He claps the book shut. "Now that I'm at it, let me get something else straightened out, insulin related. Insulin's what controls the sugar uptake by the cells, and I wonder whether the receptor proteins alter the insulin molecules." Muttering, he pulls down his weighty biology textbook, the repository of much of his science mumbo-jumbo, including that "pulvilli" word back in Chapter 9 he scrounged for to help her out. She needed just a single piece of terminology to capitalize on the houseflies' agility, but he had to go on a long, roundabout ramble about the Malpighian tubules in houseflies.

So it's not diabetes. Partly pacified, she says to herself, Well, his avidity isn't really a deterrent. Phloem sap, she's learned, is what gobbed up the rug at Mary Beth's office. Wade pointed out the textbook's cutaway diagram and explained that the phloem contains a high percentage of sucrose, making it sugary and sticky. It's very unlike the innocuous xylem sap which travels the opposite direction inside a tree, upwards toward the leaves. Or the needles, if it's an evergreen like the office one that crashed or like her scruffy example still pining away here in the kitchen.

Er—wait—isn't this merely a semantic distinction, "leaves" versus "needles"? Technically doesn't the term "leaves" signify foliage of any type? Bladed or not? So would it be fair to speak of her Christmas tree's—um, her Christmas tree's—um, um—?

But Wade, his molecular facts locked up, is filling the doorway, coming once more to her rescue. "C'mon, Anna. Let me." He seats himself in the chair beside her again and gets down to chafing each of her grim piggies, in turn, with his large, capable hands. "When will you ever learn?" he asks. "Why must you jump to mad conclusions?"

"Mad. You're saying I'm mad."

"No, you have a lousy habit. These leaps of the imagination."

"Crazy leaps, uh-huh. I'm crazed—this Abraham-and-Isaac mess is just because of my crazed mind. That's what you think, isn't it?"

"No, it's not."

In the pause that follows, the querulousness drains from her limbs. Her tippy-toes are pinky-pinking and attaching again to her feet, and a curious, warm hum is setting off in her head. "Ah-h-h," she breathes, "nice, that's better."

"Anna, your problem is, you're good. You're so good you don't even know it." He snorts. "Sometimes you can take stock in your suspicions. Otherwise, rely on other people's. Even mine. Now there's a thought, hey? Look, why not? Trust *me*—try that."

He nudges her, gently. "Did you hear me, Anna?"

22

To the south of town lies the home place of the Showalters from church, Ervin and Erma Lee: a 30-acre tract of rich valley loam, and their gray asphalt-sided house plunked amid a clutter of outbuildings. In summertime, a gone-to-seed glory hovers—clamorous pink sweet peas climb the strings Erma Lee has stretched from the porch boards to the rain gutter, weedy beds of lilies and coleus speckle the yard, and overloaded snowball bushes sag into the driveway. But winter's scene is more dissolute, the profusion laid bare, the hedgery a monochrome shadow of its former vivid jumble. Snow this first week in January has blanketed the iris stubble by Ervin's tool shed and the pyramid of discarded tires near the garage, and sobered up the small knot of beef cattle loitering near the hay barn, slime trailing from their nostrils and shuffs of steamy breath clouding around their heads. Or the animals' melancholy might be of a more mawkish nature, because for the past several days, one of their number has been hanging by his hocks from a garage beam, ponderous iron hooks threaded through his tendons.

Showalters' annual butchering used to be solely a family project, but a year or two after Wade and Anna moved into the area, the older Showalter daughter, Janice, relocated with her husband and children to Montana, and Ervin offered to let the Schlonnegers in on the operation. Anna jumped at the idea. "Who knows what's in regular feedlot beef!" she said to Ervin. She'd read an alarming magazine article at the dentist's office. "What about those growth hormones, those anabolic steroid pellets they're implanting in steers' ears—what does tampering like that do to people's genes? Not to mention the antibiotics?"

Now, Saturday, beneath the maze of cobwebby furnace ducts in Showalters' basement and a pair of bald ceiling bulbs, at a big table laid over with flattened pieces of box cardboard, Anna and Todd and Wade are hard at the day-long chore of cutting and packaging. Birdie is here too, Erma Lee's long-widowed sister. Both women are bundled into their prayer caps, like always, and old pilled everyday sweaters, and emerging below the hem of Birdie's cotton-print gardening dress is a pair of her deceased spouse's thermal long johns. Claire, the other Showalter daughter, and her husband, Dan, have come over from Pendle Mills. They've brought their nine-year-old, Joshua, and another kid—a knock-kneed, frightfully skinny boy with brown teeth bulging from his mouth—who's mostly preferred to lurk on the broken-down porch glider over in the corner. A while ago Joshua was zigzagging around and around the perimeter of the room on a beat-up scooter, perilously close to people's shins, and now he's demonstrating for his wary chum the tin-can stilts Ervin made when the girls were little: two 40-ounce great northern bean cans to balance the feet on, with holes punched in the upended bottoms and long pieces of baler twine fed through to grip as handles. Clankety-clanking along, Joshua has to keep the twine taut enough to bring the cans down squarely, if he doesn't want to hit the concrete with a splat and crack open his head.

"Let's fetch another piece, Dan," says Ervin, switching off the bandsaw and depositing sections of rib on the table.

"Can we help, Gramps?"

"No, I need your dad." But Joshua dumps his game as the men exit for the garage and races out into the cold, and the other boy duly tags along.

"Who's the little friend?" Anna asks.

"Our foster child," says Claire. "Aaron."

"Foster? Oh dear me, you're brave. How long have you had him?"

"All of a week and a half."

"From an unhappy home situation, I guess. A Bill Arnold type of father, except worse." Anna catches herself. "Oh well, you know. Bill can be mean."

"Aaron's parents are estranged, I can say that much," Claire murmurs.

"I understand—it's all supposed to stay confidential. Mary Beth gives me an earful sometimes about her more dire cases. You're so selfless to be doing this."

"He doesn't know yet that he's safe," says Erma Lee. "He needs some time."

Whomp, the door slams. The boys are back. "I don't wanna," Aaron is objecting, rubbing snow from his face. "I'm not playing." He dodges in between Wade and Anna as if for protection, even though Joshua has given up pursuit.

Anna smiles down on him warmly. "Looks to me like you're a good brother for Joshua."

"Yessum."

His eyes follow the tugging blade of her knife, and the flight of the patch of rib fat when she pitches it on top the scraps in the dishpan that will go for hamburger. She pares off another piece and gives it a flip. More pieces—*ffft*, flip, *ffft*, flip. "Them's ladder bones," he observes.

"Why, you're quite right! Good ribs for barbecuing." She found a recipe yesterday she can't wait to try, Barney's Humdinger Australian Outback Sauce. It includes a half cup of Worcestershire sauce (not the usual sissy teaspoon), an entire garlic bulb, and two tablespoons of instant coffee granules. "Have you ever heard of putting coffee in a barbeque recipe?" she asks Birdie, squinting through the lightbulb glare.

"Coffee? My, my."

"That there thing, what's that?" Aaron asks, gazing at the pearly, glinting ball attached to the fearsome-sized femur bone Wade has cleaned of its muscle hanks. "Uck, what's that runny stuff?"

"You've got the very same joint in each shoulder and hip," says Wade. "Imagine that. And your bursal fluid allows you to walk and run and bat baseballs without hurting. Minus the lubricant, your joints would click and grate with every move."

"But I ain't no dinosaur like that'n."

"No."

A blast of cold sweeps in with Ervin and Dan, and their load bounces down onto the table. A lackluster maroon, the carcass is banded thickly with the same kind of hardened white fat Anna is peeling from the ribs. Choking the cavity is a ragged mass of tallow, evidence of supplemental corn feedings. "The guy was a biggie all right," says Wade. "He was a good boy. He always cleaned up his plate."

"Yessir."

Wade fingers around at something gray and stringy hooked to a front-quarter lump of meat, near a grotty mass of transparent red bubbles. "Here, check this out. The artery that carried the blood down to the leg? See how strong and thick it is? Very critical, because vessel walls must sustain the blood's systolic pressure. They're constantly pulsing."

Good grief, thinks Anna, here comes another of his spiels. "Oh, stop it," she says. "It's Saturday." She pokes Aaron. "Just wait till you get to high school and land somebody like him for your teacher, ramming you with all the facts."

"Yeah," says Todd, "lucky you. Dissection labs, cadavers. Bugs, worms, barfy frogs in formaldehyde."

"If the vessel doesn't keep dilating and contracting to push the blood along," says Wade, "the cells won't receive their oxygen and sugar. Joshua, you get over here, too." Wade is knifing down, separating the muscle. "See how this vessel gets smaller and branches out? Oops—where did it go? Do you see anything? Nope, you don't, but the arterials are there, tinier and tinier. They carried the plasma with its leukocytes and erythrocytes and platelets."

Bonking the handle of his knife against Aaron's head, he says, "Ancillary capillaries are so microscopic, the erythrocytes must travel single file, transporting oxygen to the muscles. But you want to know something?" He puts his face close to the boy's, scarily. "The white cells—leukocytes—can pass through the vessel walls. Fighting off germs, the leukocytes can act like ghosts."

"Bugger germs," contributes Joshua. "That's how my teacher says."

"Yep, pathogens are pervasive little codgers."

Todd says, "Some bulldoze right through the host tissues."

Wade slaps at a sticky hunk destined for the oven or crockpot. "I can't say about steers, but do you know how far a full-grown person's vessels would measure laid end to end? Close to one hundred thousand miles. Astounding. How do scientists ever arrive at such calculations, anyway? When they're mere creatures, themselves—just bone tissue, nerve, and muscle? Just meat?"

"Meat and speck," Ervin clarifies, chuckling. To Aaron he says, "That's what the old-timers called fat—speck. No speck on you, but your new family is gonna fix that."

Ervin steps to the bandsaw with a section of untrimmed leg and flips the switch to start the blade jumping, and Aaron troops over and watches him aim the bone into the blur of teeth. *Gggggggg, SHEEEEeeeee, gggggggg, SHEEEEeeeee, gggggggg, SHEEEEeeeee.* The bone's every trip through, the high, petulant whine of the blade disallows any space in the air for words. But afterwards, Birdie takes up the educational cause. "Those'll just be soup pieces," she says. "Here though, see this roast? It's got a good marrow bone. Sometime when Claire does a roast, you can scoop out a little marrow onto a piece of bread. Dash on the salt and pepper and you'll have you the best sandwich."

"No, I disagree," says Erma Lee. "Tongue is the thing for sandwiches, in my opinion."

"A tongue?" squawks Aaron. "Uck. Uck. Yer makin a joke."

"She's not," says Anna with a giggle. "Don't worry, I'm on your side. I tried it once. Once was enough, believe me."

And then Erma Lee turns on the grinder and waves the boys over to feed the hopper. Flaps of meat and fat suck into the maw of the gnashing, slurping machine, and loopy ropes of burger squeeze out and plop lazily into the tray. But Anna is still remembering that dish at the church potluck, soon after her family started attending at Conoy. The neat, blocky slices of flesh resembled Melba toast. Fattish and pale, they'd been baked in a rich cream sauce. "Mmm, delicious," she raved to the person across the table, but a moment later, "What? What did you say? What?"

Somebody brought Donna Rhodes over. "It's Nelson's favorite," Donna supplied, shy but eager. "You scrub the tongue good, and boil it, you know, and skin it." She smiled in her tentative way. "You skin it while it's still hot—that's important. Then you just trim off the roots and small bones and carve it up however you like."

Anna took one more bite and grabbed her napkin. The animal had lapped bawdily at its nose drools and worried its cud, and now its sandy, spongy appendage lay on her plate. It was too much a rank actuality. Her mind could no longer mistake it for a euphemistic cut of meat—she lacked the needed objectivity.

Hacking up another sliver of scrap for the grinder, Anna thinks, Well, so what's new? "Why can't you treat an issue objectively, Anna?" Wade has often asked. "Why not assess a question on its own merits? You shouldn't go only on your feelings—your gut response." Yet isn't this empathy just part of her makeup? And *no* feelings—there would go a person's essential humanity. The person would lose even his dumb-animal functions. Worse off than the lower beasts, he would be just a vegetable, a piece of boring organic material.

She thinks about that common poser, "mind versus matter." Why, it's an inconceivable divide. To tidily distinguish between the nerve functions, between thinking and feeling, is impossible, really. Furthermore, only the finest of lines separates "perspicacious" and "crazy"—and there's the rub. At least, she decides, even in her berserk periods she's still recognizably human. She's not *in*human, anyway.

Anna limbers her fingers briefly, then snatches up a new section of beef bone. Knitting her brow in thought, meditating over the sorry—and wondrous—attributes of the preeminent order of species, she begins chipping away at a knot of gristle that seems unduly stubborn, coming from a creature who's given up the ghost.

THAT WASN'T RIGHT, calling it "melancholy." Showalters' steers, out by the barn, weren't holding a funeral yesterday. Cattle don't experience vacillations of mood. They're too dumb for grief. They're not *mute* dumb, no—they bawl. But it's more of a rote instinct.

And whereas a bovine's oral instrument, one not severed at its base and cooked, cannot emote significantly, in contrast Anna's tongue, vibrantly in motion this morning at church, is framing tunes varied and undulant and shaping syllables arranged according to the arcane rules of the English language, all to the honor and glory of her Redeemer, *Lord Je-sus en-throned on high, enthro-o-oned, enthro-o-oned, I bless your name.* In charge of this part of the service is Conoy's praise-and-worship team: Donna at the piano; Scott, the pastor, and Jack Nussbaum, Susan's nattily dressed husband, chording on acoustic guitars; Larry Arnold summoning occasional throbs from his electric bass he got for Christmas; Heatwoles' Marvin thumping a pair of sticks against a red snare drum; and the Nussbaum twins and Lorna Forry leading out on vocals.

The lyrics on the wall, high up, to the side of the cross window, go fuzzy and jerk out of view when Nathan Forry, the eleven-year-old on the front bench who's assigned to the overhead projector, picks up the floppy plastic to lay another song in place, "I Will Call upon the Lord." That one is followed by "Mighty, Mighty Savior," and "For I'm Persuaded," and "He is Exalted," and "Lord I Long," *Lord I long, Lord I wait, let your good-ness and mer-cy manifest in me.* Anna's neck is developing its familiar crick from her craning backwards to see, but she loves these ditties, loves singing them. She's never understood why Wade isn't as appreciative. "Here we go again," he'll grouse in an undertone, making like he's about to dry up, if Donna swings into an extra repeat or two of a chorus. But doesn't drawing out the worshipfulness like this help people to center, get them into the right frame? Aren't they supposed to be stilling their souls? What's his main pain?

By "Lord, My Life, Soul, Heart," *Lord my prai-ai-aise I bring you, Lord my li-i-ife, my sou-ou-oul, my hea-ea-eart*, the room seems bathed to Anna. Though no fancy touches are evident—the candles' stale carbon wicks are sunk in their pools of hardened wax, and little more than the stern January cold is glancing off the windows—the music has set a-strum the cords of her heart. The team's faces are flushed and brimming. Lorna's eyes have clamped shut. She's waving her upraised arms in a gentle, swaying fashion, and the twins are into the motions, *You left your thro-o-one in glory, brought me to-o-o the light, took my pai-ai-ain and trials, perished o-o-on the cross*, and Anna is lustily immersed, her tongue tripping through its paces and her cardiopulmonary members pumping enthusiasm and energy. Not until the final run-through, when Donna takes her hands from the piano keys and signals to the others on the team to rest their instruments, leaving only the aching, soft-throated choral sounds swelling across the sanctuary, does the twins' pantomiming penetrate Anna's gauzy fog: *You left your thro-o-one in glory* (a finger pointing upward), *brought me to-o-o the light* (both arms spread wide, invitationally), *took my pai-ai-ain and trials* (both arms pressed against the chest in an *x*), *perished o-o-on the cross* (one fist pounding the other, like a hammer sinking in a nail). The sinister intent, harsh and inexorable, sends shudders down the knobs of Anna's backbone.

Always, the last song before the children's story and the sermon is done in the plain, traditional four-part harmony—no band. "Number 259 in the Evangelical Brethren hymnal," announces Scott, his guitar hanging off his neck. He raises his arm to direct as Donna hits the starting notes for the soprano, alto, tenor, bass. From not far behind Anna comes Peg's reedy vibrato, and Wade by Anna's side lets loose a semi-musical rumble, and Anna takes hold of a corner of the book he's holding and joins in on "When I Survey the Wondrous Cross." But midway through *See from his head, hi-is hands, hi-is feet, sor-row and love flo-ow min-gle-ed down*, her mouth's tool of speech lays itself down, too thick and freighted, its little string of muscle underneath rendered flaccid and useless. Those nails driven in by the soldiers met marrow. The one soldier's spear rived Jesus' side, rending sinew and flesh. Jesus was the meat.

After the service, Scott nabs her in the lobby. "Anna, you're just the one I wanted to see. Can you do the story for the children next Sunday?"

Why is he picking on her again? It hasn't been all that long since she took a turn. "Well, I don't—I'm not real—"

"I'll be focusing on the priorities of the Christian life, on ordering our time and energies and commitments." Scott nods at somebody behind her, shakes hands with a couple other people, and turns back to Anna. "So what do you think? I've titled my sermon 'Keeping God God.'"

Her sharp intake of breath goes unnoticed. She shrinks back, more into herself. He's rubbing his palms together briskly like it's a done deal and hitching his shoulder in the same funny manner she's noticed in other men, as if the fit of their suit is a botheration. "Whatever the Lord lays on your heart, Anna. You'll do it, won't you?"

"I don't quite know if—"

Oh. Her old story about Elijah, maybe. The whoosh of fire, and the crowd's acclaim: "The Lord he is God! The Lord he is God!" Anna swallows weakly. "Okay," she says, "I guess. I can try."

23

Toward the end of Tuesday afternoon Anna is at another impasse, suctioned to the desk chair, the computer studiedly humming but the lines on the monitor frozen in place, not jumping antsily with every rinky-dink rectification. She's printed out the part in the last chapter containing the church-potluck episode, and the drama has flattened on the page and staled from her over-and-over rereading. Also she's undecided about "nose drools." Should she say "snot," instead?

At the familiar chatter of the windowpane, the low-grade Richter shock waves from the school bus's chug-a-lugs riding up the glass, she rolls her head around on her neck and swallows back a yawn. *Chushhhhhhh,* the brakes. The sound is more of a hiss, these days. It's a brand-new bus (probably the brakes are hydraulically operated), with one of those awful, piercing lights on top. She had to creep the whole way into town behind it this morning, trying to duck her lids just enough to screen out the worrisome blink, blink, blink, blink without running the car off the road. Her annoyance resurges as she leans back and observes, past Todd ambling up the drive with his jacket open to the cold, the bus picking up steam on its way up the road and clearing the knoll with a dizzying parting shot.

"Hey Ma, I'm home."

"Hi there."

"Did you get groceries? Did you remember peanut butter?"

"Uh-huh." Clicking out of her file, *MySo-to-SpeakBookCh22*, she hears the fridge door's yielding sigh and the fruit drawer bumping open.

"Guess what now?" Todd calls. "Another one of those quack deals. Mrs. Stanley is gonna give extra-credit points for the cash register tapes we bring in."

She's suddenly out of her chair and mashing her papers into order. Scuttling for the kitchen, she declares, "Are you serious? That is so disgusting."

"Yep, that's the plan." After producing an apple from the new bagful, he brings down the jar of Peter Pan Crunchy from the cupboard and peels back the foil seal. "Mrs. Stanley says Pantry Pride is participating in some kind of technology-and-education program. The store donates funds in exchange for customer receipts. She'll knock the nine-weeks' homework scores up as much as ten percent, depending on the cash totals."

"But what does a grocery bill have to do with Spanish? What's the point? That's just plain wrong!"

Anna has always deplored this sort of thing. Wade, too, of course. Grade fixing! Some teachers offer bonus points if the students show up on Fridays wearing the school colors or if they attend certain extracurricular events, so it's not just Mrs. Stanley. But she's especially notorious. During the time Mary Beth took Spanish, Mrs. Stanley's church was sponsoring a food drive for the needy, so she set out a giant cardboard box with the promise that contributions would cancel out uncompleted assignments. With Jonathan's class, she had a campaign going for soup-can labels. "I just don't understand," says Anna, as Todd jabs a knife down through his apple, intent on slathering the two halves with the peanut butter. "How can a teacher of her ilk hang onto her self-esteem? Can't she see she's a discredit to the profession?"

"She's an old bat, Ma."

"Well, I don't know about *that*. 'Old bat,' that's not very respectful."

Tsk-tsking, she drops the Peter Pan's oily moon of foil and the twistie from the apple bag into the waste can in the cupboard under the sink and bangs shut the door. After pondering briefly, she swings it back open. Todd wouldn't try to earn himself a fudged grade, surely not. Still, what if it's a temptation? Bent in front of the waste can in such a way as to block his view, she picks through for the long paper tail of grocery prices and, pinch, pinch, pinch, reduces it to nibbles.

Flushed from her efforts, she warns, "I don't ever want to see you get-

ting snookered into one of those schemes. Always, *always* cherish your intellectual integrity. It's just not right, defrauding the system like that. Cooking the books, or whatever you call it." He nods affably as he takes an
enormous chunk out of his apple and she adds, "Maybe Mrs. Stanley just
thinks she's extending mercy. But how's it merciful to let students get away
with a minimum of learning? They'll find themselves at a terrible disadvan-
tage once they're out in the real world. Huh, tactics like hers just provide a
false sense of security. She's fooling people into believing in cheap grace. Actually, there's no such thing. Cheap grace!"

He bites off another chunk, and through a mouthful of mush he says,
"Preach it, lady."

He steps around her to knee-up his backpack onto a dining-table chair,
and she says, "Wait, wait. Can you move to the other table? I need to take
care of the wash—would you mind bringing it in for me?" Everything
promptly froze to the lines yesterday afternoon; she had to keep running
back into the mudroom to blow on her fingers. Now, beaten dry by the
wind, the clothes will come in redolent of chimney smoke and that sharp,
high, mossy scent of raw air. "Oh, never mind," she says hurriedly. It looks
like he's brought home most of the books in his locker. "You're saddled to
the gills with homework—I'll go out."

So a short while later, back in the warm environs, her basket balanced
across two chairs, she's busily sorting and folding. The bath towels, weather-
drubbed and plump, and washcloths and dish towels, she stacks according
to their kind in satisfying, squared-off towers. Next she smooths the handkerchiefs and orders them into spruce parcels. After those, it's Wade's undershorts. Methodically she configures each to the bureau-drawer
specifications, once over, twice over. She quarters another pair, and another,
and another. The thin blue lines on the elastics remind her of the racing-
lane dividers on the high school's sports track. The fancy designing is supposed to alert the wearer to his creeping corpulence? To his need to jog it off
instead of grow a worse paunch and turn into a Frank or Herbie? Why do
people let themselves go? Thank goodness these 34-36s of Wade's practically hang off him.

Doing the 30-32s, Todd's, she cues in to his mumbling. Propped on his
forearms over his Spanish book, his clavicles jutting out like coat hangers,
he's rehearsing his vocabulary words. "C-a-m-b-i-a-r. D-a-ñ-a-d-o, d-a-ñ-a-
d-a. T-o-d-a-v-í-a." The buzzy back hairs on his head are almost close
enough to the lamp to spark from the heat. "L-a l-l-e-g-a-d-o. D-e t-o-d-o-s
m-o-d-o-s." The way he's bellied klutzily across the back of the blue-painted

chair, rocking it on its rear legs, the tense shapes of his wallet and box of Tic-Tac mints in his hip pocket are protruding like unfortunate deformities. Why can't he just sit down?

"E-l b-a-r-r-i-o." She pulls from the wash heap her white cotton bras, puritanical no-bones affairs, and pats them into halves. "V-a-l-i-o-s-o, v-a-l-i-o-s-a. P-e-r-d-o-n-e." Next, the schmaltzy black number given to her by Wade at Christmas. She disentangles the skinny satin straps, nests the lace cups like soup bowls, slips the back bands under. "R-i-c-o, r-i-c-a. D-o-l-o-r-o-s-o, d-o-l-o-r-o-s-a." But the bra with flowers, spattered pansies, can't be folded due to the underwires. "E-v-i-t-a-r." To be truthful, underwire bras give her the willies. "Those stays?" she asked Mary Beth once. "In a car accident couldn't a pointy end twist cockeyed and punch through the person's sternum?" Mary Beth let out an imitation shriek. "Yay, punched lungs!" She twirled her finger in the air and tapped her head to signify the idiocy. "Mo-o-om."

"C-a-l-i-e-n-t-e," Anna catches, starting in on her panties, high-rise ones she shouldn't have bought, inclined to bag out behind like balloons. "D-e-s-a-g-r-a-d-a-b-l-e. C-o-n c-u-i-d-a-d-o. P-o-c-o d-e-s-p-u-é-s. P-r-o-n-t-o. M-u-c-h-í-s-i-m-o." She pancakes the undies atop her bras. "A-h-o-r-r-a-r," Todd concludes, and he lets out a noisy spew of breath exhaust, *fffff.*

"Quiz me on some, Ma."

"Want me to? Sure. Give me your book."

She calls out the words' definitions, allowing time for his pencil scritching. "Upset." *Molesto, molesta.* "To suppose." *Suponer.* "Tour." *La excursión.* The undershirts she's attending to now, Wade's, appear to be stricken with liver failure. They're about jaundiced enough in the pits to be chucked. "For example." *Por ejemplo.* "With pleasure." *Con gusto.*

The T-shirts, though, can still boast their health. She folds a favorite of Wade's displaying the periodic table, and another that touts, "Teachers Have Class." One of Todd's has the famous, round face of Gandhi printed on in purple and his list of seven deadly sins. Todd's red one reads "Evolve, Don't Replicate," and depicts a scabrous lizard with paddleball eyes. "Tomorrow," she enunciates. *Mañana.* "Suitcase." *La maleta.*

She matches up the athletic socks belonging to Todd, fagged crew-tops in need of suspenders. "When." *Cuando.* "Information." *Los informes.* Last she mates Wade's more upstanding dress pairs, their ribs still sucked in. "To understand." *Comprender.* "Incluso." *Even.* "Reason." *La razón.*

"Check everything," she says, handing back the book. "See if you passed."

Into the basket she bundles her items for their ride upstairs, all but the dish towels, and moving over to take a look for herself, she pokes her snout within close range of Todd's paper. *La razon,* he's written. "Hey," she pounces, "huh-uh-uh. Ra-ZON. You're supposed to have an accent above the *o.* Don't you dare tell me Mrs. Stanley would let you get away with that."

"Naw. I just forgot."

"I sure hope so."

"If we skip a mark she takes off points."

"Then she's not doing everything wrong. She's at least that strict." In an amiable manner Anna tweaks her son's ear. "You know yourself how it is. With language, if it's not right, it's wrong. You have to get every jot and tit-tle, be so, so, so—"

"Every what?"

"You have to cross your i's, dot your t's. Be precise."

"Ma-a-a."

"What? What did I say? Oops—cross your t's, dot your i's." She tacks on, more to herself, "Oh my. That story of mine."

"Story?"

Snagged by an unexpected thought, she doesn't respond immediately. She stands there squeezing her lips and unsqueezing them. "Why, one up in my box. One of my tenth-grade masterpieces I've never before offered up for human consumption." She clucks quietly. "I guess I should get it." Her arms wrap around the wash basket. "But maybe it's too bonkers to use."

Upstairs in the hall she parks her load, for the meantime, and steadied on the wicker stool, gray fluff wafting down from the drafty insulation-fringed hole in the ceiling, she forages for her item. Hm. She pudges up her eyebrows at the story's title. The *l* is so smeared, anybody else would take it for a lower-case *i* and read the word as *titties.*

For a quiet few minutes she squints over her prose—her smudgy, ob-noxious underlines, garbled incidentals, and hashed logic.

Jots and Tittles

Paragraphs again, yippee, because Annie liked doing paragraphs, she did. Once Miss Barrick had read in front of the whole eighth grade Annie's about what to do when the boy doesn't like you back but she went in after school and cried in front of her and now they had an understanding, Miss Barrick knew to respect her confidences. She licked her pencil and made ready now. They were done with the Aesop fable in their book about the boy who cried wolf so Miss Barrick put on the blackboard, Why Honesty Is Important.

The other students around were rustling around and this boy in front of her was digging for ear wax, the worst habit, and Annie said in her head, Okay, get going. She wrote down <u>Jots and Tittles</u>. You didn't really need a headline for a plain paragraph but Jots and Tittles, wasn't that a socker? This was the small exact things in the Bible laws.

<u>Here are some rules I could suggest</u>, she put. <u>First, every little teasing thing is not a lie. My sister Margie and I used to like petunia crackers. When we said yum! we just meant the make-believe tea party kind of yum. We didn't mean hardy and nourishing</u>. They didn't eat the leaves. Just the petunia part, they put it in between two saltines like a sandwich and there wasn't much of a taste, just a fluttery something mixing in with the cracker chew-up. What their playmate Wanda'd said in Sunday school though, her kind of teasing, that was wrong. Annie'd seen her eating the Sunday school paste out of the jar and said, "Ick. Paste is made out of horse hoofs. You could get sick." Wanda'd said, "Leastaways I don't eat petunias like these two girls I know." The Sunday school teacher, Mrs. Wert, burst out laughing, she was picturing Annie and Margie as petunia eaters but they'd never ate petunias plain, Wanda made it sound like petunias plain.

<u>Number two</u>, she wrote. <u>The whole truth doesn't always show, but if it's not on purpose then it isn't the person's fault, something bad they did. Like, in my school picture can you see the back of my head? No. But it's not like I'm dressed worldly</u>. Same way with the Bible school pictures. Every year, the last day of Bible school everybody jam piled along the curb for a picture. The way it turned out you could hardly see the children in the back row but they were all there, weren't they? You couldn't see Raymie Egger's shoelaces were untied and going down the sewer grate, neither. The ladies that came over from the Waterbury and Jackson churches to help out were missing their one arm, just the lonely half of their pair was crooking in a pose and the sleeve was creasing at the elbow joint. Not true though! You couldn't see their bun neither and maybe not even a scrimp of their prayer cap, so were they some kind of worldly Evangelical Brethren offshoots? No.

<u>The third thing is, probly it's not wrong if the person is ignorant and it would be too hard to explain the exact truth and so you don't. We know a blind and deaf man named Clyde Bailey. He has my mother's name wrong. When he says, "Myra, is that you Myra,"</u> she

motions his hand up and down. Up and down is supposed to mean yes, and how is she Myra? But she's not wanting to slighten his feelings. Anyhow, if Mama ever tried to straighten Clyde out and re-spelled it M-Y-R-N-A, Clyde might butt in before she got to N. He might say, "Heh heh Myra, I knowed it was you already."

Fourthly, if somebody asks you something and it's too embarrassing you don't have to exactly answer. This isn't lying, not answering. Or anyhow I should say I hope not because that's what I did. A couple summers before over carnival time this neighbor boy Teddy from down the street was going by eating his wiener and watching her and Herbie in the yard catching lightning bugs. "Hey yous," he said, "you want my wiener?" She said, "Herbie, you want some of Teddy's wiener?" She never said yes or no herself. But Herbie ran up and snitched it and gobbled it up. She was planning she'd bring it in the house so number one, she could chop off the end that had Teddy's germs, and number two, she and Herbie could share. She thought she'd get a taste at least, it was in a paper boat and had mustard on. Imagine somebody just throwing away their wiener.

Lastly this. Pretending isn't bad except if you're trying to convince yourself and then after awhile you can't tell what's the truth anymore. She'd done something awful gullible when she was still a pigtailed girl of eight years of age. Mrs. Overholt had given Mama some peewee eggs from her pullet hens, no-yolkers, for angel food cake, but playing house one day Margie and Annie asked could they have them. Mama said yes and mashing them up on a concrete block out in the yard Annie got it in her head that the goopy gunk might turn into bubble gum if she'd let it sit. She'd been hankering and hankering for some that tasted better than Wanda's already been chewed variety. With this fanciful desire stirring in her she laid the goop on a board and all afternoon she let it to the mercy of the sun beating down. Ha ha. Did it gum up? Change its constitution? Ha ha.

Well you can see how the jots and tittles are crucial, she wrote. These are just some samples.

Uh-oh, on Monday when Miss Barrick distributed back the paragraphs Annie almost fell out of her desk. D, she'd never got a D. Here's what Miss Barrick had put, "Next time, Annie, heed the assignment. I didn't assign 'Extenuating Circumstances' or 'Shaving It Close.'" Whatever that meant. Annie must of mistook the topic. Honesty, right? What could she even say? Miss Barrick, I, I, I? Try and excuse herself for her poor feeble handiwork, no, so before Mr. Plugged Ears could turn around and act nosy she folded it up till it was enough scrinched to save in her diary.

But with that diary long departed, her ruination of a treatise—except for here—is lost to history. Anna wishes she could see the teacher's corrections.

Lagging, still distracted, she places the story by the stairs and returns the box to its cubbyhole. Trudging in and out of the bedrooms and bathroom with her laundry basket, putting the wash away, she hearkens back to the muffly, cloistered nook at the mission where she produced her adventure series for Miss Fritz. Up in the second-floor Bible school room above the chapel, wires were crisscrossed overhead like tic-tac-toe lines, strung with old blankets for partitioning off the different grades, and for two weeks in the summer, the room was a hive of industry. The drawn curtains shielded flannelgraph boards, boxes of supplies, and small clutches of squirmy children—any late-arrivers had to find their way up the back stairs behind the men's anteroom, creep along until they reached the familiar voices of their class, and grope amid the folds of bedding for an opening. But the rest of the year, the compartments stood hushed and stuffy and forsaken.

"You want to do what?" Daddy asked. "Take the typewriter over there?"

"Just sometimes. If you don't care." And thus equipped, deep in the innards of the room, saddled up to a table, she parsed out her plots and plunk-plunked away, advancing at poky-pecky speed. *But Herbie ran up and snitched it and gobbled it up.* "Gobbled" seemed an especially juicy vocabulary choice, each letter honking like a turkey, *g* (honk), *o* (honk), *b* (honk), and lofting into the hemming-in blanket and plunging head over heels down onto the table, outwitted.

That bubble gum recipe, though. Humph. Anna bumps her wash basket against her bedroom doorway but reroutes herself. *Pretending isn't bad except if you're trying to convince yourself and then after awhile you can't tell what's the truth anymore.* Is belief nothing more than pretending? No, but faith—Abraham's kind of faith—and Elijah's when he took on the prophets of Baal—demands of the believer an unwavering determination. Mired as she is, where's her conviction and trust? Pursuing this question, she makes an unstable attempt to deliver to the dresser drawer the too-high pile of pristine hankies, and it collapses and they pelt silently onto the bedroom floor. Trust in *what*, even, she can scarcely say anymore.

24

Mm, not a plastic cow. The fumes—mercy. What about—um—how about the little insignia doohickamajiggy, USDA CHOICE, SATISFACTION GUARANTEED, in this ad for sirloin tips in Pantry Pride's circular? Clip it to use instead? Okay. Now what else? Mm, a hot pad. Well, this old ratty thing should do—nobody will see the grunge. Then a cake tin, too—hm, get one all blacked up? Well, here's the aluminum pan Wade brought home from school—it still contained half the pie, lemon meringue—no one in the teachers' lounge wanted to finish it off and he fed it to the chickens. Is this too flimsy? No, probably not. Now, the alcohol. Maybe keep it in the bottle if there's a usable screw-on cap? Sure enough, that will work. And then matches, of course. And the brown sugar—let's see, let's see—maybe just take a whole bagful—

"Bye, Ma," calls Todd. "Dad, I'm off."

"You're picking up Marvin?" says Wade. "Are you taking anybody else?" Saturday nights when Conoy High's basketball team, the Cyclones, has a home game, sometimes Natasha and Nicole beg a ride too, or others in the youth group. "Fill up on gas while you're in town, all right?"

"Will do. It's just Marvin and me."

"Have fun!" She waves Todd out the door. "See you! Bye!" But the sugar is still uppermost in her mind. Why bother with a measuring cup? Why not just dump a few lumps into the pan?

Okey-dokey, she tells herself, some ought to be up here in the cupboard, behind the bags of confectioner's sugar. She roots around. "Hey! The brown sugar—where's the brown sugar? I didn't know we're out! Hey, wait wait!"

She flaps out the sidewalk in Wade's slippers, no coat, waving wildly at the car starting to coast down the drive. "Stop! Stop!" Todd brakes, and she knocks on the car window, gets him to roll it down. Dancing in the cold, hugging her arms, she beseeches, "Brown sugar! I need brown sugar! After the game can you stop at Pantry Pride? Please?"

"Sure. If I remember."

"Except—no, wait!" By now her teeth are chattering and the harsh cold of the driveway gravel is knobbing up through her slippers' soles. She gazes at the path illumined by the headlights. "I have a better idea. Stones. I'll just use stones. Never mind, okay?"

"Whatever, Ma. Whatever you want."

The taillights wink redly, marking his pause at the driveway's end, and the pebbles chunk against the wheel wells as he vaults out onto the road.

BUT DO THINGS ever go as planned? Ever? Fittingly, the Sunday-morning scene with the children up front for story time, before Scott's sermon, commences on a shaky note. Feeble green-infused light slants through the sanctuary's side windows, and the fractured-cross window's rays create bare, green glimmers. The long-legged candles, congealed and indifferent, lend only a token ambience; but faint suggestions of warmth emanate off the palm plants that flank the candles, the silken fronds powdered with scatter-shot motes of yellow hitting down from the rafter's tilted-just-so spotlights. At the side of the pulpit, Anna is posed primly with the cluster of youngsters, her gored black velveteen skirt lapping around her ankles and cloppy clogs, and out across the sanctuary the necks of the congregants stretch and crane as she rustles her still-unopened grocery bag. But the certain fate of her paper stand-in for the toy cow has temporarily receded in her mind, as well as the dramatic subtleties of her Bible story's theology, because her pantyhose feels too cinchy and twisty around her tremulous upper thighs.

AFTER CHURCH she joins her husband and son in the car, unloads herself of her storyteller appurtenances and her black Goodwill handbag, and expels a loud, flustered sigh.

"Oh me. Did it again. One more fiasco."

"Not really," says Wade. "The pyrotechnics were entertaining."

"That leak, at first I couldn't think how to proceed, other than to maybe warn everybody to stop, drop, and roll."

Wade's keys bang in surprise against the dashboard instead of locating the ignition, and Todd says, "Ma-a, what for? Aluminum doesn't leak."

"There was a nick. A big nick. I didn't see it in time."

She leans her head back, her eyes fluttering shut, and for a few racing seconds she lets the rest of the picture replay itself against her lids—more of the details: the grocery bag she'd brought along up front, squat and emptied; the children's faces before her, round blurs of curiosity; her strike-on-the-box matches ready on her lap while she drizzled the capfuls of alcohol over her mound of rocks in the pan and the scrap of advertisement and prattled on. "Nine. Ten. Eleven. Twelve. The-e-ere we go. I used my brother Wesley's cow when I told this story many years ago, so those children didn't have to rely quite so much on their imagination, did they? I pretended it was water in my jar and I had them close their eyes for Elijah's prayer, I didn't want them to spy my match, but that Benny, he peeked! Okay now, watch. I'm not Elijah, this isn't how he did it, oh no, but I don't think Pastor Scott wants real live fire coming down from heaven and engulfing our church." It wasn't until she dropped in the lit match that she realized.

"A nick," Wade is repeating. "What do you mean, Anna?"

"Just that. A cut." Where a scratch in the pan marked the journey of somebody's knife sawing down through the crust, she spied a half-inch gape. Oopsie. The next instant, a blue nebula of flame swayed across the moat around Elijah's altar and surged up the stones, as intended, and hot tongues began ragging and leaping along the pan's edge. But into her head sprang visions of the sogged hot pad igniting, and then the stiff green polypropylene fibers of the podium carpet, releasing a deadly vapor.

She blitzed around in her mind and glanced up frantically. Scott's glass of water stood on the pulpit ledge, placed there by the usher during the opening hymns. She bounded up to grab it, nearly stumbling over the cord of her clip-on mike. No, too piddling! She smacked the glass down and darted over to Wade sitting along the middle aisle. "Your jacket. Give me your jacket!"

"Anna." Uncertain, he unfolded his arms.

"Quick! Now!"

He was bent front slightly, his tie looping out from the buttoned-down, gaggy part of his shirt collar, and because he didn't respond further, she yanked on the tie and then yanked on the gray herringbone wool of his lapel. He shucked himself free. With the jacket wadded in her arms she raced front, snatched up the water glass again, and socked down next to the pie pan. "Whew! You never know!" She signaled to Scott watching from the front bench. "Pastor, as the children go back to their seats will you finish the story? Go, children. Off you go. Go, go, go." Swinging Wade's coat, she shooed, shooed.

"Yes indeed, folks," Scott was up now and moving forward, jovially rubbing his hands, "upon beholding that mighty demonstration of God's power, of fire striking from on high and consuming Elijah's sacrifice, the people bowed to the ground and in one accord made their confession. Can we take up their cry? 'The Lord he is God!'" He paddled at the air to coax forth more enthusiasm. "Again! 'The Lord he is God! The Lord he is God!' Amen, amen! When Elijah stepped out on faith, God provided. What a resounding confirmation! Would any person present that day, anybody who bore witness, ever slip back again into Baal worship? I daresay not! Those onlookers had tasted anew of the Lord's might. They'd tasted anew of the same victory and power and saving grace that God imparts today, to all who come under the blood, who turn over their lives and determine in their hearts to keep God God." Scott swiveled to face her. "That's one we'll not soon forget, Anna. Thank you." Hunched on the steps by her pie pan, the sweat spreading retroactively in two rings beneath her armpits, she managed an obedient, foolish smile.

Returned to her seat for the remainder of the service—Scott's sermon, sharing time, and the offering—with her paraphernalia inert where she'd left it, she sometimes jerked her eyes in that direction, as if the carpeting might spontaneously combust. A silly fear, sure. But scrambling for a contingency plan, was that so stupid? "What else could I do?" she asks, tight against the car door, as Wade swings out of the church parking lot. "I sure made a spectacle of myself."

"Nah, don't worry about it."

"You stole the show, Ma."

The blond hairs on his fist above the steering wheel spiking in the noontime sun, Wade moseys them past the sign in front of Hamburger Heaven with the day's specials chalked on. They pass Twin Kiss's larger-than-life ripple cone peeling its paint, and the north-side-of-town houses, their shingles grayed with five-o'clock shadows of highway exhaust. At the stoplight he blinkers and turns onto the old bridge, and as the car thumps over the spacer cracks in the concrete and the oncoming traffic swooshes rhythmically by, she scowls out the window at nothing in particular, other than her ineptitude.

On Route 519 the fields slide past, patched with fading brown snow, and the staccato fence posts and the parcels of vast, bony woods. Todd taps her shoulder. "Wesley's cow? You said you used Wesley's cow. Did you mean a stuffed cow?"

"No, no. A puny little plastic thing. So my meltdown—I guess I fumigated everybody."

"The whole gosh-darn bull," Wade says to himself.

She gapes at him. "What?"

"Elijah's. Did he flay it first, do you suppose? The passage never says, does it?"

"Flay?"

"Skin it. For the Levitical burnt offerings sometimes the hide was given to the priest."

"How do you know that?"

He shrugs. "That messianic rabbi. According to him, for those sacrifices they burned everything but the hide. Burned the head, the guts, the fat, everything. But for sin offerings, only the fat."

"Oh-h-h. I forgot all about him. Justine's cousin's uncle-in-law or somebody? Tha-at's right." A convert from Judaism, he presided over a Seder meal at church, an elaborate, drawn-out affair. He brought along matzah and horseradish for the Seder plate and conducted the longsuffering Passover verses and prayers.

"Only the fat?" Todd echoes. "They wasted the rest of the carcass?"

"The priest used the blood, too." Wade looks over at Anna. "Hide or no hide? What do you think?"

"Hm."

Todd's kneecaps pummel at her back, through the car seat. "Ma, you should've had actual meat. Bacon. Or one of those Vienna sausages."

"That's an idea. Well, I was just trying to make a point."

"Not pig," says Wade. "No pork."

"Oh, right." Anna nods. "I didn't even think of that."

Relaxing, she frees the strands of hair caught in her neck scarf and jigs around to unbunch her coat under her legs and straighten her skirt. "Justine sure was upset during sharing time."

"I guess so."

"Has Frank ever talked about back trouble? Before now?"

"Don't know."

"A bad back—that's not very lucky."

She thinks about the ruddy, bobbing triangle of Frank's face in Sunday school this morning—the way it jutted out from his forward-sloping shoulders, above his barrel belly—and about his moist pink lips, set treacherously close to his chin. Except for a remark or two he stayed quiet in class. He wasn't his usual self, palsy-walsy and droll. Then upstairs in church, probably hurting, he had to latch onto the bench in front of him to heft himself off his duff. Even before the usher reached him with the roving mike, Justine's snuffles started up. She had a Kleenex pressed to her eyelids, and emotional splotches, almost the same crazy shade as her hair, were coating her neck.

"I got awake Tuesday morning around four o'clock with terrible pain in my back." Frank sounded grainy, worn out. "Couldn't even get out of bed. Couldn't move. Justine had to bring me some 600-milligram Ibuprofen. The MRI showed no evidence of prolapse. Maybe dehydration at the D8-9 disc, but that's to be expected at this stage of the game—anybody my age. So why an attack like that, I dunno. I'm not so bad now, but the doc says I must stay on the Ibuprofen to counter any inflammation. If there's a repeat attack he'll order a myelogram for a better look at my spine."

Frank's stomach draped over the bench gave a twitch, Anna remembers, and his voice broke. "The doc talked about surgery. I dread going under the knife, but if that's what the Lord wills, so be it. In the meantime Justine and I earnestly covet your prayers."

Scott had been jotting down the praise reports and concerns. Hallelujah to Jesus for sparing Tom Hurst's life when his car hood flew up while he was in the passing lane on the interstate, allowing him to see in front of him only a wall of metal decorated with the tiny Chrysler emblem. Thank the Lord for the recent conversion of Clement Finkbinder, Birdie's nephew. Hooray to Stacey Rhodes for placing first in the botany division in the eighth-grade science fair for her project on aphids. Commit to the Lord Dottie Miller's pulmonary embolism—for the sake of her relative in Nebraska in critical condition, Susan had waved a sign-up sheet with 15-minute prayer slots, 6:45–7:00 a.m., 7:00–7:15, 7:15–7:30, on around the clock. The pastor planned to mention all these specified needs in his lengthy sharing-time prayer, but as Frank spoke and Justine's sobbing intensified, their misery took hold of Scott and he dropped his pen. "My brother, I'd like to offer up a special word on your behalf. Can we gather around, folks, and together approach the throne of grace?"

Different people were already jumping up, collecting. "Are you coming?" Anna whispered to Wade. "Come on." They joined the swarm—

Susan and Jack, Rhodeses, Kings, Hursts, and others, even Brenda Arnold—congesting around the Beckers, each gripping another's suit shoulder or sleeve.

Scott let out all the stops, then. "Oh, for Your healing power, kind heavenly Father! Oh, that You would spare Frank the scalpel!" *Yes Lord. Yes Lord.* "Oh, that You and You alone would cure his impairment!" *Yes, yes, heavenly Father.* "Oh, that You would restore him to full and complete health!" *Grant a healing, oh Lord, oh yes Lord, amen, amen.* "Oh, that You would bind up any and all afflictions and work a work in his life!" *Thank you Lord, thank you Lord, thank you Lord, yes, yes, yes, thank you Jesus.* Each fresh burst of fervor from Scott got borne along by everybody's under-the-breath refrains.

In the car, remembering Justine's smeared mascara and Frank's hopeful, loud amens, Anna twiddles again with her skirt and smooths the velvety nap. She tries not to picture any philanderer scenarios. It's often a struggle, keeping a lid on her imagination. "I guess," she says hesitantly, "somebody beefy like him should try to lose weight."

"Frank's a regular blimp," says Todd. "That much baggage, it's no wonder his spine is out of whack."

"I just meant, he's—you know, heavy. Don't be unkind."

"Can't he help it?"

"There could be a glandular problem." She ponders. "He might be a good candidate for one of those gastric overpass operations where they clamp the person's stomach."

"Bypass," says Wade. "Gastric bypass."

Todd says, "If he'd go for liposuction surgery they'd take out the fat by the bucketful."

"Oh hon," she chides.

"Fat like Frank's," sniggers Todd, "adipose tissue as high as his in triglycerides, would've outclassed a bull's. Frank's pot gut on the altar—ha ha." At this, Anna's eyes pop out like Martian saucers and her hands shoot up to protect her titillated, tingling ears.

25

Typically, Saturday morning allows Anna a reprieve of sorts. Instead of the bed jolting cruelly in the pitch blackness when Wade lunges for the clock to punch the alarm dead, consciousness comes creeping in stages easily borne. While she quiescently zones in and out, the room lightens by shades—the windows take shape as the sky blooms peach pink—and beneath the tangle of bedding her husband groans in contentment, rubs his hairy belly, pulls his lumped pillow closer to hers, and wraps around her again. The day doesn't break shatteringly.

This Saturday though, the clangor intrudes at the usual wretched school-day hour, 5:30. The vague outlines of her dream brusquely disintegrate and scatter when he thrashes up from oblivion. She claws confusedly at the inky air, rakes his arm, and flops back in disappointment. How could've he neglected to unset the alarm?

"Sorry," he rasps, his cranky back to her. Legs swung over the bed's edge, he scratches at his groin whiskers. In the morose, gusty darkness, the front yard sugar maple's branch stretching over the porch roof grazes the window and taunts. To atone for himself he adds, "I'll bring your coffee. First I'll light the fire and mark those papers I didn't get to last night and see to the chickens."

The dresser drawer squeaks, giving up a pair of undershorts. She hears his jeans whump upwards, the clink of his belt buckle, the door to the hall wedging softly shut—he must've folded a hanky and stuck it in the crack, because without something stuffed there, the broken latch of the door allows it to drift back open. Sneaky footsteps sound on the stairs. Kindling twigs snap, and a log thumps into the wood stove. Then she hears the radio—can't he turn it down a little lower?

She sleeps, though. When sounds hit again—Wade's anklebones popping in the hall, and his wake-up whistle to Todd—the brazen sunshine is flooding in. The bedroom door gives at his kick, and beneath her lids the bold blue of her Christmas coffee mug registers.

Dopey, blinking, she strains for her nightie flung over the iron headrail, while he makes space on the night table for the coffee and his *Conoy Gazette* and bowl of raisin bran he's brought along and throws the blanket off the bedside chair for a place to camp. Once she's decent, she settles the bed pillows behind her back, bolstered with the blanket, and takes up her hot toddy. "Um," she croaks, the first swallow wondrously scorching her passages, "Daddy's Bible. I need that, too—I'm still reading in his. Do you mind? It's downstairs by the sofa."

"How about mine?" Wade's spoon clangs. Cereal bowl at a chancy angle, he digs beneath the library books on the night table's lower shelf for his NIV. "Where is it? I thought I had it up here."

"Under the bed, maybe? Ooh, watch it! Don't spill."

From the depths comes, "Anna, there must be ten *Newsweeks* here."

"Oh, I know. I'm so behind." *And so tied up,* she doesn't say. Though maybe the opposite is truer. *So untied up. The worst kind of drifter.*

"Aha, found it." He drops the Bible on her lap, sits back with an oldie magazine rather than the newspaper, and resumes his breakfast.

"My, you're sweet," she says, squelching a giggle—the coffee taking effect. He's usually opposed to eating anywhere other than smack up against the table. "You didn't have to bring your food upstairs just to be sociable."

"I was hoping to salvage the morning, reinstate myself in your favor."

"Oh you."

She has often despaired at his habit of stuffing his Bible with unrelated information, and it's no surprise now to find a scoring grid for a long-ago biology test bookmarking a spot in Genesis. But she cocks her head at the block of verses underlined emphatically with teacher-pen red. "You sure clobbered things, here."

"What? Oh, yeah. Sometimes I use that story to introduce the genetics unit—Mendel's experiments with peas and dominant and recessive genes, and the resultant work on sex linkage, hereditary factors, chromosomal transmission. It makes a pretty good lead-in."

She skims the familiar passage about Jacob's gambit with the cattle he's herding for his father-in-law, Laban. Granted permission to cull any imperfect newborn goats and add them to his own flock, Jacob places in the adult goats' watering troughs some tree branches with sections of the bark peeled off, in the hope that the animals mating in front of the troughs will bear mottled offspring. The nannies produce lots of streaked, speckled, and spotted kids, sure enough, which boosts his take; but it's not because of his branch tricks. "'Streaked,' hm," says Anna quietly. "Doesn't it say 'ringstraked' in the King James? I think so. Why'd the translators make that change, I wonder? 'Ringstraked' is better, if you ask me. More pocked sounding."

She pushes back her frowzy hair. "So what do the students say?"

"About the story? They're amused. I'm just sparking interest in the subject—the Bible isn't supposed to be a science book."

"But then don't they look at Jacob with ridicule? Doesn't it seem like you're ridiculing?"

"No, not really."

She'd best get busy. Onward and upward! Often she fights a temptation to shirk on her devotions, plus a rattledness takes over, much as when she's writing. Maybe because she's acting under obligation, she must continually gurgitate and regurgitate the sentences to derive every last modicum of essence. But is this any excuse? The Bible is slip-sliding off her legs and she makes a grab for it, pulls her knees up to her chest, arranges her nightie to stretch leotard-like over their cauliflower knobbiness, draws up the quilt, and rests the book. All right, maybe this next chapter in Genesis will do. Fifty-five verses, though. Well, okay. That's not overly overly long.

Reading, she peruses the lines again and again, her ocular muscles as nervous and jumpy as rabbits. In this part of the saga, Genesis 31, Jacob secretly flees with his accumulated wives, children, and herds, but Laban takes chase, and when he catches up to the caravan he accuses Jacob of filching the household gods. Unaware of the theft, Jacob tells Laban to search everybody's tents. Wade's page cracklings are distracting Anna and she must apply herself mightily to shut them out and stay on track. A sudden twist of thought, though, brings her to a stop. "Huh. Would Scott dare to read this out loud? Over the pulpit?"

"Mm?" Wade is engrossed in his *Newsweek*.

"Here where Laban is all wrought up about his idols? He gets to

Rachel's tent—she's in there sitting on her camel's saddle, you know, where she's hidden them—and she claims she can't stand up because of her period. 'I'm having my period,' she says here. Period! I can't see Scott reading that."

"Mm."

"How's it stated in the King James? 'The curse of women is upon me,' something along that line. Not 'I'm menstruating.' Nothing that blunt."

"Aren't you dawdling, Anna?"

"Dwaddling? Oh dear, I guess I am. Sorry."

"No, dawdling. It's not 'dwaddling.'"

"It is too."

"No."

"Yes. I heard that word all the time, growing up. Mama would go, 'Now girls, no dwaddling.'"

"No, Anna."

"But—but—" She holds her tongue, just sends him a look. "Okay then. You want me to prove it? You want to see for yourself?" With that her legs slide flat, collapsing her bedclothes teepee, and she skids down from the bed and pads off.

"Aren't you up yet?" she calls to Todd, dragging the wicker stool from the bathroom. She yawns open the ceiling-hole board in the hall and smashes around in the box for her story. Wade can just quit his scoffing. Back in the bedroom, she says, "You never believe me, do you? You always assume I'm mistaken. Meanwhile you're the world's foremost expert. Okay, so I'm exaggerating, but you ought to have enough common sense to realize that once in a while I could use somebody in the peanut gallery rooting me on. Just once in a while!" Peevishly she thrusts her story at him. "It's puerile, I know, but I don't care. Go ahead, read it. Dwaddle! I should know what I'm talking about!"

How Many Pork-n-beans

Mama had her finger at 1 Thessalonians 5:17, same place Preacher Yoder was, but second grade age Annie just watched his spit come flying out. Mama'd fixed him a cot up in the Bible school room so he could stay all through Bible conference, she'd given him the goose pillow and her best seersucker spread. "Thus we pray without seizing," he hollered out. "In prayerful submission must we await the resurrection, but by setting our minds on our Lawd's return may we speed the day. Even so come, Lawd Jaysus. Can I hear an amen to that, brethern and sistern? Amen."

Next he wanted a Timothy verse, 1 Timothy 2:8, and she budged against Mama to read herself about men lifting up their holy hands to pray instead of raging in a fury and doubting. He hollered, "Only in holiness and surrender, my brethern, doth we beseech the Lawd to hasten the day. Amen amen."

Then something in the next verse fooled her good, verse 9, not where the preacher was. "Mama," she whispered, "you think that means if you're a grown lady? Pigtails aren't wrong if you're still little, are they?"

"Shh. What? Pigtails?" said Mama, and Annie said, "Right there, that part about no braided hair or gold or pearls."

"No, broided," said Mama. "See the o letter? Sort of like embroidered, in Bible times rich ladies wove ribbons and jewels through their hair to look all queenly and haughty. Shh now, pay attention."

She did because there was more spit juice and when he re-mindered how the clouds would part for the Lord at the last trump and the dead would rise in the air and the elect still on earth, Annie made in her head like the dust-to-dusted Evangelical Brethren's ghostly skin and bones were knitting together and whizzing up through the coffin lids, and like the living were joining up too, not their clothes though, dropped off and left in forgotten little piles on the grass, their girdles and slips and their underarm sweat shields like what Mrs. Overholt pinned in her sleeves. But the preaching went longer and longer and she had to go to the bathroom.

She'd never took a shine to the one out in the ladies' anteroom because a PU smell came up the pipe and the commode ran and ran till somebody jiggled the handle, she'd always go over to the kitchen and go in the pantry under the stairs that had a commode back at the end where the ceiling slanted down, a handy dandy place to sit and hum Bible school songs like "I Will Make You Fishers of Men" and "Deep and Wide" or check the stockpiles of cans Mama got on special or read the Egbert's Cleaner bottle and toilet paper wrappers or play she was blowing the hugest whopper in a bubble gum contest. "I have to go to the bathroom," she whispered. Mama said, "All right but hurry back, don't dwaddle."

But when she got back Preacher Yoder was dabbing up his fore-head sweat in conclusion and talking low like. He was saying low, "I sense tonight a special need among us and would appreciate if our song leader could lead us in a hymn of invitation as we come before the Lawd and seek His will."

"Five hunnert sixty-six," Mr. Wert said, "five, six, six, 'Just As I Am.'" He blew the pitch and got going and over the singing Preacher Yoder asked, "My brethern and sistern, is Jaysus knocking at your heart's door? Won't you leave your heavy burden at the cross?" Somebody in the back, their sad wails were starting up and he started reading out of 2 Timothy 3 about the wages of sin and the last purilous days when men would be covachewus, boasters, proud, false accusers, blasphemers, incontinent, and disobeejent to parents.

That one, disobeejent to parents, his eyes dug into Annie and she felt like he could tell her heart about jumped out her throat. Mama's trilly alto was going up and down the song notes and Annie'd been trying to copycat but now she was too choked. All of a sudden the preacher hollered, "I see you sister, yes yes, God bless you," and Mama turned half around and then glanced down at her girl and saw the teardrops rolling down. "Annie, what's the matter Annie?" she said and then's when Annie put her hand up, stuck it up.

After church he said, "Come along, come along," and he had her and the neighbor lady Agnes Retzlaff kneel down by the couch with their heads pushing in the cushions while he led in a word of prayer. "Thankee thankee dear Lawd for the cleansing blood of Jaysus. Thankee thankee Lawd. Thankee thankee. Thankee thankee Lawd for bringing our sister Agnes to a saving knowledge of Thee and thankee thankee for the contrite spirit of this young child, tender and sensitive to Thy leading." Agnes was helping out with little yelps.

Then she went home and he took himself upstairs and Daddy and Mama came to Annie on the couch. "Well well well," said Daddy, "you let Jesus into your heart."

"I was counting the cans," she said, "one pork-n-beans, two pork-n-beans, three pork-n-beans, four pork-n-beans, and seeing how to sanitize bedpans right and playing binoculars with the toilet paper cardboard, dwaddling like that."

"Annie, what?" said Mama.

"Disobedient, he said, and pointed his snozzer right at me."

"At you?" said a flabbergasted Mama. "What? No, he was looking at me, he was concerned about Agnes, he wanted me to move back and lay hands on her."

Mama said to Daddy, "And here I always bemoaned her stony heart, I thought she'd never darken the church door." Agnes lived two blocks down from the mission by herself but not like a recluse hermit, she kept her front room blinds pulled down the whole sufferable summer and covered up the furniture with sheets. Whatever she was saving it up for. Anytime Mama and Daddy paid a call, "Why, if it isn't Reverend Farber," she'd say like a good token Christian, and go and get her peanut butter fudge and serve it up on a big glass cake plate. So Mama'd took the politeness as, thanks but no thanks. Wrongly. And herself, Annie'd jumped to conclusions again like with the braids, leaped before she looked right. She was still saved, right? By hook or by crook.

At the end, finished reading, Wade fails to conceal a horse whinny. She lets it pass, languidly nipping her tongue at a thread pulling loose from the binding of the quilt that now covers her all the way up to her neck. The Bible is back on her drawn-up knees, but part of the time he was reading, her head was in her plot. "You gave the man quite the vocabulary," he says. "But 'seizing'?"

"Uh-huh, grabbing. It did fit. No grabby prayers, no trying to sway the Lord."

"So a word is however you take it, Anna? That makes it the gospel truth?"

"What do you mean?"

"That's your pattern, you know."

"Wade!"

"You're too literal."

She gives a maniacal sputter. "'Literary,' I thought you were starting to say. I wish!"

He solidifies his jaw, grimaces the muscles. "How many of these minor epics did you produce?"

Anna doesn't answer. She's put the has-beens, those already entered on the computer, back in the attic. They're not in the Tingley box, just along-side it, protectively swaddled in the insulation. They'd been downstairs, mingled with her wreckage of other papers.

"Look," he says, "don't let me hassle you. All right?"

"Okay, if it's not dwaddle I apologize. But—well, even Shakespeare. Shakespeare is replete with misappropriations." Hurriedly she backpedals. "I mean, malapropisms. So nobody's perfect."

"It's not your malapropisms. They're not your downfall."

Wade rouses himself to leave. He reclaims his newspaper and tucks it underneath the *Newsweek*. "I'm still not done grading. And I've got to work on the Sunday school lesson."

"You're teaching Sunday school? When did Susan call?"

"A couple nights ago—I guess you were in the shower. Jack has a convention. She's going along."

"Where? Belmont again? That would be fun." Anna indulges in a small stab of envy. "Hotel buffets. Splurging at those cute boutiques."

"Nah. You'd find it entertaining for two minutes. Oh, shoot, I didn't let the chickens out."

This late, still jailed, they're probably frantic. They must be pecking claustrophobically on the coop windows, stirring up the nesty feathers-and-poop dust, scolding. Well, them instead of her, for a change. Let *them* feel skanky and heckled and at loose ends. She'll laze here in tranquility a bit longer. Alone, postponing taking up her mantle of responsibility, Anna indolently shlishes the Genesis page frontwards, flat, frontwards, flat, limping its starch. The pouring-in sun is scarcely fazed by the puddly, thin cotton curtains; even as she watches, the monkish, chaste old-plaster walls of the room take on a warmer cast and the nicks on the black-painted bars of the bed's foot rail grow softer and more quaint. She was so excited, acquiring this bed at Davy Jenkins's auction. Wade hauled it home in pieces and reassembled it, but when he went to lower their old bedsprings into place, it crashed down through—the side rails were too widely spaced. "What was wrong with our other bed?" he fumed. "Now we'll have that to get rid of." It was nearly midnight but he had to trot out to the garage to saw slats.

"I hope I'm not being too demanding," she said. "I just think it's so old-fashioned and beautiful." Well, it really is. Sometimes she's been right. Because the slats and the wooden blocks Wade put under the legs to prevent scratches on the floorboards jack up the mattress to an uncommon height, a person almost needs a stepladder, or a handicapped ramp.

The piles of laundry waiting downstairs in the mudroom cross Anna's mind. Shucks. Shilly-shallying, the fraying quilt grazing her chin, loath to lock her eyes in concentration, she steals a few guilty minutes more.

26

Searchingly Anna runs her thumbnail along the point of her chin, her expression anxious in the ladies' room mirror. "I have this one hair that keeps sprouting like a boar bristle," she murmurs. It can grow out a whole quarter-inch before she notices. Hm, no traceable tiny shaft, so she's good for now.

"Maybe a sow bristle," says Peg, done pinning her doily on and finger-fluffing her bangs. "Oh, pish! I didn't know I splattered stuff." Spots of donut grease from breakfast are parading up her mohair sweater set.

She douses a paper towel with soap from the dispenser, but Anna is sure any Band-Aid approach will prove futile. "See there? Some got on your skirt, too."

Panting, observing herself in the mirror grinding the paper towel across the worst spot, Peg grumbles, "Just look at me. Sag, sag. Talk about the belly of the whale."

"No. You're so perfect and skinny. *I'm* the dump." Anna turns to view the pouch of flab below her own waistband. Well, it's not Frank's lard. Maybe it's more like a scant two-cup measure of I Can't Believe It's Not Butter.

With a snort Peg directs her paper towel into the trash can. "What are women our age supposed to look like anyway? Mermaids? Would you believe my mom has gone back to wearing a girdle? Isn't that nuts? The bondage! Is she worried my dad might trade her in? Jay says I'm only getting better—bless his heart. As long as he's happy, huh?" She strikes a magazine-model pose with one leg splayed fetchingly, stretches out her stocking, and snaps it like silly putty. "Ooh la la!"

Suddenly giddy, Anna adds her laughter to Peg's rippling out the low door vent. "Age over beauty!" she bleats. "Yay for us!"

But when Peg sails into Sunday school ahead of her, speeds for the chair on Wade's right (leaving her with the only other empty one, halfway down the table on the opposite side), and bends in to give him and Nelson a hello and a sample of cleavage, Anna wonders if her friend is turning into a sleazeball.

"You've all studied the chapter in Romans, I hope," says Wade. "So first off, a quiz." He sits back with his notes, disregarding the general all-around groans. This is a favorite strategy of his when he teaches the class—a quiz. It's merely to get the ball rolling; the papers never get collected and scored. "The back of your bulletin will be fine. Everybody ready? Just one-word answers, please. Number one. True or false? 'I am justified, declared righteous.'"

On her paper Anna puts "true." Not that she's so confident. But righteous doesn't imply no sins ever. Justification isn't something a person particularly deserves.

"Number two. True or false? 'All people are justified.'"

Well, now. Anna doesn't know what to put down. Some people don't behave justifiably, for sure. Or, wait, that would be "defensibly," not "justifiably." At any rate, they don't notably demonstrate changed lives. So no, she can't answer with "true." But to say "false"? How would it be right to assign "false" for other people if she's put "true" for herself? Wouldn't this sound like she considers herself superior?

Uncertain, she lets number two blank.

"Number three," announces Wade. "True or false? 'I am reconciled to God.'"

Slowly, not with the rigor of a good student, Anna writes "true." Her choice seems devious, not reflective of her prevailing emotional state. Even now, her chest is seizing up.

"Number four. True or false? 'People can be justified without being reconciled.'"

Too bamboozled, she abandons the rules. *Huh??* she scribbles on her paper. *How?? How in the world would that be??*

Quiz completed, the class members' reactions come cropping up like interesting bouncy bubbles. "Listen, old pal," says Nelson, "justification and reconciliation and salvation aren't iffy guessing games. The answers are found right here in the Bible. Justification comes only through the blood of Christ."

"And first the person has to believe," says Donna, reasonably. "Believing is the important thing. Salvation hinges on belief. The Bible makes it clear that we're saved by our faith, not our works."

"Yes anyway," says Justine. "What would evangelists be for, otherwise? If people didn't need to get saved? What are missionaries for?"

"I wonder that myself," Wade says.

"You don't either," Justine retorts, shaking her red-thatched head.

Oh, come now, Anna wants to soothe, this wasn't a for-real exam.

Wade says, "Hold on, let me explain. Uh, how can I put this?" He hesitates, ticks his pen point in and out. "Didn't Jesus die for us all? While we were still sinners? Wasn't it sinners being justified? Hasn't Jesus' death on the cross made us worth something, no longer base and vile, and enabled us to come boldly to the throne of grace?"

Offhanded about it, he adds, "But even if people *don't* take that step? If we're insisting people must believe to be saved, that they must attest to a faith experience, then aren't we making belief and faith out to be works? I know, I know, this isn't what any of us grew up with—the idea that faith might be neither here nor there. But doesn't the usual theory strike you as somehow screwy?"

Somebody's gurgle of disapproval comes traveling down the table past Anna. Wade ignores it. "Personally," he says, "I have a hard time believing that all the unreached souls who've never heard the gospel are damned to hell."

"You mean—but if—" Peg is fluttering weakly, her smile frozen in place, not playful.

Wade shrugs and levers his great big elephant foot up across his knee. "Somewhere else in Romans, not here in chapter four, doesn't the apostle Paul say that the law and the knowledge of God are written on the hearts of people everywhere? That when anybody spurns God's law, naturally their conscience is pricked? They're ashamed, or fearful, and maybe they decide some sort of noble gesture will absolve them—some sacrificial deed. But it doesn't. The sins repeat. Paul also tells us that on our own we're hopeless and our righteousness is like filthy rags—that we're saved only by God's mercy."

"Still, we have to accept," blusters Nelson.

"Sure, we first ask and then accept," says Brenda.

"Wait," Wade says, "I'm not done. Follow me, here. Are you following? *Only by God's mercy.* Our attaching a qualifier, insisting that some performance on our part, some particular stated conviction, must precede forgiveness, just indicates that we're stuck in the old thought patterns—that we're acting on the same primal impulses as those of Cain and Abel and everybody else in the Old Testament who tried to curry God's favor by bringing sacrifices. We're 'in' because of what we believe? That's poppycock! It can't be people's *understanding* that entitles them."

"No," says Frank, "but the way you're talking, a person could get away with murder."

"No, that's not it at all. I'm saying that only God's love redeems us. Otherwise, we're creamed. Is it possible to rate the many different evils that might be entrapping us? Superciliousness, unbelief, ignorance, hatred, greed, lack of exposure to the gospel message—for which of these will we be damned? Where's the line?"

By now, quiet Donna has her Bible at the ready. "But what about Abraham in today's lesson? Here in verse three?" Softly she tappy-taps the page. "He believed God and that's what saved him."

"Abraham, yeah. Quite the geezer."

"Wa-ade," says Anna. Geezer? Was that necessary? Nobody's going to take it for a joke, given the set of his mouth and the ditches across his forehead, all the way to where the green would start if he had any hilltop foliage. His bald dome, the waxy sheen of sweat, is catching the wink, wink, wink of the overhead fluorescent tube. Apologize! she thinks. Don't be a turd!

But something on his mind seems to cohere, for suddenly, jig-a-lig, that shiftily, he's off on a new tangent. Another murky kettle of fish—oh please. Wait a minute! she silently demands. Slow down, Wade—explain! He's saying something about Abraham being the father of many nations. Saying that if Ishmael was in historical fact the firstborn son, then exactly which nation should've been designated the favored? That much she garners, but otherwise she's lost, seriously lost. Twitters and jibbers of dissent are rising up all around the table, but Anna feels like she's circling her arms in slow motion, straining against a muddy, noiseless, underwater current.

"Enough, enough." Nelson's commanding voice puts a stop to the flurry and catches up even Anna. "No question about it, the Jews are God's chosen people." Deliberately he zips open his own Bible and hunts down Donna's verse. "Furthermore, let me quote Romans 4:3 in its entirety. 'The

Scripture says, "Abraham believed God, and because of his faith God accepted him as righteous."' There you have it."

"Believed God how?" says Wade.

"Enough to obey," Nelson replies. "God said leave your country and go to a land I will show you, so Abraham went. Picked up and moved, pronto. He also relinquished his only son."

"Not his only one," says Wade.

"His promised son. Not the illegitimate one."

"No use for the bastard, you guess?" Wade tilts himself back, at a precarious incline. "Do you ever pity Hagar for her pawn role? What do you make of that wrinkle in the plot, anyway? God promising a son to Abraham and Sara, but Abraham taking up Sara's offer of a concubine since she's over the hill, herself? You think Abraham isn't party to the tryst? You think it's his wife's fault—she's pulling his strings? 'Holy moly, why's the wench in my bed?' and in he leaps? He's not being untrusting and faithless?"

Stiff in her seat, Anna stays quiet. Her facial features feel too eked, constrained. Her lips feel like they might fall off. Down the table Peg is maybe tugging uncomfortably at the neck of her sweater, acting not one bit the flirt, and Brenda is perhaps turning an interesting heliotrope hue underneath her makeup. But Anna is busy with her own issues. In a distant way, almost without regret, she admits to the ironies—to her judgmentalism. Who're the wayward ones, here? Who're the dalliers in risky business, the dabblers? Who's convinced about what's right and what's wrong, about what's true and what's false?

THE LAST PERSON'S HEELS have disappeared around the bend of the classroom doorway and Anna is distractedly helping to pile Wade's things together to take them along up to the sanctuary. "Whose *Newsweek* is this? Is it ours? Did you bring it?"

"Yeah. I didn't get to that."

"Get to what?"

"That article. Check it out—it's quite good. It just goes to show. Sacrificing children is as old as the hills."

"Which article? This one? Huh, I never saw this. Why, *why* is everything going past me?"

"What else can you expect, Anna? If you're just pitching your magazines under the bed?"

She peers at the photograph: a mummified corpse of an Inca girl, age eleven or twelve, discovered by archaeologists at a dig in Chile. "Sacrificed?

She was sacrificed?" Magazine in hand, stumbling back and bumping into Justine's Christmas bulletin board gone pallid, Anna asks, "How could they tell?" She brushes off a limp curlicue of ribbon hooked onto her sleeve and examines the photo again. "Ugh, that's how a mummy looks?"

By leaving the child on the mountain to die, the Incas hoped to placate their gods. Maybe hoped to stave off drought, with everybody's maize stalks dried up and raspy and the potatoes just hard little polyps on the vines.

There's a sidebar piece, too, about the prevalence of such religious practices in early civilizations. Besides children, the Incas' objects of sacrifice included beer, pepper, corn, cloth, and animal blood—llama blood, especially. Llama? wonders Anna. Why llama?

According to the text, the Aztecs were similarly disposed. As she studies the accompanying illustration, a pen-and-ink drawing, her stomach does a sick flip-flop. A sword-brandishing Aztec priest is holding up a freshly severed heart like a county fair blue-ribbon red beet, cooked and drippy, while the manly but eviscerated sacrifice victim remains pinned across the rock altar by the priest's helper warriors in feathered headdresses.

Wade is standing by, waiting, his eyebrows nearly up to the tree line. The longer she lingers on the drawing, the more nauseated she grows. Before the start of Sunday school she felt lightheaded and hungry, having consumed nothing at home but coffee, too rushed about getting off to church to touch her bagel with grape jelly. In front of the ladies' lavatory mirror she remembered it longingly. But now, her biliousness. "Think 'Neanderthal,' Anna," says Wade. "Put it in context. Those Genesis characters were Neanderthals, essentially. Next to antediluvian. Aboriginal. They were primarily pagan, and nomadic."

"What does nomadic matter?"

"It doesn't matter. Knowing that aspect just helps us understand the archaic mentality. The superstitiousness. People slaughtered an animal or forfeited one of the tribe to mitigate the collective guilt—to spare themselves from the gods' capriciousness. If you take the facts and givens, Anna, what's there to conclude? Ancient humanity just didn't grasp God's higher designs and unconditional mercy." Wade is searching her face, intent. "That scapegoat ram, though. Lucky Abraham. Lucky Isaac. Saved by the bell."

In the picture, the beet's aorta is still gulping moistly, in the manner of the lips of a fish out of water. Down through the heating ducts is coming the the jubilant, rich waves of congregational singing, *Redeem-er Lord, might-y and true, for-e-ever I offer up all glo-o-ry to you.* Anna lifts her baleful eyes to her husband. "Can you go find Todd? Can we just go home?"

27

Vapid, witless creatures, they're constantly stretching out their necks, clawing the soil, pecking pecking pecking. Unlike commercial-raised layers penned in windowless buildings, fed the XLA 18% protein mash and stripped of their souls, Wade's hens devour just about any garbage. She's seen them feasting on a copperhead snake Todd killed with a hoe, groundhogs that the dog treed, and the rats from the crawl space under the house where Wade mined with snap traps (he allowed the cat to glut itself first). On Anna's forays out to the coop with the tin pitcher she employs for kitchen scraps, sometimes she can't get it emptied before the chickens catch up to her, crowding and cackling underfoot, and the shower of potato peels, apple cores, coffee grounds, and pasty lumps of oatmeal down onto their heads puts the birds in a complete dither of ecstasy. Even chicken skin and gristle and those drumstick shards she circumspectly culls when fixing soup, they'll gobble gobble gobble. Their own species! It's plain-down cannibalistic. Practically the only handouts they'll ignore are peach pits and citrus rinds.

Last evening she set the roaster pan of beef rib bones from supper on the porch to allow Popper and the cat first dibs, and this morning, armed with the remains and her pitcher of junky pickings, she's gingerly sidestepping the chicken yard's snow-and-ice patches, afraid her feet might shoot out from under her and land her on her back. The strewn waste wouldn't matter, of course. But spilled, herself, mightn't she, too, get taken for a food sacrifice? *Ga-gack, ga-gack, ga-gack,* the birds are chortling, scampering to meet her on their scrawny stick legs, *ga-gack, ga-gack, ga-gack.*

Carrying her dumped containers, she beats a cautious retreat. On the safe side of the gate, wedging the board that serves as a makeshift crossbar, she casts an oblique glance at the chuffy, dry cobs scattered around Wade's store of fencepost logs where the chickens are fond of digging their dust holes. While hulling the popcorn, Wade must've left enough kernels for them to glean. Those Incas offered their precious corn, thinks Anna, deterred by the reminder of that *Newsweek* article. And beer! They meant to get their gods drunk, or what?

"I wonder what it was Cain brought?" she asked last night. "What exactly did he sacrifice?" She'd been traveling in her mind back to her baptism classes at the mission, and Bishop Strite with his ancient, droopy jowls. "I know, I know," she added with a frown, "Abel's fatty portions made a pleasing savor, but Cain's lesser gift, just some fruits of the field, counted unto God as a provocation." *Prah-ah-voh-oh-ca-a-tion,* as the bishop put it. His words always held an odd, quavery timbre. "It was something or other Cain grubbed up, sure. But, like what? And how'd he know God was cross?"

"Cross?" Wade at the dining table was helping Todd with his math.

"Enough to make Cain slink around the way he did, in a big snit."

"You mean did God's judgment bolt down from on high?"

"I just—"

Wade contemplated. "Maybe Cain's offering lay untouched on the platter, rotting and drawing flies, whereas Abel's got carried off secretly by a raiding coyote, and the food's disappearance was taken as a sign."

"A jackal," Todd suggested. "Wouldn't a jackal be more like it?"

"Oh, stop it," she scolded. "Jackal! Who says there were jackals?"

"Think figuratively, Anna. Think about it figuratively."

"Why? Why do you say that?"

"Cain and Abel don't have to be specific historical characters. The lesson in the story—that's what's of import."

"But if—"

"God was perceived as rancorous, vengeful. That was the perception." Impatiently Wade jabbed his pencil at the air. "Listen, Anna. Reading anything you have to take into account the context. Back then the sun revolved around the earth. The earth was flat—any poor blokes who walked to the edge fell off. The earth was only so many genealogies old. So what other ill-conceived ideas predominated? If you can't look to the Bible for scientific and geographical accuracies, neither can you demand from it the definitive facts on the world's early cultures. Given that the Bible is more of a folk history, a storybook, what sense does it make to put yourself in a bind over this or that anecdotal detail?"

"But this isn't just some minor stickler thing I'm asking."

"Any storyteller is allowed to take liberties. You know so, yourself. You said as much in your speech at Rawlings Lake. So don't keep mining for aspects you can't quite wrap your mind around. Don't keep sweating over questions you can't realistically expect to resolve."

"You think I'm just some dumb sucker. Uh-huh, you do." Unsatisfied, she ensconced herself in a dining-table chair. "Okay, but I still wonder. The Cain figure brought a plateful of vegetables instead of a fine juicy joint of lamb, but what kind? *Which* vegetables? I just need the scenario."

She thought suddenly of the flip chart by the cash register at Rite Aid. In the afternoon, at the store, there at Wade's request to pick up a case of distilled water for school, she'd seen the chart. Waiting for the clerk to ring up the customer ahead of her, she'd browsed the colorfully illustrated, flip-down cards pitching the antioxidant benefits of various fruits and vegetables. "Well," Anna muttered slowly, pinching at her lower lip, remembering, "I guess if a person just approached it in terms of the vitamins—the nutrients. You say it's all in how Cain and Abel saw things, right? So since they didn't understand, didn't see the incredible nourishment value in a ho-hum plate of vegetables, then even between them they *had* to view Abel's meat as preferable."

"His prime leg of mutton, I take it," Wade grunted.

"Sure, whatever. Weren't they big meat eaters? Didn't they subsist mostly on their hunted-down game and their fatted oxen they roasted on spits? So because Cain's sacrifice wasn't meat per se, it didn't fill the bill. Look at the difference it might've made if they'd been better informed! I mean, if they'd had any grasp of their own dietary needs and body chemistry—free radicals, amino-acid building blocks, all that."

"Free radicals?" asked Todd. "Now what've you been reading?"

"Yes, the disease causers. Those snarky particles that lower the body's resistance till, bingo, along come the plants' phytochemicals to the rescue. Isn't it amazing when you realize about the powerhouse bonuses found in commonplace scratch-dirt foods? Take, for instance, those antho—antho—um, what are they? Anthocyanides? No, that doesn't sound right."

The one flip card at the drugstore had indicated that the pigment in tart cherries supplies ten times the anti-inflammatory relief of aspirin. She'd felt like running back to the pharmacy counter and collaring Mr. Treadle. "A single piddling cherry, does that mean? The cherries in one slice of pie? Or what? What help is it if the statistics are confusing? And shouldn't there be a disclaimer about maraschino cherries? The sugar and additives! What a miserable excuse for food!"

"You're referring to anthocyanins," said Wade. "Yeah, the zeaxanthins pack a punch, too. And the alpha and beta carotenes, and lycopenes, and luteins."

"Yes, yes! But the antho—whatever—are way high on the ladder. They're found in the greatest concentration in blueberries. Oh, hey! Didn't you mention some experiment where they fed pureed blueberries to elderly rodents? Rats, maybe? And the animals showed improved memory and motor skills?"

"That was in *Science News.*"

"Blueberries, huh. Brain food." Anna chuckled. "It's all so interesting. My, just think about it. Wasn't scurvy a problem? Weren't people in those primitive societies hit with all sorts of epidemics? Pellagra, beriberi, rickets? Pernicious anemia, maybe even scabies? If Cain had been more knowledgeable, instead of drowning in remorse over his disdained sacrifice he could've deduced that God in fact wanted *him* to be the one cleaning up his plate. Cain could've read the situation that way, which would've put a whole different slant on the story." She gave a heartier chuckle. "This is pretty silly, though. Here I am, presuming any old figment of the imagination!"

Silly or else knuckle-headed, thinks Anna, still huddled by the chickens' gate and reappraising last evening's chance epiphany. It almost puts her in a humor again. But her lips feel too clunky to comply with a grin, too stilted and encumbered by the deep-freezer morning air.

Lesser gift, the bishop said. As it were, Cain didn't put himself out enough. Well, personally, she can believe he might've been a bit of a bum. His produce was maybe second-rate. Back in the house, in the cheer of the kitchen, she drums up some possibilities. He simply went out and gathered a couple of stolid, paunchy butternut squashes, didn't inspect the undersides first for slugs or rot. Or he dug up potatoes disfigured by scab. Her refuse pitcher washed, she places the roaster pan beneath the spurting faucet, adds a squirt of Palmolive, and begins working her scrubby over a crusted, burnt spot. Or perhaps he picked some too-long-gone green beans, the strings as tough as shoelaces and the pods knobby and bent up with arthritis. With slacker contributions like those, how could've he stood a chance?

The Band-Aid meant to safeguard her weather-cracked fingertip slips free as she's scouring, still molded into its stuck-on shape, and she skims it out of the greasy water and worms it back on. But suppose Cain had baked his squashes? Dabbed the melty, tender meat of each half with pats of butter and sprinkled on salt and pepper? The memory of Birdie King's butternuts, ones Anna fixed this same way last fall, makes her stomach cave in with a sudden longing. A nasty onslaught of bugs, *Anasa tristis* nymphs, had destroyed Wade's vines, so when Birdie brought to church some of her crop for the taking, Anna helped herself. It was the deprivation, partly—had Wade's plants begotten squashes prolifically, she wouldn't have swooned over every meal she made with them. "Incredible, oh my word, incre-e-e-edible," she'd moan at the supper table, to Todd's annoyance. He'd ask Wade, "Is it time yet to send for the men in the white coats?"

All summer long, through to the end of harvest season, Birdie does this—shares. She sets up a card table in the church foyer and puts out her free-for-all garden surplus. Picturing to herself the shoe-shined eggplants, rotund tomatoes, fingerling okra pods, permanent-pleated Chinese cabbages, and other delights upon which the nongardeners descend after the service like eager magpies, Anna nods sagely. In a way, those goodies represent Birdie's own personal offering-up to the Lord. They're her succulent buds of kindness, laid out like perfect, yielded fatlings, needing only to be cooked. Properly prepared, they make scrumptious dishes. Wouldn't it have been possible for Cain to finagle something as fine? If not some to-die-for squash, then how about a batch of chow-chow? Suppose he'd picked his green beans at their most toothsome stage, chopped them into tidy lengths, and cooked them—as well as the cauliflower nibs called for in the recipe, and the pearl onions, cute ears of baby corn, lima and red kidney beans, diced celery, and red peppers? And then poured over his beauteous melange the sweet-sour solution? If he'd offered up an ample, stunner jarful of this concoction, what then?

Anna badgers away at her roaster pan and dreams on, plucking from her mind more zesty words to evoke Birdie's card-table selection. The wispy sugar peas, promising a sheer, unmitigated taste of earth and sky. Her buttercrunch lettuces, the leaves rippled and fragile. The beet greens, provocatively piquant, their bright ferrous veins fanning like fingers, and piled separately, the bulbous tubers themselves. Beets, hm. If Cain couldn't have pulled off homemade chow-chow, what about pickled beets? Canned ones, guaranteed *Clostridium*-free? The behemoth effort would've counted for a lot. When it comes to the Detroit Reds Wade always plants, on the day of reckoning it takes some get-up-and-go on Anna's part to put herself to mustering from the scorched earth the dusty, ossified clunkers and scrubbing them out by the garage faucet, mud streaking her legs. Cooking the beets, no matter how low she turns the burner under the kettle, it invariably simmers over and the juice runs in maroon rivulets down the front of the stove. But once they're packed in the jars and she's added the salt and spices, and the vinegar-sugar brine, sending the bay leaves and mustard seeds and peppercorns deep-sea diving toward the bottom, she feels so very proud and satisfied. Wouldn't pickled beets from Cain, ones like those in the lineup in her hutch, have been enough to please God?

She winces at the thought of her quart in the cellar with the questionable bubble of air. But what if Cain had eked the lid off an assuredly safe jar, put half the contents aside for supper, and then hard-boiled and peeled some eggs and dropped them into the jar with the remaining slices, beneath the liquid, to soak for a day or so? Pickled beets *and* eggs, how about that? What if he'd set out his treat for the Lord God on one of those fancy slotted plates? wonders Anna, reaching again for descriptives. The eggs circling like dazzling spicy-sweet yolk-set brooches, the pink blush of their rims spreading into the golden centers, and the beets arrayed slippily in the center of the plate, resembling crosscut sections of Christmas-tree trunk, with their xylem rings exposed and the lifeblood seeping away?

The shed blood. Bashing her scrubby at the pan's grime, she remembers the way Bishop Strite enunciated—*bluh-uhd.* As he pointed out in baptism class, Abel's sacrifice, though acceptable to God, was just a foreshadowing. F-o-r-s-h-a-d-o-w-i-n-g, she maybe spelled it, adding to the list of important words she'd started in her journal. The lone child among the acolytes on the bench in the men's anteroom, she was also the sole notetaker. Or f-o-r-s-h-a-d-d-o-w-i-n-g, perhaps. Neither Abel's deed nor anybody else's offering of a beast, the bishop explained, could provide lasting expiation. E-x-p-e-e-a-t-i-o-n, probably. Only in the fullness of time would once-and-for-all forgiveness come, by way of God's own Lamb, through the shed blood.

Sitting in front of the class, Norman Strite often propped his one knee over the other, causing his pant leg to hike up and expose the puny whiteness of his skin and his leather garter strap with its little wire hook that bit down on a button's worth of sock top. The sickly nakedness made her squirm—as did the reverberating ring in his voice which made it seem like he was speaking from a cave where bats hung like boiled spinach by their sticky feet. His pronouncements hallooed eerily off his jaws. *Bluh-uh-*

uhd—maybe he strung it out more. Anna pauses a moment from her task, seized by the irony. The words' hollow tinge, their shivery cadence, is what spooked her? Not their purport?

These last several days, she's been sampling around in Leviticus. For the person bringing the animal, and for the priests, there existed certain set procedures. *And if his oblation be a sacrifice of peace offering, if he offer it of the herd; whether it be a male or female, he shall offer it without blemish before the Lord. And he shall lay his hand upon the head of his offering, and kill it at the door of the tabernacle of the congregation: and Aaron's sons the priests shall sprinkle the blood upon the altar round about. And he shall offer of the sacrifice of the peace offering an offering made by fire unto the Lord; the fat that covereth the inwards, and all the fat that is upon the inwards, and the two kidneys, and the fat that is on them, which is by the flanks, and the caul above the liver, with the kidneys, it shall he take away. And Aaron's sons shall burn it on the altar upon the burnt sacrifice, which is upon the wood that is on the fire; it is an of-fering made by fire, of a sweet savour unto the Lord.* The same as with Abel's crackling, snapping meat, she guesses, the sacrifice's smoke signals and steam wound cloyingly up to the heavens and suffused the anticipative nos-trils of the Almighty God. Or the anticipative *flared* nostrils, she proposes to herself, feeling gutsy. The flared, quivering, craving nose holes. No, *craven*—the flared, quivering, craven nose holes of the carnivorous God.

She tips her pan to release the lapping flotsam, creating a flood-swell that sucks loudly at the drain, and when the tide recedes, left behind in the strainer basket are some bloated shreds of Showalter steer. She may as well deliver these, too, to the chickens, instead of right away dirtying the washed pitcher. She'll pander to *their* craven appetites. Slipping back into her jacket, she wonders if she's being maudlin again. How's she supposed to ever get back on a friendly footing with Harold Epp? What could she even say to him now, in a letter? *Dear Mr. Editor, remember me, your old contrib-utor? Probably not—out of sight, out of mind, like they say. But I don't guess I'm dried up yet. It's more like I'm in disarray. Your rejection of "A Two-faced God?!" was a blow to my system and I wonder now about the fairness. You called the ar-ticle melodramatic, I think because I was grieved at God and I questioned a sa-cred cow. Melodramatic! I'm afraid there are lots worse things! Apparently you deemed me too weak in the second story for taxing intellectual pursuits—and I agree, I can't help my IQ. But please, shouldn't even your common, ordinary, run-of-the-mill type person be able to work through the basic Christian teach-ings and find some peace and hope? The levying of blood in the olden Bible times—what kind of a gory ruse was that? If, like the Evangelical Brethren in-*

sist, killing is always always always wrong, then don't we have to say God goofed with things? I'm serious. The only other choice would be for us to recant. So yes, now my quarrel with the Abraham-and-Isaac story is just the tip of the iceberg. My confidence in God's higher purposes has only grown shakier. And people's pious, sanctimonious platitudes aren't any help—whenever there's something being questioned, everybody just says airily, "But it's in the Bible, it's in the Bible!" You too, right? Am I right, huh? About this much, anyhow?

Outdoors, watching her step as she coldly wends her way toward the chickens, Anna goes on making conversation. Into the frozen-numb atmosphere she murmurs, "Mama, I can't lay my quagmire of doubts on you. You'd have a conniption. But like Margie that time you hustled her back upstairs with her loot from your closet, I need to know. Blood? Why blood? This needs elucidating. What am I missing? Mama, how can any bloody sacrifice ever be *redemptive?*"

She'll only throw the meat over the fence, not try to navigate all the way up to the coop. "Yoo, yip, hey! Here chickchickchick, here chickchickchick." Giving her strainer sludge a pitch, she mumbles toward the sky, "Clue me in, please? Thou, shalt, not, kill? Then why oh why the guts and gore?"

These last questions go unmet, but not her niggardly scraps and her once-again emancipated Band-Aid, undone by the force of her motion. The inedible crumb, upon striking the tundra earth, is the first to be pecked up by an overzealous, salivating hen. Anna doesn't care though. Maybe even Wade, the big-cheese authority, wouldn't mind, if he knew. Unlike with cows, a little plastic doesn't matter. Chickens' gizzards, Wade has told her, can surmount almost anything.

DING-A-LING-A-LING.

"Mom?"

"Mary Beth—oh, it's you."

"What'd I catch you at?"

"Not much. I was just sitting here."

"Entertain me then. My client didn't show. We bend over backwards trying to schedule appointments for people and at the last minute they plead some dire unavoidable emergency."

"So have a heart."

"No! It happens over and over—people aren't responsible."

"Mm, no," sniffs Anna, "I guess they're not."

"Is something wrong, Mom? Now what's happened?"

"No, no. I just wonder if I'm really nuts, or what? Maybe this tack I'm exploring is entirely baseless. Maybe I'm only conjuring stuff up."

"What tack?"

"Chow-chow—is that so offbeam? And pickled beets? Wouldn't you say those foods are tantalizing? What would you choose? What would be exceptionally delicious and enticing?"

"You're getting company?"

"No. Just say what, okay?"

"Pie." Mary Beth hasn't even debated. "One of your pies."

"Pie? I was meaning a vegetable."

"I'm still mad I didn't get any of that grape pie, Mom."

If Cain could've whipped up a pie? thinks Anna. Raspberry? Raisin? Shoofly? Probably not—no. In her experience, if that counts, any number of things can go wrong with a pie. The gluggy crumbs, for example. Or if it's apple pie, which she lids over with a second circle of pastry, the crust wants to brown before the fruit softens. And cherry pie can be ruined by too much cornstarch; instead of the desired delicate, shaky consistency, a few cherries gooshing out and falling over themselves when she cuts a piece, the texture is thick and cranky. Pumpkin pie, if the filling ingredients aren't thoroughly beaten they'll separate during the baking, which results in an eggy layer sunk queasily along the bottom. Lemon meringue—well, she's never achieved as miserable a specimen as the one Wade brought home from school. Agar pie, Jerry Funkhouser dubbed it, out of earshot of the teacher who'd brought it in. No, but her meringue can come out of the oven all lofty and golden and gorgeous, only to shrink in the fridge and turn weepy. The watery runoff sops into the crust, and—

"What? I'm sorry, Mary Beth—I wasn't listening. Look, not pie. Huh-uh. I should've said foolproof, too—what would be delicious and foolproof, both? Despite all the pains you take with a pie, there's no guarantee. Lemon meringue, once in a while you get that soppiness, and with shoofly pie the middle goes dippy, and—"

"Well, you asked. To me, 'tantalizing' suggests something fussy, besides dessert-y and sinful, but now you're saying this special food can't be at all tricky? Okay, lemon bars, then—I vote for lemon bars. Oo-o-o-oops, maybe not. *Aaggh.*" A scream of laughter rushes up the phone cord and assaults Anna's ears. "I just remembered! Wow, Mom. Ha ha ha. Oh, guess what, I think my person just came. Bye!"

Hanging up, Anna shakes her head. Did she need yet another reminder of her mental inanity? Mary Beth dredging up that scene she made?

Pea season—it was pea season, she remembers. The onset of summer vacation. She'd helped Wade in the morning with the picking, maybe three bushels, and overseen the interminable shelling party, with the forced slave-labor conscripts engaging in races and pea shoots and contests to see who could sing more off key. Although a mountain of work still stared her in the face, like an ignoramus she'd given in when Mary Beth begged her to help make lemon bars to take to Bible school, the sugary, sticky, pudding-y kind with a shortbread dough on the bottom. "Let the mess go," Wade said after supper. "If you get done with the blanching before I'm back from town, go take a bath. Let the dishes for me."

"A bath! If only! Can you find a T-shirt for Todd that's not ripped? Please? Jonathan, get upstairs and wash your face." She noticed Mary Beth was ripping off a length of tin foil to cover the lemon bars. "No!" Anna yelped. "Don't take the whole batch! Your class can't eat that many. Here, let's pack some in a bag."

Her hands were wet, and when she singled out one of her quart-size freezer bags for Mary Beth, a tiny bit of water trickled down into it. She dabbed at it with her dishtowel and ran out to the porch where the fan sat. Wade had used it to winnow the peas. With it switched on high, she puffed the plastic in the wind for a few seconds to dry out the inside. "Here you go," she told Mary Beth, running back in.

But as Mary Beth jimmied up the first bars with the pancake turner, Anna impetuously snatched back the bag and plunged it into the sink, down into her pan of cold water and blanched peas, pushing the puckery, underdeveloped ones that had been bobbling around on the surface coursing over the edge. "Mom!" howled Mary Beth. Breathless, she yanked open the drawer for a bagel bag and threw it at her daughter. "This one instead, okay? Just use this."

She quailed from explaining, right then. She was too embarrassed. On the porch, holding the bag in front of the fan's spinning paddles, she'd all at once recalled that American Legion convention at a Philadelphia hotel with a faulty ventilation system that dispersed a rare, previously unidentified aerobic bacteria—the fatalities that resulted. Couldn't those same gram-negative rods Wade had explained about, *Legionella pneumophila,* be residing in the fan motor? Couldn't they be flying by clumps into the freezer bag? Back in the house, as she'd watched Mary Beth lip the bag against the floury edge of the pan, Anna's farfetched thoughts had stood up on their wimpy trotters and stampeded. The utter horribleness! Sending her daughter off with poisoned food and knowingly causing children's deaths? Dear Lord, have mercy!

Murderous versus crazy—she had to make that choice. At least she didn't go so far as to dribble Clorox or some other disinfecting substance down the fan's motor-housing holes, after her family left for Bible school.

Unexpectedly Anna finds herself giggling. In the solitude of the kitchen, producing unfettered, burp-like intimations of glee.

ABOUT THE GUNKY edges, though.

With her fruit pies, this is always happening. Toward the end of the baking time, the juice starts to burble and leak through the topping crumbs or the seam of the double crust, and some slops up the rim, and as the drippage on the floor of the oven *blip-blips* and turns to char, the siege of clouds pouring from the vent tips off the smoke detector. She used to have to offer voluble excuses for the mucked-up crimps.

It's funny—Birdie is the one who set her straight. Anna had asked her over for supper. She'd invited the Showalters, too—Erma Lee and Ervin. Anna was making her apologetic noises and pulling from the cupboard her huckleberry pie with jellied bruise-blue blobs hanging off the sides, when Birdie broke in. "Homemade!" she cried, palms pressed to her bosom in rapture. "Now *that* is what I call a treat to the eyes. I declare, I cannot for the life of me see why anybody pays for those perfect cardboard store pies."

"Oh, but—" quickly Anna recuperated. "Well!" She scooted her dessert onto the table, with the pan turned in such a way that Birdie could easily cut herself a piece from the worst-gobbed part. And ever since, Anna has been partial to that moochy effect, to the way the syrupy piping around the crust jazzes up the look.

Which means Cain could've gotten away with a certain qualified hodgepodgedness. Or so she supposes.

28

She stepped into the house a short while ago, in time to catch the phone.

"Where were you, Mom?"

"Jonathan, oh! Let me catch my breath." She pushed out of the way her store bags, grappled with her coat buttons. "In town. Errands. Wal-Mart, the Goodwill. And I wanted to take a little something to Mrs. Snipe, because—"

"Who?"

"Nobody you know. The grandmother of a student—she sent a recipe to school for Wade. Naughty me, I've put off and put off thanking her. There was some three-bean salad from Sunday in the fridge and I settled on that, because it wouldn't be obligating—I didn't want to start up another round of favor exchanging. I had to ransack the phone book for her address, and then—"

"Hey Mom, I've a quick question."

"Oh, but the dumbest thing happened. I mean at Wal-Mart, where I went first. Work gloves for Wade, a few groceries—that's all I was after. Let me tell you, nobody's ever beat out their price on orange juice, and their lunchmeats aren't bad, either! So back at the deli, I couldn't help spotting their three-bean salad—I had to take a minute to compare, you know. The

exact same ingredients, and $3.59 a pound? Something you just dump to-
gether? I felt like asking the lady, 'Where's the sense?' Anyhow, I went on
about my business, I rounded up the stuff on my list, and I was wheeling
my cart toward the checkout when suddenly I got this weird twinge about
my handbag propped squat open on the baby seat with my three-bean salad
down inside. You could see it was in the same kind of deli container. It still
had the Pantry Pride sticker that said how many ounces of pepperoni, but
all the same, I was afraid the clerk might take me for a thief. Might think I
hocked Wal-Mart's three-bean salad."

"Mom, no."

"I know, I know. But I had to stop right then and there and cover it over
with Wade's hanky I had along. I used that." Halted beside the bulk-candy
shelves, she'd fixed it like an unbefitting fist-lady cap, rumpled and snotty,
down overtop the offending bean brains and subjugated them. "So I guess
it's on their security cameras now."

"But you had no reason to be paranoid."

"What's that got to do with anything? I'm just telling you how I felt.
Like I'd engaged in some sort of criminal behavior, and if I were to do anything else shifty, such as glance behind me or otherwise act self-conscious, I
might raise suspicions. Even though I was as innocent as the day is long!"

"Right."

"I mean, there's no law against bringing beans into the store in your
handbag. Unless it's one I invented just today. It's like I hatched up my own
new rule and incriminated myself. 'Absolutely no agricultural products allowed down in with the customer's lip balm and keys and cell phone,' or 'If
the customer has a sheepish look on her face, well then!'"

"I wouldn't make too much of it, Mom."

"Well, but see—and this is what's so interesting—I'm thinking that
maybe—*maybe*—it was this same type of thing going on back in the Old
Testament with the sacrifice rules. The Old Testament sacrifices. All those
cautionary codes and restrictions—maybe the people just concocted
them."

"Huh? You lost me there."

"People had their guilt feelings, naturally. Laboring under guilt—isn't
that just part and parcel of the human condition? On their own, couldn't
the people have cooked up their grisly altar-pot rules? Is this too farfetched?
But it still doesn't explain why—why a—" Anna mashed her shoulder into
the Coca-Cola magnet on the refrigerator and winced. "Oh dear, am I rant-
ing, by any chance? What am I saying? I don't even know! Why'd you call?

What did you want?"

A certain shirt, it so happened. Heavy duty, hooded, with the Brownsville State logo on the front. Jonathan's description didn't ring any bells.

"Long sleeves, Mom," he repeated. "No pockets."

"I haven't seen it around, no," she told him. "I don't remember it from Christmas vacation either. Have you looked in Crater's closet? Does your dorm have a lost-and-found? Why's it so important all of a sudden?"

Oh-h-h. A pair of jeans he'd thrown in with a load of wash had turned everything blue. His only other hoodie, included. "Well, there's nothing to do about that!" she exclaimed. "Except walk around in blue underwear. I guess that's how a person learns. Somebody with an engineer's mind, though—I'm surprised."

Pulling on her lip, she pondered her words. Against the backdrop of the boisterous dorm he'd turned silent. "But who's perfect?" she added. "Who's infallible? Who's never ever had to eat crow? Nobody *I* know."

"Good point."

"No problems, the person would have to be dead!"

"Mom, I have a class now, but if you find that shirt can you put it in the mail?"

"I'll sure do that. What's the class?"

"PDE. Partial differential equations. The take-home exam is due. It took me three hours."

"Does Crater study as much as you?"

"No, but he gets by."

"I don't see how you're able to apply yourself."

"There's a room in the basement I can use. Nobody goes down there. It's my cell."

"Cell?"

"No amenities. A couple of old chairs, a table."

"Just so you're not turning into a monk."

"Fat chance of that. Mom, I've got to go."

Upstairs in the boys' room, her head to the floor, scanning the various objects moldering under the bunk bed, Anna sprang upon the idea of putting to use her and Jonathan's exchange. It would neatly feed in. She could skip the handwritten first draft, too. She trotted back downstairs, and without even resorting to her omnipresent fold-out chart of jabberwocky scribbles, she lit into Chapter 28, pulling the words out of thin air, as it were. At least the dialogue would help bulk up the manuscript. Much to her gratification she succeeded in clipping right along, *bunk-rap-rap-rap-rap-bunk rap-rap-rap-rap-bunk rap-rap-rap-rap-bunk rap-rap-rap-rap-bunk rap-bunk rap-rap-rap-rap-rap-rap-rap-rap-rap-rap-rap-rap-rap-bunk-rap-bunk-bunk,* undeterred by the usual hamperedness, transcribing almost verbatim down to the final parting shots, *rap-bunk rap-rap-rap-rap-rap-bunk rap-rap-rap-bunk-rap-bunk.* But now she's just sitting here festering, in a state of suspension. Her jitterbugging words on the monitor have given way to the inky night scene. Where can she go with this, pray tell? The computer-programmed stars keep shooting from their black-hole center and streaking across the stygian sky, world without end—the tumbling Pleiades, Scorpius's fleet, Betelgeuse, Sirius, Belta Centauri, the Crab Nebula dust. Mutely the universe speeds on by.

OH. AND THEN NOBODY was home when she stopped at the Snipe place. She didn't tell Jonathan. For all he knows, she did her Christian duty. An old beat-up vehicle was parked in the turn-around, right by the door, but no one answered at her raps. The entry once served as a garage, was her guess. The remodeler put in any old kind of junk windows, with tiers of boards for indoor plant shelves, and they were crammed now with geranium starts in mayonnaise jars. Waiting, her present clutched close to her coat, she made out a chest freezer, mud boots, a hunting rifle, worn-raw linoleum. An overhang at the back of the house, large enough to be a carport, held cords and cords of firewood, and while she watched, a squirrel rushed back and forth on top of the logs, *chhht-chhht-chhht*ing, peckish and aggravated. Or better yet, peeved, p-e-e-v-e-d, *rap-rap-rap-rap-rap-rap,* if her thesaurus is to be trusted.

But Jonathan ought to be back from class now. She'll give him a call.

"Jonathan? It's not under the bed, anyhow. Your shirt. Look, I couldn't deliver that three-bean salad. I forgot to mention that nobody came to the door. It could be I even had the wrong Snipes."

"Okay."

"You did all right on the test, you think?"

"I don't expect any big screw-ups."

"A professor giving out take-home tests—I don't understand that. Somebody could cheat."

"Sure, it happens."

"Proofs? Were you writing proofs? Three hours! Now me, I would conk out, not having the foggiest notion of what the subject matter entails."

"In one part we had to prove the orthogonality of—"

"Wait wait wait. Spell that."

"O-r-t-h-o-g-o-n-a-l-i-t-y. The orthogonality of the sine and cosine functions under integration from negative pi to pi."

"*Pffft.* Ridiculous! Wait, tell me more."

The students also had to lay out Fourier's series for a quartic polynomial and find the roots of Bessel's function of the second kind. Tolerantly Jonathan briefs her on the puzzler nomenclatures. "What else do you want to know? You still want more? There's more. What's going on, Mom? I don't get it."

"Me either. Which doesn't make for the jolliest of moods. Um, do you capitalize just 'Bessel'? Or is it all one big title?"

In the study again, Anna expunges with one nimble keystroke the onrush of celestial bodies and enters for the record the postscript scraps of conversation, *rap-rap-rap-rap-rap-rap-bunk rap-rap-bunk rap-rap-rap-rap-rap-rap-rap-rap-rap-rap-rap-bunk rap-rap-rap-bunk.* With unaccustomed acumen she parlays every suggestible tidbit of malarkey, *rap-rap-rap-rap-rap-rap-rap-rap-bunk rap-rap-rap-rap-rap-rap-bunk rap-rap-bunk rap-rap-rap-rap-bunk rap-rap-rap-bunk-rap-rap-rap-rap-rap-rap-bunk rap-rap-rap-rap-rap-rap-bunk rap-rap-rap-rap-rap-rap-rap-bunk-rap-bunk.* But after her keyboard chatter ceases, the screen reverts to its former vista.

The monitor's twinkly white jewels pop up, speedcoast according to their established orbits, snuff out. Pop up, speedcoast, snuff out. Back to feeling uninspired, she goes for the roll of clear packing tape so she can shore up the disintegrated spine of the thesaurus. All the while she's struggling with a ticklish piece of tape, trying to get its positioning fair and square, the frugal rays of February sun passing through the study windowpane and arriving in real time at the speed of light find only those electronic facsimile stars to hit on—the screen's feigned, racing-by, supernal denizens.

29

In Wade's grip, in certain now-and-then moments, she can let go. His bodily bulk quells her thrumming, under-the-skin disgruntlement. Her pique temporarily muffled, she drinks in his raw, reassuring earthiness. She'll detect on his breath his raisins, or the onions he put on his hot dog, or the peanut butter and car-a-mel from his moose tracks ice cream. Or she'll get, rising off his neck, faint leavings of the corn and moldy hay in the wintered-down feed shed. There'll be the unmistakable tinge of gasoline or bar oil clinging to his coveralls, when he's been up on the hill with his chainsaw working on firewood. On schooldays, late afternoons, the smell of his clean, confident perspiration wafts from his shirt, and the sharp, saccharine nip of some science-lab compound. Today when, just in the door, he backs her up against the kitchen stove to kiss her suckingly on the lips and nibble at her loop earrings (tiny little ones, not like Susan Nussbaum's on Sunday as lunky as inner tubes), Anna catches a more rife, but not off-putting, chemical odor. The rice kettle behind her *phlupp*s approvingly as she gives way and basks.

But then she thinks of his pate, probably smarmy from the pores' day-long oozefest. She extricates herself, tips off his beret, and grazes her fingers across the glistening barebald skin. "Oof," she reproaches. "Hon."

He says, "I'll have to run back to school tonight. Once the fruit flies emerge from the pupal stage it's only ten hours till they mate. For the data to make any sense they must be virgins, and I've collected a batch, but I'll need—"

"Virgins?"

"I'll need a couple dozen. So I'll sort them again this evening, get a second batch."

"That's how you say it in class?" she asks, scooping the hat off the floor. "Virgins?"

"Yep. It's one of the better experiments when it works. You crossbreed the sepia-eyed normal-winged flies and the red-eyed with vestigial wings; the white-eyed mutants and the red-eyed; the white-eyed mutants and the sepia-eyed—all the possible combinations. Then you use the new batches to chart the phenotypes, recessive versus dominant. But everything depends on getting the flies sexed before they're fertile."

"How do you sort flying-around flies?"

"I don't—they're anesthetized. I use a triethylamine product, FlyNap. Bug ether, so to speak. *Drosophila melanogaster* gas."

"Huh, so that's what tickled my sniffer. But I always thought mutants were neuter. Sterile, I mean. Like with donkeys. No no no, mules. Mules, right? Because they're inbreds." Anna turns the hat over and studies the suede's lining. There's a dark stain of sweat. "Ugh. Rank." She frowns. "Didn't Todd tell you he'll need the car after supper? He's supposed to go over to Heatwoles. Peg said he and Nicole and Kimmy could just meet there. She didn't see why they should waste a regular youth-group night just to make their posters for the hoagie sale."

"Well then, I'll go as soon as he gets back." Wade lunges for his hat. "Give me that. It's not that bad." He stops by the living-room closet to throw it in and hang up his jacket before retreating with his briefcase to the study.

A few minutes later, back to chopping the celery for Marlene Wagler's recipe for chow mein in the newspaper, Anna remembers her green notebook journal still open on the desk. The back flyleaf, pinned down with her gummy coffee mug from the afternoon, bears her lexicon from baptism class. She was fact-checking those two spellings today—it's e-x-p-e-e-t-i-o-n, actually, and f-o-r-s-h-a-d-i-n-g. As Bishop Strite sonorously lectured from his chair, God's eye homing down, down, down past the spotty ceiling of the anteroom, past the fly-smirched lightbulb and pull chain, past her jabby wing-bone behind bosoms and the bend of her back, to follow the wake of her pencil traveling the paper, must have quailed. *Nonconformd,*

carnel, purety, propitchiation, holy matrimoney, sanctifyed, innerrent, damma-
tion, furnication, adultry, nashing of teeth, redempted, hippocrisy, nonresistince,
depravaty, supsitutionary atonment—in time, her list took on the appearance
of a crooked chimney column. Not that Wade will give it a second look, but
her unpleasant mangle of papers is lying right there, too, and he likes all the
desk space he can get. "I'll move my stuff," she calls.

Confiscating it, thrusting all but the mug up with the books shelved
above the desk, she takes a peek at what he's reading. "That's weird," she remarks. In the *Popular Science*—which likely came from Jerry Funkhouser,
because sometimes he pawns off his classroom copies—a close-up photograph shows a hot-water bottle of sorts containing a white liquid. It reminds
her of milk of magnesia.

"It's Oxycyte," Wade says. "A blood substitute, completely synthetic,
made from PFCs. It was successful with mice, so now they're using it on accident victims in a pilot trial. I should photocopy this, require it as supplemental reading for the tenth-grade unit on the circulatory system."

"Oh, that's an IV bag. The patient's blood turns pink, you mean?"

"Good grief, no. Not from a few milliliters."

She chews on the nub of her little finger and considers. Out of nowhere
she says, "Tell me something. Make sense of the stabbing part, will you? The
water and blood that ran out when they pierced Jesus' side—explain that. It
came pouring out in two separate streams, or what?"

"Maybe not pouring."

"But was it separated? Or was the blood just watery?"

"I can't say. Ask a hematologist. Conceivably the red cells were starting
to clump."

"They were visible red-cell clumps?"

"I guess just clots."

"In clear fluid? Transparent?"

"Clearer than normal, anyway."

"But Wade, no! Once the person is dead, doesn't their blood thicken up?
Coagulate? From rigor mortis setting in?"

"Not right away. Not where it's pooled. From his stance below the cross,
the soldier could've pierced up through the diaphragm into the heart." Wade
reflects. "Which suggests another possibility—the serous fluid. The thin yel-
lowish substance that's found between the pericardium layers."

"You could've differentiated it from the blood?"

"Well, I doubt it. There's hardly that much."

"It gushed. 'Forthwith came there out,' it says in the King James."

"Nah, it wasn't like when you stick a steer."

"Stick? What are you talking about? You shoot the steer."

"You stun it."

"What?"

"When you bleed a steer, it's only been stunned by the bullet. The heart is still pumping."

"The steer isn't *dead?* You stick it *live? Does it feel* this?"

"I don't think so. Probably not. It's not like being crucified."

"Wade, you're awful." She skulks from the room and returns to her cooking.

LATE IN THE EVENING, about to head back to school, the headlights streaking across the wall in announcement of Todd's return, Wade is at the closet inspecting his aforementioned haberdashery. He appears to be having second thoughts about it. "See?" says Anna, close at hand in her bathrobe, plucking at her terrycloth sleeves. "Was I right, for a change?"

For him to verbally concede—is that asking too much? He just tosses the hat back in and retrieves instead an old stretched-out stocking cap of Jonathan's. Crammed down around Wade's ears, it engenders a suitable loser effect. Going out the door he catches the keys from Todd, and soon the car lights flit along their night path in reverse, up next to the ceiling.

"Aren't you loaded with homework?" she asks her son, when he tracks upstairs for his shower.

"Nope. I can finish it during first-period homeroom."

"Oh. Okay."

On tiptoe she explores the closet shelf but finds no hat. It isn't snookered on a hanger in the closet, or on the shoulder of a coat. Nor is it hung up on the sweeper, or the shoe box holding seven years' worth of credit-card statements and canceled checks, or Mama's bag of sewing leftovers. Anna drags the bag out, the brittle, crackly plastic ripping away in her hand and the bowels spilling, but the hat isn't along the back wall of the closet. It fell into the cranny between the Christmas boxes, maybe? She nabs the umbrella from the shelf and fishes with the tip. Aha—up leaps her hooked Catawally catch.

Grungy, oof. But she can't leave the thing at the dry cleaner's. What about the solvent's possible lethal effects? Residual chemicals absorbing topically and dispersing into Wade's bloodstream? At the sink, she blips dish detergent on the hat and works the detergent in. She rinses and squeezes the hat under the wide-open faucet, rinses and squeezes, rinses and squeezes, disregarding the yells and wall thumps coming from upstairs, Todd's signals of distress about the water pressure that has slacked to a piddle. "Sorry!" she offers when she hears him emerge and stomp to his room. She whisks the hat outdoors to pin it to the side-porch clothesline.

"Todd?" she calls, going around switching off the downstairs lights—she'll leave the pair of electric candles at the kitchen window lit for Wade. "Did you hear me? I said I'm sorry!"

In the bathroom, Todd's toothpastey spittle rises up to greet her. She chases it down the washbowl drain herself, for penance, and then tends to her own last-minute ablutions. Deciding to let the wall lamp on, she just spanks lightly at the shade to scatter the dust. But the punched-tin nightlight below, plugged into the same socket as the lamp, catches some of the fallout; when she puffs at it, dead bugs fly up, a whole raft. Wee, mite things, nameless fairy specks, not fruit flies, they were clogged down around the screwed-in part of the bulb. She wonders about the poofy, dry carcasses—the flammability. A dumb thought! Still, who knows? She tugs the nightlight loose, dislodging more bodies which go cascading into the washbowl. With a second, harder puff at the bulb's base, she drives off any lingerers. Duh, now she's maybe spewed her own spit all over the prongs. Afraid of shocking herself, she deposits the nightlight on the windowsill instead of plugging it back in.

She leans into Todd's dark doorway and murmurs, "You'll forgive me, I hope. Love you. Sleep good." He grunts and rolls to face the wall. The bunk bed grunts.

In her bedroom Anna riffs her toes through the snarled, upturned fringes of the rug, a minor habit she's gotten into to forestall anybody from tripping in the dead of night and bamming their nose on the foot rail of the bed and sustaining cerebral damage. She's heard of a case like this—the woman fell against her kitchen counter and rammed her nasal bone up into her brain. Anna also bails off the dresser a billowy Wal-Mart bag holding only the receipt for her new six-pack of panties, the comfortable kind, not sexpot high-risers. She folds the plastic several turns, mashily, and weighs it down with her hairbrush. She doesn't want the bag lofting over to the bed on a chance middle-of-the-night wisp of north wind and landing on Wade's face, or hers, and cutting off the oxygen.

Coiled into a ball under the covers, thrashing her soles against the bedding to raise some warmth, she hears the car. Then the kitchen door. She hears Wade taking the steps two at a time, his ankle joints grinding. She listens to the rain in the bathroom, its gentle pelts against the old, soft sheet she made last week into a liner for her cotton Battenburg shower curtain from the Goodwill. There's a cozy feel now when you're showering—a muffled drumming instead of the water hitting against an unforgiving plastic curtain, amplified like killer hailstones. Doesn't Susan's gold-bulrushes shower door make it seem like she's in a car wash?

Waiting for the pipes to shut down, Anna wishes she would've checked the freezer, behind it where the motor makes a sort of hot-air pocket. The situation this creates is something she worries about more in the summer, when the mudroom stays stifling hot even through the night, and the motor's humming spells are practically nonstop in response to the onslaught of strawberries, peas, cherries, green beans, and corn. But even now, isn't there a risk? Next to the freezer stands the jumbo cardboard box into which the paper trash from the household waste cans gets put till there's enough to lug to the burn barrel, and if somebody was incautious when emptying the can with her scratched balls? If a wad missed the box and coasted behind the freezer, into the cobwebs, mightn't it heat up enough to ignite? Or mightn't a cobweb itself start on fire? Anna means to stop herself, but more thoughts press in—visions of the first smolders, negligible strings of smoke, a fuzz-winged moth corpse from last summer sparking, and the picayune blaze leaping to the next parched insect shell and engulfing more bugs, their feather-light, lethal husks, and the conflagration spreading—

She gives herself up to the derangedness and slinks back downstairs.

Hanging across the freezer, shafting the flashlight down behind it, she hears Wade's low summons. "Anna, hey."

"I'm just seeing to something," she calls. "I'll be upstairs soon!" No curveballed strays catch the light, so that's good. As a precaution though, she catches up a few zephyr-like spider threads with the dust brush and knocks them into the trash box. She squashes the contents further down and pushes the box a bit to the left to give the freezer extra breathing space. There, that's better.

When she scuds from the mudroom, Wade is still in the hall. His head is looming over the banister. "I'm coming," she hisses, passing the closet. "I told you I'm coming! Oops, hold on. These materials. I should've taken care of my mess." She wheels back and switches on the end-table lamp.

She's had the collection since last summer, when Margie brought Mama for a visit. Margie staggered up the walk with the bag extended at arm's length like an undue burden, while Mama, entirely pleased with herself, brought up the rear. "What a person doesn't find in their attic!" Mama was saying. "Scraps from way back, Anna. I plumb forgot I had them. You can thank Rita—she was up there hunting for Herbie's diplomas. Now you girls can each make yourself a quilt. You'll have to decide between you who gets what."

"But I never sew anymore," said Margie. "Where do I put this, Anna?"

"All of it for me? Can't I just donate it to Conoy's sewing circle, Mama? Sometimes the ladies put together crib comforters."

Anna wasn't sure the group would welcome any old scrimpy, grab-bag thing. Wouldn't they prefer actual yard goods, substantial lengths straight from the store? She still hasn't checked with anybody. On her knees now, raking from the closet the no longer bound-and-gagged fabric, she thinks it's too ragtag an assortment.

"Anna, can't that wait? Get up here, will you?"

"You could find me a bag that's not torn! Oh, never mind, that's all right, I'll do it. Wade, you should see this! Huh, Margie's yellow-marigolds dress. And my blue plaid with the box pleats. *Pfft*, dreary. I kind of thought so then, too. My my—this one, this one, this one—drab, drab, drab. Oh, but look, here's one of Mama's I loved." The dribble of brown cloth with delicate octagonal designs punctuated in their centers with red spots, when Anna holds it to the lamp, assumes a sweet, burnished glow.

"Anna, come. I'm hitting the sack."

"Good, good! I'll be up."

Inspecting again, however, Anna decides the spots look like Wade's fruit flies' eyes, astonished and bulgy, maybe infected with conjunctivitis. Or like a steer's drained, last-ditch drips. She hurries to finish. Relegating the tails and flutters of discarded yore to their former obscurity, she chokes them up in a new bag and knots the neck.

She thinks suddenly of Wade's hat. If it stays too long on the line, won't it be left with a permanent dent from the clothespin? She hops barefooted across the porch to find the suede frozen hard as a board. But she's pleased by the trenchant, soapy tang when she dares a whiff, back in the house. The lining seems spiffed enough. Not wholly *redempted*, but worthy of Wade's cranium. She places the hat over a jar of peaches from the hutch to thaw and finish drying. Hm, no, that will make the crown poke up. Hm. The rice kettle in the dish drainer—maybe use that, turned upside down? Yes. It's more the girth of his head, supplied as he is with superior knowledge. Not that he has the answer to every piccalilli hypothetical question, when it comes to the spiritual. He's not all that much of a genius, spiritually. Of course, who is she to judge, anymore?

30

Her next chapter just won't take off. She's sick, sick, sick of these false starts.

When Wade calls on lunch break, the kitchen floor is strewn with her mashed tries. "I'm not getting anywhere with this," she groans. "I'm just nitpicking, nitpicking."

He clamps down on the carrot he tucked into his briefcase this morning along with his cheese sandwich. The loud report of the beaver-tooth-marked end snapping off makes her cringe. "Is it the writing part or your subject matter?"

"I guess the wording, mostly."

"You have to put a lid on the perfectionism, Anna. Not pay fanatical attention to every slight kink. You have to spit out something and go on, keep on moving your pencil."

"Instead of masticating, masticating. Yeah. Who said that? The mother in *Glass Menagerie,* but what was her name? Not Miranda. Um. Um. Oh, come on. Who was she? See? I can't *think.*" Enervated by the effort, Anna slumps her shoulders and sighs. "My lot in life, I guess."

"Just get your sentence down. Say it any random way." Another crack resounds meanly in her ear. He never even peeled the carrot. He gave it a rough swipe under the faucet, scarcely washed it. "Then charge on ahead.

None of this waffling and second guessing."

"That doesn't work. It just doesn't. I'm inflicted with some kind of mental submandibular paralysis."

"Go for a walk. Get outside, Anna. Get off your duff, get your endorphins going." The principal's voice interrupts, crackling over the intercom in the teachers' lounge. *CAFETERIA ACCOUNTS ARE DUE TOMORROW, NO EXCEPTIONS. ANOTHER REMINDER TO ALL AFTERNOON VO-TECH STUDENTS: PLEASE DO NOT, DO NOT BOARD THE BUS UNTIL THE 12:20 BELL. A THROUGH K SENIORS, YOUR YEARBOOK PHOTOGRAPHS CAN BE PICKED UP IN THE OFFICE STARTING ON MONDAY.* The static-filled squawking makes her feel like she's on the line with an emergency 911 dispatcher. She doesn't need Wade preaching at her. She hangs up with a bang.

In a move to divert herself, she attempts to clean up a couple of problems in the last chapter, insignificant diddlysquat complications. But her snailpoke progress reduces her to tears.

IT'S THE DUMBEST little things that bog me down," she says tonight. "I'm telling you, I'm demented."

"Nah," rebuts Wade behind her in the steamy mirror, the shower spout dropping its last dregs. "Not demented." He slaps his washcloth at his yawning underarms and slick chest, the black hairs uncoiled and swollen like sidewalk worms, *Lumbricus terrestris,* after a rain. "Just touchier than all get out." He wrings the washcloth soulless, the collected runoff drumming into the bathtub, and next swats over his shoulders. Always and always his mop-up proceeds along this same order of events: bald top, scritchy beard stubble, tautly banded trunk and arms, hangdog privates (unless Fido has risen unprovoked), and legs as hunky and stalwart as those of Michelangelo's David, *swat, swat, swat,* the excess on his washcloth launching to the four winds. As a midget of flyaway water hits the mirror and bobbles uncertainly downhill through its fog and another splashes into the commode to set adrift in the flinching sea, he says, "What is it now? Give me an example."

Pressed against the washbowl to meet her clouded face in the glass, probing with a tweezers for that chinny-chinny-chin pig bristle of hers, Anna resists. "Don't make me say! It's all so dumb."

In bed a few minutes later, she crowds up to Wade. On nights this cold he's her furnace. She tugs the quilt higher, and the tousled top sheet. "I could try Prozac. Or Zoloft—I saw this ad."

Bonk. Todd's door. Does he have to get mad about scant peeps of conversation coming from his parents' room? How's he going to manage in college? Cope with the bull herds crashing around in the dorm? But she obligingly adjusts her volume. "All the side effects, though. Kind of scary."

"Not Zoloft, Anna."

With a shudder she grates her toenails up his shin. "Well, *something.* Before I'm too far gone."

"Nah."

"Yes. It's driving me bonkers. Like, a person's wing bones, you know? 'On-behind bosoms,' do I say? Or just 'behind bosoms'—*be*hind, not be*hind.* See? You don't understand, right? So how will any readers? How am I supposed to put it intelligibly? And that's just one needless little sideline—the bosoms." She pulls away and socks at her pillow to reorient the stuffing. "Bazooms, I used to think. You know, zoom zoom, bigger and bigger. Aunt Dolly's, especially. That's how I said it, till tenth grade when Miss Fritz read to us about the skipper's daughter with her boozum white as the hawthorn buds. Boo-zum. 'Peek-a-boo,' that connotation. Or, 'Boo to you.'"

"Anna, you're the limit."

"I *know.*"

"Use the correct term, why don't you? Scapula."

"No, that wouldn't work."

"Suit yourself, then."

"It's *not* boo-o-o, is it?"

"No."

"Did you learn that poem in school, 'Wreck of the Hesperus'? I loved it. 'Colder and louder blew the wind, a gale from the northeast; the snow fell hissing in the brine, and the billows frothed like yeast.'" She huffs softly. "I wonder how much I can still dredge up." She squirrels nearer to Wade and nudges him. "You want any more? Hon?" But his lower jaw is slackening. His visage is losing its striving consciousness. *Men.*

His teapot whistling starts up and she must throw her body across his to turn off the light.

No, she suddenly thinks, it's not submandibular paralysis. That diagnosis she came up with today on the phone, trying to explain herself to Wade, wasn't right. No, she's suffering from a subluxation—a subluxated cranial joint, to borrow from Dr. Goebbels back in Pottstown. Her dislocated cranial plates have injured the soft tissues and warped her mental processes.

Wade settles down to steady chugs, but she gets to brewing over whether that Goebbels guy Mama had her visit, soon after her baptism, was a plain-out quack. Mama was so concerned about the insomnia. She didn't perceive what was actually going on, Anna figures. It was just that some nights she got stuck. Ducked under the sheet, offering up her urgent last-minute snatches, she couldn't wind up. "Forgive me for all my sins, dear God, please dear God, please, in Jesus' name, amen," she'd try to pantomime, over and over. "Please please forgive me for all my sins, dear God, please dear God, please, in Jesus' name, amen." Somehow she'd muff it. Between her aborted efforts she'd lay listening to the mission house's aches and pains and sighs.

Finally she'd leave her bed to pad over to Mama and Daddy's room. The jukebox music from Hickey's beer joint across the street still plinked away, and pale patches of incandescence played across her parents' lumped forms in the bed, from the lit-up, milk-glass-paneled mission sign that jutted from the building's corner downspouting and advertised to all the night, JESUS LOVES, JESUS KEEPS, JESUS SAVES, JESUS HOLDS. Daddy would emit a grunt and go back to his snoring, but Mama would prop herself up enough to inquire phlegmily, "Whahisit, Anna? Whahsa matter?"

But she couldn't exactly verbalize the trouble. Roosted in the armchair by the window, she'd pick at the upholstery nubs. She'd let in just enough light under her eyelids to assure herself that the chair with her in it wasn't slowly circling toward the ceiling. She'd choke back her buzzy, protracted yawns, trying not to crack her jaws. After a while, too dead spent to hold a thought in her head, she'd trundle back through the hall and fall down flat in her bed and sink into the land of slumber.

She was nodding over her books at school, Anna remembers, even letting her head bump down onto her desk, and Mama's anxiety grew. She heard Mama say to Daddy one evening, "I hardly know where to turn. Could a couple of those treatments hurt any? Verna Pyles says that Goebbels doctor has done wonders for her nerves."

"Verna?" Daddy sounded dubious.

"Oh, I know—her cure-alls." Verna took great stock in her evil-odored syrups and the gobstopper calf-feed pellets she bought from the Watkins dealer, mineral supplements really, in brown jars. Mama didn't go for the Watkins man's sales pitch. "But this is different, isn't it? Verna claims up and down those spinal adjustments make all the difference in the world. Would a doctor like that just be picking people's pockets?"

Ha, thinks Anna. Overtaxed as she feels at this hour, she pushes away from Wade and tumbles out of bed. Blindly she feels around for her robe and the slippers with malformed toes. In the sloughy darkness of the hall, poised on the wicker stool, breathing hard into her sleeve, she hoists the attic-hole board upwards and takes the Tingley box from its nook. She retires with it to the bathroom and situates herself on the floor. Here by the tub, on intimate terms with the underbelly of the washbowl and aided by the lamp's frazzled, lukewarm spill, she can shop through the green journal. She intends to find her version of events—her recounting of the first chiropractor appointment.

Here it is, yes. *After school mama said your coming with me. We'll see abot this, she said. Just this once anyway.* If she concentrates, she can remember Mama traipsing her down Front Street, past Cut-Rate Pharmacy, Woolworth's, Shapiro's Shoes, Hammond's Bar & Grill, to a door with RAYMOND P. GOEBBELS, CHIROPRACTIC painted on the glass, ARTHRITIS, HEADACHES, CARRIAGE DISORDERS. And she can remember a rickety flight of stairs. It led to a stark, bare-walled room and a table padded in chilly vinyl, bolted to the floor.

Mama said, if only somthing could help. He had this shaver thing, it vibrated like daddy's shaver. He ran it up my back slow and the register needle went thisaway and thataway like it couln't make up it's mind and a paper came out the machine with marks on. Then Dr. Goebbels compared the jiggles on the tape. He kept murmuring into his double chin, stirring the tubercular clabber in his lungs, coughing rustily. At last, tapping at one particular spike, he turned to Mama. "You'll note, Mrs. Farber, the misalignment. The subluxation isn't severe, I'm sure. Trust me, it's nothing a few manipulations can't rectify."

He got me down on my belly, din't let me fix my box pleats. Then crunched on my backbone, pow pow. It happened too fast to hurt. A friendly, prickly warmth radiated, an effulgent glow that spread across her scapular bumps and down her lower torso, met her legs and her knee socks, and melted into her shoes. *It wasn't terible terrible. I sat up, but when I was gettng down off the table, oopsy daisy my dress was mashed good and sound, stuck under my hind. The dumb slidey screech, I couldn't stop it. Like a fart.*

The doctor's whacks didn't take care of her prayer-time ailment. Not even after a second appointment, and a third. But unbeknownst to anybody, and partly by accident, late one night she discovered a little trick. She was starting out that last part again about being sorry. How many tries, already? As before, she felt her mouth noiselessly curling down wrong on the d in "God," threatening to shape the word as "Gah." Nonetheless she went through with it, "Gah." The next "God" too, she articulated wrong, "Gah."

She did it on purpose—she planted her molars, mutely pushed out the mis-
nomer, and concluded on that foolish, near-blasphemous note. "Forgive
me for all my sins, dear Gah, please dear Gah, please," she pleaded, "in
Jesus' name, amen."

She was shocked at her brazenness. But the muscles of her body un-
clenched. Very soon her mind went floaty as a cloud and she somersaulted
down the grassy green hillocks and over the cliff edge into sleep.

The next night she drifted off even before Mama and Daddy came upstairs.

So here's the question she phrased later, in her journal. *What if did I
singe my conshus?* A person could come to ruin in that exact way, she knew.
One wrong deed could lead to the next and the next and the next. The in-
stigator would suffer fewer and fewer pangs, as time went along, until their
conscience got burned to a coal black.

Anna thinks fleetingly, So what might I imply, now, from my present
deviated state? But she's too close to lunacy, and too pooped, to probe that
subject, yet. Her head feels too swarmy and come-around-again spinny.
The way she's backed up to the bathtub, the porcelain's cold rancor is seeping into her spine. She's lonely for Wade, for the toasty closeness of him,
even for his teapot steam. She'll let her reading material here in the bathroom to wait for morning. Maybe she'll allow the box itself downstairs, to
boot. She lids it shut though, as solicitous of the diaries and the remaining
stories as of their counterparts wallowing overhead in the insulation, barred
from the house air. Conversely, true to her loosey-goosey self, before *shluff-
shluff*ing off to bed she softly palms Todd's door open so that he needn't be
reinhaling his own stale carbon dioxide the rest of the livelong night.

31

But are any of these unused installments the least bit relevant? wonders Anna, the Tingley box in front of her in the sunlit kitchen.

Well, maybe this one—the story about her soup strainer.

"Now, can you point to a consequence?" she remembers Miss Fritz querying of the tenth graders. "Yes, Anna?"

"The skipper just poohed the old sailor. Scorned his warnings. Said don't worry."

"But what resulted? Remember, we're talking here about cause and effect. In this case, effect."

"Yes ma'am, I know. He was just some old nut-head that didn't care beans what anybody said. Him poohing, that was the consequence of his lofty attitude."

"Oh. Why, yes, of course. And as a result? That is to say, con-se-quent-*ly*?"

"Sure, their deaths. He and the maiden froze stark stiff. But Miss Fritz, it never said he bound *himself* and then her. Just her."

"No, Anna, look again. Look at the stanza ending with 'a frozen corpse was he.' Now check the next line of the poem."

"It says he's lashed to the helm, sure. But you don't get told that until after he's dead. You don't know at first. You shouldn't have to quail around rightening all your wrong slants."

"Or perhaps you should. You're expected to draw your understanding from the clues. That's what is meant by the word 'infer.' The reader must fill in the blanks—must make certain inferences." And her teacher continued on, leaving Anna behind in the dust, for in her mind she was starting to formulate a more expedient title for the tale she'd begun the night before on Daddy's typewriter. She would need to xxx out the other title, or start over.

M-o-r-a-l-*e,* she thinks, ha. "Annie's Suffered Morale"—that would've worked.

A Morale about a Suffered Consequence

It was a pass out tracts Sunday and the mission help was done having sandwiches so Mrs. Overholt who'd took oversight since time memorial handed the packets of Gospel Messengers around and told everybody their routes. Like she always did. "Annie and me'll take both sides of Grackle Street," she'd say, or some such street, and "Ralph, you get Chester Street," and on down her paper that had her harvestfield map on it. That Sunday it was likewise, Grackle Street for Annie and her.

At the stop sign Mrs. Overholt was putting the string from off their tracts up her sleeve to save and Annie busied herself posing blase like in the Sears catalog with her one saddle shoe pitching outwards raffishly. "You ready?" asked Mrs. Overholt. "Remember not to put them in the people's milk box because they'll just end up to be padding under the bottles, and their mail box is their private property so not there either."

Annie'd done this enough with Mrs. Overholt, she knew the mail slot in the front door was the best preference. And otherwise Mrs. Overholt'd put the tract in the screen door handle. But Annie didn't go for that second way, usually if there wasn't a slot she put the paper under the porch mat, designed and artful so the corner poking out would catch the people's eye. And it was no different today, she marched from house to house dropping the Messengers down the slots or fixing them under the mats and not fooling around, or leastways not until she got to this pink painted house. On the one side lived the Hustons, very nice and cordial, but the other half had these people living there with a retarded son. Mama always said be friendly, he can't hurt you, but still Annie was intimated by this great big boy named Buddy. He'd frivol the whole summer away just bouncing in the porch chair. If he got excited he'd squeal "Ooo-ooo-ooo-ooo," nothing meaningful, and drool and motion with his fingers, they stayed stuck together and curled down in knots.

She didn't so much mind some unfortunates, Pyleses' mongoloid girl wasn't so bad, Lulu, frowzy and chubby and always going up to passersby not of Pyleses' acquaintance. Or Tommy Clark, he was only crippled, he still had his perspection. But Buddy. The one thing worse was the time Daddy'd taken her and Margie to feed the ducks at the Waterbury park and somebody'd come toward them pushing a baby buggy and without a thought Annie'd run up for a peek at the baby, only to see it had a head like a basketball, it stunned her so bad she started bawling. So that was how she learned at a very young age about waterheads.

But Buddy wasn't out on the porch today and she carefreely trod up the steps. Inside the father walked past the screen door in his undershirt, scratching his stomach and hardly giving her a passing look. Not acting nosy herself either, Annie went to deposit the Messenger but here under the mat was last month's tract. All tracked up, probly hers, one she'd put. Stooped over thinking, she didn't know whether to leave it be or fix it again on display with the fresh one. She couldn't make up her mind and choose betwixt the two. Move it or don't? The headlines on the front said loud and clear, IN THE WORDS OF THE APOSTLE PAUL IN ROMANS 3, THERE IS NONE RIGHTEOUS, NO NOT ONE. THERE IS NONE THAT UN-DERSTANDETH, THERE IS NONE THAT SEEKEST AFTER GOD. THEY ARE ALL GONE OUT OF THE WAY. WITH THEIR TONGUES THEY HAVE USED DECEIT, AND THEIR FEET ARE SWIFT TO SHED BLOOD. FRIEND, HAVE YOU YIELDED UP YOUR HEART AND LIFE TO THE LORD? ARE YOU WALKING IN HOLINESS AND OBEDIENCE? She couldn't just take it back, it wasn't mission property anymore.

Leave it be, she decided, and just put the new one in the door handle, do Mrs. Overholt's way. She was fidgeting the new tract into place when Buddy saw her. In there he was in the parlor rocking and now he started his expleting, "Ooo-ooo-ooo-ooo."

"Buddy boy, what?" Annie heard the mother asking from over by the TV where she couldn't at all see out on the porch. "Does the cat want let back in? George! George! Yoo-hoo. Where'd you go? Can you let the cat back in?"

"It's nuttin, Sally," the father answered from back the hall, "it's just one of them little missionary gals. Gots on her soup strainer."

He never would of said it for Annie's ears, he never considered about his words carrying. But she was still caught unawares and flabbergasted. And she didn't want the mother knowing either, it didn't take her long jamming the tract in and getting herself out of there. Escaped to Hustons' side she almost didn't think to leave their paper, which she realized though in the nick of time. Then she steamed on to the next house and all the rest of the passing out job she wished she could be under a bucket. Who else called it her strainer? For soup!

First she thought, Okay Annie, that's just how it is, you're just different from the world, remember Daniel in the lions' den. But then she thought about her posing and posturing, how she'd aped after the catalog worldliness. She was too hoity. Elsewise getting nabbed for her soup strainer wouldn't of been some big insult. Being seen as some kind of a retard herself. So that's the morale of this story, the person getting in the truest way what they deserve. And sometimes it serves them right getting took down a peg.

Her one leg mixed up in the blue-checkered tablecloth, Anna messes with the pages. She unsnags from the cloth, snags, unsnags, snags. She kicks free of the hem, Wade's refugee moccasin swinging off her weather-chapped heel, and claps her foot onto the chair rung.

In a dilatory way, she kneads the wafer shape of her contact lens beneath the pulpy skin of her eyelid. She chases a minute lachrymal blot, yellow like hollandaise sauce, on her cheek. Mechanically she grooms her eyebrow stragglers. She chips at the lip of her coffee mug with her fingernail. Ever since the other night, that question has needled her: *What might I imply, now?* The domino effect can hardly be disputed. On corn day at Heatwoles, gathered around the corn crates with her church people and discussing, she flipped her lid, in a manner of speaking. Her comedown at the hands of the editor followed, leaving her flamming around for her faith. At long last, feeling up to snuff, she tried for a more substantive article about Abraham but flopped at it. Flip, flam, flop.

And pridefully acting upon Wade's suggestion that she take a more personal route and address head-on the challenges in holding to one's firm, fixed beliefs, she only leaped from the frying pan into the fire.

What's the famous adage? Murphy's Law, is it? Yes. *Everything that can go wrong, will.*

MAYBE THIS IS a bit flimsy—maybe she's straining too hard for analogies. But doesn't pride *always* play a role? Her curbside footsy-wootsying down by the Grackle Street stop sign, in her story—ha. There's no question vanity was readily making inroads. And fashionwise, certainly, one thing just led to another. With worldliness pulling at her, she only slid on down *that* slippery slope.

She remembers the catalog game she and Margie invented, in which they took turns choosing the best frocks on the Misses pages.

"Tucks down the front, that's chick," Margie asserted one day, defending her selection.

"'Cheek,' you mean."

"Huh-uh."

"Uh-huh. 'Cheek.' Go ask Wanda."

With the outdated catalogs they crafted paper-doll ladies, backing them with cereal-box cardboard so they'd stand upright. Old Sunday school offering envelopes, the dolls' closets, held their many outfits. The glamour queens lived in a broken overnight suitcase Aunt Dolly had thrown out—it had a dapper red handle—and in one of the satin pockets Anna had found a spent tube of Aunt Dolly's lipstick, so she luxuriated in rotating the Luscious Cherry butt upwards and applying an imaginary layer, pancaking her lips to grind it in.

That was in grade school—the innocent-looking make-believe—but the allures gained a toehold.

During her first years in high school, Anna occasionally chomped at the bit. "Maybe a shinier material, Mama? Maybe swishy?" Or "How come it's got to be this baggy?" But the regimentation pretty much held. The summer after tenth grade, though, she took to pestering Mama for honest-to-goodness dressy, stylish shoes.

"With pointy toes, Mama. Aren't I next thing to a woman? Tie shoes are for little runts, for babies. Look at my busts. I'm not some puny little scruff anymore. Ple-e-ease?"

In Shapiro's store stood one of those X-ray machines—the customer could feed in a nickel to view the shadowy semblance of their entrapped phalanges. Anna's peering from the gloom didn't look damagingly squished. But Mama still had her reservations. "I just don't know," she wavered. She grabbed for Herbie and sat down. "Such points. They're too extreme."

Perched sidesaddle on the clerking stool, her hose crinkled from her trips up the ladder in the back room for more try-on samples, Mrs. Shapiro jingled her shoehorn against the chrome. Anna watched for the softening of Mama's chin, for the little giving-in flickers. "Aren't they perfect, Mrs. Farber? A perfect fit?" Mrs. Shapiro heaved damply with conviction, her eyeglasses chain strafing her low-cut taffeta blouse and her divulged, poached flesh. "Such darling pumps—you like them, yes?"

To Anna she said, "You want them boxed up?" The woman patted Mama's knees. "Will that be all, Mrs. Farber?"

Back home, Margie as her audience, Anna pranced in front of the oval bureau mirror that distorted their likenesses, making their bodies bandy and elongated. "Not right!" Margie cried. "What about me? Ma-a-ma! Why'm I stuck with these old barrels!" So Mama had to purchase a second pair of hussy-style shoes. Eventually she scraped up enough money for Mary Janes like Wanda's, cutesy and pert, and Margie quit her mooning. On Sundays Anna and Margie paraded over to the mission chapel, a chummy twosome as full of importance as Banty hens.

Then skirt lengths entered in. In eleventh grade Anna sewed herself a gored jersey number, wine red. Smashing, she thought. But the first time she put the skirt on to go anywhere—oh no. Margie, too, grasped the incongruousness: in the mirror beveled frontwards on its hinges, the fuddy-duddy expanse of material kerblammed around Anna's calves, piteously at odds with her shee-eek shoes.

Downstairs Daddy and the boys already had their coats on. Wesley was chanting, "Grogans first! Grogans first! Grogans first!" Shortly they would be going around to all their friends—Pyleses, too, and the Clarks, Finkelsteins, Nickels, and Agnes Retzlaff with her peanut butter fudge. Last year the Grogans' door had flown open before Mama could even fix the pitch for "Joy to the World." Mrs. Grogan was pumping her arms in welcome and shouting, "Come on in afore you git frostbit!" Caroling in the parlor, *Let e-e-vry-y hea-ea-eart pre-pa-are hi-im roo-oo-oom, and heav'n and na-tu-ure sing, a-and heav'n and na-tu-ure sing,* Anna and her siblings had ogled the festive spread in the next room—the punch bowl of eggnog reigning over the table, the ribbon Jell-O, the fruitcake Billy said could make his grand-pappy drunk. Below the Christmas tree lay a preposterous pile of presents, and Mr. Grogan's electric train clackety-clacked around a ring of track, chasing its tail.

Still assessing her skirt, Anna knew it would drag below her coat, one Mama had unearthed from last year's Evangelical Brethren outreach box. Anna held off a few seconds longer. Haltingly she rolled her waist elastic like the wax paper on a sandwich, folded once, folded twice. By now Margie had bounded off the bed to study her own image. As her body undulated sickishly with the warp of the glass, the pout on her face assumed enough dimension that Herbie's parakeet, Sammy, could've lit there. In rapid succession she tucked her own waistband once over, twice over.

Anna smacked at her buried placket button. It made a fat lump. She smacked at it again, to no avail. "We'd better hurry," she said. "Come on."

Mama stood by the coat rack now, too. As her daughters descended the stairs, the glove she'd been pulling on slipped to the floor. "Oh," said Mama. "Anna, I should've helped you mark your hem." Mama's hand went up to her mouth. "Why, Margie. Girls, I'm surprised. You go back upstairs and change."

Climbing the steps Anna felt cheap and exposed, like a harlot. She swung the wardrobe door open and stared at her dresses. "But there isn't anything that won't stick out of my coat," she choked, just to Margie.

She heard Herbie and Wesley bickering, and Daddy's, "That's enough, boys. Now hush." Impulsively her sister spun around, ran to the stoop doorway, leaned into the nerve-strung airspace, and hollered, "Tightwad old church rules! Tightwad old narrow-minded bishops!"

"Margie!" she said with a hiss, appalled, before her own dam burst. She threw herself onto the bed, burrowed in, and let her tears drench the chenille flowers of the spread. "I'm not going anywhere!" Margie muttered, addressing the wall. "I'm not, I'm not!"

When Anna's noise reduced to sniffles, Daddy was conversing in undertones with Mama, ignoring Wesley kicking at the umbrella stand. "Well then," said Mama, much subdued, "we'll stay home." And of course, who could've caroled? Who could've chimed in on a sad, bleak "O Come, All Ye Faithful," their smiles stretched falsely?

So it went. The next summer, in payment for Anna's assistance when Aunt Dolly wallpapered her dinette, Aunt Dolly furnished her with a stack of old *Good Housekeeping*s. Owlishly Anna consulted the beauty tips. She slathered her limbs with baby oil and achieved a tan. But her experiment with Sun-In turned her hair the color of calf poop. The day she fell asleep in the yard with her culottes bunched around her thighs, she broiled nearly to a crisp. "You look like a knockwurst," Margie ribbed. "A ring baloney," said Wanda. "Your yellow hair's the mustard."

When the Farbers departed Pottstown and joined up with the Evangelical Brethren at Jackson Road, home to a lively youth group, diminished buns on the girls were all the rage. Margie avowed that even if the opposite were true, even if walloping lunks were still fine and nobody were cutting their hair, she would still prefer peewee sized. The dead weight of hers gave her a headache.

"Huh-uh-uh," Anna said to her sister one evening, "I'm not gonna help do the deed."

"Okay then, don't."

"You've got some grit," said Anna. Margie reached around with a pair of scissors and took an awkward chop at her own mane. Anna watched the lank brown swatch miss the wastebasket and land on the bathroom floor.

The next day Mama went around with rheumy red-rimmed eyes.

That fall, hurrying every morning to make it to her 8:00 college class, English 101, Anna wopped and poked at her clodhopper dud of a bun. She winced, pushing in the hairpins. She'd get the one side shaped up only to have the other come unglued. "Wouldn't a nice manageable Holsum donut be better?" she said to Mama. "The bishops aren't putting a stop to things."

"No," said Mama, "they're not, and it has me puzzled. How can they justify taking the path of least resistance?"

"Or are the old rules just wrong?" asked Anna.

After a youth-group hay ride, spending the night at Judy Stauffer's place, Anna said to her friend, "Don't you feel like the sorest thumb, sometimes? Don't you get spells when you hate your looks?"

"Not really. Why? Do you?"

Anna rolled her eyes. "Why'm I the only frump in our youth group? I'll never fit in. I'm just this dumb stumblebum."

"You are not."

"Just to look normal, for once—that'd really be something. But I get the willies. Just the idea."

"What's to worry about? What's so scary? You're the most sincere Christian I know. You're not some Moslem."

"No, but—"

"Girl, you'll still get to heaven."

"But see—nobody's—well, okay, all right. But not a lot. Not a lot."

Judy's scissors went *snip-a-snip-snip*. Oops, in back Anna's hair hung at a slant. It hung crooked. Judy snipped again. Anna picked up the mirror and shrieked, "Now the other side's hanging down!"

By the finish she couldn't even pull what was left into a barrette.

The next morning she sped into the house calling for Mama. "Look at me, just look at me! How'd this ever happen?"

"Dear Lord in heaven. Oh, dear Lord. Anna, I can see where this is leading."

"I know! Put my gravy sieve over *this?* Try to plaster everything back tight again? Make myself all grim and strict? No, I guess not."

Daddy walked into the room and stopped cold. He caught up a dot of spittle at the corner of his lip. He cleared out the gurgle in his throat. "So, Anna, you too—you too." She eased past Mama weeping into her dust-cloth and fled upstairs.

Daddy never roundly reproached her. Plainly he was disappointed. But he'd not delivered his hankies sermon in a long while. As it turned out, the few times he got asked to preach at Jackson Road he stuck mostly to the Beatitudes and Jesus' prohibitions against tit-for-tat vengeance, *But I say unto you which hear, Love your enemies, do good to them which hate you, bless them that curse you, and pray for them which despitefully use you,* and Jesus' story about the sheep and the goats, *Inasmuch as ye have done it unto one of the least of these my brethren, ye have done it unto me.*

Relying on wire mesh rollers from K-Mart and stabby pink plastic stickpins, Anna cultivated a bouncy effect. She retreated from her social bloopers with a toss of her head, slopping her fluffy front strands down across her eyes. In her looseleaf binder, in the zipper bag for pencils, she kept a single prayer cap quashed into an unholy, asymmetric chunk. All through her sophomore year of college, too, there it stayed. But her junior year, waiting in the cafeteria lobby to meet up with Wade for lunch, she transferred her relic to the pocket of somebody's raincoat. She would've mentioned it to Wade, but he had on his mind the set of snow tires he wished he'd brought back from Hawk Knob. Over the weekend she'd met his folks for the first. His dad had led everybody on a hike up the back forty to a massive shale outcropping where mountain laurel spouted from the fissures, to acquaint her with the next-county ridges, washboard bumpy and purple hazed and repeating into the distance.

The August after graduation, she glided with Daddy down the center aisle of the Jackson Road sanctuary, sprigs of baby's breath wreathing her head. The chains on her sandals cut bothersome red marks across her bridges, and Mama had insisted on her wearing a slip. "It'll be too hot, Mama," she'd protested. "There's already that sticky icky lining." Sewing Anna's eyelet gown, Judy had faced it with tricot, all but the flippy little sleeves.

"A full slip, Anna. Now you mind."

"I'll suffocate!"

But in the photograph of her and Wade in the church basement gagging each other with cake, the only thing perceptibly wilted by the evening mugginess is the pink-striped gladiolus bud pinned to his shirt, from Mom Schlonneger's flower bed.

Anna hadn't trolled deep within her soul, abandoning the prayer cap. She'd gone along with the flow. She'd wanted this not to matter. She'd willed it not to matter. And as a newlywed, she gallivanted through her paces. She had her hubby, relatives, and friends; her pretty much spit-shined apartment (excluding the greasy cupboard knobs); and her copyediting job at the *Jackson Herald.* She avoided backward looks and chiefly sallied ahead. Daddy's death, though, left an unspeakable hole in the world.

Quitting at the *Herald,* pregnant, in her eighth month, left her with too much time for thinking. "The thing is, I could die in labor," she croaked one evening, supine on the davenport that could be pulled open and made into a guest bed. In the slaying September heat, the upholstery wanted to fuse itself to her legs. If she gazed down her length, her bustline made a mere foothill on the Mongolian heights. The baby's hiccups were twitching her maternity smock.

"Daddy could've been right about hair and caps," she said. "Which would make *me* wrong, shameless in my sin. What if I die not having made my peace? Jaded and unrepentant?"

"Unrepentant, nah." Wade gave her a glance and inserted his nose back into his book.

All right, she thought, I'll investigate for myself. I'll take that step—establish myself on a quest—and if head coverings are part of God's plan, so be it. Cowed by the possibility, she dabbled at the orange rickrack on her smock. She rucked and unrucked her shorts cuff. She moved to pull her hair up off her wet neck, but the oppressive heat and the gravity of her compunction pressed her deeper into the cushions. "I think I might be going bats," she whimpered.

Sunday after Mama's fried chicken dinner, Anna slipped down to the basement study. She'd settled on Daddy's commentaries as the proper starting point. His papers and booklets still took up the desk, filmed over with a year's worth of dust and divested of all purpose and intent. A pall hung in the room, an absence of spirit. She recalled Daddy's distress, at the hospital. "All the things I didn't get done," he'd wheezed. "If only I—if only I could've—" She'd dodged around the IV pole for his hand and said firmly, "No, Daddy. All the things you *did* get done. Think about *that.*" But her words hadn't eased him much. At the very end, she and Herbie had stood by helplessly. They'd witnessed his struggling, comatose breaths and the chill stealing up his arms. The final rattle died away and he was gone. Nobody home. It was just his jaundiced, papery husk.

The various commentaries she browsed after Mama's Sunday dinner didn't agree on the interpretation of 1 Corinthians 11:1-16. "One thing's for sure!" she chortled a few days later, dumping onto the bedroom dresser the Clyde Bailey bandanna hankies she'd found at K-Mart near the wrist-watches counter, displayed in parcels of three. "That passage never suggests the Evangelical Brethren caps and straight pins. How come I never, you know, never really *thought* about that? Until now? I mean, I *knew* better. The woman was just supposed to keep her headpiece on, her long, drapey sari or whatever they called it in Corinth. Nobody was saying she had to get-up herself in some bizarre-for-the-times, out-of-style hat!" Anna ran her hand over her sweaty face, then slung one of the hankies onto her head and tied the ends in back, underneath her locks too swamped by the humidity to be exhibiting their ordinary spunk. "Whew, this heat!" She flopped onto the bed to fan herself with the store bag.

Wade stood over her, stymied.

The night her pains began, 2:00 a.m., she didn't take time to fasten on a bandanna. Racing to the hospital in Waterbury, digging marks into Wade's arm during her contractions, at least she wasn't throttled up in her headgear. In the delivery room she bore down with a fevered intensity, *Jesus, Jesus, help me dear God, help help help,* and afterwards, spared from hemor-rhaging to death from placenta previa or a burst artery, her wrinkled babe attached to her breast, she lay back in a sweet-by-and-by bliss. No head hanky, but her pleas had still reached heaven.

Then life turned upside down. Those first weeks and months of new motherhood, the responsibilities consumed her. She fretted over the chances of the baby reacting to immunizations—of the MMR antigens col-luding and metastasizing—and over the alarming new findings on cold viruses' longevity and resistance to antibiotics. Also, could traces of caffeine in breast milk cause DNA mutations in an infant's cells, or developmental delays? Not that Mary Beth showed any danger signs. Anna pored over *Par-ents' Magazine*s, reading articles about the grave upshots of ear infections, the different vaporizers on the market for treating croup, and the perils of feeding honey laced with *C. botulinum* spores to a baby under twelve months of age. She checked continually on Mary Beth's breathing when she slept, bending to catch the in-and-out lisps. How could've she heard wound up in a head cloth? And one day, emptying a chest drawer to make more room for Mary Beth's sleepers, snap-tab undershirts, Kicky Sockies, blan-kets, diapers, and safety-catch diaper pins topped with yellow ducks, Anna happened upon the bandannas. With nary a quibble she added them to her pile of unwanteds destined for the thrift shop on Jackson Road.

So I acted pragmatically, yes, notes Anna—I took the liberty to use my common sense. Stoic for the moment, fiddling with the coffee grounds in her mug, using the retracted tip of her mechanical pencil to push the slurry up the sides, she faces this next question unflinchingly: mustn't any Christian use the frail, God-given wits they were born with?

32

"Ma, you gotta get a move on. We're picking up the tomatoes."

"All right."

"At Pantry Pride. Peg's doing the Wal-Mart stop—they promised better deals on everything else."

"I'd expect so."

"Beckers'll be there early too. Peg wants all the chopping done on ahead."

"What?" Anna's cereal spoon parks in the air en route to her mouth. "Done before ten o'clock? You never told me that." *Calling all helping hands,* last Sunday's bulletin note read, *young and old. Youth group and any available parents, please be at the church on the dot of ten on Saturday. We hope to get the hoagies made by 11:30, the proceeds as always to benefit the Evangelical Missionary School of the Good Samaritan. Thanks and God bless, Jay and Peg.* "Then you're going along too, Wade."

"I am? Sure, if you need me."

Recklessly she staggers the dishes in the sink. She washes her hair, leaning over the bathtub while droplets from the obstreperous shower head ping down onto the spout. She pulls on jeans and rushes downstairs. She runs back up for her sweater—the red one with hangdown pockets, probably the reason somebody donated it to the Goodwill.

"I'll drive if you don't care, Dad," she hears, and Wade's grunt of agreement.

And, "An-na, get out here!"

She dives into the car as Wade lurches his front passenger seat back a notch for more leg room, and they peel out onto the road. They pass the mailbox and the winter-weary still-naked red oaks fronting the neighbor's field that's marked with crusty dimples of light overnight snowfall, and Todd swerves to miss the shoulder gully. The car jerks when he wrenches the wheels again, this time for the curve, but the road isn't slick and he confidently zips up the incline. "Oh dear," says Anna with a start, "did I unplug the blow drier? I forget. That outlet in the bathroom heats up—I don't know if I ever told you, Wade. Is that anything serious? If I put my hand against it, it's hot. Is that normal?"

Her brush was clogged with hairs, too. Scrambling, she maybe plunked it down too close to the open end of the blow drier, its coils behind the wire cage still glowing orange.

Addressing the egg-like rise of Wade's head above the neck rest, she accuses, "You didn't have to yell at me like you were calling the dog."

"I meant no ill, Anna."

"Even so! A little respect, how about?"

What good is the car heater? Shivering, the goosey cold hackles spreading up her back, she pulls her coat tighter around her. "Todd, let me pick through those tomatoes before you pay. If you're getting a whole case, it'll most likely include seconds."

"No, they'll be okay."

"The produce manager won't mind one bit. He's supposed to be accommodating. The store shouldn't charge for seconds."

"I'll handle it myself, Ma. You're not going in with me. Stop being a ding-dong harp."

"Hey, you."

"Anna, lay off," says Wade.

Hffff.

"You've got to choose your battles," her husband warns. "You can't fight them all."

Perhaps he's planning to say more. But remarkably, the back-seat furor subsides. The dust settles. The rest of the way into town, little flights of hymn choruses, brief impromptu bars from assorted songs, are all she emits.

While they're waiting for Todd to emerge from Pantry Pride, she says, "I suppose an impediment doesn't especially matter, since the tomato gets all hashed up, anyhow. Imperfection, I mean. By the time it reaches its promised destination, the hoagie'll be a soggy, undefinable mass, mostly. Oh, that's right, the lettuce and tomatoes go in a separate bag, don't they? Forgot that! Huh. Well, that's the breaks."

In the silence that follows, she speculates about a microscopic speck of *E. coli* harbored by a lettuce shred in a hoagie purchaser's sealed-up baggie maybe duplicating by the process of fission to the fatal teeming point.

CROWDING THE CHURCH KITCHEN are jars of pickles, mayonnaise, and vegetable oil, sundry paper supplies, lots of meats and cheeses, and the waxed-cardboard produce boxes. Past the counter-high serving slot in the wall with its accordion-pleated door that can be pushed shut during wedding receptions and other special occasions, in the open eating-and-fellowship area, Peg is coaching Marvin and Todd on how to arrange the tables for the assembly line. Employing a slippery cleaver-sized knife from the utensils drawer, Anna is steadily coring and slicing the tomatoes. She's always found challenging these pitch-in-and-help, church-family occasions—it's good to see everybody kowtowing to their different tasks, not acting too high and mighty to serve.

To Wade working alongside her: "These are about what I expected."

"Uh-huh."

"Pink rubber, more or less," she snorts.

"Sure, they're bred for hardiness. For marketability. They're crocked with enough pesticides to pass for embalmed."

"Don't *say* that."

Justine chopping lettuce chimes in. "Yeah, Frank won't touch shipped tomatoes with a 10-foot pole."

"I won't what?" says Frank. "Nope nope nope, Crystal," he growls at his daughter assigned to be his colaborer on the onions. With his elbow he corrals her back to her heap of papery skins. "Nope, a little water coming out your eyes won't hurt you."

"Do it the way I do at home—hold the onion under the faucet," says Anna. "Give that a try."

"Say, Frank, how's your back treating you?" asks Peg, approaching the serving window. "You're still on Ibuprofen?"

"Oh, I'm bearing up, bearing up."

Her trademark freckles crimping across her nose, Justine whispers to Anna, "He's not doing so hot. I keep waiting for the other shoe to fall."

Anna wonders, Other shoe? How many shoes do you have?

"Peg, what's the total figure for the orders?" asks Frank. "How good's the youth group making out?"

"We still don't know the exact net. The kids sure pounded the pavement, didn't they? Like I told Jay, all their enthusiasm, don't they deserve to see where their money's been going? Or at least see that level of poverty somewhere, firsthand?"

"That's a thought," says Justine.

"I just wish our church could send them on a mission trip," says Peg. "The short-term service-adventure type of thing the other churches around here are always reporting on. Wouldn't that be great, Crystal? Marvin, hey— where's that brochure?" But he and Todd are banging folding chairs onto a cart, making too much of a racket. "Oh, wait, did Jay maybe leave it in the youth classroom? Hold on."

A trip? Passports? Fly the youth group to Tegucigalpa? Anna is surprised.

In a matter of seconds, here comes Peg again, waving a paper. "Got it! You all look at this. Tell me what you think."

Wade rips off a paper towel to clear a space. He flattens the brochure open on the counter so the Beckers can see too. Squinting, Anna leans in. GO TEAMS, INC., hm, is that the organization? Or just the designation for the service groups?

"Interesting," says Frank. "Yup, plenty interesting."

"That's what I say." Peg nods vigorously. "Their mission emphasis looks to be right on target. Their operational setup, too. They'll provide a financial statement upon request."

"They send teams to Honduras?" asks Wade. "Tegucigalpa?"

"I don't know." Peg pokes at a tomato core in Anna's pan. "Puerto Rico is mentioned, and Belize and Guatemala. I wouldn't insist we stick to Tegucigalpa. Would you? Just so it's a place like that, somewhere really poor."

Wade says, "Don't the local churches send out their own evangelists?"

"Well, I'm sure, yes. But think how limited they are in resources."

One picture shows skin-and-bones children with swollen bellies, lined up to receive their bowls of foo-foo porridge or whatever, their indigenous staple. In another, teenaged participants wielding long-handled paint rollers are transforming a dingy concrete-block classroom to a bright peacock blue. In several photos a tent revival is in progress, and the blurb states, "Without supplying for the souls, too, the world will be lost." Something about the grammar seems shifty, but Anna can't quite put a finger on it.

She moves her lips inaudibly, intent on a volunteer's testimonial. *"Lord," I said as our bus rolled along, "on my own I can do nothing, just make me an in-*

strument." Within minutes of our arrival at Escobal I saw an old man sweeping sticks from his yard and went over and lent a hand. I collected up a basket of debris and when I got done the man was weeping. He couldn't believe he mattered enough for anybody to notice and carry the burden. I told him that's what Jesus did, he took our burden. So another seed was sown, praise the Lord. She wonders, Is a more in-depth program available then, for follow-up?

"The need in these places, wow," says Justine. "The spiritual need."

"What would it ever cost to go there, though?" says Anna. "Tons, I guess."

"So?" rejoins Frank who has lumbered over to the luncheon meats in Styrofoam trays on the far counter, glimmering under plastic wrap. "What's the meaning of sacrifice, anyway?" She turns to see him weasel forth a salami slice. With a few practiced flicks of the wrist, he rolls up the meat to pop it between his wet teeth. *Oink oink,* she thinks, dismayed at herself.

"That's the big thing, I know," says Peg. "Really, though. No sacrifice, no gain. Can't we pare back expenditures? Give up some nonnecessities?"

So give up your 10-packs of Swiss Miss cakes, Frank, thinks Anna. Sacrifice your Doritos and Cheez-Its and Pringles. Mounds bars. Peanut M&Ms. The pasty pink meat is studded with peppercorns and pallid snips of fat, and with every swallow his gullet wobbles. "Yes well," she says, "about sacrifice, maybe it's not everything it's cracked up to be."

Justine looks at her. "You want the kids going after the high-roller life? Not knowing from personal exposure about the tragedy in the world? The hand-to-mouth existence the other half leads?"

"That's not what I meant."

Wade is still focused on the brochure. "This Go Teams organization. They're a pretty fundamentalist bunch."

"Oh, you bet," says Peg. "The youth, when they fan out on their community-service projects, find opportunities to lead people to the Lord, one on one. And everybody's welcomed to the evening services where many more get converted. That's the main thrust—bringing folks to salvation."

"I led my friend to Christ," says Justine. "Diane. In fourth grade, out on the jungle gym."

"You're kidding," says Anna. Ineluctably, the street meetings back in Pottstown come to mind. "Did—did you—did you have her pray the sinner's prayer, or what?"

"She repeated something after me. I explained that her sins were washed in the blood. Jesus died, Jesus paid her ransom."

"You said that?"

"What was I supposed to say?"

"Bulls? Goats and bulls? You told her that Jesus, in dying, took their stead?"

"No, I didn't say *that*. Do you expect me to completely remember the train of conversation?"

"But why would've God exacted a ransom?"

Justine's auburn-fringed head snaps around on her neck. "Why are you grilling me? Bulls, shmulls—what do I care? That's Old Testament stuff. We're mercifully delivered from all that."

"From presenting the fleshpot delicacies, uh-huh. Pigeon parts, ram suet, lamb kidneys with the fat on, wrung-off pigeon heads, calf gall bladders."

"Ugh. Anna. What is your *point?*"

"Just that, I guess—ugh. Why would've God wanted gross-out guts?"

"Whoa whoa whoa," says Frank, "take it easy. Let's not get the cart before the horse. Let me see that info again. Hand it here, Wade, if you don't mind. If this group is spreading the simple gospel message, then I'm sure satisfied. Aren't you?"

Frank's thumbs are squishy from his sampling, and he's floundering around for something to use to clean them. "No more paper towels?" says Wade. "My fault. Hang on, I'll get another roll."

"They're on the highest right-hand shelf in the closet," Anna calls as he disappears into the hallway. "I think!" She clanks her knife onto the counter and scurries off in pursuit, down the corridor to the double-doored storage area next to the men's and ladies' restrooms. She finds him craning toward the economy pack of Bounty towels, 2-ply, extra absorbent, behind the plastic tablecloths on the shelf.

"Wade!" Out of breath, she steps backwards to allow the door to shut on itself and about knocks loose the wet mop clamped to the large, wheeled bucket the janitor rolls out for linoleum cleanups. But the mop head only rams into the box holding the candles for the annual Christmas Eve service, petite white tapers with paper collars to catch the wax drips. Not only do the collars save the sanctuary carpet, also they insure that some little child won't disturb the magical scene—the individual flickery, lit faces of the thronged congregation, and the joyous caroling—with a scream of pain. "Wade!" she gasps again. "I couldn't help it! I'm such an imbecile."

"What'd you do wrong? Speak your mind?"

"I—but I—"

"Anna, we're with friends. What are friends for? We don't all have to see eye to eye."

"No, but—"

"Relax." Bounty roll in possession, he looms close and chucks her chin. "I'll give you anything that foreign-missions outfit is raking it in."

"But you don't *know*."

"And you're no imbecile—you've a nimble wit. You're doggone funny."

Did she hear right? *Nimble* wit? Not *thimble?* Taken aback, she trails him out of the closet and tags in his shadow back to the church kitchen.

The subject there has turned to Crystal's gym teacher, Ricky Wallizer, and his wife, Carmen, who've adopted an Oriental baby. From Cambodia, Justine is sure. Or no, Vietnam. More parents and the rest of the youth group have begun piling into the fellowship hall, bringing along the snow on their shoes and spates of crunchy winter air, and when Peg requests her help in assessing whether the configuration of the tables will allow the sandwich making to proceed expeditiously, Anna hurries over. Susan throwing off her coat displays a striking cable-stitched turtleneck and Anna hears Brenda exclaim, "It's gor-r-r-geous. Wish I could wear clothes like that! I go for that gold—it's exactly your color."

"Honestly? I wondered if it makes me look dumpy." Happily Susan hugs Brenda. "I found it on sale up at the mall, at Bon Ton—way marked down. Thanks, really!"

Donna, placid and rosy, joins in the complimenting, and Anna smiles along.

Noontime, riding around town, Wade at the wheel so Todd can unload his hoagies, she keeps to herself. While the motor idles, beyond the vaporous glass of her rear window the people's doors fly open and shirtsleeved arms relieve the bearer of his cylindrical, paper-wrapped bundles. Occasionally somebody wags a hello at her. The brick fronts go past, the vinyl sidings, the porch posts, the lawns that are starting to dry in the sun and lose their snow lace. Mrs. Munk, Todd's English teacher, who requested six for her family, no onions. Bill Langdon on Mineral Street, responsible for Jonathan's guitar lessons. The Kelley brothers, Terry and Roger, at their automotive-repairs business. The Schildts' home, where Mary Beth loved to babysit. Fritsches, Brukers, Ulreys, Kratzes. Todd jumps back into the car and Wade inquires, "Where next?" and revs them onto the street. Stop and start, stop and start, stop and start. Her mind on what's transpired, and on the state of her manuscript, Anna only chirps up once in a while with some bland, unobjectionable comment.

33

"Hey," says Todd, in the kitchen. "Hey—turkeys."

Lacking her son's eager-beaver fascination, Anna only glances at the four muscular, majestic birds strutting, where the gangly greenbrier brambles on the slope angling up from Coldbrook Road give way to a stand of redbuds and persimmons. But Wade grabs his binoculars. "Unh, unh, unh," he gloats, "would you look at that."

"Can you please take care of this junk?" she demands. Why should the welter of jackets and lesson quarterlies and papers from church this morning, on the table, be her job? "Help me out, will you? Come on, Todd. Get the place mats and bowls." Still not pared out of her nylons, she clippity-clops her black felt-vamped clogs back to the sink and tugs the crockpot's umbilical cord from the outlet. "I'm still worried about Susan. About her reaction. People are talking, I'm positive."

Anna and Wade have already gone over the events in Sunday school—on the way home Todd got the rundown. It wasn't exactly pretty. Anna thinks again about how Susan, abetted by her hefty red Unger's dictionary, was ticking off the different gems on the foundation walls of the New Jerusalem, the abode of the resurrected saints of all ages, when Donna put up her hand.

". . . jasper, topaz, sapphire, sardonyx, calcedony, beryl, and emerald,"

Susan finished. "It's all in the book of Revelation." She caught her breath, tipping for a moment on her heels, before rounding out the picture. "And the city's twelve gates are solid pearl. Yes, Donna?"

"The splendor, that's true." Donna dog-eared a corner of her bulletin uneasily. "I shouldn't say this, I guess, but spending eternity singing "Holy, Holy, Holy"—you know, bowing down and worshiping for eons on end—doesn't seem to capture my imagination like it should. I don't think about it with a deep longing."

"Well, I can sympathize. It's too far beyond us to comprehend. With our mortal minds, we're incapable."

"But our desires should line up. Should fall into place. Here I am, wanting to stave off heaven. I'm afraid I'm not the best Christian."

"Same here," said Brenda. "I sure know what you mean." She smacked at her saggy pocketbook on the table in front of her, intending to remedy its posture, but it keeled over with a *thwop* and disgorged her keys, loose change, Kleenex, eyeliner, tampon case, cocoa-butter stick, and other doodads. She lunged for the open roll of Life Savers tumbling across the table toward Jay and Peg. "Jeez, if anybody's a weak Christian it's me."

"We've all fallen short," said Susan. "We've all made mistakes."

"No, but I never feel like I can reach that real nice, unselfish spiritual level. How does anybody even know they'll *get* to heaven?"

"We're saved," Susan reminded.

"Well, but the verdict isn't till judgment day. So how can anyone be honest-to-God sure? What if we just *think* we're saved?"

Anna jumped in. "It's a terrible pickle. I mean, for us all. Because we can so innocuously stray across that line of demarcation separating the sheep and the goats. Almost unwittingly. The Bible says we're saved by faith, right? But how's a person supposed to always stay really really really true and convinced the whole way back to the dimmest recesses of their cranium? Rabidly confident, all the time? It's too hard! Well, I guess there's that little 'out' clause that says we're the recipients of grace—that it's nothing we can contrive. Which makes us not all that responsible, then. Going by appearances, at least. People are all the time accepting salvation, but look how they act afterwards! Any old way!"

Frank sitting next to her declared, "So we've just got to leave it up to God."

How's *that* any comfort? thought Anna.

The chair on her other side, Wade's, had slammed down on all four rubber tips. Wade bent around her, practically squashing her. "A God who banishes the malingerers to a burning lake?" he asked Frank. "Are you content with that? A God who in his lovingkindness and for his pleasure creates humans, but to punish them for their dereliction, condemns them to a place of everlasting torment?"

Justine poked her head around Frank's and stared. Somebody accidentally struck their knee against the leg of the table, setting it to quaking.

Susan turned and took the chalk from the blackboard ditch. She rubbed the holder end against her chin, deliberating. Alternately, she made tiny repetitive clockwise circles in front of her, like she was practicing her penmanship. She put the chalk back down. No fluttering, her mouth pooched the whole way out to China, she looked long and hard at Wade. "There *is* a hell. Unless you think it's just a fundamentalist construct."

Fun-da-men-ta-list. She ground out the word in unhappy, tight bits.

No, it wasn't a fun class, Anna tells herself, investigating in the drawer for a pair of hot pads. So who're the turkeys here? she wonders. Wade's comment yesterday about the Go Teams bunch, and her outburst—and now this! Why'd Wade have to add fuel to the fire? "Don't you agree, hon?" she asks. "Haven't they been gossiping? Somebody's told Susan all about the Sunday school class she missed—that quiz you gave—and they've passed on our big discussion we had yesterday before she showed up to help with the hoagies. Advised her in great, juicy detail."

Anna removes the crockpot lid, sniffs at her chili. "But what good it'll do me to speculate, I don't know." She plunges her longest-handled ladle into the grub. "You guys, can you get moving?" she huffs. "Lift a finger, okay? Todd, put the place mats around."

"I forget where I saw this poster," says Todd, "but it said something about how we get a hell of our own making."

"Yeah," replies Wade, "I've heard that quote."

"Mr. Barnard says hell is a pack of nonsense. He says there're maybe a few deserving. People like Hitler."

Wade starts gathering up the paraphernalia from the table. "My next chance to teach Sunday school, I have in mind to give one doozy of a quiz. I've already prepared it."

"Oh no," squeaks Anna.

"Number one, What's our purpose in studying the Bible? Number two, Do we adhere to every word? Number three, Since we don't, why not? Number four, If only a small minority element can claim they were born into the true religion, what are the mathematical odds it was us? Number five, What allows us to thumb our noses at other belief systems?"

She spends a moment digesting. "Uh-huh, all right. And then what will you say to the answers?"

"Yeah, Dad. Let's hear it."

"I'll suggest that we get frank about the Bible's antiquity and its cultural biases. And freely confess to how little we know about the metaphysical. Darn it, what warrants this holier-than-thou arrogance? What's the point in hanging on to these pharisaical attitudes? Why are we so full of snobbery and self-satisfaction? How did we turn into self-righteous prigs?"

"Snobbery, Wade?"

"Cool," says Todd. "'Prigs,' that's cool."

"No, it's not!" she cries. "Wade, you're unfair."

"Possibly. 'Fair' might be a matter of perspective—it might all depend on which side of the fence you're on."

"But if—"

He cuts her off. "I say it's high time for a reality check. Do the folks at church expect sinners will burn forever? Honestly expect that? I don't think so. I don't think anybody much does. Ha, another quiz question—here we go—ready? Number six, Are we counting on a sulfur-and-brimstone hell? If so, why aren't we racing like mad to get everybody and their grandmother converted in the next ten minutes?"

"Boy oh boy, Dad."

"In point of fact, I'd better not sit around waiting for my next chance to substitute for Susan. Not if the youth group is talking about a mission trip. One of these Sundays I'll just spur some good healthy back-and-forth debate in class about that. I'll ask whether we want our kids peddling hellfire and damnation."

"Wade, what is going *on?* What're you after? Are you going to keep pushing the envelope, pushing the envelope?"

"Aw, Ma."

"Stop that. Stop calling me 'Ma.'" Flailing her hot pads, she asks Wade, "You want to be making enemies at church? You want us turning into pariahs?"

"Of course not."

"You said yesterday they're our friends, remember? Well, I hardly knew what to do when Susan scrooged up like that, this morning in class—"

"She what?"

Anna doesn't quite want to say. "Oh, just—"

"Diddled her eyelids?"

"No, when she—" Anna shakes her head. "Never mind."

Has he never noticed Susan's one strange mannerism when she's displeased? Why, Anna picked up on it their very first Sunday at Conoy. She'd asked Wade after church to reclaim Todd from the nursery, and forging out the door in search of Jonathan and Mary Beth, she saw a few items lying in the middle of the parking lot, including Jonathan's little guitar she'd made for him out of rubber bands and a Velveeta cheese box. Over by the high wire safety fence guarding the embankment that cuts sharply down to the Catawally were her children. In the company of another youngster, they appeared to be sucking the nectar out of some honeysuckle blossoms off the profusion of vines climbing the fence. When the new pal dove for another flower, the sight of her panties peeking out below her frilly polka-dotted skirt reminded Anna of those yard-art mushrooms planted all over Conoy in people's front lawns (if you took a second look, the mushroom was really a doubled-over old grandma, just her bloomers and her obscene, chumpy legs).

Then the door behind Anna swung open, and the woman coming out—Susan—extended a larky handshake. Anna had in mind to say a little something to get acquainted. But Susan's eyes flitted across the parking lot, and she let out a "Toodle-doo!" and took off down the steps. "Ellie! Girlie, girlie! Children!" She screeched to a stop by their dumped possessions. Besides the cheese box, there were story papers from Sunday school, some packs of candy, and Ellie's small New Testament, and Susan plucked the book from the macadam, her mouth swelling out in indignation.

Anna bustled over to help collect everything. The candy belonged to Ellie, too—Brenda Arnold's Ellie, Larry's sister. The child wasn't even a relative of Susan's, wasn't hers to boss. Crouched by Susan, almost knocking heads with her, Anna stole another appraisal. Close up, her lips were even puffier. Like pumped-up bicycle tires, Anna decided. Maybe a pair of pincushions, or the leftover butt from a pot of chicken-corn-and-noodle soup. "Your Bible, Ellie!" Susan hailed loudly. "Come right this minute!"

After Anna shooed Jonathan and Mary Beth into the car, Jonathan asked, "Mommy, why'd that lady get mad?"

"Oh no, sweetie. Just vexed. What if somebody'd run over you children's stuff? Right out in the parking lot—was that any place to put your treasures?" Having missed the encounter, Wade was buckling Todd in, and Anna landed hard in her own seat and started gabbing up a storm. "Wasn't that a great bunch in Sunday school, hon? Such a lively discussion! What'd you think of that one couple, the Nussbaums?"

Later she did fill Wade in on the run-in. But divulging her chicken-butt thoughts—that would've been mean. Plain mean. Even now, *especially* now, she'd rather not.

From the living-room closet where he's hanging up the coats comes another of Wade's volleys. "Friendship implies a mutual respect, Anna. And objectivity and open-mindedness are basic in any sound relationship. That sort of generosity is all I'm after. People have to be more charitable in their thinking."

"Well then, *you* be charitable, too. You hear? Because people are sincere. That spiel Susan went on about scriptural inerrancy, after you challenged Frank? Didn't you see how whole-hog in earnest she was? When she said our church ought to be more rooted and grounded and the whole class nodded along, I wanted to crawl underneath the table. I feel like you—I—we—like we're alienating everybody."

"I hope not." Wade has propped himself by the doorway. "Let's not go blowing things out of proportion."

"How'd we ever get into such a morass?"

"Don't overreact."

"This isn't contributing to my sanity any, if you want to know."

"Then buck up, buttercup."

"Was it Frank who told about yesterday?" shrieks Anna. "Was it him?" She rolls her eyes in exasperation, then flaps her mouth shut because Todd is listening. No doubt Frank even repeated her litany of sacrifice parts! But a sudden bolt of self-revelation courses through her. What right has she to get up in the air about some gossip mill, given her own scummy, prurient interest?

34

I think. I think, I think. For a while, it was her theme song. She attached the disclaimer if she was relating an experience or just providing information. Suppose she'd had that same old dream in which she couldn't find a bathroom private enough. Only a commode in the corner of somebody's dining room, right out in the open, or a row of commodes in desperate need of flushing in some big hospital ward—no stalls. She'd started to pee in her chair, and she'd wakened to find her bladder about to burst. "It was this nice parlor chair," she informed Margie. "With a chintzy cushion, *I think.* I couldn't hold it anymore, is all."

Or when she reported back to Aunt Dolly who'd sent her and Wanda downstairs to Simpson's Grocery for a bottle of aspirin and a loaf of day-old bread, Anna quipped, "No bread left, too bad, so sad. Well, there *was* a loaf but that Mrs. Conklin lady got it. Here's your Bayers and all your change, *I think.*" Even when participating in meaningless banter, she had to put herself through the wringer. In the schoolyard, to Wanda's "Whatcha got in your lunchbox?" Anna answered, "Bean soup in my Thermos and a chicken-salad sandwich with my mama's pickles and *I think* Miracle Whip."

At school one day the teacher asked, "Quickly, what's the capital of Kansas? Class? Anna?"

"Topeka?" she gulped. "Yes, I think."

Mrs. Kephart paused from jabbing the map with her ruler. "Not 'I think,' Anna. Anything you say is what you think. Just say it. Skip the monkey business."

On Wednesday evening at preparatory service at the mission, after the bishop's promptings about clearing your conscience to avoid taking communion unworthily and drinking damnation to your soul, the appointed moment arrived for the examination. It was time for the members to file in small groups out to the anteroom (the ladies' side of the chapel before the men's), to stand before Strite and Herman Overholt and Daddy. Anna took her place in the anteroom lineup, everybody's carriages solemn and attentions directed at the leaders' trouser knees. The swinging door's thwumps ceased, the bishop surveyed the delegation meditatively, and he intoned, "Can you testify to peace with God and your fellow man, insofar as it lieth within you?" *Lieth*, he said. *Lieth within you.*

She imagined herself getting struck down during Sunday night's communion service for fibbing. Sunday night she would gnaw soberly on the bread, concentrating on the wracked, crucified body of the Lord, and then wallow the grape juice around in her mouth while fixating her thoughts on the Lord's letted blood—and in due course, maybe during footwashing, lockjaw paroxysms would commence, or some such horror. Swiftly down the row in the anteroom came the women's answers, "Yes," "Yes," "Yes," "Yes," mostly little peeps, and borne along on the tide, she managed a "yes." But to insure she wasn't *lying within her* she added in her head, *I guess.*

So she didn't outright fudge. And it occurs to her now, as she stares out the study window, that for all her private and not-so-private braggadocio and blustering recently, she's simply been admitting to her *I think*s and *I guess*es.

BEHIND HER, in the warm, afternoon torpor of the kitchen, the wall clock kvetches, kvetches, kvetches as the seconds hand passes the minute hand at the eleven and the hour at the two, running down the battery. Tuning in, she distinguishes also the *click click* of ladybugs colliding with the cabinets. The crop of ladybugs last fall was worse than usual, she remembers. On the days the temperature hit the eighties, the backyard air swarmed. Invading the house, they struck out across the ceilings in undefinable migratory patterns, behaving as though they had little tickers inside, *west-west, north-north, northwest-northwest,* not calibrated according to a consistent, chartable scheme. Instinctively they congregated behind the window trims, or in the covert upper corners of the cupboards, or in the secretive pockets of dead space behind the hung pictures and shelved books, ostensibly to hibernate, and although it's near the end of winter, now, she still encounters clumps—she sucks them up with the vacuum wand. Isn't it too soon for the bodies, any that are still alive, like these in the kitchen, to be resurrecting? This morning a ladybug even came hiking across the computer keys. So what's up? What's tripping the bugs' biological chronometers?

Dumb and mum and not responsible for its aberrations, an insect can only whiz its wings or haplessly perambulate. But certain advantages exist in just such a plight, undoubtedly.

On a whim she pages way back to her "Jots and Titties" story and ferrets around for any interesting clinkers. Let's see, hm. *If somebody asks something, you don't have to exactly answer. This isn't lying, not answering.* But if Susan Nussbaum were to start dredging in Sunday school for everybody's stance on salvation, how would clamming up—or sidetracking her—be ethical? Or fair? *Probly it's not wrong if the person is ignorant and it would be too hard to explain the exact truth and so you don't.* Here too, the logic seems inapplicable. Nobody at church is reasoning impaired—incognizant, or bona fide ignorant. Why should openly discussing, freely exchanging different ideas and views, be threatening?

Cogitating further, Anna twiddles her pencil point in her sweater buttonhole. The house's broody stillness magnifies the on-again off-again purring of the fridge and the occasional *zzzts* of electricity from the lamp bulb, not just the clock and ladybug sounds. The blue-tulip warmth showering down upon her bent head tempts her to sink it down onto the table for a catnap, but instead she flings out her arms, rotates them in their sockets, and squares away her hunch.

STICKY POINTS, she could title this manuscript, or *One Stickler of a Spiritual Journey.* But she can't send it to Gospel Press, the Evangelical Brethren publishing house's book division.

Their book editor she met at Rawlings Lake was friendly. He materialized out of the crowd to introduce himself with a handshake. "Thomas is the name. I appreciated your remarks."

"Why, thank you. Thomas who, did you say?"

"Bernie Thomas. My roots are here—the Thomas homestead is ten miles to the north. I bring the family back every summer."

"Oh, uh-huh."

When he informed her of his position, she lit up. "At Gospel Press?

Then you know Harold Epp personally?" Bernie's forehead shone in the heat, pale and glutinous, like her oil pie pastry. His part traveled back over his skull in an unerring white line, neatly bifurcating the spare, crinkly growth. "Well, my goodness," she said, "isn't that nice?"

Nothing more than that, though. Maybe he's not even there anymore, occupying a cubicle like Epp's, within the same maze of prefab divider-panel walls and rat-a-tat-tatting machines and suave telephone voices.

"Harold Epp has a special folder, I bet," she told Wade the other evening. "I was wrong about the waste can. About him making paper airplanes. He snuck my piece I wrote about corn day into that folder."

"Folder?"

"Yes. 'Grist for future editorials,' it's labeled. Wait—no—maybe 'Indefensible modern tacks of thought somebody should lambaste on the editorial page.' He puts in the kooky articles he receives and his clippings from unsound religious periodicals and such like."

"I see."

"Just you wait. He'll come out with a big dissertation one of these days. 'Morian Theology: God's singular purposes in requisitioning Abraham's son, Isaac, as human fodder.'"

"Sure."

It's okay. Last night, chapter by chapter she hole-punched her book pages, pasting on gummed reinforcements as she went, and she placed them in a three-ring looseleaf binder Wade brought home. A student left it underneath a desk in Wade's classroom. "Clarissa loves Tony" is splashed on the cover, written in glitter pen and encircled by a wracked heart. "I'm not sure about this spearmint stuff," she told Wade, waving her sheaf of leftover reinforcements. She pulled off a tiny circle and passed her nose along the strong-smelling sticky side. "It could attract mice, wherever I store all this."

"Nah."

"Well, that might be for the better, really. Dust to dust, ashes to ashes."

A pause. Then she said, "Anyhow, I still want to finish the thing. I might as well. You and the children can read it and then I'll consign it to oblivion. In a way, I feel like—well, like it's out of my hands, really. Like, so what if it's stupid? It's just what happened. It's just how things went. It's due to my preexisting mental condition, so don't blame me."

"Who's blaming you?"

She shrugged. "I guess nobody. I was speaking generically, I guess."

An idea tweaks at her. She could comb through her scrap bag for that swatch of brown fabric with popping-out fruit-fly eyes and clip it with her

Modess story where Mama goes into a tizzy. Oh, she could look for the piece of blue plaid, too, to flag the episode at the chiropractor's office featuring Annie's squeegee thigh noises.

Well, why bother?

A bug whirs through the kitchen haze and alights close to her papers. She dismisses it with a snick. A second one hits, but instead of meddling, Anna follows—half enviously—its feckless slog across the tablecloth's checkerboard map. Not that she begrudges the insect its simpleton existence, its cretin capacity, but with even less of an upper load she'd not be riveting herself over every word's suggestive, improbable shades and every truth's stultifying anomalies, and crazily weighing whether she's culpable for any fabrications.

35

So what's Peg to do? How's she supposed to advise her niece, help her and Gary settle their marital differences? For example, the reading. Lacey doesn't mind Gary listening to his books on tape using his headset, because even plugged in he can still be scraping paint, vacuuming, running the garbage out to the compost bin. But his reading? The minute he parks on the sofa with a book, he goes into his shell. Can't he at least sit and talk with her after the kids are asleep? She'll say, "Honey? Sweetie? What time will you get home tomorrow?" and to give her the impression he's listening, he'll adjust his whole body in her direction, all except for his eyes. He's not hearing a thing! They're usually mysteries, the Stephen King sort—cloak-and-dagger plots. He likes the action. He's worked too many hours, he's bushed, but he says he can't turn in, if he turns in too early he won't be able to sleep, so he stays up way late reading. Afterwards he's so zonked he's useless. When the baby cries in the middle of the night to be nursed, all Lacey gets is this muttering from the other side of the bed, "Shut him up. Shut him up. Hit him." In the morning Gary has no memory of it, no memory whatsoever! And then his inability to pace himself on the remodeling only compounds everything—the way he goes at the work gung-ho. The weather's good, stuff he's ordered has come in, and any thought for the family falls by the wayside. She agreed that the hole for the propane tank had to be dug, sure, but he stayed out there pushing the topsoil around till after 10 p.m., using the lights on the tractor. He stopped only because the hitch pin broke. There's no down time, no togetherness. But what's the use in Lacey haranguing him? Peg can't see how Lacey's ire helps any. Where will that get her?

"He never even remembers the baby's crying. Huh." Crook-necked, the telephone receiver clamped against her cheek, Anna has already battered the crumbs out from the little underside trapdoor of the toaster, as well as polished the chrome, run her dishcloth along the blender's grimy cord and checked for nicks, and lifted the separate clusters of silverware from their notches in the plastic holder in the drawer to swipe out the dust and food particles. Pouring Whink rust remover on a stain on the sink now, hoping it will work the magic, she says to Peg, "No recollection, that's weird."

"You said it. Still, I don't see why it's the end of the world. I tell her, 'Your cup is half empty or half full. You get to decide. You get to pick.' I try to get that into her head. Would she prefer a skirt chaser? Or an alcoholic?"

"Amen to that."

Do we know any skirt chasers? thinks Anna. Immediately, her silent, ugly comeback produces a spasm of chagrin. She means to be done with this pointing of fingers. She told Wade so last night. He said, "It's about time." She told him, "Whatever's transpired between Frank and Brenda— whatever! People are susceptible. People stumble. Anybody could be just as aghast at *us,* for sounding profligate. I mean, prodigal. Anybody could be labeling *us* as—well, I don't know what. We need our friends!"

She says to Peg, "So Lacey could focus more on the bright side. Still. You can't denigrate her feelings. They're still real."

"Well, true. Listen, can you remind Todd about the hot dogs? He signed up to help with the snack for youth group."

"Buns, too?"

"No, I have buns."

"Oh, okay. You're doing the hibachi thing again?" The group's volleyball games last fall, Jay and Peg set up their outsized charcoal grill in the church parking lot so everybody could toast marshmallows for s'mores.

"Yes—after our sword drill, a doggie roast."

"Sword drill?"

"Susan suggested that."

"*Sword?*"

"You know. The kids race to find the verse in their Bibles."

"Oh, right." *For the word of God is quick, and powerful, and sharper than any two-edged sword.* Mrs. Overholt's repertoire of posters back in Pottstown included this one, too. "I was about to ask, What's this church coming to? All I could think of was Todd's saber rattling when he was little."

Now it's Peg's turn. "Saber?"

"Oh, never mind. Not for real." She'd brought home *Harry and the Terrible Whatzit* from the Conoy library. Listening to her reading about Harry's broom-assisted assault on the horned, two-headed monster in the cellar, Todd thought Harry should've had a knife. "Knife!" she exclaimed. "No!" Soon after, she caught the boys chasing around and around the downstairs of the house, Todd brandishing the back-porch broom. Jonathan had taken his cupcake. "You both know better," she fumed. "Todd, don't you remember how Jesus made Peter put down his sword after he cut off somebody's ear?"

"Whack!" screamed Todd enthusiastically. "Whack-a-whack-a-whack!"

"Todd Gordon Schlonneger!"

She asked Wade once, "Why, please why, do these Baptists and Lutherans around here buy GI Joe dolls for their kids? And those awful sheriff holsters?" What ailed such parents? She and Wade forbade the boys dart guns and even squirt guns, and once a midget Wild West cowboy pistol that fell out of Pantry Pride's bubble gum machine. So Jonathan cut out rubber-band shooters with the jigsaw, and for a deer rifle he nailed the plunger handle to a piece of plywood cut in the shape of a gunstock. He and Todd would slink around the living room sighting into corners. "It's just a buck!" she'd call. "You're just going hunting! Okay? Just bears or deer! No aiming at people, you hear?"

Hm, Susan proposed the hunt-up-verses-in-the-Bible activity. Anna studies the sink spot that's obediently fading. "A fun, fast Bible game, that's nice."

"Susan offered to serve as timekeeper, too," says Peg.

"Fine. It's a good idea, really." Anna tries to cap the Whink, but she must put the bottle down and catch the slipping phone. Kneading the crick in her shoulder, she adds, "I'll make sure Todd stops off at the store. I'll have him get those Gwaltney chicken dogs. I've stopped buying the beef kind."

"Why so?"

"Oh, you know, mad cow disease. Aren't hot dogs mostly organ meat? I don't think brains, but who's to say? Even if the prions, those mad-cow spongiforms, do reside mainly in brain tissue, how can the packing plants

insure that none of the head meat ever falls into those humongous industrial vats?"

"You're a hoot, Anna. Such a thought has never crossed my mind."

The crunch of car tires penetrates her consciousness, and Anna jounces
the cord around the fridge to peek out the window. "Now who on earth is
that?"

"What?"

"Somebody's here. Want me to call you back? No, wait, hang on—
maybe they're just lost. Some people don't know road signs from grass."

The elderly, piranha-finned Buick tooling up the driveway rouses the
dog, too. Woofing, he streaks across the yard. He straddles the walk, block-
ing access, in high dudgeon, his tail arcing ferociously. Two women climb
out of the car anyway, clenching pamphlets. The receiver mushed against
her chest, Anna cracks open the kitchen door and storm door and sticks her
head out. "Popper!" she stage-whispers. "Shush!"

"Does the dog bite?" asks the stodgier of the pair, her smile uncertain.
She's clad in a tan clutch coat and tie shoes, and her ankles are bloated.

Anna rearranges her features into a blank book. "What did you want?"

"We'd like to offer you this free literature about Bible prophecy and the
end times. Will the dog hurt us?"

Flatly she replies, "No thanks."

The inner and outer doors shutter with reluctance, shuddering as the
repulsing air vibes lose their traction, and she tosses her hair out of her face.
"Peg? You still there?"

"Anna?"

"Popper had quite the fit. It was just some Jehovah's Witnesses. I guess
I wasn't very nice."

"They're sure dedicated. You have to give them that much."

"I suppose so. I suppose going door to door gets a little old. I
wouldn't—"

Wouldn't what? Huckster? She did that! Oh dear. If only she could
whisk back in time and telepathically suction those *Gospel Messengers* up off
the Grackle Street porches and back into Mrs. Overholt's tied-tight packet.
Prickles of contrition play along Anna's neck. Compunctedly as any Jehovah's Witness lady, she peddled the goods—and loudly hawked. What an
intrusion it must've seemed, her and Margie's singing blaring out of the
street-meeting loudspeakers, *LET THE LOW-ER LIGHTS BE BURN-
ING, SEND A GLEAM A-CROSS THE WAY, SOME POOR FAINT-ING
STRUGGLING SE-MEN YOU MAY RES-CUE, YOU MAY SAVE.*

Her remorse takes on water and forms beads which begin trickling down her skin. Making those women think Popper might attack? Letting on she might sic her pugnacious dog? The shame swells. It clammies her between the shoulder blades and wilts her hypocritical peace-principled spine and sogs down into the scruffy soles of her socks.

IN THE STUDY she runs her finger down the index in Wade's textbook. *Spongin, 796. Spongy bone, 921. Spongy mesophyll, 686.* Hm, no "spongiform." Well then, the *p*'s. *Primitive streak, 1177, 1184–85. Primordial soup, 68. Primordium, 660, 684, 736.* Okay, here, *Prion, 587.* Yep-er. Diseases like mad cow, with prions acting as the infectious agents, are labeled as *transmissible spongiform encephalopathies, TSEs.* So there, she wasn't all that off, blabbing on the phone.

The last beef dogs she put on the table, exactly three weeks ago, she fixed with sauerkraut and mashed potatoes. Over supper, Wade reminisced about the stunt he tried with a neighbor boy at Hawk Knob, Bobby Norris. Taking a cord that had been cut off of an old sweeper, they laid bare the two wires on the raw end, wrapped each wire around a nail, and anchored the nails in the opposite ends of a hot dog, after which they plugged the cord into an outlet in the Norrises' barn to wait for their shish kebab to cook. They didn't blow a fuse, but the crackling gave way to an overpowering smell of ozone.

"Wade," she giggled, "ozone? What are you talking about? That's in outer space."

"No, it's in the upper atmosphere. It's in smog, too. The charge from the nails caused the electrons to reconfigure the molecules, creating ozone."

"I don't follow," said Todd. "What kind of smell?"

"Like electricity. The hot dog tasted like it, too. It tasted horrible. No beef flavor. Nil."

"They'll ban everything beef, one of these days," said Todd, shoveling up more kraut and chopped dog.

"Why?" she asked. "Why do you say that?"

"Dad, does *Science News* ever report on studies about mad cow?"

"Yeah, occasionally there's an update. First they had to confirm that prions consumed in contaminated meat would propagate. They know now that a prion contacting a normally shaped PrP protein causes the protein to misfold, reducing its functionality."

"You just have to cook the meat, right?" she asked.

"Nope," said Todd. "High temperatures don't destroy prions. You can't cook them out."

"Oh!"

"The person goes stark raving mad before they die."

"I know *that*." She grimaced. "It makes Alzheimer's look like a picnic."

"The brain turns into a sponge—you find holes all through the person's gray matter. The term for it is 'spongiform encephalopathy,' right, Dad? For Creutzfeldt-Jacob disease?"

"So," she began, "any meat from a carrier cow could—"

"No no," Wade cut in, "it's mostly the animal's nerve tissue that's affected. That's where the prions accumulate. We don't eat backbone steak, or brains."

"But hot dogs?" she asked. "Aren't they a big hash of what-all?"

"Look, the industry is heavily monitored. They're not butchering sick cows."

After he and Todd left the table, she frantically dumped the remains— she spatula-ed clean the serving bowl and thwapped every last blob into the garbage pitcher. Her caution nearly precipitated an additional crisis. When Wade spotted pieces of hot dog in there keeping company with the slop and swill, he threatened to pick the meat out and take it to school in his lunch. Now how scientific would've *that* been—someone with his expertise disregarding a rudimentary rule of sanitation? She'd like to know!

She lets his textbook clunk shut, slides it on top of his junky stack of financial statements and income-tax papers (a job he apparently intends to let ride right up to the deadline), and huddles into herself. Nibbling on her knuckles, she ignores the drone of the computer. Her failure at saintliness strings ahead of her, a long line of consequences. She can just envision, up in some descendant's stewing-hot attic, the clincher evidence of her fall from grace. Not just the usual odds and ends from yesteryear—crazed china, broken beds, and pining picture frames—but also a long-forgotten "Clarissa loves Tony" volume, disheveled and slatternly and coated with mouse turds. Underneath will sit her Tingley box, completely collapsed but still wearing its fragment of label, and her stack of author copies of *Gospel Truth,* no thicker than it is now. Her velour chair might be languishing there too, its springs punching out the bottom and its hide as debauched as that of a terminally ill cat. Nobody will be able to bear throwing out an antique piece of furniture with such fancily carved arms.

36

Last Thursday in Wal-Mart, forking up a half-dozen cans of orange juice (Great Value concentrate, 12 fluid ounces for $1.49), she looked over to see, not far from the freezer case, a down-bellied choirboy cheeping perkily, his toes wrapped around the rack holding the insulated bags, and to her ears came the twitters of his cousins swooping around the fretwork high up next to the roof. Wade had read her a *Gazette* article about the store's trouble with these live-in finches. "Couldn't the manager bring in cats?" she'd asked. "Ones not already plied with cocoa scum?" Still, it was a jolt to her sensibilities, seeing that bird.

Home from the store, she stuck the juice in the fridge freezer, and retreating, shutting off the rush of frosty air, she thought, Ha, Marlene Wagler could do a piece about finch potpie for her "Soup's On" column. Zippily, before such a gem of inspiration could escape her, Anna grabbed the receipt to write on. *Sing a song of sixpence, a pocket full of rye, four-and-twenty twitterlies baked in a pie.* As an introduction, Marlene could use that nursery jingle. *Line a 9-inch glass pan with a circle of biscuit dough and roll out a second crust. Fix two cups of medium white sauce and add to it the following: ½ cup diced shallots, ½ teaspoon oregano flakes, 1 teaspoon coarse pepper, 1 cup hulled peas, 1½ cups boned birdflesh. Pour the mixture into the prepared crust, top it with the remaining one, and bake the pie at 425 degrees. Makes 6 servings.*

But Marlene wouldn't go for a dish that quirky—and gruesome. Anna wrinkled her nose. Okay then, she could maybe approach the newspaper's managing editor about starting her own recipe column. Explain about her bombed *Gospel Truth* contributor status and offer a new feature for the *Gazette's* weekender edition, specializing in pastries. "Pie in My Face," it could be called, or "Pie in the Sky: Heavenly Entrees and Desserts." Beyond that, no theological implications.

Then she smacked into the nearest chair with a gasp, hit hard in the solar plexus by an idea for a *Gospel Truth* article—a tack she could maybe adopt.

Friday, roughing out the article, she alternated between her old, dreaded clay-headedness and a rampant urgency. Often, sitting statue still, welded to the chair seat, she could only eyeball her scribbled fodder with menace and stump her brain over the bare-bones meat of her subject matter. "I'm just the biggest slug," she complained on the phone to Wade. "My head feels like this big mixer load of unpoured concrete. It's not like I'm *peter* petered out, but I'm too—oh, I don't know. I can't even say." By spurts, though, crystal-clear pieces of insight came to her—marvelously trenchant nuggets. She speculated on whether she might be suffering the onset of manic-depressive disease.

Saturday she gushed sentences, paragraphs. "Don't talk to me, okay?" she begged the guys. "I'm busy, I'm busy!" Singlemindedly she bored into her work. *The thing is, the ravishment of human flesh—* No, *ravagement.* Um, *ravaging?* Much better, uh-huh. *The thing is, the ravaging of human flesh violates the moral code. The notion that Jesus had to be sacrificed flies in the face of our other Evangelical Brethren teachings.* She even managed to shut out the chimney-cleaning ruckus from Wade up on the roof, his head stuck into the chimney opening, and Todd stationed below at the soot hole. Their back-and-forth shouts as they passed the chimney brush up and down on its rope and the tinkles of the creosote falling into the stovepipe crock barely reached her.

Sunday afternoon her very fingers itched, panicky about getting more words out. "Hey Anna, give it a breather," Wade coaxed, rocking her kitchen chair, amorously nuzzling her. The funky church-basement smell on his sleeves brought to mind her outlandish helping of turkey tetrazzini at the noon fellowship meal, oozing with toasted almonds. She wished she'd not made such a pig of herself. "You and Frank both," Justine had snorted cheerfully. "That dish of mine is always his number-one request."

Wade snapped her bra strap and grazed along her neck. "Come on,

Anna. How about we go look for watercress?" He wanted to check the neighbor's creek, down beyond the willows where it branches into two silvery, babbling troughs; they'd maybe find a patch. An audacious burst of sun was knocking on the kitchen-door window, magnifying the weather spots and chillblained caulking, and the inklings of spring almost—*almost*—made her cave. But she pulled away from Wade and scrawled another line.

By Sunday evening she was at the computer. Monday, adding on and nixing, she honed and stropped her *pièce de nonrésistance*. When night fell, she was still belaboring. Wade finally made her come to bed, but after he went to sleep she lay staring into the dark, too turbulent, unable to curb her hashing and rehashing. At last she twisted her body, cranking the springs, and pounded him. "Hon. Wade. Listen to me."

She slung herself across him and turned on the lamp. "That Malchus guy, you know? The high priest's slave?"

"Unh?" Wade shuddered like a wet dog and sucked up his sleep slobbers. "What time is it?"

"Did he get roped into helping? Or was he more of an accomplice?"

"Was who what? I have school tomorrow, Anna. Can we do this later?"

"When they arrested Jesus, I'm talking about. I keep wondering about those other goons too. The way they all got on the bandwagon like that, weren't they just some rabble of renegade outlaws?"

"Now's not the—"

"I mean, weren't they largely a howling, raving band of rednecks?" She slapped at Wade with her scrunchy corner of the sheet. "The riffraff, mostly? Society's dregs?"

"Is this your problem or mine?"

"Help me out, will you? Please?"

He swiped heavily at his mouth. "Anna, I have to get up in five hours, even if you don't. Give me a break."

"Wa-ade."

But he was burrowing under his pillow, seeking refuge.

She extinguished the light. He hove toward her half of the mattress and went back to heating water for tea, breathing down her neck in hampering, sedated drafts. *Men.* She was still too tight-wired, amped. After a while she wriggled free of his deadweight limbs, eased from the bed, found some clothes, and ushered herself downstairs to the kitchen, where she scarfed down several glaham clackers and a glass of milk. Wasn't milk supposed to be sleep-inducing? Didn't the sped-up stomach activity when you snacked cause the brain blood to reroute to the gastrointestinal organs? A calming effect soon took hold, but she knew she'd be hung over in the morning and tongue-tied tired.

Sure enough, today it's like she's run her clock down. She feels squishy and wrung out. She can't tell if her piece is succinctly crafted or the same dumbed-down, juvenile quality as her Tingley escapades, certifying her crackpot mentality. She's even too wimped to go pour her coffee. It's scorching to death in the pot. Her pages pulled from the printer, she's just slumped here, glazy eyed.

A Pie Would've Pleased God, Probably

"Probly," I spelled it as a child, or "probly." The word was one of my standbys. It allowed me wiggle room. Probably, I'm thinking now, God would've been okay with a nice yummy meat pie from Cain.

One made from scratch. A rich biscuit-dough crust filled with plucked, eviscerated finch carcasses in a white sauce. For a 9- or 10-inch pie, 1½ cups of boned birdie would've served.

Maybe it sounds too over the top, but why? Meat is meat. The flesh in our own supper pots once crossed God's earth or swam the sea. Creatures ourselves, we just happen to be higher on the food chain; thus the food rules are pretty much the ones we impose. We set the limits—the lesser beasts don't.

Not that this always works. When we refused to buy our ten-year-old the BB gun he coveted in the Gander Mountain catalog, on the grounds that it looked like something out of World War II, he got mad. "Just to hit birds," Todd grouched. Wade said, "Why?"

Todd went off and made himself a slingshot with a piece of flip-flop rubber and a forked stick. "If you down any birds," Wade said, "you have to eat them." What do you know, that afternoon I encountered on my kitchen sink two pearly blue eyeballs and a pair of pronged feet. Popping away on the stove in my smallest skillet were several bite-sized snitches of mockingbird. Killing mockingbirds is illegal!

Wade made Todd sit down and memorize the photos and Latin designations in a booklet I'd scavenged at the Goodwill, Twenty Favorite Birds of Appalachia.

As far as God accepting a bird pie though, this doesn't seem all that hypothetical, really. Doesn't the Cain-and-Abel account in the Bible in Genesis suggest that God took delight in Abel's meat offering? Goat liver—greasy sheep tail—who knows? And in Exodus, don't the altar stipulations delivered on the heels of the Ten Commandments indicate that God expected roasted flesh? Abra-

ham's ram sufficed on Mount Moriah, but only the cruelest of sacrifices, that of Jesus on Golgotha, could satisfy God for all time, according to the Evangelical Brethren doctrines I learned growing up. God required the slain body of his only begotten son Jesus—the butchered body. If a finch pie seems disturbing, here's what's really horrible.

The thing is, the ravaging of human flesh violates the moral code. The notion that Jesus had to be sacrificed flies in the face of our other Evangelical Brethren teachings.

The way I took it as a child, back back back in the Old Testament God spoke the commandments from a fiery cloud on Mount Sinai and then used his own skin-and-bones finger to press the words onto two gravestones. Moses took these back down to the nomad camp in the desert, only to find everybody genuflecting in front of the golden calf they'd made out of their earrings. Angrier than a hornet, he chunked the stones into little bits of gravel, so God had to start all over and spell out again. Thou shalt not make unto thee any graven image. Thou shalt not bear false witness. Thou shalt not commit adultery. Thou shalt not kill.

The rules stayed on the books, but camping wasn't the easiest life. God had to deal with all the malcontents. He let the tribe wander around on the sand dunes for forty years, but then he told the people to invade the cities taking up their promised land. Flashing javelins and tomahawks, they should run out the infidel inhabitants or behead them, and seize—or not seize—the booty (it all depended). God in his omniscience led the war generals to astounding victories by way of these grisly military campaigns—genocidal missions. Though, my Sunday school teacher never said "grisly" or "genocidal."

The rest of the Old Testament was chockablock with incredibly entertaining facts. Mama's stories in children's meeting kept us on the edge of the bench. She told about an ax that floated; a giant with six fingers on each hand and six toes on each foot; a donkey able to speak; cooking oil that never ran out; a dummy with goat's hair, which they propped in the fugitive's bed to fool his pursuers. Jesus wasn't in the Old Testament though. All this was just his ancestors' history. Salvation had to wait.

I was enamored by Jesus' birth in such an unlikely haunt as a barn, and then after he grew up, his wild miracles. He went out and collected a ragtag assortment of friends, and they ministered as his assistants while he dazzled different audiences with instant wine, fish and buns that multiplied, fixed-up legs, even the spectacle of somebody sitting up in his coffin. All through this three-year period of popularity, though, Jesus was setting his face toward his pernicious destiny, and in the fullness of time, on a dark night, in Gethsemane, these evildoer *ne'er-do-wells appeared. Peter reached into his scabbard and took a swing at a bystander, but Jesus said, "No more of this—put up again thy sword into his place, for all that take the sword shall perish with the sword." Jesus had said you should turn the other cheek, go the second mile, so right there in front of the ruffians he felt around in the grass for the piece of warm ear and pasted it back on. He matched up the edges and reconnected the twitchy nerves, allowing Malchus to get back to his rubbernecking.*

But despite his conciliatory efforts, Jesus still had to drip on the cross, between two criminals.

It made me ill if I looked too long at the picture in our storybook with his bony frame stretched out like a rack of lamb. And in the burial scene, he'd turned grayish. They'd stuck him into a cave, rolled up in sheets. His beard was too jabby. It poked out, stiff and frazzled as an old paintbrush.

I didn't wonder why God stepped outside his own parameters. I didn't ask why God forbade killing but prescribed a system of sacrifice laws rescindable only by a mob's frantic call for blood—by Jesus' violent demise, the most sacrilegious infraction possible out of all. But now I'm guessing it was just a lynching. Not just, not fair. Wasn't such an outcome predictable in light of the threat Jesus' grass-roots movement posed for the eye-for-eye righteous, puritanical religious leaders? Given Homo sapiens' *inbred belligerence and inclination to scapegoat, haven't we Evangelical Brethren misinterpreted the lurid events of Passion week? By dying wasn't Jesus squaring away humankind's price, rather than God's? No killing! No spite, no grudges, no punch-buggy hitbacks either! Instead of ditching his principles Jesus laid himself down for the slaughter.*

If it wasn't a case of God mutinying, breaking his own rules, then don't the Old Testament wars, too, demand a revisionist reading? Wasn't the warmongering exactly that? Barbarian maraudery? A xenophobic tribe claiming the sanction of its deity? Didn't this scandalize God? As for their messy sacrifice system, was God honestly hungry for beef shanks and barbecued ribs? Given the words uttered by the prophet Micah, what's to surmise? With what shall I come before the Lord and bow down before the exalted God? Shall I come before him with burnt offerings, with calves a year old? Will the Lord be pleased with thousands of rams, with ten thousand rivers of oil? Shall I offer my firstborn for my transgression, the fruit of my body for the sin of my soul? He has showed you, O man, what is good. And what does the Lord require of you? To act justly and to love mercy and to walk humbly with your God. *Didn't the sacrifice carnage sorrow heaven? The wholesale spilling of viscera outside the Israelites' camp, and the waste of that fatty flesh sizzling on the altar?*

At any rate, Lamb nailed limb-to-limb, uncooked, wasn't kosher. The stuck-deep point of a soldier's spear brought the blood spouting, but how could Mutton raw, not broiled, fill the bill?

If you're riled up now, join the club. If you can find some way to reconcile these impossible, unjuxtaposable gospel truths, please, oh please, let me know.

No, Cain's offering of dusty vegetables from his fields wasn't so swift. Hamburgers would've been wonderful. Probably most any food, had he lovingly cooked it. A steaming bird pie, just not mockingbird, Mimus polyglottos. *If not finch,* Carpodacus purpureus, *then perchance pigeon,* Columba livia. *Up on Mount Sinai God actually mentioned pigeons to Moses. Cain could've crimped the rim like an expert, brushed a glaze of beaten egg and water over the top crust, cut slits, and baked the whole thing till it turned bubbly and brown and some spillage ran jazzily down the sides. Even a vegetable potpie would've proved irresistible, I think—the white sauce crowded with slices of zucchini, broccoli florets braised in butter, bright copper-penny carrots, and caramelized Vidalia onions. Or a quiche, one boasting sautéed mushrooms and red peppers and scarlet canned tomato chunks. Vegetables instead of stilled songbirds, oh my. Yu-u-um. The rich redolence floating up would've tickled the Lord. I like to think God might be vegetarian.*

Harold Epp, she realizes faintly, is going to have a cow.

37

Bomp bom-py bomp bomp bompy bom-py, ooh bomp bom-py bomp bomp bompy bom-py is emanating from the radio, this late, and only now is Wade packing his lunch—he's honking a vague semblance of the tune and gyrating along, to his inordinate satisfaction, and sending Anna at the dining table his dumb winks. But folding the hankies left in the wash basket, awaiting her turn in the bathroom, she's thinking more about the bygone method Mama used with Daddy's. On wash days, Mama would lay down three of his dress handkerchiefs off the clothesline, blotch them with her sprinkling bottle, lay down three more, sprinkle sprinkle, another three, sprinkle sprinkle, till she had a big stack; then she'd roll it into a sausage and allow it to dampen evenly in a plastic bag in the refrigerator for a day or two, perspiring and maybe hatching that same white fuzz, *Rhizopus,* that's growing on strawberries in a photograph in the fungi chapter in Wade's textbook. But no doubt Mama's iron, when she pushed it over each hanky and ferreted into the corners, zapped any vile guck.

At Todd's hollered "I'm done!" Anna jumps up from the table and runs to the staircase. "Huh-uh," she calls, "not unless you've swept up that toenail junk all over the floor. I've had it with following you around with the dustpan. You made a grubby mess up there. It's been there for days. Tell me when you've taken care of it, hear?"

Wade's "Hanky Panky" oldie still pounding, she wanders back into the kitchen and plants herself near the stove to watch her husband closing up his carrot in a baggie. He wipes his paring knife on his pants, the same knife he used to chop off the carrot's mucky black butt, and starts cutting his cheese. *Bomp bom-py bomp bomp bompy bom-py, ooh bomp bom-py bomp bomp bompy bom-py* blares the music, sending shivery tremors up her legs and clicking dormant switches on in her head, and when Wade turns to pull another baggie from the box, she's jittering her chin in two directions and her shoulders are jerkily seesawing and her knee joints are pumping as waggishly as those of somebody demonstrating a new kind of cellulite-ridding exercise in a ladies' toning salon.

"Anna baby, yeah, whoo-ee." He gapes as she tries for a go-go-girl shimmy, but more controlled and snaky, her elbows smashed close to her ribs. *Bomp bom-py bomp bomp bompy bom-py, ooh bomp bom-py bomp bomp bompy bom-py,* "Whoo, baby." In front of his popped-out eyes she switches to a freaky, grinding cha-cha, and he goads, "Do it, baby, whoo, yeah." He's dropped his work, sent his baggie carton scuttling. "Whoo-ee, do it—show your stuff." But when he moves in, she slips him for the uncaging open space of the room. The insistent bass notes fluttering her T-shirt and thumping through every inch of her machinery, her hair a wild mass of broom straws, she flings her arms high and wholly cedes to the rhythm, rocking and heel-stomping as if in praise to the Lord.

SHE TOSSES AND TURNS in the pitch dark, or she lies catlike and immobile enough to feel the movement of the sheet, its synchronized lift and fall, as Wade guzzles in air and releases it from his chest. Once or twice she scratches the nail of her big toe along his anklebone like it's her emery board.

She leaves the bed to go for a drink. In the bathroom she worries again about the electrical outlet. Mightn't the wires be shorting when she's blasting herself with the blow drier's 1000-watt winds? Well, right now, at least, the outlet is cold to the touch.

An odor, though, gets her to ruffling up her nose in perplexity. She has a sneaking suspicion it's just the paper mill. Once in a blue moon the smell reaches this distance from Bricksburg. Glancing around, she sees that Wade propped open the window with the Band-Aids box, probably on account of his shower steam. Which helps to explain the situation—if it's the mill. She puts her face close to the gap and identifies a dim hint of rotten egg. She whiffs again, more vigorously, but not to the extent of hyperventilating. Hm.

Anna tiptoes downstairs. The gassy fetor seems to be trailing her. In the kitchen she pats at the stove top, at the spots directly above the pilot lights, in case they've involuntarily extinguished. They rarely go out, but when they do there's a slight, not imperceptible, gas stink.

The heat of the metal almost singes her fingertips. Still, she double-checks—she peers spy-like through the left front burner hole, and then the right, for the two luminous, orange-blue glimmers. All right, *all right.* As she's backing away, she wonders whether her intakes of breath at such intimate proximity to the flamelets could've, *whoosh,* sucked out the life. But with a sudden resolve, off she marches toward the stairs.

WRAP IT UP, MOM," says Todd, about to head out into the mild, dew-sparkled morning to catch the bus. "Stop your lollygagging."

She's still in her robe. More crumbs shower down onto the pages of her new article as she takes another chomp out of her bagel. "Just thinking about Epp, I lose my nerve," she murmurs, penciling in a small change. "He'll hate this. He will."

The only response is the bang of the door and the house's flinch, creating a riptide effect in her *Say nothing and look like a fool* coffee mug. She's back to using Jonathan's find because the other day, pulling the dishes from the drainer, she accidentally dashed to the floor the *If wisdom's ways* one from Mary Beth and a chunk of pottery broke off along the rim. Todd stuck it back on with Super Duper glue, but couldn't the cyanoacrylate maybe seep into her coffee with every slap of the waves against the patch line? Has anyone adequately researched the poisonous propensities of these miracle adhesives? Does a person already missing a few marbles need toxins skulking in their coffee? Never fear, she's not made mention of this new phobia to Mary Beth. She's not subjected herself to the good-natured derision, Mary Beth's cackles spewing from the receiver and escaping the walls of the house and traveling the whole way down the road to the stop sign.

Anna grinds again on the bagel. Swigs down some brew. Rests her head in her hands.

A while later, when she's layering more coffee on top the boggy grounds in the coffeepot basket leached of their zing, the sharp jingle of the phone almost makes her jump out of her skin. "Hello?"

"Oh, Anna, hi! It's just me, Susan. I was afraid I'd get another answering machine. I'm trying to pass the news along to the Sunday school class— Brenda wanted me to call everybody. Bill's father—you remember her talking about him? He's suffered another stroke, his third in two months.

Completely crippling, this time, and the hospital people are saying he doesn't have long to live. He's not a born-again Christian—he's antagonistic and bitter about religion, even more so than Bill—so Brenda's pretty worked up. She's asking for everybody's prayers. Just pray that he'll get saved."

"Sure. Okay. My, that's too bad. Tell Brenda and Bill we care, will you?"

Anna replaces the receiver and peremptorily squinches shut her lids. But how is she supposed to word her supplication? *Please dear God, please please dear God, save poor old Mr. Arnold from your snatches?* Or what? *Please please please dear God, don't dangle him over the gates of hell just yet?* Say that?

IN HER MANIC MOMENTS this afternoon she has Harold Epp poring over her words, his unweedwhacked eyebrow vegetation kinking up in pleased surprise. His second read-through, his breath racing, and moist *ahems* of admiration. Then Epp pounding his wingtips across the office carpet to the cubicle of the assistant *Gospel Truth* editor and urgently inquiring whether it would be possible to temporarily shelve the cover story in an upcoming issue.

But no. Her article is a bust. She has half a mind to reduce the pages to insulation pulp to replace some of the fluff that filtered down from the attic this winter.

Say she does send her piece? Does foist it upon Epp, and he rejects it? In that case she could still fire off a rebuttal. *Two wrongs don't make a right, sir. And such is the lesson of the cross, I suspect. People's malevolence only reaped its crop. Look, you don't have to concur with me on this. I'm not going to keep beleaguering you. But which of your own crucial, stated propositions aren't simply what you think? Aren't we all just bugs running around speaking our maybes out loud? How can Gospel Truth masquerade as a guardian of the eternal verities when it's just defending the status quo?*

No. That would hardly win his affections.

As she fine-tunes at the computer or sits lost in meditation, the minutes steal by. Off and on, the spunky feelings overtake, perhaps from her coffee, or from the metabolizing chloroplasts in the watercress she put with the hard-boiled egg in her sandwich at lunchtime—Wade went for the watercress himself on Sunday. Fixing the sandwich, she was startled by a funny *whump* and looked up from the mayonnaise jar in time to see a puny, gray-feathered body sliding down the sink window—no struggle, no resistance. A sparrow, she guessed, remembering the verse from her devotions, in Wade's Bible. God wrote it off? Ordained its demise? *Are not two sparrows sold for a penny? Yet not one of them will fall to the ground apart from the will of*

your Father. So don't be afraid; you are worth more than many sparrows.
Should've I suggested sparrow potpie? she wondered, her mound of mayonnaise quivering on the knife. But wouldn't it be—well—unbiblical to put God's protected peons in a pie?

Dependably as clockwork, her imaginings tick along in her mind, *ticktock, tick-tock.* Sometimes her mood leaps, but soon she's back to ruminating apprehensively. Lambent study-window warmth hits the desktop intermittently, and stardust streaks across the computer screen by turns, scattering fallout over Wade's income-tax pileup. Shafts of sun stripe the auction-house chair, its lap full of chapters and her Tingley box with the yoyo string slumped on top, or the rays fade out, drear and uncertain, while she questions whether she's done right by the Lord, unloading her soul.

The Author

Shirley Kurtz, Keyser, West Virginia, is the author of several children's books and a memoir, *Growing Up Plain*. Her writing has appeared in a variety of Mennonite publications. This is her first novel.